Praise for *Spells for Forgetting*

'Lush with secrets, magic, and a past that won't stay where it belongs,
this novel is (quite fittingly) spellbinding'
Jodi Picoult

'A bewitching mystery, equal parts thrilling and romantic.
Not to be missed'
Rebecca Ross

'A thrilling, rich mystery with exquisite twists. Adrienne Young's adult
debut will trick you, bewitch you and leave you begging for more'
Stephanie Garber

'*Spells for Forgetting* seamlessly weaves mystery, magic, and love into a
captivating tale . . . Deeply immersive and filled with intrigue'
Sue Lynn Tan

'With magic, murder, and prose that reads like music,
Adrienne Young weaves together an immersive tale . . . a novel
that will surely stick with me for many years to come'
Chandler Baker

'With quiet magic like wind on a spooky autumn evening,
Spells for Forgetting is so atmospheric it will leave you breathless'
Sarah Addison Allen

'Tense, lyrical, and wholly romantic'
Ruth Emmie Lang

'Haunting and mythical'
Woman

'At its heart this is a book about a community
and relationships . . . thrilling'
SF Books

'You___ _____ _____ ll ____ _____ ll ___ ___ _____ __ _____ __ _____ pages'

SPELLS
FOR
FORGETTING

ADRIENNE
YOUNG

QUERCUS

Published by arrangement with Delacorte Press, an imprint of Random House,
a division of Penguin Random House LLC, New York.
First published in the United States in 2022
First published in Great Britain in 2022
This paperback edition published in Great Britain in 2023 by

QUERCUS

Quercus Editions Ltd
Carmelite House
50 Victoria Embankment
London EC4Y 0DZ

An Hachette UK company

A CIP catalogue record for this book is available
from the British Library

PB ISBN 978 1 52942 534 5
EB ISBN 978 1 52942 532 1

10 9 8 7 6 5 4 3 2 1

Printed and bound in Great Britain by Clays Ltd, Elcograf S.p.A

MIX
Paper | Supporting
responsible forestry
FSC® C104740

Papers used by Quercus are from well-managed forests and other responsible sources.

For Laura, Brandon, and Adam
How lucky I am to be stuck with you

SPELLS FOR FORGETTING

One

AUGUST

THERE WERE TALES THAT only the island knew. Ones that had never been told. I knew, because I was one of them.

I stood at the bow of the ferry as Saoirse emerged from the mist like a sleeping giant tucked into the cold waters. The biting wind had numbed my fingers clutched around the railing and they tightened as I swallowed. I'd imagined that moment a thousand times, even on days that I wasn't completely convinced the island had ever existed. But there it was, as real as the skin that covered my bones.

I tucked my hands into the pockets of my jacket, turning my back to the sight of it. As if that would somehow erase all the darkness that had happened there. The last time I'd stood on the deck of that ferry, I was eighteen years old, and instead of watching it grow bigger in the distance, I'd watched it disappear, along with the life I'd lived there. My mother had kept her face turned away from me just enough to hide the tears striping her reddened cheeks, but I could feel in the center of my chest the words she wasn't saying. That I'd fucked everything up. And that deep down, she would never forgive me for it.

My eyes dropped heavily to the pack at my feet, where the smooth emerald face of the urn was visible through the cinched opening. Even in those final days, she'd never spoken a word of any of it. We swore we'd never go back to Saoirse, and we hadn't. That was one of many promises we'd kept. So why, after all these years, had she broken it?

The only answer to that question was one I couldn't stomach.

"Sir?" The voice was half-drowned in the wind pouring over the deck and I blinked, squinting against the blinding morning light. A woman buttoned up in the heavy nylon coat that bore the emblem of the ferry charter stood before me, hand extended and waiting. "Your ticket?"

"Oh, sorry." I reached into the bag slung over my shoulder, rooting around until I found it.

Her hand brushed mine as she took the ticket, reading the stamp that marked the date and time.

"Headed home?" Her pink nose stuck out from over the collar of the coat, her voice muffled.

The word was like ice in my throat. *Home.*

"What?" I stiffened, searching her face for any hint of recognition. But she was several years younger than I was, probably more. If she was from Saoirse, she wouldn't know my face. She definitely wouldn't know my name—not the one on the ticket.

"Sorry, don't mean to pry. It's just . . ." She handed it back to me. "It's not a return ticket. Don't see many of those on this ferry."

I cleared my throat, slipping the paper into my pocket. "I'm just visiting."

The island wasn't home, even if it once had been. And she was right. No one came to Saoirse to stay.

Though her mouth wasn't visible behind the scarf, I could see the frown in her eyes and the look edged too close to suspicion. I'd been given that look many times before.

"Well"—her gaze trailed over my jacket and down to my boots before snapping back up to my face—"enjoy your trip." There was a stiff uneasiness in the way she stepped around me, following the railing down the deck.

Beyond her, the island was now a sharp figure against the sky. A pair of white gulls glided over jagged black cliffs, catching the freezing wind that had carved the land into the shape of hungry teeth. It didn't matter how many years had passed, the memories hadn't faded.

I'd grown up being told that the people on the mainland were different from us, but living among them was the first time I really understood it. Mom had gotten better through the years at blending in and appearing at first glance like other mothers. But she still spent the equinox in the woods and the solstice at the sea. She still whispered old words over her teacups and I'd caught her muttering a curse as we passed the front door of our neighbor's house more than once.

It was clear almost as soon as we left Saoirse that she didn't want to talk about the island. That those years would be locked away in some secret place we pretended didn't exist. It wasn't the first time I'd broken my mother's heart. It wasn't the last, either.

In a blink, a single moment, every summer in the orchard, every storm over the dark sea, every night in the fishing cabin was entombed inside me like a body beneath a shroud, sealed away from the sunlight. It was for that very reason that I hadn't believed it when I read the handwritten letter folded into the will, just days after I watched my mother take her last breath.

After so many years of staying away, of never speaking of the place, she'd parted this world with only one wish—that her ashes be buried on Saoirse Island.

It had taken me four months to actually book a flight to Seattle so I could make good on her request. I'd closed the window shade as we landed, my heart in my throat. I didn't want to see the listless chain of black islands in the distance or the silvery blue of the water that only existed in the Sound. There were things that the taste of the salt-laced wind resurrected, whether I wanted it to or not, and I was already dreading the months or years it would take to put those memories back to bed.

My phone buzzed beneath my jacket and I pulled it from my back pocket, squinting as I read Eric's name on the screen. I let out a heavy exhale before I picked up my pack, hauling it onto one shoulder. I tapped to answer.

"Hey."

"You make it?"

I pushed through the doors to the ferry's linoleum-floored cabin, where green bucket seats were set in fixed rows. Behind the counter in the corner, a short man with a stained white apron draped over a thick fleece stood awkwardly, watching me over a stainless-steel coffee maker.

"Just about." I ducked low to glance out the hazy window, where the sunlight was a smear of white on the scratched glass.

"Well, I got your message. All you're really looking for is any important paperwork that might have been left there. You'll need the deed to the house in order to sell it. Titles, marriage licenses, bank accounts, whatever. And we need to get someone local to handle the sale unless you want to get stuck going back and forth to deal with all of this." Eric's gruff voice on the other end of the line was a tightly pulled tether between this world and another—my simple life in Portland and my less than simple history on Saoirse. "Any other loose ends there?"

I bit down, following the stark outline of the island with my eyes until it disappeared into the sea. There were a hundred different ones I could think of, but only one I gave a shit about.

"No. The orchard was taken care of in Henry's will." I answered, my voice catching just slightly on my grandfather's name. I hadn't spoken it in years. "It's just the house. Maybe a few pieces of old farm equipment left on the property or something."

"When do you have to be back to class?"

Class. I hadn't thought about my classroom on campus for

weeks, and the view of the orange-hued wooden risers in the light streaming through the tall arched windows made me feel even farther away. "Not until next semester. I took a leave to take care of my mom."

"That's right." His tone shifted just slightly. "Well, get all of this sorted and then get the hell out of there."

"That's the plan." I breathed, eyeing the windblown faces that filled the deck outside. It was almost the end of the season, but there were still dozens of tourists on the early ferry, headed for the orchard. "And Eric?"

"Yeah?"

I lowered my voice. "Thanks for your help with all of this."

"Pretty handy when your college roommate turns out to be a lawyer." He half laughed. "Anyway, I'm sure I owe you for one thing or another."

But he wasn't just a college roommate. He was a friend. Maybe the only one I had. He was also the only person I'd ever told about Saoirse Island, even if I'd never uttered a word about what happened there. "I mean it. Thanks."

"You can buy me a beer when you get back." He paused. "How's that?"

"Sure thing." The door opened again as I leaned into it, and I swallowed hard when I spotted the tipping masts of the boats in the harbor. "Better go. I'll probably lose service any minute."

"See you next week."

"Bye."

The ferry horn rang out as I hung up, and I pushed back out onto the deck. Below, the bow of the ship was carving through the dark blue sea, churning up a splitting trail of white foam on either side of the vessel.

I wanted to hate my mother in that moment, as I felt the deep grow shallower, the island creeping closer. I wanted to be angry or think her selfish for sending me back here. But I owed her this. After everything, the very least I owed her was this.

A few days, and then I was gone. I could turn my back on the island like I had fourteen years ago. But this time, I would never go
back. I'd lived enough years now to know that there were some
ghosts that haunted you forever.

Saoirse had secrets, yes. But so did we.

Two

EMERY

I DON'T KNOW WHEN I started sneaking out of Dutch Boden's bed in the mornings. It was just one of those unspoken rules, drawn like a thick black line around the edges of my life.

A circle of sunlight pooled on my shoulder as the sun rose behind the trees. Through the thin linen curtain, I could see the pale mist that covered the island in a heavy autumn silence. Beside me, Dutch slept soundly. The breath dragged in the back of his throat, the smell of him filling the room with the familiar scent of cedar smoke. Each time I tasted it on my tongue, it soured with the memory of the night before.

The argument had started in the kitchen, drowned in three glasses of wine, and cast in the light of the fire that had gone cold hours ago. But I'd known Dutch long enough to know how to end our fights.

I wrapped my arms around my bare body beneath the quilts, watching the early light spin his wiry blond hair into threads of gold. The angle of his chin had sharpened in the years since we were kids, the freckled skin of his face rough from the sun and salty winds. But there was a part of him who was still that skinny, shirt-less boy I'd grown up with, and maybe that was the problem.

The clock on the bedside table ticked softly, the long hand creeping its way along the dial. In another eight minutes, Dutch's alarm would go off, waking him for an early morning at the orchard, but I'd be gone before he opened his eyes. Like always.

I let one bare foot slip from beneath the quilt and slowly sat up, careful not to make a sound. The branches of the spruce outside tapped against the window as it swayed in the wind, and I watched my own reflection take shape on the glass.

That October had been one of whispers. The eyes of people in town had been drifting to the woods more and more, where not a single tree had taken the change of seasons. The long summer stretched far past its time, and though the cold rains had returned to Puget Sound, the island was still as green as July. It was strange, even for Saoirse.

Dutch didn't stir as I stepped across the old floorboards, picking up my clothes where I'd dropped them in the middle of the night. I braided my hair over my shoulder and shrugged on the soft flannel, buttoning it up to my neck before I pulled on my boots. The hinges only faintly creaked as I let the door swing open and slipped out onto the porch.

Up the hill, Nixie Thomas's house sat shrouded in the trees beyond a fenced patch of farmland. The windows were dark, the old truck gone, and I was glad I'd missed her. Her watchful eye had narrowed in the years since my mother died. So had her hearing, it seemed.

I pulled my jacket tight around me before sliding my hands into the deep pockets. The old dirt road that led to town was crowded on both sides by towering evergreens that held the island in a muted silence even when the sea was stirring with a storm.

My footsteps beat almost in time with the faint echo of the harbor bell that wove through the trees, and a sliver of sunlight glared on the face of my watch as I checked the time.

"Shit." I breathed.

In a matter of minutes, the ferry would arrive, filling the island with the tourists that came in droves this time of year to go apple picking at Salt Orchards. When their canvas totes were filled, they'd wander through the town's shops and end up at my father's pub for a glass of mulled wine or frothy beer while they waited for the last boat.

A few more days, and the ferries would stop. The orchard would be closed for the winter, and this year, it couldn't come soon enough.

The sharp snap of a limb made my steps slow, and I looked up to where a flash of something skittered ahead, disappearing around the bend in the road. A familiar prick crawled over my skin, and I knew that feeling—like a sudden fever.

When I was a child, the island's whispers had been like the sound of my mother humming to herself as she crouched in the garden, or the familiar groan of waves crashing on the rocky shore. But I'd learned a long time ago that sometimes they brought unwelcome fates.

I took the bend slowly, staying close to the shoulder of the road, but stopped mid-stride when I saw it. Beyond the grove of redwoods, the leaves of a two-hundred-year-old hickory tree had turned gold in the night. All at once.

The ancient creature glimmered like a writhing flame in the fog, every leaf painted in the saturated yellow that usually colored the island in autumn. It stood like a blazing bonfire among the towering pines.

My hands tightened around the strap of my bag as I took the last few steps to stand beneath it. Nestled on one of the lowest branches, a starling sat unmoving, its head cocked to one side. The shimmer of purple and green glistened on its feathers, the bright white flecking encircling its neck like a collar.

The starlings were late, just like the trees. By September, the birds made their way south, but this year, they'd stayed. The bird watched me in a long silence, black eyes like drops of ink, before it suddenly jumped from the branch and took flight, disappearing.

A rush of cold wind picked up the strands of loose hair around my face and I trembled, staring up into the branches. Not one flaxen leaf had fallen, but the sound of them rustling was a quiet murmur. Some incantation that I couldn't quite hear.

Down the hill, the town was settled into the fog that filled the lowlands. Only the white steeple of the chapel was visible, poking up through the mist like a reed in a pond. My eyes narrowed, watching the mist ripple over an undercurrent of reds and ambers moving beneath it. In another moment, it began to clear, and I realized my fingernails were biting into my palm.

The pointed leaves of the maple trees along Main Street shook on their branches, every one of them painted the color of blood. Nearly six weeks late, and with no warning at all, every tree on Saoirse had turned in a single night.

I knew better than to dismiss such things. We all did. It was the time of year when the veil between worlds was thin, and in that moment, I could feel the tingle of the Otherworld tiptoeing lightly up my spine.

The harbor bell rang out again, signaling the ferry to port, and I finally started down the hill. I picked up my pace, resisting the urge to look back over my shoulder, and the road eventually gave way to the uneven cobblestones of Main Street. The buildings were painted in the same shades of Puget Sound, blues and greens that melted together in the light. They were topped in moss-covered roofs, the glass of their single-pane windows catching the first bits of light as I passed.

I tucked a strand of unwieldy hair behind my ear, reaching into my pocket for the heavy iron key. The letters on the handprinted sign that hung over the walk were faded, their faces worn smooth by the sea winds.

BLACKWOOD'S TEA SHOPPE
HERBAL TONICS & TEA LEAF READINGS

When I saw who stood beneath it, I groaned, stopping at the bottom of the uneven stone steps.

Nixie was nestled into the eave beside the door, a ghost-white pumpkin covered in a blanket of barnacle-like warts propped on her hip. My favorite kind.

Her overalls were two sizes too big and the haphazard bun pinned on top of her head was unraveling.

"You see them trees?" She lifted one eyebrow.

I followed her gaze to the sour gum tree across the street. It was wrapped in a brilliant amber cloak, its reflection illuminated in the windows beside me. Like the hickory on the hill, not even one leaf had yet to touch the ground.

"I saw them," I answered, my mouth twisting to one side.

When her eyes finally landed on me, they held the look of an impending interrogation. Nixie wasn't my aunt by blood, but she'd been my mother and father's best friend since they were all kids. And to my knowledge, I'd never won an argument with her.

"Turned all in one night. Just like that. Bit of a coincidence, don't you think?" she rasped.

We both knew it was anything but. I'd been taught from a young age how to read the omens, the way children on the mainland were taught their letters and numbers. A butterfly entering the house through a window. Spotting an owl in the daylight. The thin glow of a halo that sometimes circled the moon in winter.

My grandmother Albertine would stand over me as I perched myself on the stool in her kitchen, stirring a pot of bubbling elderberries with a wooden spoon. The deep tenor of her voice still echoed within me. But I'd also been taught that there are some premonitions that stay neatly folded beneath time, only visible when looking back. I'd seen my fair share of those as well.

I came up the steps and fit the end of the key into the lock. It took three tries and a push with my shoulder to shift the bolt free, and the door swung open. The long-lived incense of lavender and sage came rolling out, breathing to life a thousand memories, no matter how many times I smelled it.

Pale light streamed through the windows of the shop, illuminating diagonal beams of dust in the darkness, and I slipped through them as I went to the rusted wall hook to hang my bag. Bundles of wildcrafted herbs dangled from the rafters and shelves lined with neat rows of brown paper bags were stacked against the walls, reaching all the way up to the ceiling.

Handwritten labels identified teas crafted for everything from anxiety to menstrual pains to relief from a sore throat. But it was the more mystical brews you couldn't find on the mainland that most people crossed the water for on those dim autumn days. Recipes for infusions to draw love, conjure luck, or beckon dreams were only a few of those that had filled the shop since its doors first opened in 1812.

Nixie shut the door behind her, finding the nearest corner of the counter to place the pumpkin. "I thought I should come check on you," she said, breaking the awkward silence between us. We both knew why she was here.

"Check on me?"

I traded my jacket for a linen pinafore apron, busying my hands with the ties.

"After last night." She raised her eyebrows, knowingly. "Hell, the whole island heard you two fighting, Em. Heard you making up, too." She set a hand on one hip, waiting. But I wasn't going to take the bait. "How many times are you going to make that boy ask you to marry him?"

"We are not having this conversation, Nixie," I said firmly. As if that would put an end to it.

"I know you don't want to hear it, but someone's gotta say it."

"You *have* said it. A hundred times." The CLOSED sign hanging on the door rocked on its chain as I turned it to read OPEN.

"Then when are you going to start listening? One day he'll stop asking." Nixie lowered her voice, waiting for me to look at her.

I swallowed against a tight throat, remembering the way Dutch's shoulders had pulled up as he stood at the sink the night before, every angle of him hardening. Nixie was right. One day, he'd get tired of asking me to move in. To marry him. To start a family. There'd be no more late nights by the fire in his cabin or weekends at the beach. The idea was as terrifying as it was relieving, and that was the worst part of all of this.

"We still on for tomorrow?" I said, changing the subject.

Nixie gave me an irritated look, finally relenting. "Yep."

The words she wasn't saying were clear in her eyes as she watched me. We weren't finished with this conversation. We never would be, as long as I kept pretending that she couldn't see right through me.

From the beginning, Nixie had never really liked the idea of me and Dutch. She hadn't bothered to keep it to herself, either. But her real fear was that after she was gone, like my mother, that I'd be left alone. I could feel her worry mounting by the week.

She leaned forward, giving me a rough kiss on the cheek. A peace offering.

The old brass bell on the door jingled as she pulled it open, but I didn't relax until she was down the steps and out of sight.

I peered up at the gray sky. It would be only minutes before the rain began to fall, but that wouldn't keep the ferry passengers away. Up the street, the low clouds drifted toward the woods, where I could still see the yellow hickory standing like a sentinel at the top of the hill. It vanished and then reappeared as the fog moved, like a candle flame flickering in the wind before it turned to smoke.

Across the shop, my shape moved over the old framed mirror. My blue eyes stared back at me, the left one aglow where the light caught the burst of brilliant green that painted a star in my iris. When I was little, my grandmother told me that it meant I was marked for something. That I was special somehow. But here I was, standing in my mother's shop, wearing her apron. I'd inherited an entire life. One I had once sworn I would never live.

I came around the crude worktable at the back of the shop and replaced the candles that had burned out before I'd finished the new batch of tea the previous night. The open page of *The Herbarium* still stared up at me from beside the row of amber glass jars.

There were two books that were passed down in the family: *The Herbarium* and *The Blackwood Book of Spells*. The book of spells was kept at my grandmother Albertine's, on the mantel above the fireplace. That would be its home until she departed this life, and then it would be given to me. But *The Herbarium* was kept in the shop.

The heavy, leather-bound book was a kind of diary where the Blackwood women recorded the recipes and herbal studies that had become a kind of textbook. The thick parchment pages were covered in botanical sketches along with handwritten notes that filled the margins. It was used by every herbalist in the family, each one adding their research to it throughout their lifetime, though I had yet to contribute any of my own.

The tip of my finger ran down the page until I found where I'd left off.

I opened the jar of crushed roses first, sprinkling the paper-thin petals into the wide wooden bowl before me. The flower dust lifted into the air and I breathed it in until the perfumed scent of the summer blooms was thick in my lungs. I picked up the jar of shaved cinnamon bark next, giving the contents a gentle shake, and in that still moment between breaths, the air grew thin and brittle. I felt the crease at my brow deepen, my head tilting as I listened, and warmth bubbled under my skin again. Softly, but it was there.

The hollow silence stretched and pulled before a sudden crack shot through the shop and I jolted, knocking the bowl from the table. The jar slipped from my fingers, shattering at my feet, and the pink tissue petals blew across the wooden floorboards as a swift wind poured through the window, extinguishing every candle in one sweep.

I froze, my fingers clenched around the flat lid of the jar so tightly that I could feel its sharp rim cutting into the soft flesh of my hand. A trickle of hot blood dripped through my fingers.

On the other side of the shop, the window's glass was cracked in a split, jagged line. I held my breath, the faint sound of whispering lifting in the back of my mind as I took a hesitant step around the table.

I could see bits of gold and crimson swirling in the air outside and I pressed my bleeding hand to my chest, where my heart was beating like a ritual drum.

All at once, the leaves had let go of the trees and were blowing down the street like a swarm of jewel-colored locusts. But it was when I looked down that the sounds of the woods seemed to race into the shop, filling the space between its walls with the cold of midwinter.

There, on the ground in front of the window, a starling lay dead. Its glossy wings were outstretched, the brilliant purples and greens shimmering and the bone-white flecking of its breast reflecting the light.

Sometimes the signs were subtle, like a fleeting shadow or an echo in the trees. Other times, the island wasn't gentle with her words.

I stood there, staring at the bird, as a painful twist woke between my ribs. And in the next breath, the ferry horn blared.

Three

EMERY

"BAD OMEN, THAT IS." Leoda clicked her tongue.

She unstopped a bottle of witch hazel and soaked the corner of a clean cloth, eyeing the cut that striped my palm. Out the window, her husband Hans picked up the starling with a gloved hand. He held it in the air, inspecting the bird for a moment before dropping it into a burlap sack.

Leoda sighed. "First the trees, now this. If your mother was here, she'd say the same."

She was right. That was exactly what my mother would say.

Leoda's silver hair was pulled away from her face, where youthful eyes were framed in wreaths of black lashes. She was a small woman, with a slight frame beneath her baggy sweater, but her voice was always too loud for the cramped space of the tea shop.

I watched Hans disappear from view, and when he returned, he had an old twig broom in his hands. He swept the brick from side to side in long, brisk strokes, kicking the dirt up into the air. When he was finished, he pulled the wool cap from his head and ran one hand through his thin, white hair.

I hardly noticed the sting as Leoda roughly pressed the cloth to my palm. In addition to running the apothecary next door, she was also the island midwife, which meant she'd delivered nearly every baby in town, including me and my parents. But she'd never had a gentle touch.

She glanced up from my hand and her mouth was twisted to one side, as if she was trying to work something out. But whatever she was thinking, she thought better of saying it aloud.

"It's nothing a little rosemary can't fix." She abandoned the cloth and took the small knife from my worktable, going to the bundles of herbs hanging from the rafters. "Where's your black salt?" She lifted up onto her toes, cutting a few sprigs of rosemary free.

I hesitated before I went to one of the small drawers in the hutch at the back of the shop and pulled it open, finding the dimpled jelly jar with a rusted lid. Inside, the finely crushed charcoal dusted the glass gray.

The old brass bell jingled as I pulled the door open and pried the lid from the jar. I leaned out over the pavement and sprinkled its contents over the spot where the starling had been only moments ago. It was customary to salt the earth where death had been to keep its shadow from spreading.

When I was finished, I glanced up and down the street, watching the leaves skitter along the walks. In the distance, a crowd had already appeared at the entrance to the harbor and one by one, the shop doors were opening. More than one familiar face was visible behind the windows.

"I think this storm will blow through pretty quick." I closed the door behind me, hoping that talking about something else would force the chill out of the air.

"We'll see," she muttered. "How's your dad doing?"

I took the broom from the corner, sweeping up the glass around her feet. "Better, I think. Like he'd tell me otherwise."

She went to the counter, taking a length of the trimmed twine I used for packages from behind the old register. She methodically laid out the rosemary and tied them together, knotting it three times. Always three.

"Well, it's no wonder he's nearly caught his death. Out there on the water before dawn in that fishing boat like he's a twenty-year-old man." She shook her head. "He's lucky it's only a cold."

She reached into the pocket of her sweater, pulling a small parchment bag free and setting it on the table. "Twice a day. Four times is better. Tastes like horseshit, but it'll do the trick." She lifted a finger into the air. "Steeped fifteen minutes, no less. You tell him."

"I will."

That seemed to satisfy her. She crossed her arms, peering through the window in the door. The light changed her blue eyes to a pale gray. "Already pouring down the street," she murmured, pursing her lips.

The people of Saoirse hated the seasonal tourists almost as much as they needed them, but we'd learned the hard way what happened when the ferries were empty.

The last of the mainlanders would be headed to the island before things shut down for winter, and I couldn't afford not to have the shop open. It was the last surge of income I'd have until spring, when the ferry schedules picked up again. Then, we'd have the whale watchers and birders to contend with. Maybe a scientist or two looking for a rare mushroom or performing water tests. In our eyes, they were all the same—strangers.

My dad had always said that they were a necessary evil, though he'd never really seemed to mind them. Not like Leoda did. The Morgan family was one of the oldest on the island, and there was no one more protective of it than her.

I watched her mouth slant, her gaze growing dimmer as a woman in a pink jacket passed the broken window with a little girl trailing behind her. I could feel it, too, the magic of the island retreating as they poured off the ferry, like water finding the cracks in pavement.

"Morning!" The woman stepped inside, her cheeks flushed from the ride on the ferry. "Cold out there, isn't it?" She pulled the gloves from her hands.

"It sure is," I said, eyeing Leoda.

She stepped backward, watching the little girl with her lips curled, as if she was afraid the child might nip at her heels.

As soon as she was clear of her, Leoda caught the edge of the door to keep it from closing. Her eyes went from me to the bundle of rosemary on the counter. "Over the threshold, dear," she rasped.

A few unsavory words I couldn't quite make out faded as she took the steps back down to the apothecary next door.

"Let me know if there's anything I can help you with." I sank to the ground, brushing the pile of glass and dried herbs into the dustpan.

The woman gave me a tight smile as she picked up a sack of tea. But her eyes drifted to the jar of black salt on the worktable, where *The Herbarium* was still lying open.

I set the dustpan on the table and lifted the heavy corner of the book, closing it with a snap.

The people who came to Saoirse didn't just come for the apples. The town had hardly changed in the last hundred years, and there were stories about the island and the people who lived here. Most of the old shops didn't have Wi-Fi and cellphones got little reception beyond the harbor, but the tourists came in droves to walk Main Street and recount those tales.

Witches. I'd heard children from the mainland whisper the word like a secret from the time I was little, playing in my mother's shop as she worked. I'd always thought that strange, because on Saoirse, the word wasn't a secret. It was deep magic that ran through the blood of every woman on the island. It seeped into the earth of the orchard, its leaves unfurling every spring, falling to rot every autumn before turning back into the ground.

For people from the mainland, the old ways had left their families somewhere up the line, untethering itself from them. But it was different on Saoirse. While the outside world was burning their witches, we were here. On the island.

"What happened there?" The woman frowned as her eyes skipped over the broken glass that filled the dustpan.

I dumped it into the trash bin. "It's nothing. Just a bird."

She studied the crack in the window behind me.

I slid *The Herbarium* from the table and hauled it up into my arms before stowing it in the drawer of the hutch. I could feel her curious stare follow me as I rounded the counter, but I ignored her. I was good at that.

When she finally started toward the register with a bag of tea in her hands, I gave her a warm smile. "Anything else?"

"That should do it."

I plucked a honey stick from the crock beside the register and held it out to the little girl, but her expression was apprehensive beneath her thick mop of dark bangs.

The woman laughed, looking between the two of us. "Well, go ahead."

The girl reluctantly took it, twirling the stick between her fingers and watching the light sparkle on the crystallized sugar inside. Her mother ran a hand over her head affectionately before pulling the wallet from her purse.

"You know, I haven't been here since before the fire."

I punched the keys on the old register, my finger slipping from the number nine as the words left her mouth. The key snapped back, leaving a smear of black ink on the receipt paper.

"Well, welcome back," I said, still holding the practiced smile.

"We came every year when I was a kid, back when the woman who owned this shop read tea leaves. My mother always got a reading." She glanced at the pine hutch at the back of the shop, where the old cups and saucers were arranged neatly.

My eyes landed on the green, gold-rimmed teacup with a crack on its lip that sat on the top shelf. I hadn't touched it in fourteen years, and I'd sworn I never would again.

"Yeah, well, we haven't offered readings in a long time." I started over with a steady hand, hitting the numbers again in a fixed rhythm.

It had been six years, to be exact. My mother was the last person to read the leaves in this shop. As far as I was concerned, it would stay that way.

"Oh." She frowned. "You really should. Adds to the whole experience, you know?"

I stared at her, studying the perfect line of her lipstick, painted in almost the exact same shade as her coat. Her manicured fingernails tapped the counter between us.

"We stopped coming after the fire, of course. Couldn't believe it when we heard. It was all over the news for months. Same night that poor girl died, wasn't it? What was her name? Lily?"

I bit down on my bottom lip when I heard it—the clinking of the teacups on their saucers in the hutch. They softly rattled and the woman's eyes drifted that way again, narrowing, as the sound faded into the soft patter of raindrops on the roof.

I dropped the tea into a bag, tying the handles closed with twine and tightening the bow with a firm tug. "That's right."

"So strange, the whole thing." She dropped her head just a little to see my face. "What do people around here think happened to her?"

I let my eyes meet hers then, for just a moment. I knew that look. The morbid curiosity. The twisted entertainment of it all. But this wasn't the first time someone had come into the shop asking the very same questions.

There was an unspoken understanding on Saoirse. We didn't talk about that night. Or Lily Morgan. Especially not to outsiders.

When I didn't answer, the woman smiled sheepishly. "Anyway, I thought it was time to bring my daughter. Carry on the tradition, you know." She patted the girl on the shoulder absently. "You wouldn't know by the look of the orchard now. Everything's so beautiful."

"Well, it's been a long time," I said. And it had been. Fourteen years. But it didn't matter how green the branches of the apple trees were now, I could still feel that black stain on the earth that the fire left behind.

I came around the counter, pulling the door open before I held the bag between us. She seemed to hesitate before she took it.

The little girl watched me from behind her mother, shrinking under my gaze.

"Thank you for coming in."

She pulled the girl down the steps and her umbrella popped open as they made their way up the walk, toward the tree line in the distance. The wind outside had turned brisk, the clouds gathering overhead like a gentle smoke.

I stepped back inside, letting the door close behind me. The shop felt empty in a way that it hadn't that morning. As if the warmth that usually hovered beneath the roof had escaped.

I reached up, pressing the tip of my finger to the crack in the window and tracing the line of it. The faint impression of feathers was dusted onto the glass where the starling had crashed into it, and my breath fogged around the tip of a wing.

The floorboards creaked beneath my feet as I walked back to the counter, picking up the bundle of rosemary Leoda had left. I twirled it between my fingers before I went to the door and lifted up on my toes to hang it over the threshold, like she'd instructed.

Maybe it was the talk of the fire or the argument with Dutch. Maybe it was the feeling that always seemed to haunt me this time of year, or the sudden turn of the trees. A coincidence, Nixie had called it. But we both knew there were no coincidences on Saoirse.

Four

AUGUST

FOURTEEN YEARS AND NOTHING had changed.

The ferry drifted to a stop, filling the clean air with the smell of burning fuel as I peered over the railing to the dock below. The gray wood planks were stained green with algae along the edges, stretching between old, rusted fishing boats and anchored catamarans.

The ferry crew was readying to leave almost as soon as the first passenger made it down the stairs, and I shouldered my pack, waiting. They'd turn the ship around and make at least four more trips before the sun went down, but the day on the island was only getting started.

A cloud of pigeons descended on the deck as the crowd thinned, scrambling underfoot for whatever crumbs had been left behind, I pulled my hood up over my hat and the metal staircase rocked as I took the steps down to the dock. The longer I went without anyone recognizing me, the less complicated this would be. But the moment my feet hit the ground, I could feel the weight of the island.

The wood planks narrowed as I followed them to the harbor and I inched away as I passed the ticket booth, where a figure sat behind the fogged glass. I kept one shoulder turned toward the boats, careful not to meet eyes with whomever it was. Maybe one of the Galloway boys or a farmhand from the orchard who'd grown too old to shovel hay. Regardless, they'd know the story, and news traveled fast in this town.

The stream of tourists poured onto Main Street, but I followed the alley behind the buildings that edged along the water. Any minute, the fishermen would be headed back in with their morning catch and every shop would have its doors propped open. It was the tail end of apple picking season, one of the busiest times of year. In another couple of weeks, the ferry schedule would change and the island would fall quiet. That was when Saoirse's demons would return and I'd be long gone before that happened.

By the time I reached the chapel at the end of the street, the rain was hitting the hood of my jacket in sharp taps. My boots mucked through thick piles of fallen autumn leaves and umbrellas opened one by one in the crowd as they cut left, toward the orchard. But I took the dirt road up into the trees to the right.

The giant evergreens that filled the woods stood impossibly taller than I remembered, and the thought made my throat feel tight. I'd never loved it here the way everyone else seemed to. To me, the island had always been a stone tied around my ankles, and everything that could have been was no more than the puddle of light on the surface as I sank. The only hope I'd had here was in the thought of leaving and I'd gotten my wish, even if it had looked different than I thought it would.

I could smell winter in the air, but it was still a ways off. It would be another couple of months before the snow began to fall and the island took on that unnerving silence. It was a hollow sound that didn't exist anywhere else. That, too, was something I'd tried and failed to forget.

The hum of an old engine sounded at my back as I crossed into the trees and I kept my eyes ahead, my grip on the strap of my pack tightening. There was no way to stay unseen on this road. The only place it led was one of the few places the tourists didn't go.

The safety of the Everdeen campus felt far away now. The old oak desk in my office, the stained-glass windows and narrow hallways of the buildings. I'd taken the job in Portland to make my life feel bigger, but even with a full classroom and the bustle of the university, it had somehow stayed small. Nights in my apartment were quiet, other than the rote greeting from the old woman who lived next door as I punched in the door code each evening. The only friend I had that transcended the bounds of the occasional after-work beer was Eric, and I'd never been any good at dating, either. That was one of many curses I'd taken with me from this place.

An old blue truck rattled past me at a clip too fast and just when I thought it would keep on going, the one working taillight glowed red. The tires popped on fallen twigs and buried stones as the truck pulled onto the nonexistent shoulder and I stopped mid-stride when I realized that I recognized it.

The last time I'd seen that truck was after Jakob Blackwood, the marshal, gave me a black eye.

The driver's-side window squeaked as he rolled it down, and one big-knuckled hand hung over the door as he watched me in the side mirror, waiting.

I cursed under my breath, staring into the trees for a moment before I started walking toward him. This was one meeting I'd known I couldn't avoid.

Exhaust pumped from the tailpipe, drifting into the road, and I stopped in front of the window. Jakob blinked before his gaze found me. His deep-set eyes were more gray than blue now, but the set of his mouth hadn't changed. He was a proud, stubborn bastard and he still hid the whiskey in his veins fairly well.

"Guess I should have known someone would have already called you," I said.

Jakob pulled the hat from his head and set it on the dash. "Get in."

I looked up the empty road in both directions before I eyed the vacant seat on the other side of the truck. I hated the man, but I'd need him if I was going to do what I'd come to do.

The pack slid from my shoulder as I rounded the hood and jerked the stiff passenger-side door open. Jakob didn't say anything as I climbed inside, shifting back into drive and taking off before I even had the door closed.

He kept his attention on the road. "What are you doing here, August?" His deep voice was barely audible over the sound of the engine.

"I don't think that's any of your fucking business, Jake."

He looked at me then, his gaze refocusing as if he was suddenly unsure of who'd climbed into his truck. The marshal hadn't taken his eyes off me in the months before I left Saoirse, and they held the same accusation now that they did then.

When he didn't speak, I reached for my pack, opening it up to take out the small urn.

He looked at it, his lips parting and then pressing together.

"Came to bury her," I said.

His jaw ticked as he fixed his eyes back on the road, but I still caught the flash of pain that surfaced there. "I'm sorry to hear that," he said, sounding as if he meant it.

The words made me grit my teeth. He'd turned his back on us after what happened. They all had. I'd grown up with Jake filling the place that my father left when he took off. He'd taught me how to fish and change a tire. Picked me up from school when it was storming.

I swallowed hard, pinning my gaze out the window, where the rain was beading down the fogged glass. I didn't like thinking about those days. In the end, he'd been just like the rest of them.

The sight of a few cottages appeared behind the swaying branches that lined the road. The Elsners'. The Hersches'. The Kellers'. I knew every house like I knew every row of trees in the orchard. I could still walk them in my mind. Sometimes, I did.

Houses, jobs, boats—they were all passed down from one family member to the next, keeping just about everything on the island the same for the last hundred years. Even the fire hadn't been able to sink it.

"She wanted me to bury her here. Is that going to be a problem?" I dared him to argue. I almost wanted him to. I wasn't the scared, stupid kid I'd been when we left.

Jakob thought for a moment, and I could see that he was weighing his options. The blowback from the town. The attention it would bring him. There was no telling how long they'd punished him for everything that happened after we left, and I was sure they had. That was how things on Saoirse worked. But I didn't give a shit about any of that anymore. I hadn't for a long time.

"Is Zachariah still . . ."

I wasn't sure how to ask. Was he still living in the old cabin? Still managing the cemetery? Was he still alive? If he was, he'd have to be pushing ninety these days.

"He is," Jake answered.

"Who can I talk to about selling the cottage?"

An expression I couldn't make out passed over his face, but when he shot me a glance over his shoulder, it was still cold and distant. I thought maybe I imagined it. "I'll send someone over."

The brakes squealed as the truck slowed and he turned the wheel, pulling into the overgrown drive. My heart instantly came up into my throat as the cottage came into view. It sat back from the road, half-covered in honeysuckle and blackberry vines. The porch was sinking on one side, the windows clouded, and it hurt even more to look at it than I'd guessed it would.

"I want you back on that ferry the moment your mama's in the ground. Understand?" Now he was the one daring me to argue.

"Believe me, I'm not spending a single minute here that I don't have to," I muttered.

Jake took hold of the gearshift, sliding it into park, and the truck jerked to a stop. "I mean it, August." His heavy words filled the cab of the truck as his hands tightened on the wheel in front of him.

There were rules on the island that everyone followed. An understanding about what was expected of the people who lived here. I'd grown up with that weight on my shoulders—the orchard, my family name. But that all changed the night of the fire.

I closed up my pack and climbed out, following the nearly invisible walk that led up to the small house. The sound of the truck faded as it pulled away and when I turned back, Jake was gone. But the coiled knot in my throat tightened when my eyes lifted to the trees across the uneven dirt road. Hidden behind the grove of redwoods was the Blackwoods' house.

I pulled in a forgotten breath when the burn lit in my chest. The thick branches shook in the wind and I could see glimpses of the porch beyond them. There was no car in the drive, but it was clean and lived in, and my stomach sank when I spotted the tended garden. There had been a part of me, a big part, that had hoped I would find the Blackwoods' house empty. But it looked like Noah and Hannah still lived there.

I pulled the key from my pocket and spun on my heel, following the steps up to the porch. My reflection was hazy on the glass as it flit across the window, but there was something out of place about it. I was a thing that didn't belong. I took another steadying breath before I turned the lock and pushed the door open. The stale scent of dust and paper met the damp air of outside and the stillness between the walls made goosebumps lift on my skin.

The years hadn't been kind to the old cottage. A dark water stain haunted one corner of the wall and the window beside the dining table was cracked. I let the pack slide from my shoulder onto the wooden rocking chair as I stepped inside and set the urn on the small wooden table. It looked as if it hadn't been touched at all, everything exactly as we left it. The dishes on the shelves. The books on the mantel. The photographs. It was all just as I'd last seen it.

That morning, we'd woken before dawn and packed only what would fit into a single suitcase. Then we'd walked the dark road into town, headed for the harbor. And before anyone even knew we were leaving, we were gone.

Five

EMERY

I WAITED FOR THE morning rush to clear out of the shop before I hung up my apron and pulled on my jacket. The café and the bakery would have lines spilling from their doors for the lunch hour, but my father would still be getting ready to open the pub for the afternoon crowd.

Rivulets of rainwater hugged the sidewalks, where bundled-up tourists were hidden beneath bouncing umbrellas. Canvas totes filled with red and gold apples were hung over their shoulders and children lugged pumpkins cradled in their arms.

Golden sunlight had burned off most of the morning fog, but it was already disappearing behind the darkening clouds. The sun would retreat as we headed into winter. With the light would go the tourists, and our island would return to the quiet town no one came to visit much except in autumn.

I pulled the hood of my jacket up and crossed the street to Adelman's Market. The wood-framed doors were propped open to the rain, and I could see Etzel ringing up customers behind the huge window. The family name was painted on the glass in old world letters that had been touched up a hundred times over the years.

"We'll need a new roof before next winter, that's for sure. Hell, all of us will. And I'll be spending the weekend mopping this floor." She prattled on to a man at the counter as I ducked beneath the curtain of rain spilling from the gutter.

"Hey, Em!" Etzel lifted a hand in the air to greet me before she went back to wrapping up a wedge of cheese in a square of brown paper.

"Hey," I answered automatically, wiping my boots on the mat.

The register was her usual spot, but her husband Rupert was missing from the short counter in the back corner where he used to stand in a white apron. He'd stopped making his famous fish and chips for an entire year after a magazine in Seattle named Adelman's Market one of the best stops in the Pacific Northwest for the coastal delicacy. For months, droves of people made the pilgrimage across Puget Sound to the market until the line reached all the way down Main Street to the harbor. Now, Rupert only turned on the fryer after the evening ferry left.

I followed the low shelf to the end of the wall and turned down the next aisle. Every square inch of the tiny market was stuffed with teetering baskets of pears and squash, loaves of bread, and jars of jam. A few of them bore my grandmother's handwriting on their paper labels.

I put a crate of eggs on my hip and plucked a baguette from the stack, my hand freezing midair when I felt the weight of eyes dance over my skin. I looked up, scanning the market until I spotted Molly Tulles and Sarah Halsted drawn together in the corner, their sharp gazes fixed on me.

Molly bounced a blond-headed toddler on her hip and Sarah folded her hands over the top of her full, round belly. I'd gone to school with both of them, but they'd kept their distance from me since graduation. Most people had.

I ignored them, tucking the baguette under my arm and going to the counter, where Etzel was already waiting.

"Saw Jake tear up the street this morning." She gestured to the wide window beside us.

"Oh?"

"That man's always up to somethin', I guess." She smirked, playing off her nosiness.

With a view that overlooked the whole of Main Street, she was usually the first to catch wind of things, and the marshal being my uncle meant I bore the brunt of the town's curiosity when something was awry.

"All right, anything else?" She rang me up and the register dinged as the drawer flew open.

"That's it." I slid a five-dollar bill across the counter, chancing another look in Molly's direction.

The sound of their whispers disappeared in the chatter out on the sidewalk, likely carrying gossip about Dutch's proposals or how I was going to be too old to have children soon. But I was used to being talked about and there wasn't a soul on the island who didn't have a theory about me and Dutch. The truth was worse than what any of them imagined.

"All right, have a good one, honey." Etzel gave me a wrinkled smile as she tucked the strands of silver curls behind her ears. Her attention was already on the next person in line.

I fit the eggs and bread into my jacket and stepped back out into the rain. There had been a time when whispers and stares had followed me everywhere I went, when the ferries were empty and the orchard was half-filled with blackened trees. Back then, Saoirse had been forced to welcome a different kind of stranger—police and detectives and forensic investigators.

It had taken years to feel as if the entire town wasn't watching me. Waiting.

I could still smell the smoke of that night and see the flames, so tall, reaching up against the black sky like writhing, angry beasts. I could still hear the sound of shouting that echoed through the woods and feel the cold that stayed in my hands for weeks after. But the worst of it all was the loneliness of the years that followed.

I put it out of my mind, taking the winding sidewalk down the hill. The faded sign of Saoirse's harbor reached out over the entrance to the empty docks, where some of the fishing boats were still missing from their slips. The windows of the ferry ticket booth were beaded with condensation, where the attendant's shape was no more than a smudge behind the glass. Beside it, my father's pub was sitting at the end of the long line of shops.

The tarnished brass handle was ice-cold in my hand as I pulled the heavy door open, and I squinted as I came inside, letting my eyes adjust to the low light. Milk glass pendants hung over wooden booths fit with worn leather seats, but the gray light of day was the only thing illuminating the pub. Behind the carved wooden bar, Dad turned a pint glass in his hand, wiping its rim before he stacked it beside the taps.

"Morning, Daddy." I wove in and out of the tables, unwinding the scarf around my neck.

He smirked, taking another dripping glass from the sink. "Don't have anything better to do on your break?"

I came to stand behind him, lifting up on my toes so I could set my chin on his shoulder. "Someone's gotta make sure you don't live on grilled cheese and coffee."

A crooked smile lifted the right side of his mouth. The scarring that reached up out of the collar of his shirt and covered half of his face was familiar now. I could hardly remember anymore what my father's face looked like without it.

The pink, puckered pattern of his skin was nothing compared to the way he'd looked lying in the hospital bed. I'd hardly been able to stomach seeing him. Not because of the wounds that covered nearly half of his body but because of the pain I knew he was in. Getting him well had been the only thing that kept me going in those days.

I set the eggs and bread on the counter and I pulled the tea from my jacket pocket. "Leoda says at least twice a day until that cough is gone."

He tossed the rag onto his shoulder and took the tea from my hands, giving the bag a sniff. "What the hell is it?"

I rolled my eyes, snatching it back from him. "Slippery elm and licorice root. And Leoda says you shouldn't be out on the water when it's that cold. At least not until you're better."

He went back to the glasses, shaking his head. "You can tell Leoda I don't give a—"

"Fifteen minutes to steep, Noah Blackwood." I cut him off, giving my best impression of Leoda. When he laughed, I shoved into his shoulder with mine and pushed through the swinging door into the narrow galley kitchen at the back of the pub. "Catch anything this morning?"

"In the icebox," he called out.

I gave the loose handle a yank and the entire thing rocked as the door swung open. Inside, a silver pail was filled with three trout half-buried in melting ice. "Might have to take one of these home with me."

"Help yourself."

I closed the icebox and took a match from the bowl on the shelf before I struck it and turned the knob of the burner. It lit with a roar and I put the kettle on, watching the blue flame beneath it.

A photograph of my mother was pinned to the wall over the stove, its edges yellowed and rippling. She stood on the road in front of our house in a white cotton dress with tiny yellow flowers. There was a mirth in her eyes, as if she were thinking something she hadn't said aloud. The tiny pieces of strawberry-blond hair that always escaped her braid blew across her forehead and I touched two fingers to my lips before I pressed them to her face.

I hadn't just taken over the shop when she died, I'd taken over looking after Dad, too.

Four years felt like an eternity, and at the same time, only yesterday. But I liked remembering her like that, instead of the version of my mother that had existed at the end.

The sound of the door to the street scraping over the tiled floor made me blink and the vision of her vanished into thin air. I pulled a cup and saucer down from the shelf and set them on the counter as the kettle began to hum.

Deep voices crept through the crack in the kitchen's swinging door as I scooped the herbs from inside the little brown bag. The dried leaves and shaved bark hissed as I covered them in nearly boiling water, and I set the saucer on top of the cup.

"August Salt."

I froze, my gaze drifting back to the door.

I knew the name. I knew it in my bones. In my blood. And the last time I'd spoken it aloud, I'd been eighteen years old.

"You're sure?" My father's voice was low. Careful. But it held a gravity that made my stomach turn.

My hands trembled as I picked up the cup and took the three steps across the small kitchen. Through the round window, I could see my uncle Jake standing on the other side of the bar. His old ocher corduroy jacket was buttoned up to his chin.

He stiffened, standing up straighter as I came through the door, and it hit the heels of my boots as it swung closed behind me. I looked between him and my dad, the unspoken storm of words between them filling the air.

Jake cleared his throat. "Anyway, just thought I should let you know. We're meeting at the chapel after the last ferry." He avoided my gaze as he turned.

"Jake?" my dad said suddenly, still staring at the bar top, where the glasses were stacked in a row of jeweled towers.

Jake stopped, and for a moment, he seemed almost afraid.

"Thanks."

Jake gave him a single nod before striding back across the pub and pushing outside.

I waited for my father to say something, still pressing the cup between my palms. My fingers burned, but I only clutched it tighter, holding my breath. "What is it?" I said.

His eyes trailed the room, looking everywhere except for the place I stood. He was rigid, fidgeting with the rag in his hands.

"Dad?" I managed to speak despite the pain strangling my throat. I was terrified of what he might say, and yet I already knew somehow.

He finally looked at me, letting out a heavy breath as he leaned into the bar with one hip. The feeling that spread through me was like ice. Brittle and sharp. His lips parted, then closed, as if he were trying to find the words. When he finally said them, the whispers that had been in the woods that morning found me again, curling tightly in my chest.

"He's back, Emery."

Six

EMERY

"EMERY, I ASKED WHEN the last time you saw Lily was."

I stared into the black window, where my reflection was illuminated in an orange glow. The fireplace blazed behind me, wood popping and sap hissing, but the house still felt cold.

"Em?" My uncle ducked low to meet my eyes. His cheeks were still streaked with soot, the outline of his flask visible in his shirt pocket beneath his jacket. He had a worried look as he studied my fingers twisted into the dirty blanket Nixie had wrapped around me.

My throat burned, my tongue still coated in smoke. The only thing reminding me to breathe was Nixie's hand rubbing my back in small circles.

"Before the party. At the pub," I rasped, not sounding like myself.

"What time?" He lifted his pen. It hovered over the notebook he'd pulled from his pocket.

Lily's face flashed in my mind, her blond hair lit like gold in the glow coming through the window as she sat across the table from me.

I pinched my eyes closed, trying to erase the image. "Lunchtime. Maybe twelve-thirty?"

The sound of Jake's pen scratching across the paper roared in my ears. "Do you know where she went after that?"

"No."

"You didn't ask?" he said, more impatiently.

I swallowed. "No. But she must have come by the house later because when I got back, I found a note on my dresser."

He nodded, still scribbling. "What did it say?"

I tried to think, sorting through the hundreds of moments spinning in my head. Lily on the dock in the rain on her birthday. Lily in the woods, chasing me through the trees. Lily lying across my bed with her feet propped up on the wall.

I sniffed. "It said to meet her at the beach before the party. But she never showed."

"Which one?"

"Halo Beach." My voice wavered.

"Did you see her at the orchard last night?"

Last night. Was it morning already? I looked to the window, where the swell of dawn was casting the sky blue. I shook my head in answer, tears springing back up into my eyes. When the ache in my throat exploded into a broken cry, I pressed my face into the blanket.

Jake set down his pen, falling quiet for a moment. "Did you see August yesterday?"

I wiped at my cheeks with the back of my hand, looking up into my uncle's worn, drawn face. For the first time ever, I thought he looked old. "What?"

"When's the last time you saw August, Emery?"

Beside me, Nixie looked as confused as I was.

"Why are you asking about him?" I said, weakly.

"Just answer the question," he snapped.

"Easy, Jake." Nixie's voice was a sharp reproach.

"Look, I need to know where everyone was last night."

"I met him at the lighthouse. Yesterday morning," I said, defensive.

Jake picked up the pen again. "Do you know where he went after that?"

My gaze narrowed at my uncle. I didn't like the look in his eye. "To the orchard. He had to work and then he was supposed to help his mom set up for the graduation party."

"Did you see him at the orchard?"

"No." I breathed. In the swarm of images racing through my head—billowing smoke, blinding flames, people running in the woods and shouting—he wasn't there.

"Jake, we need to get going if we're going to catch the ferry in time," Nixie said, getting to her feet.

I swallowed down the nausea that boiled in my stomach, remembering what my father's face had looked like when they put him into the helicopter to take him to the hospital on the mainland. They'd only had room to take my mother and she was waiting for us in Seattle.

Nixie pulled me to a stand and I leaned into her, trying to feel my feet beneath me.

"Just ask Eloise, Jake," I said unevenly. "She'll tell you. August was with her."

Jake only stared at me, his eyes running over my face as if he were looking for something there, and the faintest fleeting thought skipped across my mind.

He didn't believe me.

Seven

EMERY

I PACED THE FLOOR of the tea shop in the dark, my hand clamped so tightly to the hem of my sweater that the wool was damp to the touch.

Main Street and the harbor were empty, the light bending and fading as the sun went down over the rooftops. The hours had passed in a panicked blur with me watching the street from the window in a cold sweat.

Abbott Wittich, the editor of the *Saoirse Journal*, would be finishing his rounds, going door to door to call for a town meeting. In only minutes, everyone on the island would have heard that August Salt was back.

I watched a single leaf blow down the center of the street before my eyes lifted to the bare branches that lined the walkways. The trees. The starling. There was magic in the air, thick and fragrant. I could feel it bubbling up from the earth like a spring.

Floating lights appeared in the dark outside, lanterns bobbing in the trees like fireflies, all headed for the chapel. In the next moment, the doors down the street swung open and amber light spilled out onto the rain-soaked cobblestones, where half the town was already gathered.

I wiped my slick palms against my jeans and waited for the street to empty before I wrapped my scarf around my neck and opened the door. A shadow moved over the walk as I shut it behind me. Dutch.

His blue jacket looked black in the darkness and his blond hair was only half-tucked beneath its hood. Both hands were shoved into his pockets, his face illuminated by the light from the chapel. It reflected in his eyes as he looked up at me from the bottom of the steps.

He had the same look on his face that I knew was on mine. Dread.

"Was coming to see if you'd heard." His gruff voice was made deeper by the cold.

I hadn't seen him since our argument the night before, and I'd thought about going to find him at the orchard after my uncle came to the pub. But I hadn't been able to stomach the idea of being the one to tell him. I could hardly think the words, much less say them out loud.

August was back. After all these years, he was back.

"I heard," I said softly, hating the way it sounded.

For years, I'd have given anything to hear that August had come home. I'd imagined it a million times, until there were tears streaking my face and a pain cracking in my chest. But I'd cut that part from me long ago. So why did it feel like it was hard to draw breath?

If Dutch could see it in my eyes now, he didn't show it. August had always been the ocean between us. The past that had never let either of us go. And standing with Dutch beneath the unlit streetlamp now, it felt suddenly like we were eighteen years old again.

The sound of voices rose from the open doors down the street and I bit the inside of my cheek before I stepped around him, headed for its light.

He caught me by the arm, stopping me. "Wait a minute. You're not going, are you?"

I looked up into his face, confused. "What? Of course I'm going."

Dutch shifted on his feet, his gaze going over my head. "You sure that's a good idea?" His voice lowered.

I pulled away from him without giving him an answer. It probably wasn't a good idea, but I'd spent too long hiding from this town after August left Saoirse. I wasn't going to do it again. I couldn't.

There was a pause before I could hear Dutch's footsteps following mine across the street. The wet, fallen leaves were piled before the entrance to the chapel like seaweed left behind after a storm. Above us, the white steeple reached up into the black sky, but its bell hadn't rung even once in my lifetime. There'd been more than one soft-hearted Protestant minister who had come to resurrect the abandoned church and preach their gospel to the people of Saoirse.

They never stayed long.

"All right now, let's settle down."

Jake's voice carried through the open windows, rising over the sound of chatter as I stopped before the doors. His jacket was still zipped up to his chin, his cheeks flushed from the night air, and the dark circles beneath his eyes made him look even more tired than he usually did. He stood in the center aisle, twisting his cap in his hands when he saw me. He'd probably hoped I wouldn't come.

I pulled in a breath that filled my lungs with the cold before I stepped over the threshold and a hush fell over the chapel. Every eye fell on me, followed by the whispers. And I knew what they were saying.

"Emery and August . . ." I could hear our names tangled together in the silence, the way they'd always been. I clenched my teeth, swallowing down the hollow feeling it resurrected in me.

A hand touched my elbow and Dutch pulled me along the wall, to where Dad was standing in the back corner. His face lit with surprise when he caught sight of us, and I knew he was thinking the same thing. That we shouldn't be there.

He scooted over anyway, making room for me, and when the

woman next to him glared at us, he set his heavy gaze on her until she turned around. Dad was good at that—protecting me. Even if it had been years since I'd needed it.

Dutch fit himself behind me and the warmth of the room made me reach up to loosen the scarf around my neck. There wasn't space to breathe. Not a single person who wasn't watching me. Wondering what I would do. What I'd say.

When August left, he hadn't just left Saoirse. He'd left *me*. And I'd been dragging his sins behind me ever since.

It looked as if nearly every person on the island was present, lined up against the stained-glass windows that stretched above the pews. Each member of the town council was scattered throughout the crowd—my father, Nixie Thomas, Leoda Morgan, Zachariah Behr, and Bernard Keller.

"By now, I'm sure you've all heard that August Salt came in on the ferry this morning," Jake began.

Hearing the name spoken aloud again reignited the painful prick running over my skin. Behind me, I could feel Dutch go rigid.

"I know there are a lot of bad feelings." He continued, "This is bound to dig things up that we've all worked hard to put behind us."

"Well, what the hell is he doing here, Jake?"

I looked past my father to see Lily's grandfather, Hans Morgan, on his feet. Both hands were clenched in his pockets, as if he were keeping himself from hitting something. Leoda was seated at his side.

It hadn't taken long for Lily's parents to leave Saoirse after she died, but Hans and Leoda had stayed. When they were gone, there wouldn't be a single Morgan left on Saoirse. That was hard to imagine.

The pews creaked in the silence as people shifted in their seats and every eye turned back to Jakob, waiting for his answer.

"He's come to bury Eloise." His voice softened, and I could feel the air in the room change around the words.

The lump in my throat twisted, making me wince.

Eloise.

August's mother had been beloved before what happened. She'd been like a second mother to me and inseparable from my own mother and Nixie since they were kids.

"Seems she died a few months ago, and she requested that her ashes be buried here on Saoirse with her kin."

"Now, hold on just a minute." Leoda was the first to argue, standing from her seat at the center of the room. A deep frown carved her slender face beneath her knit hat. "You're not saying we're going to allow him to bury her in the cemetery."

Jake steeled himself. He'd been prepared for this. "I am."

"We only bury our own on Saoirse!" someone shouted, and the claustrophobic sanctuary erupted in angry voices.

I watched my father's face carefully for any sign of what he was thinking. But he was stoic. His eyes moved over the chapel slowly, the light shining in his empty eyes.

Jake lifted a hand into the air impatiently. "Now, every member of the Salt family has been buried on this island since this town was first founded," he said, louder.

Leoda scoffed, flinging a hand into the air. "Eloise gave up that right when she covered for her son."

A few others echoed in agreement. "She's not a Salt, anyway."

Eloise had become the unwanted daughter of Henry Salt when she married his son Calvin, but Calvin had run off and left her when August was only a few years old. Henry blamed Eloise, and she'd spent the rest of her years on Saoirse paying penance for it.

"Eloise isn't the only one who covered for him." Another whisper cut through the rumble of voices and I stiffened, swallowing hard. A few pairs of eyes glanced quickly in my direction, and Dutch leaned into me just slightly.

"Now, look," Jake said, more heavily, "I don't think I have to remind you all that August was never charged with Lily Morgan's murder."

Another silence fell, but this time, it was reverent. Lily's name was hallowed on Saoirse and I'd only heard it spoken a few times in the years that had passed. It wasn't just the town that had changed that night. It was the island, too. She started keeping secrets from us then, my grandmother said. And those secrets had become like the wild blackberry vine, choking out everything that came before. Before the fire and Lily.

Before August Salt.

The night of the orchard fire had folded my life into two perfect halves—one colored in amber light, fogged with hot breath in the dark of the woods, the full blood moon hanging in the night sky. And the second, wrought with missing the first. Everything had changed in a single moment. In a single breath. And I could feel that same thrumming now, faint beneath the wind rattling the stained-glass windows.

Nothing had ever been the same again.

Hans' voice took on an uncharacteristic edge of anger. "Everyone in this room knows he killed my granddaughter, Jake. That doesn't change just because *you* couldn't prove it."

My uncle shrank back at the words, the muscle in his jaw ticking. Lily's unsolved murder was Jake's greatest shame. His greatest failure. In a town where nothing bad ever happened, his job as marshal had always consisted of mediating neighbor disputes or the occasional act of vandalism committed each summer by a few teenagers drunk on cider. There had never been anything like a murder.

But it was also no secret that Jake had loved Eloise Salt, even if she never loved him back in the same way. And the belief back then had been not that Jake *couldn't* prove August killed Lily, but that maybe he didn't *want* to.

My father cleared his throat, stepping into the glow of the pendant lights. "Guilty or not . . . I, for one, don't think that Eloise should pay for the sins of her son. She was one of us."

No one argued with that. There was no dispute on the town's hatred of August, but Eloise was a different matter. My parents, Jake, Nixie, Eloise . . . they'd all grown up together like siblings.

"It's already decided," Jake said again, "August will bury Eloise's ashes in the cemetery and then he'll be on the first ferry off this island, I promise you that. Until then, he's been told to keep his distance and I'm saying the same to you all now. I don't want to hear about anyone hassling him or stepping foot on that property. Am I clear?" He let his gaze float out over the room, waiting for someone to disagree.

But there was only quiet. As if everyone in the chapel was remembering the last time we'd stood beneath this roof talking about Lily.

Jake slipped his hat back on, dismissing the meeting, and I didn't move as everyone silently got to their feet, filing toward the doors.

My father's hand landed softly on my shoulder before he wove through the crowd and I watched Leoda move in the same direction, followed by Zachariah and Bernard. Nixie wasn't far behind them and the talk of Eloise gleamed in her eyes. She looked as if she'd been crying.

Whatever Jake had decided, the town council would still have more to say about it. They took the side door out, already arguing in rasping whispers, and a few moments later, Dutch and I were the only ones left in the chapel.

"You ready?"

I stared blankly at the floor, picking at the loose thread along the hem of my sweater. I didn't know why I felt guilty any time the subject of August hung in the air. It was years after he left that Dutch and I started this thing between us. "I'm just going to head home and turn in."

He let out a long breath, but it was more sympathetic than angry, and I was glad. I didn't have it in me to fight with him. "Come on, Em. Let me walk you."

"I'm fine, Dutch," I said, a little too harshly, and I immediately regretted it.

He didn't look fazed. Almost as if he'd expected it. He gave me a single nod before heading toward the doors and he didn't look back as he disappeared in the dark.

I waited until there was only silence on Main Street before I started the walk to the house. The dirt road was almost pitch-black but I had every bend and buried rock memorized. I could walk it with my eyes closed.

Milk-white moonlight flitted through the tree branches overhead, flashing over me like distant lightning. The sky had finally cleared, the clouds peeling back to uncover the stars. But I could already smell more rain on the eastward wind.

When I reached the top of the hill, I stared at the ground and took three steady breaths before I found the strength to lift my eyes. Eloise Salt's house was tucked far back in the trees, just across the road from my own. The land was overgrown with honeysuckle and summer brush, the porch slanted with rot on one side.

He was really there, behind that door.

The night of the orchard fire, a rogue wind blew in from the sea, rolling over the island in a furious gust. And in that single moment, time split like a fraying rope into a before and an after. The snap of an old apple branch dropped a kerosene lamp into the hay beside the barn and within minutes, the fire had engulfed an entire row of trees.

Looking back, people said that the fire was an ominous warning. A kind of harbinger of what Nixie would find in the woods only an hour later, when every soul on Saoirse was fighting the blaze. The next day, Jake stood in the chapel to tell the whole town that young Lily Morgan was dead.

The cold danced over my skin, rushing beneath the collar of my shirt and making me tremble. The windows of the Salt cottage were lit for the first time since August disappeared, like eyes watching from the woods. There were times when I wondered if I'd dreamed it. If he'd ever been real or if he was a fragmented piece of my imagination, buried deep and painful within me like a splinter under the skin. But those nights in the woods were some of the clearest memories I had from before the fire. They were still painted in saturated colors, filled with breath even now.

I closed my eyes, trying to replace the images with new ones. The view of the sea on windy days or the boats in the harbor. But everything skipped back to August, as if he was intrinsically tied to everything. For so long, he was.

Eight

DUTCH

THE ROAD TO THE orchard was one I'd driven thousands of times.

The truck rocked from side to side as I made the last turn, coming to a stop beneath the sign that hung over the gate. I waited with the engine rumbling as the crowd from the first ferry crossed the road beneath it. The old, scratched letters on the wood read SALT OR-CHARDS.

It had been repainted after the fire, but years in the rain had made it nearly illegible again. That was how things were on the island. Always dying.

A little boy smiled at me as his father pulled him across the road, and I lifted two stiff fingers from the wheel in a wave.

I'd probably been about his age the first time I'd walked to the or-chard on my own, looking for my dad when he didn't show up at the house for a couple of days. I'd found him passed out drunk in the barn and had to get someone to throw him in the back of their truck and drive us home.

He was just a farmhand with hotheaded aspirations of running the place one day, but he was the only person on the island who didn't see himself for what he was: a nobody. He worked at the orchard for most of his life until he was found dead in one of the rows. A heart attack. One he wouldn't have survived the trip to Seattle for, even if anyone had found him alive. I was twenty-two at the time and I remember thinking that all things considered, that was a pretty good death for him.

Now I was sitting in the chair he'd always wanted but had never been good enough for.

The job of running the orchard hadn't been meant for me. And no one was more surprised when the town council asked me to take the manager's office than I was. August Salt was the only son of Saoirse Island who'd ever had a claim to the farm, except he'd never wanted it. That had always been my place, I thought, taking the scraps that August Salt left on the table. It still was.

I raked my rain-dampened hair back with one hand and propped my elbow on the open window, catching my reflection in the side mirror. The hours I'd laid awake in the dark showed on my face, and I'd had to talk myself out of getting up and driving to Emery's. I knew her better than she wished I did, and that's exactly why I hadn't gone. The harder I tried to draw her in, the further she drifted.

My eyes went to the closed glove box, where the leather was peeling back from the edge of the handle. The ring I'd bought her had been sitting in there for almost six years, since the day I'd bought it in Seattle. It was a simple gold band, the only thing I could imagine she'd be willing to wear, though Emery Blackwood was anything but simple.

The last few stragglers made it across the road and I coaxed the reluctant shift back into place, veering onto the narrow drive that led to the orchard house. I could feel the eyes on me when I pulled into my usual parking spot beside the barn. I'd felt them before I'd even gotten out of bed that morning.

"Hey, Dutch."

On the other side of the door, Kate was already working. Her coveralls were zipped up over her thermals to keep her warm on the first truly cold morning we'd had. She stood from the stack of crates on the ground, a drill in one hand, and her gaze had that look. The one that held questions no one had the balls to ask out loud.

"Morning." I slid out of the truck, careful not to meet her eyes.

"Morning."

It didn't matter if I was the boss here now or what pitiful shreds of respect I'd managed to gain. I'd known sitting in the chapel last night that August showing his face on Saoirse again shrank me back fourteen years in the eyes of this town.

Once, my entire world had been August, Emery, and Lily. If there was one of us, the others weren't far behind. But I tried not to think about those days. That road led to only one place.

It had taken years to go back to normal, but as the new apple trees grew year by year, so did the distance between all of us and that night. Sometimes, it felt like Lily had been all but erased from the island.

I wove through the crowded barn and unlocked the manager's office at the back corner, letting the door swing open. Inside, the stall-like room was crammed with a desk, a filing cabinet, and a corkboard on the back wall. Stacks of paper covered nearly every surface and I hit one key of the computer, summoning the ancient monitor to life.

I'd started at the orchard as a teenager like everyone else in town, hired on as a farmhand in the summers as we got ready for the harvest season. I'd gotten the idiotic idea to go to college in Seattle somewhere along the way, getting a scholarship from some bullshit math test, but it had taken one semester for me to drop out and beg Henry Salt to give me my old job back.

Now, I was managing operations. That alone would make Henry turn over in his grave.

Wide glass windows looked out over the barn floor and flits of light danced across the office as the visitors streamed past the wide-open doors. Their chatter drowned out the ache in my head. The soreness in my back.

I sank back into the chair, and took the order list from the top of the bookshelf.

"If I didn't know better, I'd think you were avoiding me, Dutch Boden."

I tore my eyes from the page, looking to the open doorway. Leoda Morgan's mouth twisted on one side as she looked down at me. I should have known she'd show up. There wasn't a single pot on this island that Leoda wasn't stirring. She'd been the one to put me in that chair and she hadn't let me forget it, either.

She stepped inside without an invitation and propped herself on the corner of the desk, folding her hands over the top of one leg. Her name had appeared on my phone screen twice since daybreak, but I'd ignored the call both times.

I clicked my pen. "Shouldn't you be opening the apothecary?"

"I think we have bigger fish to fry, don't you?"

I tapped the calculator, not looking up. "What is it?"

"You know exactly why I'm here." She arched an eyebrow, reaching behind her to close the office door. "What are we going to do about this August business?" Her voice lowered to a whisper.

I set the pen down, finally turning in the chair to face her. "He's here to bury Eloise. That has nothing to do with us," I said, trying to believe it.

"You and I both know he's not just here to bury those ashes."

A tap on the glass broke the silence and the door cracked back open. Matthew Bard stood on the other side, looking between us sheepishly. "Hey, Leoda."

"Hey, honey." She forced a smile.

Matthew hesitated before he returned his attention to me. "Sorry. Tractor's stalled out again. It's on row sixty-eight."

I let out a relieved breath, getting to my feet, and Matthew ducked out when Leoda scowled at him. She was a dog with a bone and that never ended well.

"We need to deal with this, Dutch." Her tone took on a warning as I stepped past her.

I stopped on the other side of the door. "There's nothing to worry about. Just let this blow over."

Her mouth flattened as she looked up at me. She didn't like it, but she knew I was right. Stirring things up wouldn't do any of us any good. The sooner August was gone, the better.

I fit my hat back onto my head and walked toward the open doors, where Matthew was waiting in the farm truck. Exhaust billowed out of the tailpipe, filling the cold air with a haze, and Kate looked up from the crates on the floor of the barn, her eyes squinting against the light.

But for a moment, the flash of sun lit her hair blond. Her eyes blue. And in the fraction of a second, it wasn't Kate standing there. It was Lily.

When I blinked, she was gone.

Nine

AUGUST

THE PATH I'D WORN down through the woods coming and going to Zachariah Behr's place as a kid was invisible now. I waded through the ferns and the thick undergrowth, finding my way through the trees until I spotted the corner of the cabin's roof.

The land was wilder than I'd ever seen it, and the house was threatening to be overtaken completely by the vines that snaked down the branches and fell like a curtain over the exterior walls.

Zachariah had lived alone in this corner of the woods since before I was born and other than the Blackwoods, he was the only neighbor we'd ever had. My mother had taken on the job of looking after him, and back then, he would have been out on the water fishing this time of day. But when I crossed the tree line and the little house came into view, smoke trailed up from the chimney and the chickens hadn't been let out yet. He was home.

My eyes roamed the woods around me before I followed the sound of metal clanging to the far side of the house, where the scrap lean-to shed faced the creek. The barn it was built onto was nothing more than a skeleton of wood, but the shed was still standing, its roof rusted over.

Zachariah sat on a metal stool that had lost almost all of its paint, hunched over the blades of his push mower that were laid out across the workbench. The tilted surface was littered with jars and tin cans filled with different sized screws, nails, and bolts. An empty beer bottle here and there.

His long johns were a dingy white beneath the dark blue elastic suspenders that reached over his broad shoulders. There wasn't much hair left on his head, though its remnants were combed.

The rotary file that was clutched in his huge hand stilled midair when he heard my footsteps. The old man still had his hearing, at least.

"Was wonderin' if I'd see you," he said, keeping his back turned to me.

I couldn't tell if his meaning was that he'd hoped he would or that he'd hoped he wouldn't. I decided I didn't really want to know.

"How are you, Zach?"

He started with the file again, scraping it down the blade at an angle. "Got no complaints."

"You look good."

He finally set the file down and shifted on the stool. His thick white eyebrows turned up on the ends roughly as he looked at me. His gaze studied the line of my shoulders. The shape of my face. The last time I'd seen him, I was a kid.

His bottom lip stuck out, but he didn't say whatever he was thinking.

"Jake says you're still the caretaker over at the cemetery," I said.

He nodded once, leaning into the table as if his back hurt.

"What do I need to do to . . ."

"I'll take care of it," he said, cutting me off.

So he knew. Hell, the whole town probably knew by now. But I couldn't hear any hint in his voice of whether the news about my mom meant anything to him. Maybe she'd already been dead to him a long time.

"I'll have it done in a few days." He grunted.

I waited for him to say something else. Anything. There was always a storm in his dark blue eyes.

I pulled my phone from my back pocket. "Let me give you my number and you can—"

"I don't need it."

There probably wasn't even a phone line installed in the house, I realized. And that wasn't how people did things here.

A drop of rain hit my jacket and I looked up to the treetops, where the gray had returned to the sky. By the time my gaze fell on him again, Zachariah was already turned back around on his stool, file in hand.

"Well, thanks."

I waited another moment before I backed out of the shed, my hand gripped more tightly on the phone than was necessary. I'd been well versed in the cold shoulder before I left, but after living in the outside world for so many years, the sting of it felt fresh.

Anywhere but Saoirse, I was just a normal person, but I'd never been normal here. Not even before Lily. I'd always been the heir to the orchard. Henry's grandson. The last Salt.

Bernard Keller was waiting at the end of the driveway when I got back to the cottage. He was parked on the shoulder of the road, standing on the other side of the gate, like he was afraid to open it. If I had to guess, I'd say the superstitions of the town had kept anyone from venturing too close to the cottage since I left.

When he saw me, he went rigid, shoulders straightening under the jacket he wore. It was at least a size and a half too small and his auburn hair was blown over his forehead.

The buttons of his shirt pulled as he inhaled a tight breath. "August," he said, in a poor attempt at a greeting. My name was hollow in his mouth.

"Hi, Mr. Keller."

I didn't know what else to call him. All of my interactions with Bernard had been in my grandfather's office when he handled legal matters for the orchard. He was the only attorney on the island and he'd been commissioned by the town council to step in when my grandfather came down sick one summer and refused to see a doctor.

The job mostly consisted of Bernard badgering him to deal with things that he'd let lapse or ignored altogether, like a kind of net under the business that would catch the town if my grandfather died. Most people had been sure that he would. But I hadn't been that lucky. By summer's end, the illness had gone, and we were stuck with him.

"Jake said you need someone to deal with some property matters?" Bernard hooked one thumb into his belt, tapping a fence post with the other hand.

"Yeah." My brow pulled as I studied him. He was fidgety. Nervous, even. "I'm only here for a few days, but I'm planning to sell the cottage. Can you handle it?"

"Sure," he answered, a little too loudly. "I can do that."

"Good. I'll get you the paperwork and keys before I head back to the city."

"No problem. Just drop them at the office with Claudia and she'll see to it."

I stared at him, eyeing the red glow of his skin. There were a few beads of sweat at his temple despite the cold. He looked like he was about to piss himself.

"If that's all, I'll be going then." He let go of the fence.

I watched as he fumbled with the keys and walked back to the car. Once the engine was started, he reached into his jacket and pulled a handkerchief free. He swiped it across his brow before hitting the gas more heavily than he'd meant to, and the back tires spun in the mud, sending a spray of it behind him as he pulled out.

A single bolt of lightning flashed over the treetops and I looked up, watching it spiderweb across the sky like the tangled roots of a tree. The electricity of it was buzzing in the air, and it rose sharply as my eyes fell to the other side of the road.

Everything stopped when I saw her. The biting cold crept over my skin and the woods fell silent, snuffing out the sound of the wind racing through the trees.

Across the road, Emery Blackwood stood beside the truck in the gravel drive, a set of keys clutched in one hand. Her breath fogged in the air, her chest rising and falling beneath the waxed canvas jacket.

Every muscle in my body tightened, holding me in place, and I swallowed against the painful lump rising in my throat. I'd spent countless minutes of my life imagining this exact moment. I'd played it over and over in my mind, painting the image of her from every memory. But now that I was standing there, no more than thirty steps from the person who'd haunted me for the last fourteen years, I had no idea what to do.

She stared at me, unblinking, and the color seemed to drain from her face, her lips parting. The wind pulled a strand of her dark hair across her cheek from a half-unraveled braid. The shape of her face was different now, missing the softness of youth, but she was somehow more beautiful.

She took what looked like an involuntary step backward and my fists tightened in my pockets as I searched frantically for something to say. But I couldn't stop staring at her. It was a moment split down the seams, clumsily stitched closed by fourteen agonizing years.

The set of her mouth wavered for a fraction of a moment before she clumsily reached for the door of the truck, yanking it open. I watched, frozen, as she climbed inside and the engine roared to life. Before I'd even drawn another breath, she was disappearing down the road.

I'd hoped, I'd prayed even, that she wouldn't be here. That she would have left long ago like we'd planned to. Before everything went to shit. But she hadn't.

That feeling that had climbed between my bones when I stepped off the ferry wasn't just the island or the orchard or the night that everything changed.

It was Emery Blackwood.

Ten

EMERY

I WASN'T SURE ANYMORE which were memories and which were dreams. I'd lost track of that a long time ago.

The hours had ticked by slowly as I worked, keeping one eye on the window. It took most of the day for me to realize that I was waiting. Half-hoping, and at the same time, terrified that August would reappear. The tremor in my hands hadn't left since I'd stood across the road from him, and once the shop was closed, I stayed, working late into the night on receipts and anything else I could find to do.

Knowing he was back was one thing. But seeing him, replacing the memory with something real, was another.

There were many nights I'd been so hungry for him. I'd imagine him coming back. Climbing through my window and into my bed. I would curl into a ball beneath the quilts in the dark with my eyes closed, because when they were closed, I could see him. Sometimes, I could feel his hands on me. As I drifted into sleep, I could hear his voice. The rasp it took on when he woke, his laugh, the way my name sounded on his tongue. I'd imagine him touching me, my face pressed into the pillow and the sound of my own breathing like the sea in a storm until I opened my eyes and remembered he was gone.

That he was never coming back. And the sound of my cries would turn bitter and broken.

Sometimes I would wake and for just a moment, I'd believe that he'd really been there. Because I could still feel him on my skin. Smell him in my sheets. But the remembering always found me. It was in the charred remains of the orchard and the silent island. The scars that covered my father's face. The emptiness in my life where Lily had once been. And then I'd close my eyes again, hot tears sliding down my temples, and turn back into the darkness.

It was nearly midnight when I showed up on my grandmother's porch. If there was a key to the old house, I'd never seen it. No one on Saoirse locked their doors, even after Lily.

I crept down the pitch-black hallway, to the room I'd slept in as a little girl, and fell asleep on top of the made bed with my jacket still zipped and boots still on. Here, I'd only been Emery—Albertine's granddaughter. Not the girl who'd loved the boy who killed Lily Morgan or the girl who lied to protect him.

I fell into a restless sleep, and that was when the nightmare returned.

A star-filled sky. A roaring black sea. The sound of screaming.

After Lily, the dream had found me every night without fail. But it had been years since I'd woken with the cold trail of tears stinging my skin.

I breathed, waiting for my vision to adjust to the warm light coming through the window. I could still taste cold salt water on my tongue, but the house was quiet. I sat up slowly, letting the vision recoil in my mind until it was no more than a tiny blot of black. I'd lived with it long enough to know it was never really gone.

I swung my legs over one side of the bed and blinked until my eyes cleared. The room had been my mom's when she was young, and then mine when I stayed at my grandmother's. After the fire, the four walls were a refuge, where I'd hidden from the world. It felt that way again now.

My grandmother was standing barefoot at the stove when I

trudged into the kitchen, her cotton floral robe wrapped around her small frame. She stirred the wooden spoon in a small pot with one hand and flipped a brown griddle cake with the other. Her absent gaze drifted across the kitchen, but her ear was turned in my direction, acknowledging my entrance.

"Morning." The word was innocent, but it was spoken in a careful tone. She'd been born without sight, but my grandmother always saw more than I wanted her to.

"Morning, Oma." I said softly.

The butter smoked on the cast iron, making the morning light hazy, and I went to the window, shimmying it up and letting the sweet, rain-soaked air inside. The sun was already well above the trees, painting the woods in a dusty, warm hue despite the downpour. It made the rain sparkle in the air like fairy dust.

"Heard you come in last night. I have a pot of coffee with your name on it." She pointed an elbow toward the corner of the stove, where the spout of the percolator was still steaming.

I poured us both a cup and set them on the table as she stacked the griddle cakes on the butcher block. It was a rhythm I knew. One I could predict. She poured the blueberry sauce into the green chipped beehive bowl on the shelf and I pulled the carafe of syrup from the fridge.

"I promise I didn't come up here to make you feed me." I sank back into the chair.

She followed the counter with one hand until it ended and found her way to the table, sitting down across from me. There was a knowing smirk on her lips. "I thought you liked my griddle cakes."

"I do." I smiled, setting two on each of our plates.

"So? What's up?"

"Nothing."

I answered too quickly, but my grandmother was a patient woman. She picked up her knife, feeling for the butter dish and scraping a thick mound of it off the top. I watched as she smeared it over the cakes, sipping my coffee.

Through the arched doorway to the kitchen, I could see the glow of the fire in the living room. The wood beam mantel was littered with shells, dried flowers, and half-burned candles. A perfectly oblong stone wrapped tightly and knotted with jute twine. At the mantel's center sat *The Blackwood Book of Spells*, its dark leather cover worn and soft. The thick tome was filled with rituals, charms, and lunar magic that had been passed down in my family the same way *The Herbarium* was. As a child, I would sit before that fire and flip through the thick pages, breathing in the smell of old ink and dried mugwort that was pressed between the pages. Too many of those memories had Lily in them.

"Nixie called up yesterday afternoon," she said, finally.

I closed my eyes, pressing a finger to my temple. She wasn't letting me off the hook that easily, and I could always count on Nixie to rat me out.

"She said our boy is home."

I stared at her, taking a breath before I answered. "He's not our boy, Oma."

She set her chin on her folded hands. "Have you been to see him yet?"

"No." The edge in my voice hardened the word and I pushed the tangled hair back from my face. It wasn't exactly a lie. I'd seen him, but I hadn't *gone* to see him.

"Why not?"

"Because I can't," I said, swallowing. "You know I can't."

Everyone on Saoirse believed that August killed Lily and got away with it. I'd be lying if I said there weren't times that I'd wondered if it was true myself. But the reason I couldn't go see him was more complicated than that. For fourteen years, my life had been defined by questions I didn't have the answers to. And I wasn't sure if I even wanted them anymore.

"I didn't see you at the meeting last night." I picked up my fork, pushing the blueberries around the edge of my plate.

"You know these hips. My bones get tired after sundown. I'm getting too old for town business, anyway."

I smiled at that. Albertine wasn't too old for anything.

"The Morgans weren't happy Jake's letting him bury Eloise here," I murmured.

She lifted one eyebrow. "Well, Leoda's always had a knack for putting her nose where it doesn't belong." She folded her hands together on top of the table. "I'm just glad Lily's parents aren't here to suffer through all this fuss."

Sometimes I went months without thinking about Oskar and Leah Morgan. They'd moved to the mainland a couple of years after what happened, and I'd been ashamed of how relieved I was when they went. There were reminders of Lily everywhere and I was happy to be rid of two of them.

"You should go see him," she said, gently.

The sound of her voice made me suddenly feel like I was going to cry. August's face came back to me, the way it looked as his eyes locked with mine across the road. The way his jaw clenched tight. I bit down on my lip to keep it from quivering and took a sharp sip of coffee, sniffing.

"Might not get another chance to put that heart of yours to rest, honey."

A single tear rolled down my cheek. If I didn't know my grandmother, I'd be glad she couldn't see that tear. But she had senses the rest of us didn't. She could pick up the subtle tenor of pain from a mile away.

"My heart's just fine." I set my hand on her arm, more to comfort myself than to reassure her.

Again, my eyes trailed to the book of spells. More than once, when I'd woken from the nightmares or when I was eaten up by loneliness, I'd considered coming here and opening it. Searching its pages for something that might cure me of the pain that wedged itself deep inside me when August left. I wasn't totally sure that's what I hadn't been doing when I drove to her house in the middle of the night.

"Well, what are you going to do?" she asked, holding the steaming coffee before her. A lock of her endless white hair fell over her shoulder, dropping into her lap.

The last time I'd been with August Salt, his eyes had glinted with daybreak, his mouth hot on my cold skin. Those years blurred together, in a long swath of dark wind that swirled in my mind. A clumsy stitch of broken memories I was careful not to pull at the edges of. They were sleeping monsters. Hungry. But I'd still been afraid to lose them.

"I don't know," I whispered.

It had been fourteen years since August left, but he'd never been *gone*. Not really.

Eleven

EMERY

"DUTCH BODEN, I'LL KILL you!" Lily screamed, the words breaking with laughter as Dutch hauled her up out of the water and tossed her into a crashing wave.

She disappeared beneath the white foam before springing up again, and her pale blond hair straightened down her back, almost to her waist, where her underwear was nearly over her hips.

The bottle of beer I'd swiped from the pub dangled from my fingertips as I watched them, and I pressed the bottom of my bare feet to the warm stone beneath me. It was a rare sunny day for early spring and the water was too cold to swim, but they'd jumped from the outcropping anyway. The four of us had our rituals and on days like that, we walked straight to Halo Beach after school. But August had been summoned by his grandfather to the orchard. Again.

Lily pulled the strap of her bra back onto her shoulder and when Dutch reached for her again, she trudged up out of the water, collapsing onto the blanket beside me. She stretched out, balling up the dress she'd taken off behind her head like a pillow, and I let myself fall back to lie beside her. The sky was bright and clear with a few thick clusters of clouds, a stark contrast to the slate blue of the rough sea.

I let the beer drift toward her and Lily took it, draining the bottle before tossing it to the sand.

"What the hell is taking him so long?"

"I don't know." I closed my eyes, watching the red and orange dance behind my lids.

It felt like August had spent every waking moment at the orchard that year, working before and after school, sometimes until late at night. I'd never liked Henry Salt, but I hated August's dad on those days, too, even though none of us remembered him. If he hadn't left, it wouldn't have all fallen to August.

Lily settled her cold cheek against my shoulder. It was like ice. "Let's go up to Wilke's Pointe tonight."

"And do what?"

"I don't know. Who cares?"

I turned my head to look at her. Her long arm was stretched out beside her, her fingers raking through the sand.

"We can sneak into the pub and—"

"I've hit my weekly quota of beer I can take without him noticing." I stopped her.

"Fine. Then Dutch can raid his dad's liquor cabinet. It's his turn, anyway."

Dutch shrugged in agreement before his eyes lifted over us, to the trees. "Finally!" His voice was hoarse with the inhale of the joint he was smoking.

I tipped my head back to see August's shadow painting the rocks on the path that led into the trees. He was already pulling the shirt over his head and dropping it to the ground. The sheen of sweat glittered on his skin from hours of work at the orchard and his hair fell over his forehead, hiding his eyes. But his jaw was tight, the muscles in his neck and shoulders tense.

I sat up on my elbows, watching him wade out into the cold water. I knew what that look on his face meant. He'd had a fight with his grandfather.

Dutch pulled an unopened beer from the crate, popping the top off. When August climbed back up the rocks raking the seawater through his hair with his hands, Dutch handed it to him.

"We're going up to Wilke's Pointe tonight." Lily shielded her eyes with one hand, looking up at him.

"I can't. I have to work early."

"God, you guys are so boring," she whined.

August ignored her, finding a place beside me.

I watched him carefully as he lifted the bottle to his lips again. If I asked him, he'd say he was fine. And he wouldn't talk to me in front of Dutch and Lily.

"What if we get you home before you turn into a pumpkin?" Lily tried again.

I could see the moment he realized there was no point in arguing with her. "Fine," he said, and shrugged.

I hooked my hand into the crook of his arm and squeezed gently. The water dripped from his hair, carving paths down the expanse of his back where the faint shape of a healing bruise was just barely visible beneath his shoulder blade.

"I'm fine," he said quietly, answering my unspoken question. But he didn't meet my eyes when he said it.

Lily curled into me tighter. Her fair skin was covered in gooseflesh, her cheeks pink. "God, I'm freezing."

"I told you not to go in," I reminded her.

But telling Lily not to do something only ensured that she would. Especially if it was me saying it.

Dutch picked up the flannel shirt he'd taken off and tossed it to her before he offered her the joint. Lily stared at it for a moment before she took it, taking a drag. But she left the flannel, wrapping her arms around her knees and shivering.

Dutch shook his head, a bitter laugh trapped in his throat.

"What?" Lily glared at him.

"Nothing. You're just so predictable sometimes."

There was a beat of silence as her eyes narrowed. "What the fuck is that supposed to mean?" she snapped.

I looked between them, but Dutch turned back toward the water, ignoring her.

Lily rolled her eyes. "I have to go. My dad's going to be out looking for me." She got back to her feet and shook out her dress before pulling it back on. Then she planted a kiss on top of my head, snatching up her sandals from the rocks. "I'll meet you at your house."

"Bye." I pulled my sweater tighter around me. In another five minutes, the wind would be unbearably cold.

Dutch watched Lily walk into the trees before he tossed the last of his joint into the water. "I gotta go, too." He stepped over me, dropping his empty bottle back into the crate.

"What was that?" I muttered.

"Who cares?" August said, a little too harshly. He pushed his wet hair back again as Dutch's footsteps trailed up the path into the woods behind us.

I fit myself into the crook of his arm. Lily had a flair for the dramatic and on an island where every day was nearly identical, she found her own ways to keep things interesting. I usually tried to stay out of it.

August fell quiet as the water climbed up the rocks, touching our feet.

"You wanna talk about it?" I asked softly.

"Not really." He took another drink.

I didn't push because it never worked. My eyes focused on the tinge of blue beneath his skin. The mark was almost invisible now, but there would be another. And another.

I don't know when exactly we agreed to start keeping the secret, but the older I got, the more I wondered just how much of a secret it was. Henry Salt was hated by almost everyone on the island, but he also held all the power. Without the orchard, there would be no town. But no one lived forever, even on Saoirse. At the end of the day, I realized, we were all just waiting for him to die.

August set the bottle between his feet, propping his elbows onto his knees. "Can I ask you a question?"

"Sure."

He hesitated, falling quiet for so long that I thought maybe he'd changed his mind about what he was going to say. "What if we really do it?"

"Do what?"

"Leave."

My brow pinched as I studied the look on his face. We'd been joking about leaving Saoirse together for months. Just getting on a ferry one morning and taking off. But we'd never been serious. I hadn't thought we were, anyway.

"After graduation." He paused. "What if we just go?"

I laughed nervously, pulling my arm from his. "I can't tell if you're serious."

"I am." He didn't quite look at me. Like he was afraid of what my answer might be.

I stared past him, to the water, where the clouds were beginning to darken. The sea had turned from blue to gray in a matter of moments and I could smell rain in the air. There were always kids who talked about leaving Saorise, but most of them didn't. Those who did usually returned. And the question wasn't as simple as whether or not I wanted to. Our families were on Saoirse. So were Dutch and Lily. There was the orchard. And the tea shop.

"What about the orchard?" I asked. "And your mom?"

August bristled, dragging one hand across the back of his neck. "Would you come with me?" This time, he did look at me. And the way his eyes searched mine made a sinking feeling pull at my center.

He bit down on his bottom lip, turning back toward the water. "Never mind. It's a stupid idea." I pulled my knees up into my chest, pinning my eyes to the sand between us. Neither of us had ever wanted our parents' lives, but it had all seemed inevitable. And I'd always thought that as long as we were together, it was something we could want, eventually. I'd never asked myself if I wanted to leave Saoirse, because this was where August was. But leaving . . . together? The thought was like the glimmer of light that touched the cliffs just before the sun rose. "Yeah." I breathed. "I would." The answer came so easily that it surprised me. But it was true.

August stilled. "I'm serious, Em."

I shifted on the rock, turning so I could meet his eyes. Maybe it had started as a joke, but neither of us was laughing now.

A small smile broke on my lips. "So am I."

Twelve

EMERY

IT WAS LATE AFTERNOON by the time I made it to the shop and found a note on the door.

The crowds on Main Street had begun to make their way to the pub and in a few hours, the last ferry would take them home. On the surface, it was a day like any other. But beneath Saoirse's skin, the island was humming with discontent. I could feel it in the flick of wind as I climbed the steps to the shop, my eyes drifting to the broken window.

Peter's careless handwriting ran off the scrap piece of paper that was wedged into the jamb. If I hadn't been deciphering the mail-man's notes for half my life, it would have been illegible.

Package for pickup—

I returned the key to my pocket and went back down the steps, following the slanted sidewalk. The post office was a tiny building tucked like a book between the bakery and the hardware store, with only one window that looked out to the street.

An iron bell hung from a rope on the other side of the door and it jingled as I pulled it open. Inside, the mail clerk peered up over the stack of papers on her desk. The sunlight reflected on her cat-eye glasses as unease dampened her smile. "Hey there, Em."

This was exactly why I'd wanted to avoid town and exactly why Albertine wouldn't let me.

"Hey, Margaret." I held up the piece of paper, waving it in the air. "Got Peter's note."

"Ah, yes." She rose from her chair, the hunch in her back tipping her forward and making it difficult to keep her glasses on her nose. "He said you were out."

It sounded like a question. No one missed a thing on this island, and every shopkeeper on Main Street had probably spent the morning speculating as to why I wasn't in the tea shop. After the meeting last night, there wouldn't be a mouth in Saoirse that wasn't uttering my name.

Margaret smiled up at me with perfectly straight teeth, waiting for an answer. Behind her, posters for stamps dating back all the way to 1968 hung on the wall. No one had ever bothered to take them down.

"Just checking up on Albertine." I gave her a version of the truth that would check out if she was comparing notes with anyone who saw me in that part of the woods.

"Ah. Well, all right, let me see if I can dig up that package for you."

"Thanks." The smile fell from my lips as soon as she shuffled to the back and my scarf twisted in my hands.

I knew how to play this game. I'd gotten very good at being watched, managing unspoken queries and indirect prying. Just when I thought things had finally settled, they resurfaced again in a rumor or a strange look cast in my direction in the market. People had been more forgiving of Dutch, chalking his sins up to youth, and when the town council made him the manager of the orchard, people had conveniently forgotten the past. I hadn't been so lucky.

Margaret pushed through the door again with two packages stacked in her arms and set them down on the desk, almost dropping them. I sprang forward to catch the one on top before it fell.

"Oh!" She laughed, pushing her glasses back into place. "Thank you, honey. Don't mind taking that one to Leoda, do you? Poor woman."

Leoda would find a different kind of attention from the town now that the wound of that night had been ripped back open. With Lily's parents gone, she and Hans were the only ones left of Lily's family. I wasn't sure which kind was worse—pity or suspicion.

"Not at all." I shifted the packages on my hip, dropping the note into the trash bin. "I'll see you, Margaret."

The door closed behind me and I pulled up my hood, walking toward the steady stream of smoke trailing up from the crested roof of the apothecary. Grandparents or not, Leoda and Hans were among only a few people in town who seemed to remember that when Lily died, I'd lost my best friend. And soon after, I lost everything else.

Not a single light was illuminated in the dim shop when I ducked inside. The cool air seeped through the open windows, where colored bottles of plant medicines glowed like stained glass in the open cupboards. They held everything from foraged mushrooms, to scraped bark, to tangled roots that had been washed of the earth they'd once grown in.

"Right with you!" Leoda's voice sang from the back room.

Behind the counter, an iron pot simmered on the little stove, filling the shop with the sweet scent of freshly cut sage and crushed juniper berries. Beside it, empty amber jars waited on the counter for the next batch of herbal honey.

"All right." She rounded the corner with her wet hands wadded in her apron, and her steps faltered just a little when she caught sight of me. "Oh, it's you, Em." She exhaled, smiling.

I lifted the package before me. "This is yours. Margaret asked me to bring it by."

She plucked up the glasses hanging around her neck and set them on her nose with a sigh before taking the box from me. "Good grief."

Her fingers found the little knife in the pocket of her apron and she ran it along the taped edges in three quick strokes. I took it upon myself to open it when she set it down, reaching inside to take out the rolls of wrapped tissue and stack them on the counter. For a moment, we fell into an old pattern, dissipating the tension that had hung in the air moments ago. There had been a time when I didn't know if Leoda would ever be able to speak to me again, much less look at me. But we'd all come a long way since then.

She picked up one of the bundles, half unwrapping it before she set it back down. The summers I'd worked here as a teenager, when the tea shop was closed for the season, came back to me in bright, shining colors. Each of those memories had Lily in them.

"Not there, honey."

Leoda pulled at the chain around her neck when she saw the stack of rolled paper I'd unpacked and the old skeleton key appeared at its end. It fell into her palm and she went to the glass cabinet against the back wall. When the lock gave, the door swung open.

"Mandrake," she said, almost to herself, "as medicinal as it is poisonous, I'm afraid."

She crouched before it and I handed her the bundles one at a time until they were nestled in the little wire basket on the bottom shelf. A jar of bird's feathers and a bowl filled with snake teeth sat above it alongside other items she'd collected from the island. They were the ingredients for a different kind of work than the cures and medicines she made. As kids, Lily and I had snuck the items in that cabinet for our own spells, hiding away in my grandmother's greenhouse to utter old words over a candle's flame.

"That smell brings back memories," Leoda said, getting back to her feet with a grunt. She tipped her chin to the pot of bubbling herbal honey on the stove.

I smiled. "You paid us almost nothing to make those big batches and the honey was stuck in my hair for weeks."

"Well, I had to keep you two busy. Trouble from the moment you were born, and I should know. I delivered you only three weeks apart."

I'd heard that story spoken from her lips countless times, and it always bent her voice a little, the corners of her mouth turning down just slightly.

I leaned into the counter, watching her lock the cabinet.

"Saw you at the meeting last night," she said, not looking at me.

"You think I shouldn't have gone?"

She seemed to think about it, finding a place to stand on the other side of the counter before she reached up to tuck the hair behind my ear. "No. I'm glad you were there." She looked weary, even older than her seventy-two years. She reached past me, picking up another roll of tissue, and she held on to it, turning it over in her fingers nervously. She was quiet for a moment before her blue eyes lifted to meet mine. "Did you know he was coming?"

"What?" Her words cut deep. "No. I haven't seen or heard from August since he left, Leoda. You know that."

She nodded, and her lips pressed together, deepening the lines around them. "Of course you didn't."

I tried to read the look on her face. Lily was Leoda's only grandchild, and she'd changed after Lily died. We all had. She'd never abandoned me, like so many others on the island had, but there were times when I still wondered if a part of Leoda blamed me. Maybe because I hadn't been with Lily that night. Or because I'd defended August when everyone was convinced he'd killed her. I hadn't ever had the courage to ask.

There were plenty of people in town who thought I knew where August went when he disappeared. That I'd lied for him. Betrayed Lily. Her death had garnered headlines in the city and gotten the island years of unwanted attention when the details emerged. A seventeen-year-old girl found in the middle of the woods with lungs full of seawater and no clue as to how she'd gotten there. No one could explain it.

Then only a few weeks after it was announced that August wouldn't be charged with murder, he and Eloise disappeared. No goodbyes. No clue as to where they went. He was just . . . gone.

"Why don't you come over for supper?" she said finally, coming back into herself. "Hans made an apple pie last night."

I blinked, picking up the other package and cradling it in my arms. "I can't. I'm headed to Nixie's after I close up the shop."

"All right." She stared at me silently for a moment before she went back around the counter. "Next time, then."

I nodded, watching as she dipped the long wooden spoon into the pot and began to stir. "Next time."

Thirteen

AUGUST

I PULLED ANOTHER DRAWER open, thumbing through the files with a cough buried in my chest. The dust in the air cast everything in a choking haze that diffused the afternoon light. Even with the rain falling outside and the windows propped open, that staleness had lingered, making my lungs burn.

I'd been at it for hours, combing through the paperwork that my mother had meticulously organized. The old filing cabinets sat forgotten in the back room, and through the crack in the door, I could see into the bedroom that had once been mine. The corner of the bed was covered in a quilt, and the floorboards were tinged with a thin layer of white. I hadn't been able to bring myself to go in there.

There weren't many bad memories in this house. My mother had been more a friend than a parent, and she was the only family I had besides my grandfather. And Emery.

My jaw clenched tight as I pulled the next file from the drawer. Other than a few birth certificates, an expired insurance policy on the house, and clippings from the *Saoirse Journal*, its contents were mostly from the orchard.

My dad left when I was two years old and my mother had taken his place at the orchard, managing the books and the tourist season while my grandfather ran the farming work. Henry had never seen her as anything more than a burden, but everyone on the island knew that my mother was the backbone of the business that kept the town afloat.

She'd loved the farm and I'd never understood why. My grandfather made it clear that she'd never inherit it. He would rather have watched every last tree sink into the ocean than see them fall into her hands. The orchard would only go to a Salt and he'd never seen her as one.

The cottage was the first thing that had ever really belonged to her. She'd come from nothing, and when the required seven years had passed after my dad left and she had the house put in her name, Henry was furious.

But in the end, he hadn't gotten his wish and I was glad the bastard had had to swallow that bitter pill before he died. After we left, there was no one to leave the orchard to except the town—something he swore he'd never do.

Still, Mom painstakingly cataloged order lists, equipment records, seed notes, and employee rosters, anything my grandfather overlooked or didn't bother to keep track of. Every family on Saoirse had someone working at the orchard at some point. It was the summer job for most kids and a seasonal job in the fall for nearly everyone else. Salt Orchards had built the town and then it had run it. Until the fire.

The last time I'd seen it, almost half of the rows had been burned to the ground, leaving a stack of even black stripes on the earth. I dreamed about them sometimes, and I'd wake with the smell of char swirling in the air around me before I remembered where I was. It didn't matter how far I went, the orchard and its scars had followed me.

I'd thought about going to see it. Maybe walk the trees one last time. But there were more ghosts in that orchard than I could count.

I opened the next folder, sorting through the papers and letting my eyes skim the old typewriter ink. At the bottom of almost every page, my mother's signature stared back up at me. The paper-clipped packet was a survey of the acreage that stretched up into the hills on the west side of the island. Every square inch grew apples of almost every color and I'd known more about the fruit than I wanted to since I started talking. The orchard was in our blood, my grandfather said, but to me it had always been just a curse. I still hated him for it.

I closed the file and set it on the stack to leave behind and pulled my glasses off, rubbing my eyes. I hadn't seen a copy of the deed for the cottage, and I hadn't been able to find one at my mom's house in Prosper, either. If I was going to sell the property and cut the last of our ties to this place, I'd need it.

My ties, I corrected myself. For so long it had been the two of us. Now it was just me.

The sound of a heavy knock at the front door echoed through the house as I reached for the next file and I froze, staring at the open window. I hadn't heard a car pull in, and the moment I thought it, a sinking feeling pulled behind my ribs.

When the knock sounded again, louder, I got to my feet and came down the hallway with hesitant steps. Behind the curtain, the stark outline of a tall shadow moved on the glass.

Not her. Too tall to be her, I thought. The tight knot in my lungs loosened just enough to let me breathe.

The old wooden floorboards creaked as I crossed the living room and peered over the curtain's railing. Behind it, Noah Blackwood stood with his hands stuffed into his pockets, looking out at the road. I took a quick step back, raking my hair to one side as my eyes jumped over the room.

"Shit," I muttered, reaching for the knob.

The door opened, letting the light flood in, and Noah turned to look at me. I winced when I saw it—the scars—and that sinking feeling in my gut grew heavier. They covered almost the entire side of his face, disappearing into the collar of his buttoned shirt. But that wasn't the only way he'd changed. The man I remembered as Emery's father had been ruggedly handsome, young with dark hair and a muscled frame. This Noah was almost all gray now, with deep wrinkles lining the sides of his face that still looked like him.

"Mr. Blackwood." I swallowed, trying not to stare at the rippled pink skin that striped his cheek.

He took his hat from his head, holding it before him. "August." His voice rasped as he said my name, but his eyes still held that steady kindness they'd always had. It was one of the reasons I'd always wanted his approval and also the reason he and his brother Jake couldn't be more different.

I stood up straighter without meaning to, adjusting my shirt nervously. "Do you want to come in?"

He nodded, smiling, but one side of his mouth didn't lift. "Sure. Thanks."

I moved back and he looked around the house with a curious expression as he stepped inside. Like he was remembering all the times he'd been here before. Dinners around our table. Nights in front of the fire. I remembered them, too, though I tried not to. Things were easier when I thought about the past as the time of my life that began in Prosper.

"Heard you were back," he said, looking me over. "Thought I should stop by."

"It's good to see you, Mr. Blackwood." I hated that I sounded like I was sixteen.

"Been a long time." When his eyes settled on mine, they held something else in them. A question, maybe. "I know it's not pretty but it stopped hurting a long time ago." He lifted a hand toward his face.

I swallowed, realizing he'd caught me staring. "Sorry."

"It's all right." He took two steps to the fireplace, reaching up to wipe the dust from the top of a book that sat there. "What are you up to these days, son?"

I sat back on the stool in front of the counter, grateful for the change in subject. He'd always done that—let me off the hook. And

I could do small talk. That was about all I could do. But the sound of him calling me *son* made me wince.

"Teaching, actually."

"Teaching," he repeated, as if he was trying to imagine it.

"At a small private college in Portland. The history department."

"Guess I can see that." His gaze trailed over the mantel again until it landed on the framed photograph there. He picked it up, studying the picture enclosed behind the glass. It was of my mother and Hannah, his wife. They stood side by side on the beach, a baby set on each of their hips. Me and Emery.

He stiffened a little, setting it back down. "We lost her a few years ago. Don't know if you heard."

My brow pulled. "What?"

"More than a few years ago now, I guess," he said. "Cancer."

"I'm sorry . . ." I cleared my throat. "I didn't know."

A flash of heat traced over my skin, making me feel sick. I'd lost my mother, but it had happened in the outside world. Something about this place had seemed to be untouched by time. Hannah dying was like a crack in that glass. And my mind immediately went to Emery.

"Seems right that they should be buried out there together, don't you think?" he said.

I half smiled, but the tenor of my voice shifted. "Yeah. It does."

When I looked up again, Noah was fidgeting with the brim of his hat in a way that set me on edge. "We always thought of Eloise as family. Both of you," he said, as if he was thinking the same thing.

"I know, Mr.—"

"We thought of you like a son, August." He stopped me, saying that word again. "I think you know that."

"I do."

I found my mother's face in the photograph. She, Hannah, and Nixie had been much more like sisters than friends. They were the only ones who didn't turn their backs on me after Lily. And that knowledge had turned my guts more times than I could count.

"Good. Then I know you'll understand when I ask you to stay away from Em while you're here."

An uncomfortable silence settled between us as I stared at him.

He shrugged. "I just think it's best if you leave her be."

When I couldn't stand to look at him any longer, I let my gaze fall to the floor. "I'm not here to see her." The words were true, but they felt like a lie.

"Good." Noah breathed, visibly relieved. "That's good."

It took a minute for me to get the courage up to ask. "Is she . . ." I swallowed, not daring to meet his eyes.

"She's okay," he answered. "She's good."

I nodded, unsure of what else there was to say.

He took the few steps between us and I tried not to flinch when he reached up, placing a heavy hand on my shoulder. "Now, you come say goodbye before you leave. I'm living over in the fishing cabin now."

I forced a smile, giving him a nod. "I will, Mr. Blackwood."

He set the hat back on his head and opened the door without another word, closing it behind him. The breath trapped in my chest came out in a gust and I rubbed both hands over my face, pinching my eyes closed until the sound of his footsteps faded away.

When I opened them again, my gaze went to the window that faced the Blackwoods' house across the road. I could barely make out the yellow paint on the cottage through the trees. In my mind, I could still see the image of Emery standing there in the drive.

I don't really remember when things changed between us. Emery, Dutch, Lily, and I had grown up in a kind of separate world on the island. Somewhere along the way, I fell in love with Emery in a way that I was both too young and too naïve for. I could see that now. But the tangled roots of it were still buried deep beneath the surface of me, and that pain I felt when I saw her standing across the road was still there. It had always been there.

Fourteen

EMERY

TAKING THE LONG WAY to Nixie's from the shop meant I didn't have to pass the Salts' cottage in the daylight. But avoiding Dutch wouldn't be so easy.

Usually when we fought, he'd stay away, giving me space for a few days before we slipped back into the comfort of our usual routine. Me sleeping at his house or him at mine. Dinners and weekends together. Sundays out on the boat. And maybe that's exactly how things would have gone if the last two days hadn't happened. Me, Dutch, and our problems were one thing. The past that we shared with August was another.

When his cabin came into view at the bottom of the hill and the truck wasn't in the drive, I relaxed. It was one of the only homes on the island that had been built in the recent past, and it had stuck out like a sore thumb on the wooded road when it was first finished. It still smelled like freshly planed wood on the inside, but the rain and snow had begun to paint its exterior into Saoirse's landscape, as if it had always existed there. The island had a way of doing that— claiming things for her own.

I followed the drawn-out hum of katydids hovering in the trees, the woods afire with the colors of autumn at my back. They'd surrendered to the season in only a day since the leaves had changed and the air had shifted, too, growing thin and crisp in the setting sun.

The last of the pumpkins in the field behind Nixie's house were buried in their withering vines, nestled in the overgrown patch behind the wood rail fence that surrounded the Thomas land. Nixie would let the last of them rot to seed for the next year's harvest, when the new pumpkins would cover the ground.

The house's wood siding was painted in a pale, chipped blue beneath a metal roof. The screen door squeaked on its spring as it opened and Nixie appeared, already wearing her father's old carpenter's apron.

"'Bout time, chicken!"

I held up the warm bag of fish and chips in my arms. "You want to eat or not?"

Nixie rubbed her hands together, crooning at the sight. I came up the steps, knocking my boots against the doorframe before going inside, and as soon as I stepped over the threshold, I felt like I could breathe again. Nixie was the first to catch me out, but she was also the first to let things go. I needed that right now.

She pulled two beers from the icebox and popped the lids on the opener nailed to the wall. "I've got the wax melted. Just need to do the dipping and the cutting. I'm not going to do another batch until the new year." She lifted the long silver hair from her shoulder, letting it fall down her back as she sat.

"You said that last month," I said, unpacking the cardboard boxes. The kitchen filled with the warm, salty smell of battered fish.

"Well, I can't help it if those idiots coming in on the ferry keep buying me out." She popped a fry into her mouth and picked up her beer, waiting for me to do the same. "To those bastards from Seattle." She clinked her bottle to mine.

I listened as she prattled on about supplies and the order from the store in the city that carried her candles through the winter, and when the bags were empty, I fetched two more beers from the icebox. The scene was a familiar one, and I was so grateful for it that I could have cried. For a moment, it was as if things were normal—our version of normal, anyway. The only thing missing was Mom, and I'd missed her more in the last two days than I had in the last two years.

Nixie pushed through the kitchen door and I followed her out back, where the falling sun had painted everything in the dusky blue of twilight. The red barn sat taller and wider than the little house, its doors open just enough to let a crack of orange light through.

She took hold of the iron ring with both hands, pulling one side open, and I lifted an apron from where it hung on an ancient iron nail driven into the wall. Old, rusted farming tools dangled from the ceiling and rows of strung-up yellow and red onions covered one wall, curing for the farmer's market in spring.

I took a long drink, letting the ale burn down my throat before I sat down on the stool. The metal trough was filled with clear melted beeswax that glistened in the lantern light. Nixie lit the burner beneath it and lifted the first dipping frame from the hook on the post. Together, we strung the length of wicking through the pegs, until each one held the spines of twenty-four candles.

It was a process that needed no instruction. I'd been helping Nixie with her candles since I was a child, and I had a couple of scars to prove it. Before I was old enough to dip the frames, my job had been to cut the wicking while my mother and Nixie worked over the galvanized buckets. They'd drink brandy and laugh until the sparkle of tears gleamed in their eyes, and I could almost hear the sound of it echoing in the dark corners of the barn.

"Didn't see Albertine at the meeting last night. You go up to check on her this morning?" Nixie finally asked, tying off a wick and trimming its length.

I pulled a pair of canvas gloves on, studying her. Her eyes were on the shears in her hands, but her shoulders were a little too drawn back, her jaw set. "Yeah."

"And?"

"She says she's too old for town business," I answered, picking up the first frame and lowering it down into the wax.

Nixie half laughed. "Aren't we all."

I pulled the frame back up, letting it drip before I gave it a hard shake and handed it to her. She immediately sank it into the trough of water to harden it and then lifted it back up.

"How are you doin'? You okay?" Again, she didn't look at me.

I'd been prepared for this—Nixie's gentle, loving probe that always had a way of getting beneath my skin. I wanted to tell her that I didn't know if I was okay. That when I'd seen August, it had felt like the woods would swallow me whole. But admitting that felt dangerous.

"I'm fine," I said, steadily.

"Emery . . ." Nixie's voice changed then. She turned her back to me, hanging up the first rack to cool, but when she sat back down, she dropped her hands into her lap, waiting.

I reached for the next set of wicks. "Everyone has a first love, Nixie."

"Not like that, they don't." The words struck hard, threatening to unravel the carefully constructed calm I'd managed to keep since I'd seen August.

"The two of you were . . . that was no ordinary childhood love, Em," she said, more carefully.

I bit the inside of my cheek, letting the sting gathering behind my eyes come in a painful wave. "It's been fourteen years." My voice was a little uneven now.

"So?"

"So, he left," I said, exasperated, "after all of that. After Lily, my dad . . . he just left. None of it matters anymore."

"Sure it doesn't," she muttered.

I gritted my teeth, glaring at her. "What?" I snapped.

"You think I don't know why you won't marry Dutch?" she said, matching my tone. "You never wanted to get married because you couldn't marry August. You didn't want to have children because you couldn't have *his* children." She looked me right in the eye when she said it. "Tell me I'm wrong."

I stared at her, unblinking. Hardly breathing. She'd never said it outright, but she'd accused me of it over and over in the way she looked at me. It had been laced beneath a thousand other words exchanged between us.

Nixie finished the next rack in silence, her unspoken thoughts cast over her face like a shadow. "After he left . . . Hannah worried we'd never get you back. That we'd lost you for good."

I hardly remembered the months after August left. I'd spent them beneath the quilts on my bed, letting the excruciating hours pass. I'd watch the light creep over the floorboards in silence, listening to my mother's voice on the other side of the door, and eventually I'd lost the will to even cry.

When I finally did leave my room, I'd spent every waking moment trying to discover where he'd gone. But they'd left without a trace. Not a single clue to go on.

"It feels like before," I said, swallowing, "everyone watching me, whispering."

Nixie leaned forward, setting her elbows on her knees, as if she was resisting the urge to get up and wrap her arms around me. "They're just scared. No one wants to think about the night of the fire." Her eyes seemed to glaze over with the dark memory.

Those were the words that people identified that day by keeping Lily's name as far from their tongues as possible. It wasn't the night Lily Morgan died. It was just the night of the fire.

I pulled the gloves from my hands, setting them in my lap. "You've never told me about it. About when you found Lily."

Her mouth twisted, her eyes dropping to the ground. "It's not really something I want to relive, Em."

"I know. I just . . ." I closed my eyes. "Do you think he did it?" The words strung together in a single breath.

"What?" She sat up straight, her brow pulled.

My cheeks burned hot as I watched her. "I've never asked you if you believe that August killed her. I think I was afraid of what you might say."

Nixie looked genuinely confused. "He was with Dutch that night."

"Not everyone believes that," I said softly.

Nearly everyone on the island was convinced that August murdered Lily. The question no one could answer was, why? The only thing that had kept him from being arrested was Dutch's statement to the police that he and August were at the lighthouse around the same time.

"They want someone to blame. They *need* someone to blame. This town made up their minds about August and it didn't matter if there was evidence or not. He was guilty." Nixie sighed, taking another drink. "I don't blame Eloise for taking him to Prosper."

A sound like water on rocks rattled the windows of the barn as the wind poured in, and my eyes snapped up. But before I'd even gotten the word out, the lantern flickered out suddenly, leaving only a slice of moonlight coming through the opening in the door.

Nixie cursed under her breath, getting up to rustle through the workbench against the wall for a match as I stared into the blue flame of the burner at her feet, my mind racing.

The match struck and Nixie had the lantern relit in the next breath, filling the barn with orange light. But when Nixie's eyes refocused on me, they had changed.

"Prosper?" I said, confused.

Her hands fidgeted with the next set of wicks, her gaze immediately finding the ground. "What, honey?"

"You just said that Eloise took him to Prosper."

"That's what I heard, I think." Nixie faltered over the words.

"From whom? When?" I watched her, gaze narrowed, but she stood, hanging the rack on the wall. "*Nixie.*"

She stared at it for a moment as the shifting candlelight moved over her silver hair. "I guess I figured she'd tell you eventually." She spoke so lowly that I could hardly make out the words.

My hands curled into fists in my lap. "Who?"

"Hannah." Nixie finally turned to look at me and her cheeks reddened as she wiped her palms on the apron. "They wrote letters—your mama and Eloise."

"Letters?" My voice no longer sounded like my own. It was muffled by the rush of thoughts spilling through my mind, trying to wash out the truth of what she might be saying.

"They were friends, Emery. They kept in touch after Eloise and August left the island."

Slowly, I rose from the stool with my heart hammering in my chest. "How could she not tell me that? How could *you*?"

Nixie looked panicked now. She pressed her fingers to her lips, as if trying to summon the right thing to say. "Emery, you changed after he left. You'd lost Lily and August. Your dad was hurt . . . I think Hannah was afraid that if she opened that wound up, it would never close again."

"So all that time . . . you knew where he was?" I said, hollowly.

The look in her eyes answered my question. She had known. So had my mother. I pressed a cold hand to my hot cheek, feeling like the barn was spinning around me.

"Emery."

Then I was walking. I snatched the lantern from the hook and pushed through the door, into the dark. Cool moonlight kissed my sweat-sheened skin and the smell of kerosene bled away, replaced by the scent of pine.

"Emery!"

The trees groaned as a gust of cold wind bled through the woods, and I looked up to the bits of sky that were visible through the branches. The night seemed to swell, the gooseflesh rising on my arms as I made it to the road, and Nixie's voice disappeared.

My boots hit the gravel in tandem with my heartbeat as I sifted through countless memories of my mother, searching for any hint. The tiniest clue. She had been my best friend after Lily died. She'd been the faint light that led me back from the darkness. There was a part of me that would never believe she could have lied to me. But there was a smaller, more terrified part that already did.

"*Emery!*" The faintest echo of a voice wove through the trees, finding me.

Not Nixie's. Another voice. One I only ever heard in my own nightmares.

"*Emery!*" Lily's voice sang my name, enveloped in laughter. "*Where are you, Emery?*"

A crack sounded in the dark and I whirled, lifting the lantern before me. The dim flame's light danced on the road and I searched the black, turning in a circle with my stomach in my throat.

There was nothing there, but I could feel it. Some remnant of a presence.

I started again, my steps quickening with each glance over my shoulder, and when the house finally came into view, I let out a long breath. I tried not to look at August's house across the road as I ran up the steps to the porch and opened the unlocked door. As soon as I slipped inside, I leaned my weight against it until it closed, the sweat leaving a chill on my skin.

I clawed at my scarf until it was falling to the floor and when I looked out the window again, the road was still empty. Quiet.

"It's nothing," I whispered to myself, pressing the flat of my palm to my hot forehead. "There's nothing there."

My fingers worked clumsily at the buttons of my flannel and I peeled it off, draping it over the back of the chair before going to the fireplace. The thin cotton shirt I was wearing underneath was damp, making me shiver.

I stacked three fresh logs on the grate and took a handful of kindling from the bucket, striking the long match. I stood before it, watching the flames catch the edges of the log until the comforting smell of woodsmoke drifted up to meet me. It slowed the blood in my veins as the warm light glimmered over the house and my eyes drifted from one dark corner to the next until they landed on the small rope dangling from the attic hatch.

After my mother died and Dad moved out to the fishing cabin, the small house had become mine. If what Nixie said was true and my mother kept the letters, there was only one place I could think they would be.

I stood and fetched the step stool from the mudroom, dragging it across the uneven wood floor. It clattered as I set it down below the hatch and stepped up, reaching for the length of rope to pull it open. The ladder slid free and I took a flashlight from the kitchen drawer before I climbed up into the thick scent of old paper and sawdust.

The beam of white light moved over creased cardboard boxes with my mother's scrolling handwriting in black grease pencil.

Photographs. Keepsakes. Sewing.

I lifted myself up into the small attic and slid the first one out from under a stack of wicker baskets. The corners of the box were held together with peeling strips of tape where the seams had busted more than once. I opened the lid and peered inside.

Toppled stacks of old pictures were littered over the top of several photo albums. I unearthed the first one, thumbing through the pages and turning the album upside down, shaking it. When nothing fell out, I reached for the next one.

I opened box after box, filling the air with dust, until the beam of the flashlight landed on the round edge of a hatbox. My hands froze in the air before I lifted it from beneath the stacks of paper and set it before me. I pried the lid up and my fingers clamped around its edges as my eyes landed on its contents.

Envelopes.

The lid slipped from my hands as I stared at the slanted script that covered the face of the one on top. I hesitated before I took one from the middle of the stack, sliding it from beneath a knotted length of twine and holding it before me.

There, the return address was smeared in bleeding, black ink.

Somerfield
18 Grass Valley Rd
Prosper, OR 97110

I bit down onto my bottom lip, breathing through the sting behind my nose as I opened it. A square of card stock fell into my lap and I picked it up, holding it to the light. An emblem of some kind was embossed on the center above the words EASTHART COLLEGE. I set it down carefully and the letter shook in my hands as I read the words.

Hannah,

I know I just wrote a few weeks ago, but I have no one else to share the news with. The first thing I do when anything happens around here is sit down at the desk and start another letter. August graduated from Easthart yesterday, and I could hardly believe my eyes watching him cross that stage. Something we never thought we'd see, remember? Getting him to graduate high school was hard enough. I swear you wouldn't know him these days. I'm so proud I could cry. Who am I kidding? I've cried more than a few times. I've enclosed the program and a photo I forced him to take, much to his displeasure. Some things don't change, I suppose.

My eyes dropped to the card again and I forced myself to pick it up. My vision blurred with angry tears as I opened it.

August's face peered back at me, a shy smile on his lips. The pain in my throat erupted and a hot tear rolled down my cheek. He stood in the dappled light beneath a giant oak tree and his green graduation robe was open, his hat clutched in one hand.

Behind it, a name was underlined on the roster of graduates.

August Somerfield

My lips moved silently over the name. Somerfield. Not Salt.

I closed the program and refolded the paper, not finishing the letter. The words were like a hot knife to the jagged seams that held me together. I didn't want to find out what lay beneath them.

Fifteen

EMERY

THE TRUCK ROCKED BACK and forth as I steered it downhill, toward the cabin. Dawn was just breaking over the trees, but I'd spent half the night pacing before the fire, trying to put it together.

When August and Eloise left Saoirse, they'd left everything behind. There were a few clothes missing from the closets, but the icebox was still filled with food and there was freshly cut firewood stacked on the porch. There was even mail in the letterbox beside the front window. It was as if they'd vanished into thin air.

As soon as word got out around the island, the eyes of Saoirse turned to me for a second time. Everyone, even my uncle, wanted to know where August and Eloise had gone. But I didn't know. That same sinking feeling I'd had that night returned, dropping in my stomach. I didn't know, but my mother did.

My eyes cut to the seat beside me, where the upholstery was torn, revealing the seat's stuffing. The letter I'd opened the night before stared back at me. I had spent the sleepless hours thumbing through the envelopes one at a time, studying the dates and trying to pair them with pieces of memory before starting at the beginning of the stack again. The first one had come only a month after August left.

The next, a couple of months after that. There had been at least five and as many as sixteen letters a year, each one opened, their edges softened by my mother's hands.

I hadn't had the guts to read another one, but the address alone explained why I couldn't find them.

Somerfield.

All those months searching, I was looking for Eloise and August Salt.

At first, it was just the weekends. We didn't have internet at the shop or the house back then, so I'd go into the city to use the computer, scouring the internet for any trace of August. I would wake before my parents and take the first ferry to the city, arriving just before the downtown library opened.

I started with basic strategies, plugging their names into search engines and clicking on every single result. When I found nothing, I tried each of their names with every state, hoping that I could find a location to go off of. I tried the post office next, mailing a letter to August's house on Saoirse and hoping that they had set up a forwarding address. But they hadn't. The letter arrived in his mailbox a couple of days later and when I saw the mailman deliver it, I burst into tears.

I created accounts on every social media platform I could think of and searched for his name, my heart racing as I scanned the thumbnail pictures of each profile, hoping to see his face. It became an obsession. It was all I thought about, day and night. Eventually, weekends in Seattle turned into weekdays in Seattle, and as spring turned into summer, I was almost never home.

I lied to my parents about where I was, telling them I'd gotten a job at a coffee shop in the city to save up some extra money. The charade went on for months until the day I came home after dark and they were sitting at the kitchen table waiting for me.

This has to stop.

He's not coming back, Em.

The words were like an arrow to my chest. Like the sickening snap of broken bone. I could still remember the pain in my lungs turning to fire, and a sound escaped my lips that I'd never heard before. A hollow, shattered cry from the deepest, darkest part of me.

It wasn't until that moment that I believed it. He *wasn't* coming back.

The road came to a dead end in a dense circle of trees and I hit the brakes, throwing the gear into park before the truck had even stopped. I snatched the letter up and shoved it into my pocket, pushing the old, rusted door open with a pop.

My father's fishing cabin was more a boathouse than a home. It sat on stilts in Frost's Cove, where the water was like glass in the evenings and the trees were so tall that you could make out only a tiny circle of the sky. Two boat slips reached out from the wraparound deck, where his catamaran was docked, its red and white sails rolled up tight.

I walked down from the road with the letter crumpled between my fingers. I didn't bother knocking when I came up the steps, turning the handle and letting the door swing open in front of me. The faded blue light and the smell that soaked the wood paneling found me, putting flesh to the bones of a thousand memories. It was the reason I didn't like coming to the cabin. Between these walls still lived candlelit nights and icy mornings and rare, sunny afternoons on the dock. Each one of them was colored with the same face—August. And no matter how much time had passed, the gilded edge of those moments hadn't dimmed, widening the hole inside me.

"Dad?" My voice filled the emptiness, but there was no answer.

My father spent most of his time and ate most of his meals at the pub, but it wouldn't be open for another couple of hours. Stacks of papers littered the old driftwood countertop, where a single propane burner and a tabletop icebox were stacked as a makeshift kitchen. The patchwork quilt was smoothed over the bed in the corner and my father's boots were missing from where they usually sat.

I came around the counter, pressing two knuckles to the half-filled coffeepot. It was still warm.

He wasn't supposed to be out on the water until his cough was gone, but of course he was. I went to the windows that overlooked the dock, scanning the trees until I spotted him. He was lowering his fishing pole into the boat.

There was no one I trusted more than my dad, and in a matter of moments, I'd know if he'd lied to me. I hesitated, weighing the cost of that knowledge. What it would do to me if it was true. But this wasn't just about the night of the fire and everything that came after. It was more than that.

I pushed through the screen door and took the rickety steps down from the deck. As soon as he heard me, he perked up, giving me a slanted smile.

"Hey, honey." He pulled the hat lower over his ears before he bent low to retie the line.

I stopped before him, a flash of heat licking my skin beneath my sweater.

He stiffened as his eyes focused on me. "What's wrong?"

My mouth opened and then shut. I shifted on my feet.

"Em?" His tone deepened, the way it did when he was worried. That sound, in itself, was a memory.

Before I could change my mind, I pulled the letter from my pocket, holding it between us. He looked confused, taking a step toward me so he could read the handwriting that scrawled over its surface. It wasn't until his eyebrows suddenly lifted that I let out the breath I'd been holding. I didn't even need to ask.

"You *knew* about this?" I whispered, my heart sinking.

He turned toward the water, his eyes scanning the horizon before he glanced up over my head, to the cabin. "Why don't we go inside and talk?"

"Dad." I said the word like it was the last thing tying me to the hope that I was wrong. "Did you know?"

He wanted to lie. I could see it in the way he only met my gaze for fractions of a second. "Your mother thought it was best that we didn't tell you," he said quietly.

The weight of my feet suddenly felt as if it might pull me straight through the dock, into the freezing water. I stared at the letter in my hands and a pitiful laugh escaped me, bringing tears to my eyes. "That whole time, when I was looking for him, you knew exactly where he was and you didn't tell me."

He stared at his boots. There was nothing he could possibly say to justify it and he knew it.

"How could you do that to me?" I asked, weakly.

He took a step toward me and I instantly stepped back, keeping the space between us. "I'm sorry, Em. Your mother—"

"She what?" I cut him off. "She's not here. So if you're going to try to put this on her—"

"I'm not." He lifted his hands into the air. "I'm not. It was both of us. We were afraid that you would leave. That you would go after him if you knew where he was." His voice was careful. "You weren't in any state to leave home, Emery. You were . . ." He paused, wincing. Like remembering it pained him.

But I knew. I remembered those days better than anyone. I'd fallen apart when August left the island. Not only because I'd loved him, but because I felt truly alone for the first time in my life.

"I'm such an idiot," I murmured to myself, wiping a single, pathetic tear from my cheek.

"Emery." He reached for me.

I shook my head, shoving the letter back into my pocket. "You're just like them," I said heavily. "You're just like all of them."

"We were trying to protect you."

I smiled sadly, meeting his eyes. "You sure that's all you were protecting?"

His mouth went slack, his eyes widening as I said it. And for the first time, the truth of the thing we'd never really talked about was laid bare between us. My father loved me, but there was more than one secret on this island.

I turned on my heel and I was grateful when he didn't follow. The stairs at the end of the dock carried me back up to the house and when I reached the truck, I climbed inside, closing the door with a sob breaking in my chest. The sound filled the silent cab, the keys shaking as I fit them into the ignition.

The phone on the seat beside me buzzed and the screen lit up with a text from Dutch.

Checking in. You weren't at the shop.

I stared at it until the screen went dark and I set my forehead on the steering wheel. After August left, my parents had tried to draw me back from the shadows. So had Nixie. But there was a part of me that had never left those dark corners of myself. They'd crept behind me all these years, even when I was sure I'd left them in the past.

Dutch was the only person on the island who'd understood that. In the end, it was the thing that brought us together. All we had was each other when the town flung us to the wind. But the more his hand tried to close around me, the more I wanted to run back to that darkness.

I turned the keys until the engine roared to life. The wheels cracked over fallen branches, taking me back onto the road, and the cold wind whipped through the truck, cooling my hot skin.

My parents had been right. If I'd known where August had gone, I would have followed. But now the truth was finally sinking in—that he hadn't just left the island.

I may not have known how to find him, but he'd known where I was. He'd always known. August wasn't lost. He wasn't taken away or waiting for me somewhere. He never came back.

He had never come back for me.

Sixteen

EMERY

"CANDLE?" MY GRANDMOTHER HELD the match between Lily and me, her eyes unfocused.

Lily was the one to take it, answering the question left hanging in the silence of the living room. "Air."

"And the salt?" she asked, her face turning toward me.

I picked up the little bowl she'd filled and moved it to the center of the floor. "Earth."

"That's right."

My grandmother Albertine had been teaching me how to bind herbs into charms and read the phases of the moon since I started talking, but I'd never been allowed to open *The Blackwood Book of Spells*. Not until my ninth birthday.

That's when my mother had begun to be taught by her grandmother and so on, and that's how I would teach my own granddaughter, Albertine said.

Her first lesson with the book of spells open was that every spell needed to be grounded by the four elements, Earth, Air, Fire, Water.

The candle's flame reflected in Lily's pale blue eyes as she blew out the match. The curl of smoke dissipated into the air over our heads as Albertine slid the book toward me. "Now, read it aloud."

I set my finger on the first word, following as I read. "Spells for growing."

"All right," she chirped, feeling along the floor for the single rosebud she'd plucked from one of the pots in the greenhouse. When she found it, she handed it to me. The lavender petals were closed up tight, the tip pointed in a perfect spiral. "Go ahead, Lily."

Lily's lips pressed together excitedly and she scooted closer, reading over my shoulder.

"Sun above and roots below. Wake from sleep, bloom and grow."

I stared at the rosebud, my breath held in my chest.

"Good. Now, again." My grandmother nodded.

Lily repeated the words and this time I joined her, stumbling over them until my voice found its cadence. "Sun above and roots below. Wake from sleep, bloom and grow."

The hum of heat under my skin began slowly and the rise of gooseflesh crept from my wrists up to my shoulders. The feeling was one that I recognized now—this whisper of magic.

It was the fifth time that did it. The buzz in my fingertips turned sharp and almost painful before the center of the rosebud suddenly unwound, the petals loosening their grip until they were falling open.

Lily's eyes went wide, her mouth dropping open. "It worked!"

"Well, of course it worked," my grandmother said as she laughed, reaching out for me. Her fingers felt around the bloom before she took it and brought it to her nose, sniffing. "Not bad."

She took hold of the apple on the plate, turning it on its side, and cut it right through the middle with her wood-handled knife. When she pulled the two halves apart, the seeds were tucked into the crisp white flesh in a perfect, five-pointed star. The sign of the witch.

"The first apple trees grown on the west side of the island were planted from the five seeds of the same fruit," she began.

I traced the apple's star with the tip of my finger as my grand-mother told the story again. I'd heard it a thousand times, but I'd never tired of the tale.

"By Greta Morgan," Lily said proudly.

"That's right." Albertine nodded. "Your great-great-great-grandmother grew the trees from sapling to grove."

"Until it was stolen," Lily muttered.

A frown wrinkled Albertine's brow, but Lily didn't seem to notice the shift in the air.

The Morgan family had tended the beginnings of the orchard until Greta's granddaughter married a Salt and its ownership changed hands. Now, it was passed from one Salt to the next. But almost two hundred years after the first trees were planted, the women of Saoirse were still the wielders of its magic.

"Can we do another?" Lily whined, dropping the opened bloom into the bowl.

Oma set the two apple halves on the floor between us, rocking forward to get to her feet. Her long white braid fell over her shoulder, nearly touching her waist. "All right. We'll try a daisy this time." She touched a hand to the wall, following it through the kitchen, and the screen door slammed as she disappeared.

Lily spread her hands over the open pages of the book of spells, her eyes sparkling. I watched as her gaze lifted to the kitchen, and I knew that look. Carefully, she fit a finger into one of the pages at the back of the book and opened it.

I sat up straighter, reaching for it. "We're not supposed to—"

"Shhh." Lily swatted my hand away. "I'm only looking."

I bit the inside of my cheek, watching the back door. Oma would be angry if she caught us snooping through the book, and she didn't need sight to know what we were up to.

The spine crackled as Lily let the page fall open and my eyes narrowed when I saw what looked like the skeleton of a snake drawn across the page in faded black ink. Beside it, a list was written out.

One raven's heart
Root of cronewort
Skull of a snake
Six hawthorn berries, crushed

The hinges on the back door screeched and Lily let the pages fall closed again, her eyes snapping up. Oma had a fistful of daisies from the garden in one hand and a pair of shears in the other.

"Are we ready?" She settled back down between us.

Lily looked at me, a mischievous smile on her lips. "Ready, Miss Albertine."

Seventeen

EMERY

I DON'T KNOW WHY I kept them.

I stood before the chest of drawers in my bedroom with a glass of wine clutched in my hand and a quilt wrapped tightly around me. The bottom drawer hadn't been opened in years, but its contents had been like a body buried beneath the floorboards that never finished rotting.

When my mother died and Dad moved to the fishing cabin, I hadn't been able to bring myself to take their room. It still sat unchanged across the hallway, and my own room hadn't changed much in those years, either. It was still home, but it didn't wholly feel like mine.

I sank down, crossing my legs in front of me, instantly feeling like I was back there on those dark nights after the fire. The quilt fell from my shoulders down to my waist, and I took another drink before I set the wineglass beside me. A steadying breath escaped my lips before I hooked my fingers into the knobs and the drawer scraped as it opened. Beneath a stack of folded wool sweaters, I found them.

The ferry tickets.

June 7. That was the day that everything was supposed to change. And it did, but not the way we thought it would.

I'd almost thrown them away a hundred times. First, because I was afraid of how it would look if anyone found them. People were already suspicious of August and knowing that he and I were planning to leave Saoirse the day after Lily died would only make things worse. But after he did go, the tickets had been like a last thread. One of the only things left from before.

I never told anyone about our plan to leave the island, not even Dutch. There was some part of me that thought for a long time that if August and I still had this one last secret, we still had each other, somehow. It was the pitiful hope of a heartbroken girl, and even though I knew those tickets were like a slow poison creeping through my veins, I'd kept them.

The next item in the drawer was the photograph that had been stuck to my dresser mirror as a teenager. I'd put it away after the funeral.

I hesitated before I let myself look at it. Lily's wide smile beamed up at me. Her head was tilted to one side as she sat on the dock, her toes in the water. I don't know what she was laughing about. I can never remember. A fifteen-year-old version of me sat beside her, my face turned to look at her. It felt like that was how it had always been. Me watching her. Taking my cues. Trying to mimic her carefree, spontaneous spirit.

The rain didn't stop for eight days after Lily died, and the fire department said that it was the only reason the entire orchard hadn't burned to the ground. The first drops began to fall in the early hours after the fire, while Nixie and I were on the ferry to Seattle. We spent the next four days at the hospital with my parents and when I returned to Saoirse, the rain was still coming down.

A cleansing, my grandmother had called it. The island's way of purging herself of what happened.

I could still see the casket in my mind, a gleaming black surface covered in wildflowers. The asters and red valerian and sage that marked the summer season as the solstice drew near.

I'd heard my mother and Nixie talking in the kitchen that morning about the eulogy. There wasn't a single person who'd wanted to give it. Not her parents, not her grandparents. Even Lily's favorite teacher had declined. What did you say over the body of a dead girl? There were no words for that.

No one remembered what was said, anyway. All I could recall was the sound of Lily's mother crying.

I reached into the drawer again, pushing aside a stack of papers until my fingers found the thing that I'd really been looking for—the brown file folder. I pulled it into my lap, debating whether to open it. The tickets I'd hidden to protect August. This, I'd hidden to protect my father and Nixie.

Inside, there was only a single sheet of paper. The deed to Salt Orchards.

If anyone else on Saoirse saw it, they probably wouldn't see what I did. Because they didn't know what I did.

Six months after Henry Salt died, Abbott Wittich announced in the *Saoirse Journal* that the old man had left the orchard to the town. It had been almost two years since I'd stopped looking, but I couldn't stop thinking that if I could get my hands on the will, I might find some clue that would tell me where August and Eloise had gone. I didn't. But I did find something else.

A buzz reverberated against the floor and I closed the file, pulling the phone from my back pocket. Dutch's name was on the screen.

I bit down on my bottom lip and picked up the wineglass, draining it before I answered. "Hey." I tried to keep my tone light, but it rang false, making me pinch my eyes closed.

Dutch wasn't fooled. "Hey"—he paused—"you at home?"

"Yeah, what's up?"

"I'm heading over to the shop in a bit to measure for the glass. Should I stop by and grab the key?"

"No." I closed the file in my lap. "I'll be there. I have some catching up to do."

"All right." He sounded almost formal. He was being careful. "I'll see you there."

"See you."

He hung up before I did and I pressed the corner of the phone to my forehead, sighing. There was always more unspoken than spoken with Dutch. We were a long, trailing conversation of things that neither of us wanted to say. But eventually, they came to a head. They always did.

We still hadn't talked about our fight a few nights ago, and there were only so many free passes he would give me. I'd rather it be the shop than the house, where I knew how things would go. When Dutch and I didn't agree, we made peace in the only way we did make sense—in bed.

I tucked the file back into the bottom of the drawer and closed it. A scratch against the single-pane window made me turn my head, and I squinted, trying to see past my own reflection in the glass. Outside, the arm of the aspen tree was rocking, the tip of its bare fingers hitting the pane. It wasn't until I was standing inches away that I saw the starling perched at the end of the branch. Its head cocked to one side as it watched me, almost invisible in the dark.

I reached up, touching the glass, and it fogged around my fingertips before the bird took off, leaving the branch swinging again. When I dropped my hand, the outline was still traced there on the window.

The trees may have finally turned, but the starlings still hadn't left. I didn't want to think about what that might mean, but I was sure that it did mean something.

I pulled on my jacket before I took the keys from the hook and opened the door, stepping out before I'd even looked up. I sucked in a breath when I almost slammed into the broad-framed figure in front of me.

The hood of my jacket fell back and every drop of blood in my body turned cold as a painful, piercing ring sounded in my ears.

August.

He stood on the top step, no more than two or three feet away.

Brown eyes the color of toffee met mine beneath the swinging porch light. I hadn't been able to see their color across the road when I saw him before, but I could see it now.

I watched him swallow, his muscles tensing beneath his shirt. The sleeves were rolled nearly to the elbows and his dark, wild hair was curling at the ends, his jaw covered in a scruffy beard. He stood at least a head taller than me now, but he looked the same. The exact same as I remembered.

His eyes ran over my face, like he was thinking the same thing, holding the image of me against the past. The feeling of his gaze dragging over me was like the cut of a blade.

"Emery."

It was a sound that I had played in my mind an infinite number of times. The tenor of August's voice saying my name. It nailed me to the floor, making it impossible to move.

"I . . ." But his mouth closed again, his jaw clenching.

My heart raced, my mind sifting through every awful thing I'd ever wanted to say to him. But looking at him now, not a single poisonous word could make it to my tongue.

"Hi, August." I managed to put the words together, staring at the small checks in the fabric of his shirt.

"Hi." He turned the cellphone over in his hand nervously, pressing it between his palms.

I glanced at the road behind him. Any minute, someone could drive by. "You shouldn't be here."

"I know. I just . . . I just didn't want to leave things like that—what happened yesterday."

I could barely hear him over the sound of my uneven breath. It wasn't just his voice. It was the feel of him that lingered in the air. Like the ghost that had haunted me for so long was finally flesh before me.

"Look." A bloom of red crept up his throat. It was something I recognized. "Em, I—"

Em. I couldn't bear the sound of it.

"I can't do this," I whispered.

His expression changed at my tone, softening, and the look he gave me made a burn ignite behind my eyes. Before a single tear could fall, I shouldered around him, taking the steps down to the stone path.

The wind picked up, tearing through the trees, and I climbed into the truck just as the first drops of rain hit the windshield. The ignition stuck, refusing to turn until the third try, and I shifted the gear into reverse as the lights flashed on the porch.

I willed myself not to look back as I let out the breath I was holding, but my eyes drifted to the rearview mirror anyway. There, in the glow of the porch's dim light, August stood, watching me disappear.

Eighteen

NOAH

SHE HADN'T BEEN MY little girl in a long time.

As soon as I'd closed up the pub for the night, I'd driven the single road from town to the house. It was the same road I drove every night when Emery was growing up, and often she'd be sitting beside me, her bare feet propped up on the dash. But tonight, I was alone.

The headlights washed over the gravel drive as I pulled in. Emery's truck was gone, the house dark, and I sat with the engine idle, watching the rise of the moon over the roof. Once, I'd let Emery climb up to sit on the eaves because she wanted to see the sunrise. I'd gotten up in the dark and put the percolator on before waking her, and she pulled the crocheted blanket up the ladder before stepping onto the icy shingles. There she sat, her nose pink with cold, and when the sun rose, I didn't see it because I was watching her. The way the color of her eyes changed in the light.

Much to Albertine's displeasure, we'd never planned to have children. But when Hannah told me she was pregnant, we both surprised ourselves by being happy about it and we joked that Albertine had probably gotten her way with the use of less than natural means.

I still believed that. The women had always been the ones pulling the strings on this island.

Leoda delivered Emery in the dark bedroom of our house in the middle of a storm with the power out, and the first time I'd held my daughter in my arms was by candlelight.

She looked up at me with dark blue eyes, the left one splashed with a burst of bright green. An imperfect seven-pointed star that Leoda told us was something called heterochromia. Albertine, on the other hand, said that it was a sign that Emery had been marked. That she was special.

The last time she'd looked little to me was almost a year after the fire. I'd woken in the middle of the night to a silent house. After months of Emery waking with nightmares, I'd gotten into the habit of checking on her. But that night, when I pushed open the door to her room, she wasn't there. I pulled the blankets from her bed and searched the house, calling her name out in the woods. It wasn't until I saw the faint light across the road that I realized.

I let myself into the Salts' empty cottage. It was freezing cold, but the little light over the sink had been switched on. I followed the hallway to the last room and there she was, tucked under the quilts on August's bed. I pushed the hair back from her face and pulled her into my arms and when she opened her eyes, they were red and swollen. I carried her back to the house as she cried into my shirt.

It wasn't the last time I found her there.

The cold air ignited the raw ache in my throat and I lifted my arm, coughing into the sleeve of my jacket. The sound crackled in my chest, my ribs sore. I looked at my watch again, tilting it toward the moonlight. It was almost eight and I'd waited at the house for almost an hour. I was already late.

I reversed back out of the drive with a heavy sigh and started up the road, pulling the collar of my jacket up to my chin. The heat had gone out in the truck years ago, but it didn't much bother me until January. The cold night was early for the year, even if the leaves had been late. The island hadn't followed its usual rhythms, as Hannah had called them. The late autumn had pushed things off kilter and by morning, there would be frost.

Hans and Leoda Morgan's house sat at the end of Old Pine Road in its own grove of redwoods that made the house look tiny beneath their stature. I'd driven that road many times, but not all of them were good memories. Not all of them were moments I was proud of, either. But we all did what we had to on Saoirse. That much had always been true.

The truck came to a screeching stop behind Zachariah's car, and I turned off the engine, sitting in the dark for a quiet moment. It was the last one I'd get for some time, I'd wager. Moonlight cast through the towering branches, painting white stripes in the dark, and I considered putting the key back in the ignition and leaving. But things had gone way past that now. I knew that.

The pain in my hip woke as I rocked myself out of the seat and I closed the door, tossing the keys through the open window onto the dash. The porch steps groaned as I climbed them and I knocked on the door in three steady beats. The lace curtain behind the window shifted just slightly before it opened, and Leoda stared up at me, eyebrows raised.

"Well, it's about goddamn time," she murmured, letting the door swing wide.

Inside, the fire was roaring, but the only light was coming from the dining room across the hall.

"Anyone see you?" She glanced over my shoulder.

"No."

"Good." She jerked her chin, waiting for me to enter before locking the door.

I could hear the voices before I saw them. Hans, Nixie, Jake, Zachariah, and Bernard sat around the table. In its center, a platter of pastries from the bakery was set between two candlesticks. Like we were at a fucking tea party.

Leoda lifted a teapot and filled a cup at the empty seat beside her. Mine, I presumed.

I took the hat from my head, stuffing it into the pocket of my jacket before I sat. But Leoda stood against the wall, watching me. "Well?"

My gaze traveled across the table from my brother Jake to Zachariah. The die had been cast long before this moment, but I still didn't like it.

"We might have a problem," I said, my voice hoarse. I picked up the tea and took a sip.

"What kind of problem?" Leoda waited, her mouth pressed into a hard line.

I stared into the cup for a long moment before I looked back up at her. "It's Emery."

Nineteen

AUGUST

I SHOULDN'T HAVE GONE. Not just because Noah had asked me to stay away. But also because I'd known what it would do to me.

I stood out on the black street, staring at the sign that hung over the door.

BLACKWOOD'S TEA SHOP

I used to stand beneath that window on late afternoons, waiting for Emery's mom to release her from the register. We'd go to her dad's fishing cabin and tear off our clothes before jumping into the cold water. Then we'd swim until we couldn't stand it, and lie on the dock in the sun until it went down.

The cabin was the place we'd had almost every first. The first time she cried in front of me and our first real, screaming fight. The first time she'd ever given herself to me was in that cabin and it was also the last place I'd seen her.

Now, standing in front of the tea shop, it felt like I was waiting again. For what, I had no idea.

I came up the steep stone steps until I could see her through the window. Emery sat at the wooden worktable with a laptop open and her face illuminated with the blue light. Her brow was wrinkled as she read whatever she saw on the screen, the braid over her shoulder unraveling again. She looked so much like her mom in that moment that it was almost unnerving.

I almost didn't knock, talking myself out of it several times before my fist tapped the glass softly.

Her eyes snapped up and then squinted, and the moment she made out my face she shrank back. Her hands dropped into her lap and she stared at me for several seconds, as if waiting to see what I would do. She wasn't going to invite me inside, but she wasn't telling me to leave, either. I took that as a good sign that she wouldn't throw the laptop at me if I let myself in.

I turned the knob and the bell jingled as the door opened. Above the threshold, a bundle of rosemary hung from a tied string. After years of not living with my mom, I'd forgotten those little things.

The orderly shelves of tea covered the wall of the shop, only half of the small room lit with a single overhead light. It felt smaller, the walls crowding in on every side, and the ceiling somehow seemed lower than the last time I stood beneath it.

And I wasn't the only one who had changed. Emery always said she'd never run that shop, and yet, here she was.

She was still staring at me, and I immediately thought that it was just like her to sit there, waiting patiently for me to make an ass of myself. We both knew I would.

"Hey." I breathed.

Her gaze moved from my face to my hair, down to my hands. "Hey." The edge that had been in her voice earlier was gone. Now, she only looked tired. Exhausted, even.

"Look, I know you don't want to see me. I just wasn't sure if you'd still be here, on Saoirse, and—"

"Why wouldn't I be?"

"I just meant that . . ."

"What?" Anger sharpened the words again. "What did you mean?"

I gave up. It was a stupid thing to say. "Nothing."

She bit the inside of her cheek, letting out a heavy breath. "I meant it when I said I can't do this, August."

"Well, I can't leave until we do." I just said it. There was no point in skirting around it. We weren't going to get another chance.

She swallowed, staring at the screen of the laptop before she turned it toward me. A faculty photo of me on the Everdeen College website took up half the screen.

"Somerfield," she said, hollowly.

I studied her face for any clue as to what she was thinking. It wasn't a question, but I still felt like I was supposed to give her an answer. "We changed it," I said, "after."

One of the first things my mother had done when we landed in Prosper was change our names. She was terrified someone would see the newspapers from Portland or Seattle and realize who I was.

"Well, that explains why I couldn't find you."

Heat crept up the back of my neck, making me shift on my feet. "Find me?"

"Come on, August. Don't be an asshole." She sighed.

"I'm not. I honestly wasn't sure if you—"

"Well, I did," she said flatly. "For way too long."

The heat on my skin was almost a fire now, making a cold sweat bead along my hairline. I'd known it would hurt her when I left, but I also knew that I was doing her a favor, whether she knew it or not. I told myself the same thing I'd told myself for years—that it was so long ago that it didn't matter now anyway. So, why did I feel like my chest was caving in?

"I'm sorry about your mom." She turned the laptop back around and closed it, making the shop even darker. "I should have said that earlier."

"Thanks." I cleared my throat. "And I heard about Hannah. I'm sorry."

"Yeah" was her only reply. "When is the funeral?"

"I don't know if it'll really be a funeral, but I'm waiting for Zach to tell me when he'll have the plot dug. Maybe a day or two."

"Will you let me know?"

I stilled. "Sure."

I don't know why that was the thing that made the lump come up into my throat. I turned, letting my eyes roam over the shop so that I didn't have to look at her. I'd forgotten how she did that—always looking me right in the eye like she could hear every single thought.

"So, you took over your mom's shop." I changed the subject.

For a moment, she looked embarrassed. "You probably think that's pathetic," she murmured.

"No. Hannah would have liked that."

A small smile pulled at her lips. "Yeah, I guess she did."

On Saoirse, the young inherited from the old in both life and trade. The only other option was to leave, like my dad did. If things had gone differently, Emery and I would have done the same. I tried not to think about where we might be now if we would have.

"You're a teacher now?" she asked.

"I am."

"You like it?"

I smiled, surprising myself. "I kind of love it, actually."

"Good."

When her eyes finally met mine again, I reminded myself to breathe. She was still so beautiful, in that kind of sea-swept way she'd always been. It hurt to look at her.

I drew in a long breath and let it go. The longer I stood there, the more unsure I was of what I was going to do. I had to get this over with.

"Look, Em . . ."

"You could have said goodbye." She cut me off, eyes glinting. They sparkled with what looked like tears and I willed myself not to look away from her.

I knew what she thought. That I had been a coward. That I'd been selfish. And she was right. About all of it.

"No." I paused. "I couldn't." The words wouldn't come, but I could tell by the way her mouth tilted that she knew my meaning. If I'd said goodbye, I would have never been able to leave. And that wasn't an option.

She stared at me, warring with herself over what she was going to say next. Whatever it was, I'd lived in fear of it for a long time.

"August—"

The door to the shop opened behind me, and I turned as Dutch Boden ducked inside, pulling open his dripping jacket without even looking up. When he finally did, he stopped short, eyes going wide.

His long blond hair almost reached his shoulders, streaked with sunlight. He was tall now, taller than I would have imagined.

His blue eyes jumped from me to Emery. "August." He said my name like it stung in his mouth. "Hey, man."

Emery wiped at the corner of her eye, and the air shifted in the room with something I wasn't putting together.

"Hey." I stepped forward, extending a hand toward Dutch because I didn't know what else I could do. We weren't strangers, but we weren't friends anymore, either.

He took it, shaking firmly. "I heard you were back." Still, Dutch was looking to Emery, like he was waiting for her to say something.

"Just for a few days."

An unsettling quiet fell in the shop as the three of us stared at one another and I couldn't help but wonder if we were all thinking about the only one of us who wasn't there: Lily. It had always been the four of us.

It was Dutch who finally broke the silence. "Sorry about Eloise."

"Thanks." I nodded, eyeing the bits of straw stuck to the hem of his flannel shirt. "You still working at the orchard?"

"Yeah."

"Who's running things over there now?"

Dutch and Emery shared another silent exchange before he answered. "I am, actually."

I couldn't hide my surprise at that. "Wow." That was all I could think to say.

My grandfather had tolerated Dutch, but he'd never thought much of him.

"Jake says you're packing things up over at the cottage," Dutch said.

"Packing up?" Emery echoed, the defensive tone creeping back into her voice.

"Yeah. I'm selling it."

I didn't know what that look on her face now was. Nostalgia? Betrayal? Maybe both.

"Well, let me know if you need any help. I can come by." Dutch came around the table to stand behind the stool Emery was sitting on and I didn't miss that his leg brushed her arm.

Emery's eyes dropped from mine again and her cheeks flushed, confirming it. They were a thing now. Maybe more than a thing. My eyes instantly went to the ring finger of her left hand, but it was bare, and it took every ounce of will not to exhale with relief. It was stupid, but I couldn't help it.

"Well, I was just headed out." I stepped backward, looking between the two of them. "I'll see you guys."

I pulled the door back open and drew in another breath that made my lungs ache. My feet came down the steps more quickly than necessary, and before I'd even crossed the street, the shop door was opening again.

"Hey! August!"

I stopped, hesitating before I turned around. We didn't need to do this. In fact, I didn't want to.

Dutch's even pace crossed the street until he reached me. He was smiling, but it was thin. I could see right through it. "That was kind of weird back there."

"Kind of."

He ran a hand through his hair, taking on that air that he used to have when we were teenagers. Like he was in control, even though we both knew he wasn't. And just like back then, I let him have it. "Emery and I have been together awhile. Didn't mean for you to find out like that."

I shrugged. "It's been a long time, Dutch. I think we're good."

He lifted his chin, looking down his nose at me. There was something he wasn't saying.

"What is it?"

Dutch took his time, looking up the street toward the woods before he answered. "I don't know, man. You leave without a word and then you just show up out of nowhere . . . I guess I just don't really know what to say."

"There's nothing *to* say." I was trying to give him an out, but he wasn't taking it. He'd never known when to shut his mouth.

"You sure about that?" He paused, lowering his voice. "I mean, how could you just take off like that after . . ."

"After what?"

Dutch's voice lowered. "After what I did for you."

My eyes went over his head, to the cracked shop window. The light was cast onto the street in a diagonal line. That's what this was about. Emery. "Does she know?"

"No."

That time, I did exhale. I didn't want to admit it, but the possibility of Emery knowing everything made my stomach turn. If I had to guess, I would have said that Dutch felt the same.

"And I think it should stay that way." He leveled his gaze at me.

"I get it. You don't want me messing anything up for you."

"Come on, August, I just don't want Emery—"

"To find out I'm not the only one who lied that night?" I cut him off.

Dutch leaned back, his expression instantly changing. The timid friend walking on eggshells he'd been inside the shop a moment ago was gone now. He matched my cold stare wordlessly.

"I told you. I'll be out of here in a few days," I said, heavily. I turned on my heel, pacing up the street and leaving him standing in the dark with the glow of the shop behind him. "It'll be like I was never here."

Twenty

EMERY

I THINK I'VE MADE *a terrible mistake.*

I sat on the living room floor, the quilt pulled tight around me. The fire had almost gone cold, but I couldn't feel the chill. I'd lain awake in the dark for hours with the sound of the woods coming through my window, afraid to fall asleep. Because when I did, I knew what would come.

Albertine had warned me when I was little that there was no such thing as nightmares. Not really. Dreams carried all kinds of messages, some of them unpleasant, but they were messages all the same.

They started the night I came back to the island, after staying at the hospital in Seattle with my dad. I'd tossed and turned in my bed, thrashing in a cold sweat until the screams woke Nixie and I opened my eyes to her standing over my bed, shaking me. It took months for them to fade with the help of one of Albertine's charms, bones of crow.

But going to my grandmother again was a last resort. She would press beneath the surface until she found the aching wound, and I couldn't bear that.

I'd never told anyone what I saw on those nights, fearing that if I did, it would somehow cross from the shadow of my mind to the light of day. It had been years since I'd heard the screaming and woken with the numbing cold in my fingertips. But it had been three nights since the starling flew into the window, and with each one, the dream had returned.

I finally got up and lit the candle, dragging the quilt behind me as I came down the hallway to the living room. There was a whisper in the air when I lifted the lid on the box. For a moment, I thought it was some kind of warning, my mother touching the veil of the Otherworld in a last plea from her to let the past go.

But I couldn't let go. My mother had never been one to keep secrets. Yet she did. Fifty-eight of them. And all this time, they had been up there in the attic. Just waiting to be found.

I pulled the envelopes from the box, sorting them on the floor before me. The postage dates spanned eight years, beginning one month after August and Eloise left Saoirse and ending four months before my mother died.

We'd never kept secrets from each other before. It wasn't until after the fire that my parents started lying to me. I could hear it in the lilt of their voices, when they smiled too wide or when they didn't quite look me in the eye. It was little things at first. Futile attempts at distracting me or sugarcoating something that was overheard in town.

The memories whirled into blurred colors and shapes. Those nights had been cold. Lonely. After August left, I cried myself to sleep every night, watching my father's shadow beneath my door, and I stopped leaving the house. It was months before I'd even let Dutch come over. A few times a week, he'd show up on the porch and I'd refuse to come to the door. So he and my dad would sit out on the steps and talk awhile until he left.

Eventually, I stopped looking for August, but I didn't stop thinking about him.

Every autumn, when the crowds filled Main Street, I would watch out the window of my mother's shop and imagine him appearing in the stream of faces. More than once, I even thought I saw him.

It took longer than I wanted to admit for me to realize that I couldn't cut him from me. That some part of him had been fused to places I couldn't even see. It followed me wherever I went. And each day when the sun went down, I dreaded that moment that the aching would find me again.

There were bad nights and then there were worse nights, but every single one of them, I was alone.

Faint sunlight was lifting over the trees outside by the time I summoned up the courage to pull the first letter from its envelope. I held my breath, biting the inside of my cheek as I began to read. Eloise's slanted handwriting pulled across the pages in even, practiced lines.

Hannah,

We've made it to Prosper, and it's just as beautiful as I remember. Beautiful, but it's not home. The house we've rented is furnished. The neighborhood is mostly quiet, but the sound of traffic on the main road is a bit grating. We'll get used to it. I think we'll get used to things. We both just need a fresh start. A clean slate.

Please write and tell me how the orchard is getting on. I'm desperate to know. And please don't tell anyone I've written. Please don't tell Emery.

Love,
Eloise

I swallowed, staring at my name written in Eloise's script. We'd always been close. We were family. August wasn't the only one who'd broken my heart when they left.

If this was the first letter she'd written, then my parents had known about her plan and where she was going before August and Eloise even left. I wondered now if they were the only ones.

I refolded the letter and slid it back into the envelope. The next one was posted two months later.

Hannah,

August started at the community college last week. Never thought I'd say those words. He's never wanted to go to college. I guess that's one good thing that's come out of this mess. He's quiet and I admit it's been worrying me. I'm trying not to ask too many questions or bother him, but you know how I worry.

I've found a tea shop in town, but it's nothing to yours. Can I burden you with a small request? I would be so grateful if you'd send me some tea from the shop. I started a job working at a café while August is at school and so far, it's fine. I've been thinking I might sell the cottage on the island and give the money to August for school. I don't know. It feels too final to sell that house when it's been in the family so long. Henry would probably have a fit.

The sea is different here. It feels and smells different. So do the trees.

Love,
Eloise

Hannah,

My grandmother used to always say that if you left the island, it would call you back. I think that's true. I dream about it. Sometimes I feel like I can feel its fingers in the air, pulling me back north to Puget Sound. We don't belong here.

Sorry for the sad letter. I'll do better next time.

Love,
Eloise

Hannah,

I think I've made a terrible mistake. I woke up a few days ago and August was gone. I thought he'd left early for class, but when he didn't come home by afternoon, I spent the whole night pacing the floor. I didn't want to call the police. I don't want them finding out about what happened. I don't want anyone here to know.

He was gone almost two days and then he showed up late last night. He went back to the island. I could almost smell it on him, Hannah—that smell of the woods. I honestly don't know what he was thinking. He's promised me that Emery didn't see him and I think he's telling the truth. I think he just wanted to see her.

I don't know if I did the right thing by bringing him here. I don't know what the right thing is to do anymore. He's not happy. He sits in the chair by the front window with his headphones on and listens to music, and I don't know what he's waiting for. I think maybe he hopes . . . I don't know. I hope August didn't do anything stupid while he was there.

Love,
Eloise

He came back.

The words blurred in my vision as angry tears filled my eyes and I closed them, searching the hazy memories of those awful days— when I was so hungry to see him that the pain of it had suffocated me, he'd been there. Somewhere.

I tossed the letter aside, reaching for the next one. And then the next.

Hannah,

I've just finished reading your letter and I don't know what to say about this news. I have no words for it. I cannot imagine a world without you in it.

You saved my life once. I wish I could save yours.

Love,
Eloise

I sighed, refolding the paper carefully. I'd known for a while before we found out about the cancer that something wasn't right with Mom. The light around her had changed.

When she told me, she knew she wouldn't get better. The tea leaves had told her that much.

Hannah,

I've been thinking that I needed to write this particular letter for some time but I haven't been sure how to do it.

All I can think is that I wish that night hadn't happened.

I know what August did is unforgivable. I've thought so many times about how you think you know your child, and then they do something that terrifies you. Something that opens a darkness.

I froze. The letter shook in my hands, my palms suddenly slick with sweat.

I'm so sorry. For everything. I can't tell you how sorry I am. Every day I wonder if I did the right thing. I don't know the answer to that question. It changes each time I ask it. Sometimes, I wish I could go back and do it all differently. There's no going back, is there?

Do you remember when we use to go up to Wilke's Pointe with stolen cider from the pub and lay on the rocks and talk about when we were older?

You are my dearest friend. My oldest friend.

Love,
Eloise

I read it again, over and over, each time searing like a burn.

What August did.

What August did.

What August did is unforgivable.

I only knew a few people on Saoirse who believed August was innocent back then. But when he and Eloise disappeared, leaving everything behind, it was enough to convince most of them that maybe he *had* killed Lily. That they wouldn't have run away if he wasn't guilty.

In the weeks after Lily's death, I'd tried to make sense of it. I'd asked him more than once to take me through that night and every time he answered, August had given me the same story. He'd gone to work at the orchard and then he met Dutch at the lighthouse. Thinking of it now, I couldn't quite hear his words. I couldn't make out the clear image of the memory as he said it. He was at the lighthouse with Dutch. That was the only thing I knew.

But this letter sounded as if even Eloise knew something I didn't. This letter sounded like . . . an admission.

Twenty-One

AUGUST

THE TASTE OF BLOOD was dry and cracked on my lips.

I walked up the dirt road, sidestepping the river of rainwater that rippled over the rocks. The cottage was dark when I came around the bend, and I thanked whatever God there was that Mom hadn't waited up for me.

I lifted the gate latch slowly so it wouldn't squeak and came up the path to the porch before I unzipped my jacket. The winter storm had blown in as soon as the sun set and I was soaked through from the walk. My clothes were dripping wet and I didn't want to risk Mom hearing me, so I stepped on the heels of my boots, pulling them off and leaving them beside the front door.

I'd never had a key to our house because no one needed to lock their doors on Saoirse. That was the kind of bullshit that people said to pretend like it was safe here. I knew better.

I slipped inside, coming down the hallway to my room with light steps, and I relaxed when I saw that Mom's door was closed and the lights were out. She was asleep.

My bedroom was dark except for the beam of moonlight coming through the window. I peeled off my T-shirt and let it drop to the floor, bending low before the dresser mirror. My shape surfaced in the darkness and I leaned into the light so that it hit one side of my face. The blood was dried down my chin, but it was nothing I couldn't clean up and blame on orchard work.

I winced, pressing a fingertip to the cut on my lip. The dark purple ring that hung below my eye was another matter.

"Fuck," I whispered. I'd have a hard time explaining that.

"August?" A small, sleepy voice sounded in the dark corner of my room and I jolted, hitting the dresser with my knee.

My eyes refocused in the mirror until I could see Emery sitting up on my bed, her eyes squinted. "Hey," I said, too loudly.

She was in one of her huge sweatshirts, her hair messily falling into her face, and there was a book open on the bed beside her. She'd fallen asleep in here.

"Where were you?"

I turned my back to her and snatched the wet shirt from the floor, wiping at my face. I dragged it from my forehead to my throat. "Working at the orchard." I tossed it into the laundry basket before taking a pair of sweatpants from the drawer.

Emery was quiet for a moment. It felt like she'd been watching me more closely by the day. "This late?"

She didn't believe me because she wasn't stupid. Emery knew me.

She slid down the edge of the bed and rubbed her face with her hands, still getting her bearings. But once she was on her feet, she walked right into my chest, waiting for me to put my arms around her. Her hot cheek was like an iron against my skin.

"You're cold."

When she looked up into my face, I leaned away from the light.

"What's wrong?" She sounded awake now.

I let her go and pulled on my sweatpants. "Nothing. I'm tired."

When her hands reached for me, I tried to slip free of them.

"August." She turned me around to face her. "What's going—" Her eyes went wide as my face caught the light. "What happened?"

"Nothing."

"Did he do this?" She reached for me again, taking hold of my jaw. "August," she said, louder.

"You're going to wake up my mom." My voice was a hoarse whisper. That was the last thing I needed.

"I don't care."

I stared at her, not moving. "It's not a big deal," I said, exhausted.

"We need to tell my parents."

I went rigid. "No."

"Then Jake. He can do something about this, August."

The pit that lived in my stomach made me feel like I was going to vomit. "You swore you wouldn't," I reminded her.

Emery watched me through the dark, her mind weighing the cost of breaking the promise she made me. I could see it. But telling Jake would only make things worse for me and my mom with my grandfather. I wasn't going to do that to her before Emery and I left.

"It doesn't matter. In a few months, we'll be gone," I said.

It was a secret we hadn't breathed to a single soul. We'd scraped enough money working at the orchard and the pub for the next year and would spend the next twelve months traveling until we found a place to land. A small suitcase, an old jeep, and about a hundred places we wanted to go. That was the only plan.

"What do you think your grandfather will do when he realizes you're gone?" she whispered.

"I won't be here to find out."

Her eyes traveled over my face again.

"Don't say anything to your parents. Or Jake."

"I don't know."

"*Please.*"

She was silent a long time before she turned toward the door and I stepped around her, holding it closed.

"What are you doing?"

"Getting something to clean that up." She pulled the door back open, disappearing into the hallway, and I listened as she opened the cabinet in the kitchen.

I let out a painful breath, finding my reflection in the mirror again.

I looked like him. My dad. Every picture that filled Mom's photo album. The older I got, the more people said it, and it was always laced with a shameful whisper about what he'd done. But I couldn't even find it in me to be angry that he'd left us. Couldn't blame the bastard for wanting off this island.

Twenty-Two

EMERY

THE LETTER HAUNTED ME through the long, slow hours in the shop.

With only a few days left in the picking season, the town was overrun by the second ferry and the bell on the door hadn't stopped ringing. I punched the keys of the register, refilled the herb canisters with new supplies and kept my hands busy with one eye on that cracked window.

That starling had been more than an omen. Something dead had woken.

What August did.

I'd never really let myself think it—that August could have actually hurt Lily. Even after he'd gone, leaving me to fend for myself on Saoirse. Even when the whole town was convinced he was a murderer. I'd defended him.

But the letter in my pocket told a different story.

As the minutes ticked by throughout the afternoon, I considered a thousand scenarios. That maybe there was an accident and August was there. Or maybe he'd found Lily before anyone else did and lied to keep it from looking like he was involved. But none of it explained why he would have lied to *me*.

As soon as the last customer was out the door, I pulled off my apron and locked up the shop without bothering to do the receipts. There was only one person on this island I could go to with that letter. Nixie. Even if she'd lied to me, too.

I couldn't remember the last time I'd gone more than a day without talking to my dad. I'd avoided the pub and he hadn't stopped in the shop, which meant he was treading carefully. Mustering up the courage to come and test the waters. But I was still angry, and I didn't know how long it would take for that fire to die out. It was too many years of lies. Too many nights being tortured with the not knowing. Right now, Nixie was no more than the lesser of two evils.

I made it to the top of the hill, peering down at the house that sat on the slope. Smoke drifted from the chimney and again, I tried talking myself out of it. The moment I'd read Eloise's words, I'd known what I had to do. The letters weren't just the lonely correspondence of two friends. They were evidence. A piece of the puzzle that Jake didn't have fourteen years ago. What I couldn't work out was why my dad had kept it from his own brother.

The sound of music carried up the road with the cadence of night in the woods. Nixie was playing a Joni Mitchell record and that boded well for me, I thought. She'd have a bottle of wine open and we'd both need it.

A sharp ping sounded as I made my way down the hill and I stopped when I spotted Dutch watching me from behind the open hood of his truck in the drive next door. His hands were covered in grease.

"Em?" He tossed the wrench he was holding into the toolbox at his feet.

My hand instantly slipped into my pocket, finding the letter. He was never home before nightfall. Not when the orchard was this busy. "Hey, what're you doing?"

He looked down at the engine, as if confused by the question. "Working on the truck." His voice had a tone that I knew well. "What are *you* doing?"

He stepped around the hood, coming to the fence that stretched between his land and Nixie's. I hesitated before I followed, meeting him halfway.

"I was just stopping by to pick something up."

His eyes moved over my face, deciding whether to call me on it. Dutch always knew when I was lying. "I called you earlier."

"Sorry." I glanced over my shoulder, to Nixie's darkened porch. "The shop was packed all day."

Dutch studied me for another moment before he let out a long breath, rubbing at his brow with the sleeve of his stained shirt. "What are we doing here, Emery?"

"What?"

He shook his head. "You've been dodging me for days. I think I deserve an explanation."

That, he was right about. He'd had unending patience for me, waiting out my dark moods and hoping I'd come around to what he wanted. We'd been down this road many times. Now, on top of everything, I was hiding something from him.

"I don't know what we're doing," I admitted.

"Why won't you just talk to me?"

I leaned into the fence post, my mind skipping through every way to end this conversation I could think of. I didn't have time for this. "I'm talking to you right now."

"This feels like before. You look . . ." His gaze ran over my face. "Are you sleeping?"

Before. He was talking about the nightmares.

"A little," I answered honestly. "I'm just . . . August being here is dredging up all of this"—I sighed—"and I had this fight with my dad . . ."

His expression instantly turned from defensive to concerned. "Your dad? What happened?"

"Nothing. It's stupid."

"Then why are you so upset about it?"

"I'm not," I said, irritated. "I mean, I am. I just . . ."

"Don't want to talk to *me* about it," he finished. "That's nothing new, I guess." Before I could answer, he pushed off the fence and turned his back to me. "The glass for the window will be here in a few days," he called out.

When he reached the truck, he lifted the hood up and let it slam down. Then he was stalking up the drive to the cabin. I watched him go, ashamed that I was grateful. I should have stopped him. Asked him to come back. Told him that we could talk over dinner. But I didn't. I wouldn't.

And he didn't expect me to. Dutch had put up with my shit for a lot of years.

I watched the light flick on behind the windows. I'd asked myself many times if his home could ever also be mine, and even in the rare moments when I could get my mind around the idea, the answer had never been yes.

I put my face in my hands, trying to soothe the ache in my head.

There were more layers to this than wanting different things. After August and Lily were gone, we were the ones left behind. It was suddenly just the two of us and when you took away everything else, it had really just been the fact that we were lonely. Together. We became villains in the eyes of Saoirse because without August, there was no one else to blame. I figured we might as well bear their hatred together. It wasn't a romantic story by any stretch, but it was our story. And there was no changing it.

I followed the half-sunken pavers up to Nixie's porch, looking back once more to Dutch's cabin. None of it was fair. To either of us.

Nixie was standing in the kitchen when I came through the door, but she didn't look up from the cutting board. Like she'd been expecting me.

"That didn't look good," she murmured, tipping a chin to the window that overlooked Dutch's property down the hill.

"Would it kill you to mind your own business?"

"Might." She smirked, running the knife through a thick bunch of parsley. The bright, green smell of it filled the air. But her mirth gave way to something else as she gestured to the blackberry wine on the counter. Her favorite. "You here for an apology? I know I owe you one."

"Yes, you do." I took a glass from the shelf and helped myself, filling it with a generous pour.

Nixie set down the knife and took a sip from her own glass. "I know I should have told you. A long time ago."

I slid onto the stool, facing her. I wasn't going to tell her that it was okay, because it wasn't. But Nixie had a way of seeing me that no one else really ever did and although I didn't like that there was no hiding with her, she was often the only one I really trusted. I'd learned the language of my parents, finding ways around their fussing and their worry. But it seemed that Nixie had learned mine.

I pulled the letter from my pocket and set it on the butcher block between us without a word.

Nixie read the address before she put it together. "Oh." She frowned.

"I need you to read it," I said, my stomach twisting in knots.

She looked like she was going to argue until I lifted my glass, taking several anxious gulps.

"You all right, honey?"

"Not really." I breathed.

I watched as she picked it up and carefully lifted the flap of the envelope. Once she read it, there was no going back.

Her eyes ran over the letter slowly, but her expression didn't change. She said nothing when she glanced up at me, and then she was reading it again, from the beginning.

"The words are the same the second time. And the third," I said. "I've read it a hundred times."

She set it down on the counter without refolding it.

"What do you think it means?" I asked, my voice small.

"I think"—she paused—"I think there's no way for us to know what it means, because Eloise isn't here to tell us. They were her words."

"But Nixie, it says—"

"I know what it says," she said, exasperated. "You asked me what it *means*."

"I think there's only one thing it could mean."

Her lips pressed together. "You don't believe that."

"Maybe I should have. All along."

That was the crux of it. Nixie had been right that night in the barn. It was no ordinary childhood love between August and me. It was something else entirely. And even if I'd wanted to, I didn't know if I could have seen things clearly. I don't think I would have believed it even if it came from his own lips.

"I think she was saying that he did it," I whispered, "and I think I have to give it to Jake."

Nixie stiffened. "Em, listen to me. You're upset about your parents and Dutch. About August being back. You need to take a breath before you make your mind up about anything."

"This isn't just about August, Nixie. It's about Lily. I can't just keep this a secret." I flung a hand at the letter. "The only reason he wasn't charged with her murder is because there wasn't enough evidence, right? Well, *this* is evidence. What if this is what could prove that he did it?"

"Maybe it would. Maybe it wouldn't."

"If he . . . if August killed Lily, we have to know. Her family has to know. *I* have to know."

Nixie was quiet a long time. Her gaze drifted past me, to the fire, and I could see the words turning in her mind. Finally, she picked up the bottle of wine, refilling her glass nearly to the rim. When she was finished, she filled mine.

"You do what you have to do, Emery," she said, "but if you're going to cut this wound back open, you better be damn sure you're right."

Twenty-Three

AUGUST

I'D FORGOTTEN THE RAIN. The Oregon coast and the streets of Portland saw their fair share, but Saoirse was different. The rain this time of year was heavy and thick, with a sweet smell that clung to you wherever you went.

After two days of digging through every scrap of paper at the house, I'd finally given up the hope that I was going to unearth the deed to the cottage.

Eric's next best guess was the records office, and though Saoirse didn't have much, it did have one of those. The records office, the marshal's office, and the *Saoirse Journal* were one and the same— a small red brick building that sat at the end of Oak Avenue only one block away from Main Street. The only other building that shared the crude, gravel lot was an old ice-cream parlor that was shut down in the colder months. From the look of it now, I wasn't sure it had been open in at least a few years.

Jake's truck wasn't parked in the lot and that would make this easier. The less I had to see of him, the better.

The latch on the door stuck, and I leaned my weight into it by memory, lifting up on the handle until I could push it open. I'd come here a lot as a kid, when Jake had been something like a father or an uncle to me. But it was the times after Lily that I remembered most about being in this place.

I lifted the door on its hinges to get it closed again, eyeing the hallway that led to his office. Two of the three lights were burned out, leaving only the one that hung over his closed door.

The smell of ink and stale cigarette smoke hung in the still air, threatening to dig up those days from where I'd buried them. For weeks after the fire, Jake had hauled me back in here to ask more questions, looking for the tiniest crack in my statement or maybe hoping I'd eventually make a mistake. But I didn't. It hadn't taken me long to figure out that he had nothing to go on. All I had to do was stick to my story.

"Can I help you?" Sophie peered up over the stack of papers on her desk. The old woman had worked here for as long as I could remember. She had to be nearing a hundred years old.

"I need to access the city records for a deed," I answered, keeping my distance from the desk. I didn't like the feeling of being back beneath that roof and I'd learned to keep a wide berth from the residents of Saoirse.

The moment she recognized me, her silvery eyes narrowed. She didn't move.

"Just need a copy of the deed to the cottage and I'll be out of your way, Sophie. Couldn't find it at the house."

She rose from her chair slowly, her gaze going to the hallway, as if she was hoping Jake would appear. She was afraid of me. "Don't want any trouble," she said.

I lifted my hands into the air. "I'm not going to give you any."

"Good." She kept an eye on me, picking up the ring of keys from her desk and shuffling to the wall of file cabinets. Half of them were rusted from the damp air, plastered with peeling handwritten labels. "Four Poplar Drive, isn't it?"

"Yeah."

She searched for the right drawer and pulled it open with the key still dangling from the lock. Her small hands flitted over the manila folders inside, but she paused every few seconds to glance back at me. There was no telling what kind of stories they'd all conjured up over the years. Enough time had passed for them to paint me into whatever they needed. In this case, it was Lily's killer.

Behind her, the old rotary printing press still looked as if it was in use for the *Journal*. Abbott Wittich had taken the small weekly newspaper over from his uncle when he was maybe twenty years old, and he'd run it with only Sophie as his receptionist and one or two boys from town who delivered the papers.

Dutch had worked here for an entire year before I'd gotten him the job at the orchard, and I still remembered the ringing and clicking of all the turning brass cylinders and the slide of the paper on the big rolls. Abbott would stand over the massive contraption with a burning clove cigarette in his mouth and the sleeves of his crisp white button-down shirt rolled up to his elbows. It was a wonder the place hadn't burned to the ground.

"That's odd," Sophie murmured, her hand freezing midair before she pulled a folder from the drawer.

"What?"

She set the folder on top of the file cabinet and searched through the tabs again. "It's not here."

Her mouth twisted as she closed the drawer. When it was locked, she took the folder from the top and came back to the desk. She placed it in front of me.

The label on the file was printed with a typewriter. 4 POPLAR DRIVE—SALT PROPERTY. But when I lifted the top of the folder, it was empty.

"Might not have been filed when it was changed into my mom's name," I said, thinking aloud.

"No, it was filed." Sophie set the folder down, pointing to the label. "Did it myself. The orchard, too, when it was signed over to the town after Henry died. But I didn't see it in there, either," she thought aloud.

"Can't you email it to me or something?"

Sophie stared at me, her brow wrinkled. Of course she couldn't.

"Well, where else could it be?"

"Beats me. You'll have to order a copy from the county office on the mainland."

I sighed, letting the folder fall closed. I didn't have that kind of time. The county offices were in Seattle and it would take an entire day to make the trip on the ferry, get to the records office, and then get back to the island. But the house couldn't be sold if I didn't have the deed.

"Damn it," I muttered.

The door opened and the woman who stepped inside froze, eyes going wide when she saw me. The copper red hair was a dead give-away. Clara was one of the Hersches' daughters. She'd been a few years younger than me in school, and from the look on her face, she knew exactly who I was.

"Thanks." I pushed the folder back across the desk and zipped up my jacket, shouldering past Clara. I could hear their voices before the door had even closed behind me.

Four days and I was no closer to getting this done than when I'd first stepped off the ferry, but I wasn't leaving Saoirse until every loose end was tied off. Until I was sure I'd never have a reason to come back.

But I should have known the goddamn island wasn't going to make it that easy.

Twenty-Four

JAKOB

I GLANCED UP TO the calendar on the wall before I scratched the date at the top of the report. James McAlister had been waiting at the door of my office when I climbed out of my truck to report his fishing boat stolen. It was much more likely that the rusted, moments-from-sinking vessel, which hadn't been seaworthy in years, had sunk in the cove.

The words on the copied form were almost illegible in places, a reminder that the ink needed to be changed. But my eyes were the only ones that would ever see the report anyway.

I signed my name at the bottom and drained the whiskey in my mug. It still smelled of coffee, with a brown ring from yesterday staining the lip, but the sink in the small kitchenette that I shared with the *Journal* had been clogged for weeks.

The door down the hall scraped and Sophie's high-pitched voice sounded a moment later, followed by another.

As soon as I heard the footsteps, I pulled the drawer of my desk open, dropping the bottle of whiskey inside. I wasn't supposed to drink on the job, but "on the job" in Saoirse was the equivalent of being a babysitter. Usually.

I stood, tossing the report on top of the others I had sitting in the wire basket behind the desk as Emery came through the door.

"Em," I said, smiling.

I couldn't hide the surprise in my voice. It had been a long time since the days she used to show up unannounced at my office with a sandwich from the pub or a pie from Nixie's.

But she didn't smile back. "You all right?"

Most of her hair was wild and waving where it stuck out from the knit hat she was wearing, her big blue eyes roaming the room. She used to look tiny in this office.

She pulled her hands into the sleeves of a thick green sweater I recognized. In fact, I was pretty sure it had been Hannah's at some point. "Yeah, I'm good."

"Haven't seen you at the pub the last couple of days."

She shrugged, picking up the paperweight on the desk and turning it over in her palm. It was a flat, round stone from the beach covered in faded blue paint with a tree on it. She'd made it for me in kindergarten.

"I've just been busy with end-of-season stuff. You know how this time of year is."

"Yeah, I know." I leaned back in the chair, watching her. Something was off. "What's going on?"

"Thought I'd come see how you were doing"—she paused—"you know, with everything about Eloise."

I felt the frown pull on one side of my mouth. The whole town knew how I felt about Eloise Salt, even long before she married Calvin. And maybe Emery was the only person on this island who would understand that even if it had been a long time, it had still cut deep when August pulled that urn out of his pack.

"I'm okay."

Emery turned the stone in her palm once more before she placed it back down. She stared at it.

"You sure that's the only reason you came by?"

She pulled the beanie from her head and ran one hand through her hair. "I wanted to talk to you." Her eyes shifted over the room, not landing on me. "Confidentially, I mean."

"All right."

"It's a question, actually."

"Well, lay it on me." I waited.

Her lips pressed together, making her look like the little girl who used to stow away in the back of my truck. "Back then . . . after Lily"—she hesitated—"you were so sure that August killed her. I want to know why."

That was the last thing I'd guess she'd want to talk about. I set both elbows on the desk. "Where's this coming from?"

"I've just been thinking about how we never really talked about it. Not really. My parents, you, Nixie . . ."

"Well, you were just a kid."

"But I'm not anymore. And I want to know."

"This about him being back?" I didn't like saying his name. Not unless I had to.

"Maybe," she admitted. "But I've wanted to ask you for a long time."

I drew in a long breath, thinking. It wasn't exactly policy to share details about an investigation, but it wouldn't be the first time I hadn't followed protocol. Especially when it came to Emery.

"You sure?" I asked.

She really thought about it, searching my face before she nodded.

"Well, I'll start with the facts, I guess." I knew the details backward and forward. I'd been through them a thousand times. "August was the only one unaccounted for that night when the fire broke out. No one knew where he was," I began. "Eloise was frantic, thinking maybe he'd been lost to the blaze, and several people remember her looking for him and saying she hadn't seen him before the party. He was supposed to be there early to help her get things situated, I guess, but he never showed."

"But he was at the lighthouse. With Dutch."

"He was," I admitted. "He was there sometime before the party.

They claimed they were smoking joints up in the lighthouse and we did find evidence of that. But the timing wasn't ironclad. Dutch made it to the orchard just before the fire. Where was August?"

Emery had no answer for that.

"So, there was the matter of August's whereabouts, and that was strange. There weren't any clues at the crime scene. All Lily had on her was a small book of matches, but when we got the autopsy report, that's when things really didn't add up." I tipped my head to one side, trying to read her. "You sure you want to hear about all this?"

"I'm sure," she said again, resolved.

I sighed. "Well, none of it made any sense. Lily had drowned. Her lungs were filled with water from the Sound, but none of it was on her hair or her skin. When Nixie discovered her in the middle of the woods, she was bone dry, even her hair, makeup still on her face. And when the dress she was wearing was analyzed, they didn't find any seawater on it except for a bit down the front. Other than that, there were just a few drips of wax and some dirt. No footprints anywhere near the body but hers. The other odd bit was that there was seaweed in her stomach."

"Seaweed?"

I nodded. The oddities in the report were what had caught the attention of the news outlets. There was no reasonable explanation for how she'd gotten there and too many unusual details.

"When we found out that Lily was in a relationship—"

"A relationship? What are you talking about?"

I paused, remembering. When we'd questioned Emery about that, she'd been insistent that it wasn't true. "The report concluded that Lily was pregnant, Em."

Emery stilled, her lips parting. "What? That has to be a mistake."

"It wasn't."

"She was my best friend, Jake. I would know if she was sleeping with someone. Lily had never even had sex. With anyone. We talked about it."

"Then she lied. We found contraception in her bedroom and her parents confirmed that they'd also suspected she was seeing someone before she died."

Emery paled.

"Look." I lowered my voice. "I don't see why all of this matters now."

I could see the moment she started to piece it together. Her eyes cleared, focusing. "You think she was sleeping with *August*?"

I hesitated, resisting the urge to reach for the mug again. "I do."

"How do you know it wasn't someone else? Someone off island?" She was defensive now. We hadn't had this fight in a long time. It was exactly what I'd wanted to avoid.

"Honestly, that's what we thought at first. Earlier that day, Albertine had called and said she thought someone was in the house. A break-in, maybe. I went up and checked it out myself, but I didn't find anything. We chalked it up to some wind, but then when we found Lily, I did wonder if maybe we missed something. But there was nothing stolen. Nothing out of place. No other reports of that nature."

Emery didn't look convinced.

"We started going through the ferry tickets over the months leading up to her death, but found almost no repeating passengers. If someone was coming to visit her, there was no paper trail of that."

"Maybe she was going to the city then. Hopping the ferry to go see a guy or something."

"No trace of that in the tickets, either. The manifests are kept for years, Em."

She was breathing harder now, her hands gripped to the arms of the chair. We'd agreed, all of us, not to tell her any of this. But Hannah was gone now, and I didn't see what difference it made as long as it helped Emery see reason. She'd always been blind when it came to August, and I understood why. I'd been the same way before what happened.

"There were no signs of struggle at the scene or on the body. Whoever was there, she knew them. She wasn't scared, didn't fight."

"Everyone knows everyone on this island," she said.

It wasn't until that moment that I realized she was trying to convince herself, not me. "Then who? Give me one person you think may have killed her." I waited. "August is the only one who wasn't at the orchard close to the time that Lily died."

She pressed a hand to her mouth. "You're wrong." She spoke against her fingers. "You have to be wrong."

"I think that Lily and August had something going on. It happens. But maybe Lily was going to come clean. Maybe it was getting too hard to hide. Or maybe she wouldn't let him break it off. Could have been anything. The only reason he wasn't charged with her murder is because there was no physical evidence tying August to the scene where we found Lily. And he had an alibi, even if it was a flimsy one."

Emery closed her eyes, taking a measured breath.

"If he didn't do it, then why did he and Eloise run?" I asked.

"They didn't run. They were run *off*. No one gave him a chance, Jake. Everyone thought he killed Lily. How could they stay?"

My voice lowered. "There's also the matter of the family history."

"What family history?"

"Henry. And Calvin."

"What does this have to do with August's father and grandfather?"

I waited, trying to think of how to say it. "They were violent men, Emery. Both of them."

Her face turned to stone and I met her eyes. She knew. Of course she knew. We all did.

"It's the kind of thing that's in the blood. It was no secret that Henry had a temper on him, but you were too young to remember Calvin."

That was a thread I didn't want to pull. There was a freight train of darkness behind it.

Emery sank back into the chair and a heavy silence filled the small office. "You didn't know August," she said, finally.

But I did. I'd loved that boy like he was my own.

My brow furrowed as I watched her. This wasn't just closure. There was something else. "What's going on, Emery?"

She shook her head. "It's nothing. I just . . . him being back is stirring everything up, I guess."

Emery had never been a good liar, but she'd gotten better at it. The first time I caught her and her friends on the beach drinking stolen beer from the pub, it had taken her all of three minutes to burst into tears. But now, she looked me in the eye, unflinching.

She was hiding something, but she wasn't going to trust me with it. Not yet.

"You know you can tell me anything, don't you?" I said.

"I know, Uncle Jake."

I nodded, giving up. Pushing her wasn't going to do any good. "He'll be gone in a day or two. Hang in there, Em."

She tried to smile, but it wasn't reassuring. If anything, it worried me. "Thanks." Emery stood, straightening the paperweight on my desk before she left.

I stared at the yellowed keyboard in front of me as Sophie called out a goodbye, and as soon as I heard the sound of the door scraping, I picked up the phone. The distorted minor tones of the numbers chimed in the receiver as I dialed, and when it started to ring, I pressed it to my ear.

"Hello?" The voice on the other end of the line crackled.

"Hey, it's Jake." I rubbed the place between my eyes with one knuckle. "She was just here."

A pause. "And?"

"She was asking about Lily. Stuff about the investigation."

A long exhale sounded, followed by silence. "All right. I'll deal with it."

Twenty-Five

AUGUST

THE BEAM OF THE flashlight swept over the balcony of the lighthouse, catching my eyes and I hissed, turning away from it.

"Sorry!" Lily's laughter lifted over the sound of the waves below.

I looked down to the beach, but I couldn't see her and Emery on the rocks except when the flashlight occasionally caught one of their faces. It was a cloudy night, hiding the moon, and we'd been drinking cider since sundown. At some point, we'd thought it was a good idea to hop Nixie's fence and steal a wheelbarrow full of pumpkins. Getting them to the beach was one thing but hauling them up the steps of the lighthouse was another.

"Ready?" Dutch shouted beside me, picking up another one.

"Ready!" Emery answered back.

Dutch swung the pumpkin back in both arms, flinging it over the railing, and we both watched as it hurtled into the darkness. The flashlight's beam followed it all the way down until it smashed into the rocks, exploding.

The girls cheered. "I give that one an eight!" Emery called up.

"Nine!" Lily followed. "I'm pretty sure there are pumpkin guts in my hair!"

Dutch set both elbows on the railing, tucking his hair behind his ears. He still had that glazed look in his eyes, but my buzz was wearing off, making me tired.

"How many are left?" I reached back, pressing a thumb into the sore muscle at the corner of my shoulder. "I gotta get home."

"Just one, Cinderella." He rolled his eyes.

"I have to be at the orchard by five." It was almost two in the morning and I was already dreading the hangover I'd have the next day.

"Poor August Salt, with his inherited family business and a job he'll never lose," Dutch muttered. He was still smiling, but I knew him well enough to hear the hint of bitterness in the words.

"It's not as sweet a deal as you think." That was putting it lightly.

"Oh yeah, what would be so great about all that? I sure as hell wouldn't want that problem."

I couldn't blame him for being resentful. Dutch's dad was the most pathetic creature on the island and he never held a job for more than six months. He went from fishing boat to fishing boat, running out his luck every time. Eventually, he cycled his way back through.

"Sorry, man. I didn't mean it like that," I said, sinking down to haul up the last pumpkin.

"You never do."

I set it back down, looking up at him. "What?"

"Nothing."

I fell quiet, letting the fuse burn out between us. Dutch was an angry drunk and nights like these usually shook loose the things he wouldn't otherwise say. It would pass. It always did.

The truth was my future had been planned out and written in stone while Dutch's would never be certain. Not until he was out from under his dad's mistakes and making his own way in the world. He would gladly trade places with me and vice versa.

"Do you want me to see if my grandfather has any openings for farmhands in the spring?"

Dutch's eyes lit up. He pushed off the railing, turning toward me. "Really?"

It only occurred to me then that I should have offered a long time ago. But he'd never asked. "Yeah. It's not a big deal."

"Do you think he'd take me on?"

I shrugged. "Maybe. If I ask him to."

Dutch grinned. "Yeah, man. That would be awesome."

"Might be able to get him to take your dad back, too."

"Seriously?" It almost made me sad to see how excited he was.

I smirked. "Maybe between the two of us we can keep an eye on him so he doesn't get himself fired again."

Dutch laughed. "We can try. But he's got a talent for fucking up."

"Yeah, he does."

"How is he"—Dutch paused—"your grandfather?"

Again, the flashlight's beam skittered across the face of the lighthouse's balcony.

"Same," I answered.

It had started with a cough. Mom had tried to get him to go to the doctor in the city when it was clear Leoda's cures weren't doing any good, but he'd refused. I didn't know why she wasted any time worrying about the cruel bastard. Slowly, the color had left his skin and for the last few weeks, I'd caught him wiping blood from his lips with his handkerchief.

"If he's going to die, I wish he'd get on with it," I said, the words drifting into the wind.

When Dutch said nothing, I blinked, turning to look at him.

He gave me an unnerved look. "That's fucked up, man."

"Yeah, I guess it is," I realized. But it was true. The best thing that could happen to me was the old man dying.

"Come on! You guys making out up there?" Emery shouted.

Dutch let his head fall back, calling out over the sound of the wind. "Yeah, we are! You gotta problem with that?"

"No, just hurry up! We're cold!"

Dutch sank down, lugging the pumpkin up into his arms. We'd saved the biggest one for last. "All right! Bombs away!"

He turned in a circle, flinging it over the railing. It flew up over our heads before it started to drop, and we both leaned over the side, watching as it disappeared.

Twenty-Six

EMERY

I PULLED AT THE nettle stalks along the fence, tearing them out of the soft earth.

The northeast corner of the land was all but overtaken by wild herbs this time of year, and we always harvested them in the days leading up to October's full moon. The patch would die out in winter and then return in the summer, but there was a year's worth of nettle here that I'd dry and use for the tea shop. What was left I'd give to Leoda to use in her medicines at the apothecary.

The chore was a welcome distraction. Sweat trailed down my back as I tore them out by the roots, more roughly than was necessary. My wrists burned where the barbs had grazed my skin, despite my long sleeves and gloves. I ignored the sting, reaching for another handful and yanking. When they didn't budge, I leaned back, groaning as I pulled, and they lifted from the soil all at once, sending me backward.

I hit the ground hard. "Goddamn it." I flung them onto the pile, sitting back up.

I pulled off my glove and unbuttoned my sleeve, cinching it up so that I could see my elbow. The skin there was scraped and raw.

My phone hummed from somewhere behind me and I turned to see Dutch's name on the screen. He hadn't called since I saw him on my way to Nixie's, but he was finally breaking his silence. I instinctively reached for it, but my hand trembled over the phone, waiting for it to go to voicemail instead. I couldn't avoid him forever. I knew that. But the last thing I needed was another fight about a wedding ring.

I pulled the glove back on and picked up the spade, raising it over my head and driving it down into the earth. The pain that had surfaced in my jaw woke again, and I had to force myself to unclench it, breathing through the erratic pace of my heartbeat.

The letter was now tucked beneath the sweaters in my bottom drawer with the ferry tickets and the brown folder, but it pulled at the edges of my mind all the way from the house. Eloise's handwriting was like a loop of images replaying in my thoughts. They were followed by my uncle Jake's words.

Lily being pregnant changed everything, but still, none of it added up. We told each other everything. Every secret. Every embarrassing thought. She was the first person I'd gone to when August and I had sex the first time and she'd never hidden her crushes or the things that happened with guys she was fooling around with from school. There was only one reason I could think of that she'd hide it from me. That maybe Jake was right. Maybe it was August.

My hands stilled on the nettles and I sat back on my heels, staring into the trees. I'd gone to see Jake to give him the letter, but as I sat there in his office, I couldn't bring myself to do it. I didn't know if I could believe that August hurt Lily. It didn't fit with anything else from that time. But I had to admit to myself, for the first time, that it was possible.

And Lily wasn't the only one who'd kept secrets. I had, too.

August had hidden the bruises well enough or explained them away for a long time before I started putting it together. But the older we got and the more nights we spent together, the less easy they were to miss.

At first, he lied to me about it, but over time, his responses were less insistent. Eventually, they turned into an uncomfortable silence when I asked. When he finally did admit it to me, he never answered my questions or gave me details. He did, however, make me promise not to tell anyone.

It wasn't a hard leap to believe that Jake was right about Calvin, either. He'd left his family when we were babies, and I'd never gotten the sense that anyone was too broken up about it. Henry, on the other hand, was a different story. Everyone in town knew he was difficult and that he was hard on August. Always. But he was also the most powerful man on the island and no one dared to step out of his good graces.

I'd promised August I wouldn't tell anyone, and I'd kept that promise only because I knew we were leaving. Looking back, that had been the wrong decision, but we were kids. I somehow always forgot that we were just kids.

"There you are."

I jolted at the sound of my father's voice, nearly jumping out of my skin. I looked up as he took off his hat, holding it before him. His denim jacket was unbuttoned, his cheeks pink. He'd probably just come in off the water.

"Heading over to the pub and thought I'd stop by."

It was the last weekend of the tourist season and the ferries would be light for once. Half the shops in town had already closed, but there was always a demand for beer.

I tossed the spade to the ground and stood, wiping my forehead with the back of my arm. "Hey." My voice was cold. Colder than I meant it to be, and it looked as if it hurt him. "You still drinking that tea that Leoda made you?"

"Three times a day, as ordered." He tried to lighten the tension.

I nodded. I didn't know what to say. There had never been something unmended between us. I couldn't even remember the last time I'd been angry with my dad.

He nudged the tipping pile of nettles at his feet with the side of his boot, pushing it back into place. "I think we should talk," he finally said.

"All right. Then talk."

His eyes traced the tops of the trees beyond the fence. I didn't like seeing him like that—unsure. "I know it wasn't right to keep all this from you. I've known it a long time."

I stared at him.

"I didn't mean to blame it on your mother, either. I agreed not to tell you about the letters. We thought we were doing what was best for you. And we were wrong."

The morning August left, I was waiting for him at Halo Beach. It was a Saturday and I'd told my mother that I wasn't feeling well so that she wouldn't ask me to come help her at the shop. As soon as she disappeared up the road, I slipped out and ran the broken trail through the woods.

It had been two weeks since Jake announced that August wouldn't be charged with Lily's murder, and that night someone threw a stone through August's bedroom window. The town was still pressed beneath darkness, unable to breathe. And August was at the center of it all.

We started meeting at Halo Beach because Eloise didn't want him to come into town. Not until things calmed down, she said. And August didn't want me coming over anymore. He'd been pushing me away, slowly. It began with little things. Being the first to let go of my hand. Not quite looking me in the eye when we were together. I'd felt the divide between us growing by the day, but I was convinced that he'd come back to me. That he'd come back to himself.

I waited on the rocky bluff for two hours, my feet dangling in the wind, and when I finally decided he wasn't coming, I figured Henry had called him to the orchard.

My parents were waiting for me when I got back to the house, and I stopped at the gate when I saw them sitting on the porch. The looks on their faces were ones I had never seen before and the sight made my stomach drop. The scars on my dad's face were still red, but they'd lost some of their brightness, and after almost a year the look of constant pain had left his eyes. But I could see it there in that moment.

They're gone, baby.

The words twisted in the air, losing their meaning. And then I was running back across the road. Up the drive, where Eloise's truck was parked. I pushed through the door and the house was empty.

He was gone. August and Eloise were gone.

Looking at my dad now, the memory didn't feel so long ago. That look on his face was too familiar.

"I went to see Jake yesterday." I took off the gloves, brushing the dirt from the suede. "He still thinks August killed Lily."

He nodded. "I know."

"But you and Mom never believed that. Why?"

One side of his mouth lifted. "I don't know. We cared a lot about August. You know that. We cared about Lily, too, and it seemed just too hard to think he'd ever have done something like that."

But he didn't sound as convinced as he used to. In fact, my dad looked a little afraid, and that made me even more uneasy. Maybe the reason we hadn't been able to believe it wasn't because it wasn't true. Maybe it had just hurt too much.

"I wish you had been honest with me."

"I do, too."

That was the worst part of all of this. I loved my father and I didn't know if there was anything he could do that would change that. What they'd done was undeniably wrong, but there was no undoing it now. And even if they had told me, that wouldn't have changed the fact that August left.

I stared at the ground between us. "There's something else we need to talk about, Dad."

"Okay." He waited.

We'd never spoken of the folder in the bottom drawer of my

dresser. He didn't even know it was there. "Is the reason you never told me because you were trying to protect me, or did you have other reasons to keep August from coming back to Saoirse?"

"What are you talking about?"

"This isn't just about August," I said, looking him in the eye. "I know what you did. You and the town council."

His face was twisted on one side, the scars unmoving on the other. "Em—"

"I've seen it. The deed to the orchard."

He went rigid.

"I know you love me, Daddy"—I swallowed—"but I don't trust you anymore. And I don't know how long I can keep your secrets."

I stepped past him before the lump rose in my throat and he didn't stop me.

My father was a quiet man. He'd always been that way. But since my mother died, he'd been a drifting thing, living out there in the fishing cabin by himself. We'd both lost her and we'd both been changed by the years, but for the first time in my life, I wasn't sure I knew who he was.

Twenty-Seven

AUGUST

I COULD BREATHE IN the city.

Seattle wasn't Portland, but I exhaled as soon as I stepped off the ferry and onto the loading dock. The skyline was half-hidden in the morning fog, buildings peeking through the thick white drifts. But that rotting-sweet smell of the island was gone, and so was the sick feeling that had lived in my gut for the last several days.

As a kid, I'd always seen the island as a prison. We didn't talk about my dad much. No one did. My mom didn't bring him up and I never asked my grandfather questions because when I did, he took his anger over his son leaving out on me. Emery's mom, Hannah, was the one who eventually told me that he'd up and left one night, taking his boat across the sound to Seattle and never coming back.

Almost immediately, I began to fantasize about doing the same exact thing. I remember the first time I realized that one day, if I wanted to, I could leave. I'd been up on the most remote rows of trees in the orchard clearing a patch of poison oak by myself. My grandfather saved the worst jobs for me and I almost never had help, except when an older farmhand like Zachariah took pity on me.

I was taking the shears to another vine, and when I heard thunder,

I looked out past the water. Far in the distance, a black tangle of clouds was drifting over the sea. But it wasn't moving toward Saoirse. It was moving away from it. It occurred to me suddenly as I looked down to my scraped arms that I understood why my dad had done it. Henry Salt believed that the orchard was in our veins, and it was true. It had drawn my blood many times. But there was one thing that divided my dad's story and my own. There wasn't anything on Saoirse that he couldn't leave behind. Not me. Not my mom.

But I had Emery. And she was the only thing I'd ever missed after I left.

I walked up Fourth Avenue, weaving in and out of the crowds on the sidewalk. I liked that, too, about cities. The fact that you could disappear. I hadn't really felt that until I moved to Portland for school. Before then, I'd never shaken that feeling of being watched, like even from all the way across Puget Sound, the island's eye was still on me.

The Recorder's Office of King County was one of several city buildings that lined the street. I pushed inside, shaking the rain from my jacket, and followed the placards until the hallway opened to a waiting room. On the far wall, two women sat behind a glass window.

The one on the right waved me forward, her eyes still glued to her computer screen. "Can I help you, honey?"

I pulled the paper from my pocket, setting it down. "I need to get a copy of a deed."

"All right." She slid the paper toward her and stood. "Just a minute."

The woman on the left stopped typing and, though I didn't look, I could feel her attention on me. A sharp prick crept up my spine, making me sweat. My face had been all over the news when the Seattle Police announced that I was a person of interest in Lily's murder. I told myself that it was years ago, that no one would recognize me. But still, I always had that drop in my stomach when I caught someone staring at me. It happened all the time. On the train downtown, in the middle of class, even when I was walking on campus. Like my body couldn't forget that feeling I'd lived with for so long.

I finally glanced up, and her eyes dropped back to the keyboard. Maybe she did recognize me. Or maybe my face had been just familiar enough from the news headlines that she thought she knew me from somewhere. I wasn't going to ask. But when a small smile broke on her lips and she blushed, I realized it was a different kind of fascination that had drawn her gaze to me. I'd never been much good at that, either.

The first woman reappeared around the corner and her chair rolled as she sat back down. "Looks like that should be filed over at the records office on Saoirse Island."

The younger woman looked up again, curious. It wasn't just what happened the night of the fire. There were a lot of rumors on the mainland about the people who lived on Saoirse.

"It's not. I've already been there," I said.

She frowned, reaching into one of the open trays of paper on the left side of her desk. "Well, fill this out and we can have a copy sent to you."

I stared at the paper as she slid it toward me. "Can't I just get a printout or something?"

"We don't keep the archives here."

"A digital copy then? There's gotta be a way to get it now."

"We only do physical copy requests. Just jot down your address and I'll process it."

I leaned into the counter, trying to think. "How long will it take?"

"A few days. Maybe more."

I blinked. "I don't have a few days. I need to get this dealt with."

She finally tore her eyes from the computer screen. "Well, I don't know what to tell you. This is the system we have to request copies." She plucked one of the pens out of the cup to her right and held it out to me.

I reluctantly took it, finding a seat in one of the chairs and fishing my glasses out of my pocket.

The blanks on the page looked up at me. I couldn't have the deed sent to the cottage because by the time it arrived, I wouldn't be there. I didn't want to chance it being delivered to my apartment in Portland. Half the time, the mailman shoved envelopes into the wrong boxes.

I pulled the phone from my pocket and found Eric's number. The ringing made the ache in my head throb as I filled in my name on the first line of the form.

"Still alive?" he answered, the sound of his voice drowned out by the background noise.

"Still alive. Where are you?"

"Waiting for a client. I meet this guy at coffeehouses because he has a thing about offices," he said, annoyed. "Too corporate. Makes sense except this guy is as corporate as you can get."

I laughed. "Bet you're wishing you'd listened to me when I told you to go into civil rights law."

"If I had, I'd be living in my car right now." He scoffed. "What's up?"

"I'm having a problem getting ahold of the deed for the cottage. It's not at the house and it's missing from the records office."

"Missing?"

"You'd understand if you saw the place."

"Got it."

"I'm at the county office in Seattle trying to get a copy, but they have to mail it. All right if I just have them send it to you?"

"Sure." A scratching sound cut over his voice. "I'll take a look when it arrives and give you a call."

"I can just deal with all of this from there, right?"

"If by *you*, you mean *me*, then yes. It's not as simple as just selling the house if it's in your mom's name. You'll have to probate it, prove she's deceased, all of that."

"I found someone to handle the sale."

"Good. We can do it all remotely as long as you have the paperwork. And I'd get whatever you want out of the house now so we can have someone go clean it out, unless you sell it furnished."

The thought of the house sitting empty, with all of the furniture gone and my mom's things missing, made my throat feel dry. We hadn't lived there in a long time, but it still felt like a place she existed. "Okay. Sounds good."

"I'll text you where to send it."

"Thanks."

I dropped the phone into my lap and finished filling out the request form. When my phone buzzed again, I copied down the address Eric sent and signed my name.

But my hand slipped as I went to lift the pen, and the black ink pooled on the paper as I stared at it—the name. I'd been August Somerfield for so long that I hadn't even thought about it in years.

But that's not the name I had written. I'd written August *Salt*.

Twenty-Eight

EMERY

I SAT BEFORE THE fireplace, holding the letter in one hand and a glass of wine in the other. Eloise's words stared back up at me like a riddle I'd never have the answer to.

I didn't know what happened that night in the woods. What I *was* sure of was just how much power was in this letter. If I gave it to Jake, I knew exactly what he would do with it. In minutes, he'd be on the phone with the Seattle Police Department. It would be a match to strike in his attempts to go back and right his own wrongs. Fix what he'd broken. In the process, he would destroy August and the life he'd found outside the island.

I swallowed hard, imagining it.

I hadn't craved freedom the way August had when we were growing up, but I'd craved space. Possibility. I hadn't dared to dream it until the day he first asked me to leave with him and then it became an all-consuming thought. For the first time in my life, I had no idea what may lay ahead, and I found the feeling intoxicating. After eighteen years of knowing exactly what the future held, I wanted more than anything to take a path with no visible destination. I wanted to take it with August.

In the end, he was the only one who got what we wanted.

Eloise's handwriting moved over the paper in patient strokes, but I could swear that the pain of what she'd written was visible in the script. My thumb ran over the address in the top left corner as I read it again. For years, I'd have given anything to have an address. A phone number or an email. Anything. All that time, it was right here.

Nixie was right. We would never know the letter's meaning.

I held it to the light and the warmth buzzed under my skin, making the shadows in the room swirl. Before I even realized what I was doing, it was drifting toward the flames. Like the weight of the air was pulling it forward, my hand following. I breathed slowly, watching the fire lick at the corner of the paper, and a single thread of black smoke appeared as an ember ignited. But just before the page caught, the faint sound of a heavy knock echoed through the house, making me freeze.

I blinked, staring at the letter, and the heat on my skin was instantly replaced by a sharp chill.

What was I doing?

I looked around me, confused. The light from the fire danced along the walls as I set down the wineglass. I'd been seconds from burning the letter. But I couldn't remember even thinking to do it.

Another knock rang out and I stood, pulling the paper inside the blanket. I crept across the floor, holding my breath as I came around the corner of the hallway. I knew as soon as I saw the shadow on the glass. The shape of his jaw. The curling ends of his hair.

August stood beneath the swinging porch light, looking out at the dark road. When he saw me through the window, his gaze ran from my face down to my feet in a way that made me feel unsteady.

The taste of smoke still coated my tongue as I tucked the letter against my nightgown. Beneath it, my heart was racing. A fleeting thought skipped through my mind as I watched him on the other side of the window. August's mouth pressed to Lily's. His hands around her neck.

I pinched my eyes closed, trying to erase the image. I crossed the living room, pulling the door open, and August left one foot on the bottom step as he looked up at me. The shoulders of his jacket glistened with the rain.

"Hey." He swallowed. "I was just going to tell you that Zach came by. The burial is tomorrow at two."

My hand tightened around the edge of the door as he came one step higher. I didn't know if it was because I was scared of him or if I was just scared of what might happen if I was close enough to touch him.

"You asked me to let you know, so . . ."

"Thanks."

My gaze went across the road and I tried to make out the shape of August's house set back in the woods. But it was dark, invisible. The sound of wind in the branches and water running in rivulets down the road cloaked the island in a hush. But I could almost feel it— someone watching. If anyone saw him here, I would never hear the end of it.

His eyes traveled past me, to the inside of the house. "Your dad said he's living over at the fishing cabin."

"Yeah. He moved out there after Mom died. It's just me here now."

He nodded. "I thought maybe Dutch lived here, too."

The comment caught me so off guard that my cheeks instantly flushed. "No. He's got a place over by Nixie's."

He studied me, considering whether to ask more questions. I could see them stirring in his eyes. That much about him hadn't changed. But I didn't like that I could still read him like that. He was a language I hadn't forgotten.

"Sorry, it's none of my business," he said.

It wasn't. So why did I feel like I'd somehow been caught?

"When do you leave?" I asked, hoping it sounded like an innocent curiosity.

Part of me knew that the sooner August was gone, the better. Things would go back to normal with Dutch, even if our normal wasn't what either of us really wanted, and the town would eventually put the past back to sleep. But there was still the letter. There were still Eloise's words. And I didn't know what to do with them.

A glow of light flared behind the trees in the distance and I stilled, my eyes scanning the dark. When I saw it again, I sucked in a breath, my hand slipping from the doorknob.

Across the road, a bright amber flash twisted in the wind. The same light that I'd seen that night at the orchard. Fire.

"August." The word was a breath.

He turned, searching the darkness, and the light appeared again. A tall, writhing flame. A sound escaped his lips that I couldn't make out, and he took off, feet hitting the gravel as he ran.

I let the quilt slip from my shoulders and fall to the ground before I snatched the phone up from the table by the sofa. A moment later, August had disappeared on the other side of the road.

"August!" My bare feet took me down the steps, and then I was running after him. Past the gate. Into the trees.

I followed the sound of his footsteps up the path toward the cottage. I'd lost sight of him by the time I passed the hedge and I came to a stop when I saw it.

It wasn't the house. It was the truck.

I took the last few steps and August appeared on the other side of the trees, at the mouth of the drive. He stood there, frozen, as the glow painted half his stricken face in light. The entire truck was engulfed in flames, filling the air with thick smoke.

"What . . . how?" I stammered, breathing so hard that my head was light.

"*Bastards.*" He pushed into the bushes that lined the house, yanking the water hose free. The spigot turned with a rusted squeak and he came back with it running.

I tried to catch him by the arm as he walked toward the truck, but he pulled free of my hands. He shielded his face, spraying the hood, but the flames only grew, reaching up over our heads and touching the lowest branches of the pines. From where he stood, he was only a moving black shape against the light. But it was no use trying to put it out. The entire cab was burning.

"Get back!"

The blaze swelled on the passenger side and the window shattered. But he only moved closer.

"August!" I stumbled forward and wrapped my arms around him, using all my weight to pull him backward.

When I got him into the grass, I put myself between him and the truck, holding tightly to his shirt with both fists. "Are you crazy?"

August's eyes focused on me, as if he was only just remembering that I was there. His chest rose and fell under my hands and he stared at them before his gaze slowly rose to meet mine. I could feel his heart beating beneath my fingers.

"Are you trying to get yourself killed?" I shoved him hard.

He dropped the hose and the cold water pooled around my feet as the fire's heat stung my skin, giving me goosebumps beneath my nightgown. Standing there in front of him, with that look on his face, was like being eighteen years old again. The feeling put knots in my stomach.

The phone shook in my hands as I found Jake's name, but there was no service. I pushed past August, watching the bars with my breath fogging in the cold, and when one finally appeared, I hit dial.

August watched me. "What are you doing?"

I pressed the phone to my ear.

"I'm calling Jake."

He shook his head, the expression on his face resembling something like pity. "They're not coming, Em."

I stood there, rigid, as the ringing on the other end of the line went on. And on. No one picked up. I wiped the burn of smoke from my eyes, dialing again. Still, there was no answer.

Thunder broke in the sky overhead, followed by the tap of rain on the rocks. My hand felt numb as I hung up, the phone dangling from my slick fingers.

"They're not going to set the fire and then come put it out," he said.

"What?"

"You think this truck just burst into flames?" He almost laughed. "Come on."

I stared into the fire until my eyes ached, nausea rolling in my stomach. He was right. Someone had set it.

"Em."

"Don't call me that," I snapped.

Another crack of lightning unleashed the rain, and it began to fall, making me shiver.

"They did this. You know they did."

They. He wasn't just talking about Jake. He was talking Saoirse. All of *us*.

"No, I don't." I didn't look at him, because I couldn't. I didn't want to think about what he was saying, what it meant.

"You can't seriously still believe that these people—"

"Why? Because I'm still here?" My voice rose. "You don't get to disappear and go make a life for yourself and then come back and pretend like you know everything about us. Not everyone on this island is your enemy. Some of us have been paying for our loyalty to you for a long time, August."

He fell silent, the look on his face changing.

"Why did you come back here?" I said, weakly.

His jaw clenched. "To bury my mom."

"Is that all?"

Again, he said nothing. And what could he say, really? What was done was done.

"Look"—his voice was suddenly softer—"I'm sorry. For all of it."

My hands fell heavy at my sides. "Are you serious? *Now* you want to apologize?"

August exhaled. "I wanted to apologize the other night. But I didn't know what to say when Dutch showed up. I know things weren't easy for you after what happened, and I—"

"How the fuck would you know? You weren't *here*." I glared at him, furious.

"I know."

"You left."

"I know," he said again.

"You left *me*." I almost didn't recognize the sound of my own voice. "And I don't care if you're sorry."

I shoved past him, breathing through the sharp pain in my throat as I followed the light of my front porch across the road. The door was still wide open, and I climbed the steps with my frozen, bare feet, slamming it behind me.

A moth danced around the light hanging over the dining table. Beyond it, the fire in the living room had shrunk down to embers and the house was colder, the warmth sucked out into the wind.

I looked down at my numb hands. The creases were marked black with soot and I reached up to pull a leaf from where it was stuck in my braid. If someone had set the fire . . . of course someone had set it. But if it had caught the house, if the wind had pushed it just a little farther before I saw it in the trees . . . I didn't want to think about what could have happened.

This town had seen what a fire could do.

I flipped on the switch in the bathroom, catching my own eyes in the mirror. A fury burned behind them that I hadn't seen in years. It was both familiar and foreign. And the thought that kept finding me was that I was feeling *something*. That fact alone was a stark contrast to the numb emptiness that had marked my life for so long. It almost scared me.

I turned the knob on the tub and sat on its side, pulling my foot into my lap. There was a diagonal bloody slice along the arch where I'd stepped on something. Maybe a stone. Maybe glass.

I pulled my nightgown off as the tub filled, dropping it on the floor. It would have to be cut into rags or thrown in the garbage. There was no getting that smell out—I knew that from experience, too.

Slowly, I lowered myself into the hot bath and let myself sink under the surface. The roar of the water filling the tub drowned out the rush of thoughts skipping through my head, but when I came up again, I still felt like I couldn't breathe.

I pulled my knees into my chest, hugging them to me. I'd thought nothing could be worse than when August left. But it turned out, his return hurt even more. If I just hadn't seen him. If Nixie hadn't mentioned Prosper. If it weren't for the letter—

I watched the ripple on the surface of the water, my heart stopping. *The letter.*

The water sloshed over the lip of the tub as I stood, snatching the robe from the hook. I wrapped it around me as I came down the hallway dripping, my eyes flitting over the living room. The blanket I'd had wrapped around me was still on the floor where I'd dropped it in front of the door.

I picked it up, shaking it out frantically.

Nothing.

The sound of my own breath rang in my ears as I turned in a circle, studying the room. I pulled the cushions from the sofa and scoured the floor before checking the papers on the kitchen counter. When I didn't find it, I went to my room, crouching down beside the bed and pulling the hat box of letters from beneath it. I clumsily thumbed through the envelopes. It wasn't there.

My hand pressed to my mouth, my pulse skipping unevenly as I looked down the hallway, to the front door. I'd been standing right there with it in my hand when I saw the glow of the flames across the road. I'd dropped the blanket and ran and . . .

I got back to my feet and found the flashlight in the kitchen drawer before I pulled the door back open. It hit the wall with a crash as the wind poured into the house, and I went out on the porch, searching. The beam of white light moved over the wooden slats in a jittery sweep before finding the steps. Then the yard. I followed the stone path all the way to the gate at the road and when I reached it, I turned around, looking at the house.

The windows were lit, the porch light swinging in the wind. The door was open, just like it had been when I came back from August's minutes ago.

But somewhere between the moment I saw the fire and the moment I came back through the gate, it vanished.

The letter was gone.

Twenty-Nine

AUGUST

I WASN'T GOING TO take the alley this time.

Main Street was busy. The last of the season's tourists filled the walks, bundled in their parkas and their hats with bags of apples on their shoulders. They'd taken the early ferry, headed to the island for the orchard, and the bakery, and the beautiful views of the sound.

I'd spent eighteen years on Saoirse. Long enough to know it was all bullshit.

The smell of smoke still clung to my clothes, my hands blackened with the remnants of the fire. But the thing that had turned my guts standing there in the dark wasn't the burning truck. It was Emery.

She had every right to hate me. It made things easier if she did. But the sound of her voice when she said that I left her had been a knife between my ribs. It was true. All of it.

The boats anchored on the dock rocked in the wind, masts tipping like metronomes as I passed. Just beyond the harbor, there was a line of people streaming out of the pub. I followed it, pushing open the door. Noah would be swamped with the weekend breakfast rush, but I knew what else I'd find inside.

Jakob Blackwood.

"Hey!" The man at the front of the line threw his hands into the air, but I ignored him, heading straight for the bar.

Jake sat hunched on his usual stool over a steaming mug of coffee, and I thought for a moment how pathetic it was that the man had had a regular stool for that many years. Every day was the same on this island.

Noah saw me first, abandoning the cup and saucer in his hands to come around the counter. He walked straight toward me, opening his mouth with a warning, but I didn't take my eyes off of Jake.

I pulled the rusted door handle from the pocket of my jacket and dropped it onto the bar. It clattered sharply, making Jake jump, and he turned on his stool with wide eyes.

"What the hell are you doing?" His coffee sloshed from the cup.

Around us, Noah's patrons stopped mid-bite to watch.

I jerked my chin at the door handle. "This was you, right?"

His brows pulled together before he picked it up, inspecting it. "What the hell is it?"

Noah stepped in front of us, blocking the view of the tables along the bar.

"Someone set the truck on fire last night," I said, watching him carefully.

His gaze lifted again, meeting mine. "What?"

"Last night"— I spoke more slowly—"someone set the truck in the drive on fire."

Noah looked between us warily. "All right, maybe we should take this to the back," he rasped.

I fixed my stare at Jake. "No. I want to hear him say it."

"This is the first I'm hearing about it." He spat, shoving the handle into my chest.

"You think I don't remember how things work around here?" I took a step toward him. "When people don't fall in line, they're made to."

"You don't know what you're talking about," he growled.

"I told you I'm not leaving until I bury my mom's ashes, and I meant it. You can burn the whole fucking house down if you want."

Jake slid off the stool, standing eye to eye with me. "If you're accusing me of something, then you'd better go ahead and say it."

"I don't have to." I scoffed. "Everyone in this town knows what you are. I know what you are." Before he could say another word, I took hold of his jacket. "You're still the guy who beat up a kid because you couldn't deal with the fact that you can't do your fucking job." I leaned in closer. "But I'm not a kid anymore, Jake." I let him go.

Noah studied him. From the look on his face, that was one of Jake's transgressions he *didn't* know about.

To me, Noah had always been Emery's dad, someone I felt like I had to convince that I was good enough. Jake had been something else. Not quite a father and not quite a friend. But in the end, he was just beating the shit out of me like my grandfather did.

When Jake didn't deny it, Noah looked to me. "All right, I think it's probably time for you to get home, August."

Jake was Noah's brother, and even if the two of them weren't cut from the same cloth, Noah had had a lot of practice cleaning up whatever messes Jake made. Seeing the two of them there, side by side, I couldn't help but think about my mom. How they'd stood on the other side of the line from her, too.

"She hated you," I said, before I'd even thought it.

Jake went still, his brown eyes narrowing on me.

"Both of you. You turned your backs on us and she hated you for it."

I knew that each and every word would cut like an uneven blade. I wanted it to. Noah wasn't lying when he said that Eloise had been family. They'd both loved her.

The brothers stared at me, speechless, and I turned on my heel, stalking back through the pub until I was pushing out onto the street. I pulled the cold air into my lungs, trying to cool the fire in my chest.

What I said was true. My mother had been like a sister to the Blackwood brothers. But when the town came for blood, they cut her loose.

Thirty

AUGUST

WE WERE SIXTEEN, EMERY just barely.

Her dad's fishing cabin was on the east side of the island, and on clear nights you could see the city lights from the end of the dock. We would lie out there on a blanket, backs flat on the wood, and when the tide was high, we would dangle our legs over so that our feet touched the cold water.

I loved her long before that. I don't really remember a time that I *didn't* love her. But that summer was different.

Emery had shifted from the girl I'd always known into something else. She was quieter. She was, impossibly, more beautiful. Her laugh was shy and the things she wanted to talk about had changed. And when she touched me, her hands lingered in a way they hadn't before.

It was a full moon. I remember that, because she lifted a finger into the air and traced it on the black sky. It was bright, its edges yellowed like old paper, and giving way to the color of warm copper. The blood moon.

She pulled off her white cotton dress and we jumped into the dark water like we had on many other nights. She hooked her arms around my neck, and I could feel her naked body beneath the surface, goosebumps covering the curves of her. The only bit of warmth was in the places that her skin touched mine, and I loved that feeling.

There were so many times when I thought that her existence just felt like an extension of mine. Like this part of me that lived outside of my skin. I'd watched in a kind of silent awe as her body changed in those years, and I wanted her all the time, but I'd never had her completely.

I pressed a kiss to her throat as she looked up at the moon. Her face was washed white with it, and she whispered, "Swear that you'll love me forever."

I almost laughed, because she knew that I loved her. But she looked down into my face, and she wasn't smiling. She looked like she was going to cry.

"What's wrong?"

"Swear it," she said again.

The water lapped quietly against us as I studied her. "I'll love you forever," I said. "I swear it."

Two tears fell in tandem down her cheeks, caught by the corners of a smile that finally broke on her lips, and I wrapped my arms around her so tightly that I couldn't feel her breathing against me.

"I'll love you forever," she whispered. "I swear it."

I didn't know it was strange, because Emery and I had just always . . . been. I didn't know that teenagers didn't usually fall into that kind of love, or that there was anything unusual about us at all. I just knew that she felt like air to me.

That night, we sat in front of the fire, our hair still wet, and Emery had her cold feet tangled with mine to warm them. Our parents didn't like it when we spent the night at the cabin, but I could already tell that Emery was going to fall asleep. I pulled the quilt up higher so that it covered her shoulder and she blinked, like she'd forgotten where she was.

She pushed herself up, swinging one leg over my lap, and she looked down at me with her hair falling around her face. I let my hands find her knees, sliding them up her thighs. The air was cold, but beneath her dress, she was warm.

She reached down between us to unbutton my shorts, and I kissed her when she came low, finding the band of her underwear along her hip with my thumb. I wasn't cold anymore. The room grew hot around us, even though the fire was dying out, and I sat up, pulling her beneath me.

We found our familiar rhythm, hands moving in a pattern that they had a hundred times, but Emery slowed, going still. I pulled back to look at her, and her chest was rising and falling with deep breaths.

Her lips were wet, her eyes almost scared. "I want to," she whispered. "Is that okay?"

It took me a moment to realize what she was asking. We hadn't really ever talked about going all the way. It was just this unspoken thing we'd sidestepped before that night.

"Yeah"—I searched her eyes—"that's okay."

Suddenly, I didn't know what to do. How to touch her. Like I'd forgotten everything in a split second. I watched as she pulled the dress over her head and the firelight moved over her olive skin like liquid.

"Are we doing this?" I spoke between heavy breaths, smiling.

The corner of her mouth lifted and she nodded, like she was admitting to a secret, and I came back down to her so she could fit herself against me.

Her hands moved down my back as she kissed me and I had the same feeling I had each time we stood at the top of the cliffs at Wilke's Pointe. Like I could feel in every cell of my body the distance I was about to fall.

I reached between us, waiting for her to look at me. When she did, I pushed into her slowly, and her eyes closed. She held on to me, her head tipping back with her lips pinched between her teeth, and it was the first time I'd ever felt that pull—that soul-deep tide that drags you under until you can't breathe. It was the only time I had ever felt it. And I don't know if it was being young, or being stupid, or if it was just what first love feels like, but I didn't want it to ever stop.

That night we learned to make love. Over time, we got good at it, and that tiny sliver of space between us vanished. There was no fraction of a second that I didn't want to be with her.

It was the single best moment of my life. The color of her bare skin in the firelight. The feel of her. The sound she made as she moved against me. At times, I'd even felt like that one memory was the only thing that was keeping me breathing. And there were a million times after I left Saoirse that I wished to God it never happened.

Thirty-One

AUGUST

ZACHARIAH BEHR HAD BEEN burying people on Saoirse for most of his life. Now, it was my mother's turn.

The cemetery sat in the middle of the woods, surrounded by a rusted iron gate that was pitched in an almost perfect square. Inside, the stones that marked the graves were covered in moss, some of the inscriptions only barely legible.

Every single member of the Salt family had been laid to rest in that ground except for my father. The newest headstone among them was Henry Salt's. The granite was still shining in places, having spent only eight or nine years standing in the sea winds.

I hadn't expected anyone on Saoirse to come to my mother's burial, but I wondered who'd been there for his. The whole island, I guessed. He was the last Salt to live here, and though the man had never been called generous or kind, he'd somehow managed to find it in himself to leave the orchard to the town. That was something, I guessed.

His name stared back at me.

HENRY FITZ SALT

It was a black rectangular stone that was polished so smooth that I could see myself in its reflection. The suit jacket was one I'd bought for a lecture I was chosen to give for the heads of the departments at the college. At the time, I'd been proud to wear it. Looking at it now, I suspected I'd never put it on again.

The gate to the cemetery opened with a screech, and Zach came up the path. His hair had been brushed and he'd shaved, revealing the severe jaw and dimpled chin that I remembered most about his face. But the limp he'd always had was more pronounced now, making him sag on the right side as he moved.

He gave me a simple nod as he reached me.

"Thanks for doing this," I said.

Zach had never been one to care much what other people thought, but he also didn't like complications. The town couldn't be happy about him helping me.

He cleared his throat. "She'd have done the same for me, I suppose."

She would have. That was true.

"Are you ready then?"

I glanced back to the closed gate on the other side of the cemetery, half-hoping that Emery would be there. It was covered in a thick carpet of Virginia creeper that had begun to turn gold. In another week, it would be orange, then red.

She wasn't coming.

I hadn't seen her since she walked back across the road with the glow of the fire at her back, and I guessed that I wouldn't again. I'd known when I apologized there would be no forgiveness, but I'd done it because I owed her that. Still, the most pathetic part of me had hoped as I buttoned up my shirt and tightened my tie that she would come. It didn't matter how grown I was or how hardened I'd become from what life had brought. I didn't want to stand over my mother's grave alone.

"I'm ready," I answered.

My mother's urn was suddenly heavier in my hands. The trees

creaked as they bowed in the wind and the distant sound of the water crashing on the rocks wove through the woods, finding me. I looked at it one last time before I handed it to Zachariah.

He gently touched the engraving on its side. My mother's name.

Zach's thick white eyebrows lifted. "The more years I live, the harder it is to outlive the young."

He was old enough to remember my mother as a child. He'd always seen her that way.

I watched as he placed the urn in the ground. The emerald green surface was the same color as my mother's eyes. That's why I'd picked it. They'd never dulled as she got older, and I always thought that was strange. But my mother was strange, like the island. She had never really belonged in the outside world.

I'd known the weight of what I'd done, even back then. That this island had been a piece of her she had to cut out. For me. And I don't think she ever stopped bleeding. More than once, I'd thought maybe it had actually been the thing that made her sick, growing inside her over the years.

Zach's gaze moved past me, suddenly refocusing, and I turned.

Emery stood on the other side of the rusted gate in a simple black dress with buttons down the front. She reached up, tucking her hair behind her ear nervously as she watched me with an expression I couldn't decipher. Like maybe she was seconds from turning around and walking away.

I stilled, unable to hide the overwhelming relief of seeing her there.

She waited another moment before she finally made up her mind to push the gate open, and she followed the winding path through the cemetery. Her long brown hair was loose and pulled over one shoulder instead of tied up in a knot or bound back in a braid.

When she reached me, it took every bit of my restraint to keep from touching her. I hadn't expected that when I came back—the instinctive reflex I felt every time she was near me.

I looked down into her face, following the seven points of the

green star that sparkled in the iris of her left eye. The last time I stood
that close to her, I was memorizing the shape of it. Spinning the pattern into a single, unspoiled memory to take with me when I left. It
was the last time I saw her, but I was the only one who'd known it
was a goodbye.

"You didn't have to come," I said.

"Yes, I did."

Her gaze lifted above our heads and I followed it to the low
branches of the pines, where there were at least a dozen starlings
perched in silence. Their feathers were puffed out against the cold
wind, their yellow feet clutched around the spindly wood as they
watched us.

Emery's mouth flattened into a straight line.

Zach cleared his throat, making us both turn. He stood over the
hole in the ground, a small, worn book in his big hands. "May I
begin?"

I nodded and Emery took the place beside me without a word.

Zachariah opened the book, reading aloud in his crackling voice.
"Eloise Amelia Salt was born under a waning crescent moon on July
tenth, nineteen fifty-one. She was the daughter of Walt Carter and
Serena Hubbard, an only child."

I'd heard Zachariah speak over the open graves of others on
Saoirse, but the words felt different, hearing them read over someone I loved.

"We now lay her to rest in the same ground on which she was
born."

I breathed through the ache in my throat as Zach carefully lowered himself to one knee and took up a fistful of dirt, scattering it
over the urn. I followed, doing the same, and then Emery sank down,
scooping a handful of earth into her palm. Her fingers closed over it
for a moment and her lips moved over words I couldn't hear before
she opened them again. A gentle wind wove through the trees, blowing it from her hand and she let it fall into the grave.

A tear dripped from the tip of my nose as I stared at the ground, and her small feet reappeared beside my boots as Zach's voice drawled on. It was lost in the sounds of the island, and from the corner of my eye, I could see Emery's hand reaching toward me. I could hardly feel it as her touch traced over my knuckles, pulling my hand from where it was clasped with the other. Her fingers wove into mine, and the faint tingle of warmth bled through me, bringing the feeling back into my skin.

My eyes traveled up her arm to her shoulder, her throat, her face, where the cold wind had pulled a few strands of her hair across her forehead again, turning her cheeks pink.

She'd looked at me like she hated me as we stood in front of the burning truck, but there was also something comforting about it. It felt like before. When angry words between us had been like the waves that crashed around the island. It had never mattered what was said, because we always returned to each other. Like gravity.

For the tiniest sliver of a moment, I forgot the last fourteen years. The fire. The months that followed. The half-life I'd made when we left. For a moment, there was no *after*.

Thirty-Two

NIXIE

THE STARLINGS AND THE sea had the same sound, almost exactly.

I stood on the rocky shore watching them, fishing pole in one hand, a pail in the other. It was Monday, and for once, the ferries would be empty. The orchard was officially closed and life would tuck into the much-needed rest that winter would bring before spring came to wake it. But the island wasn't sleeping.

The birds moved like a thick, drifting smoke across the sky, taking shape and then instantly shifting. They floated up into the low-hanging clouds over the sea before plummeting down with a sound that reverberated in my bones. Then the edge of the mass almost touched the water, pulling up and bending its form again.

I'd lived my entire life on the island, and I'd never seen the star-lings linger so long. Before the first frost, they were gone. But there were thousands of them, and the swarm was growing by the day.

My head tipped back as they roared overhead, nearly blacking out the light. In another breath, they disappeared altogether, vanishing beyond the trees.

The *Saoirse Journal* was on the porch when I returned to the house, lying on the second-to-bottom step. The cover story was folded over, but one word was visible in bold type, facing up: SALT.

I set down the pail of cod and crouched low, unbinding the paper and unfolding it before me.

FIRE AT SALT COTTAGE

The charred remains of a truck were pictured below the headline. Eloise's truck. It had been Calvin's before that, but no one thought of Calvin anymore. The few of us who did wished we hadn't.

I hung out my waders and drank a full two cups of coffee before I finally walked the road with the *Journal* tucked under my arm. With Hannah gone, there were certain things that were left to me to handle. Emery was one of them. This was another.

Hannah, Eloise, and I had sworn ourselves to be sisters when we were ten years old. Hannah's and my kin were long rooted, respected residents of Saoirse, but Eloise had been cursed with a drunk fisherman for a father.

We'd been there for each other growing up, and that didn't change when Hannah and Eloise got married. We'd had to keep our promise then, too. We'd bled for each other, sacrificed for each other, and hell, we'd done some dark things. But it had been a long time since I'd had to face those demons.

When I turned off the road, Leoda Morgan was on the porch, sitting in her rocking chair.

The old house's windows were open to the autumn breeze, a practice that most residents of the island would partake in today. It was a last chance to air out the house before the cold set in, and it wasn't just the stagnant air we were ridding ourselves of. Albertine Blackwood always said it was also a way of shaking the tourists out of our bones. Cleansing the island of whatever shadows they'd brought with them across the Sound.

"Nixie!" Leoda greeted me with a rare, relaxed smile. That should have been my first clue.

I lifted a hand in greeting and took the winding path up through the tall grass. I'd have to tread carefully if I was going to keep the peace. Leoda's ire wasn't known to fade quickly, and her seat on the town council was a weighty one. I'd learned the importance of making sure we were on the same side.

"I've got a fresh pot, if you'd like it," she said.

I untied my scarf. "I would, thank you."

Leoda rose from the chair as I sat and she disappeared into the house, fetching a second teacup. When she returned, she set it down on the small table beside me and filled it. Her feet were bare despite the chill.

"As happy to see them go as I am, aren't you?" She arched one eyebrow.

That was one thing Leoda and I saw eye to eye on. We'd never had any qualms there. The tourists descended upon the island like locusts, picking it clean, but there was no arguing with the fact that we needed them. Without those full ferries, the island would die. It almost had, once.

"I've lived with them this many years. I suppose I can stand a few more."

Leoda laughed, "Come talk to me when you're my age."

I studied her. Lily's grandmother had always been something like a mother hen to everyone on the island. It wasn't until I was older that I understood she was more raptor than prey.

"We'll see if I make it that long," I said, without thinking.

Leoda paused at that, surveying me with a curious look.

I hadn't thought about the words before I spoke them. "Sorry, I don't mean to be grim."

The truth was the news about Eloise had brought my own end into sharp focus. The time of year didn't help, either. Samhain was right around the corner, and I could smell the decay of fallen leaves and fermenting fruit in the air. It was the season of death.

The two sisters I'd made blood oaths with on the stormy beach one summer night were both gone. I could almost hear their voices whispering to me from the other side.

I took the paper from beneath my arm, setting it on the table between us.

Leoda stared at it, but she said nothing.

"I hope I don't have to ask."

She pursed her lips. "I hope you don't, either."

I sighed, swirling the tea in my cup. Leoda was the person you went to if you wanted to get something done on Saoirse. But she was a train that, once moving, was almost impossible to stop. "Leave him alone, Leoda. He'll be gone in a few days."

"That's what Jake said when he arrived, and now he's been here more than a week, Nixie. Sophie says he's been to the records office, and I'm not the only one who thinks his departure is overdue."

So, she hadn't acted alone. She never did. But if August was sniffing around Henry Salt's will, there'd be no reasoning with her.

I finally looked at her, studying the lines around her eyes. To her, we were all still kids. Me, Noah, Jake, Hannah, Eloise. But somewhere between blinks, we'd grown old. We'd grown into a lot of things.

"Is this what we are now?" I said, more heavily. I was really asking. It was difficult to remember what kind of people we'd been before.

Leoda raised the cup to her lips again. "Let's not pretend that your hands are any cleaner than the rest of ours. When you came to me for what needed doing, I did it without question."

I stared at her, my blood running ice cold. We'd sworn we'd never speak of that night. But there was a warning in her voice. A threat, even. "I know."

When I went to her all those years ago, I hadn't known what would follow. I couldn't say that I regretted any of it, either. But I wasn't sure if Leoda knew that I could see it was all part of the same intricate web, and I wondered if any of it would have happened if I hadn't knocked on her door that night.

"I'm the last Morgan on this island, and that's a responsibility I take seriously. I know you have a soft spot for that boy because of Eloise, but you need to remember it's Salt blood in his veins."

That's what this really came down to for her. The orchard. It was always about the orchard. After Lily died and her son and daughter-in-law left Saoirse, people wondered if Leoda and Hans would follow. But she was as much a part of this island as the cliffs or the woods or the coves.

"We've all done things for the good of this town, you included." She took her time, finishing the last of her tea. "He never should have come back here, Nixie. So, let's make sure it doesn't happen again."

Thirty-Three

EMERY

THE TREES HID THE scars well.

I climbed to the top of the ladder with the cloth sack draped over one shoulder, ducking through the branches. From this high up, you could hardly tell where the fire had blown through the orchard. But I could still remember the blackness of the earth where the flames had been. The smell that had hung in the air afterward.

It had been a beautiful day on the island. I remember that, because I remember the dappled light on the lawn in front of the school during graduation. But hours later, a single wind rolled over the sea ahead of the oncoming storm. It crashed up the bluff before tearing through the orchard and when it found the weakened branch on one of the oldest trees, the glass lantern fell.

By all accounts, the town shouldn't have survived it. The annual tradition of riding the ferry to the island each fall was overshadowed by the news coverage of a dead girl, and there wasn't much reason to visit when the orchard was closed. It had taken years, but the new trees did grow. The ferries returned. And Saoirse went right on living.

I wedged the heel of my boot into the crevice between branches so I could reach higher. The apples on the topmost branches were always left behind by the tourists, but we would make use of them in preserves and jams and vinegars that would be sold through spring and summer in the shops.

Every year, the orchard called for volunteers to help wrap up the last of the season's work and every year, we answered. Closing up the farm was a responsibility that stretched beyond the payroll. It was something we all did—together.

I yanked another apple from the branch and dropped it into the sack. My fingers were already numb and I'd left my gloves in the truck, but the day was colder than expected. By nightfall, when all the clearing and pruning was done, there would be supper and mulled wine at the orchard house. I'd been dreading it for days.

I'd come because I was expected to, and because I didn't need to give anyone more reason to talk. But it had already begun—the watching. The wondering. And someone had already taken matters into their own hands by setting fire to Eloise's truck.

August was right. No one had come. The phone at the marshal's office had gone unanswered each time I called it, and I imagined my uncle at his desk, watching it ring as he sipped whiskey from his coffee cup. The thought made me tremble.

I didn't want to think about the possibility that Jake had set the fire himself, but I knew my uncle wasn't exactly the upstanding marshal that outsiders might expect him to be. I had a hard time believing that my dad would have set a fire when he bore the scars of one. But Dutch . . .

The front page of the *Saoirse Journal* was plastered with a photo of the blackened truck that sat in front of the Salt cottage, and by now everyone on the island would have heard about it. But this wasn't the random spark of a bonfire gone rogue or a discarded cigarette butt. Someone had set that fire. And they may have also stolen the letter.

I'd gone out in my wellies and nightgown as soon as it was light enough to see, searching the yard, the garden, the ditch that stretched along the side of the road. I couldn't remember setting the letter down. I'd had it in my hand and then I didn't. I told myself that the wind could have blown it out the front door. That it could have skipped down the road in the pouring rain and if it had, there was no way it survived the storm that blew over the island throughout the night. If anyone found it, it would be no more than a smear of white pulp in the dirt.

But there was a tingle over my skin as I peered through the branches of the apple tree, studying the faces I'd known all my life. More disturbing than the idea of any of them being responsible was the fact that I could believe it.

"Em."

I jerked, catching myself on the limb overhead as I looked down between my feet. Dutch stood at the bottom of the ladder, my gloves clutched in his hand.

My breath fogged in the air as I regained my balance, and I tried to slow my racing pulse. "Hey."

He took hold of the ladder, and I hesitated before I climbed down with the weight of the apples pulling at my hip. When I reached the ground, he lifted the bag from my shoulder, handing me the gloves. "Saw them sitting on the seat in the truck."

I took them, sliding my hands into each one as he watched me. "Thanks."

Dutch looked more like himself than he had in days, and I wondered if it was being in the orchard that did it. Here, he was in charge. He controlled things.

"I finally got a call from the city," he said. "The glass for the window will be here Friday."

I nodded, looking for the anger that had been in his eyes the night I went to see Nixie. But it wasn't there now.

He stepped past me, setting the hat back on his head as he walked toward the end of the row. I swallowed hard, changing my mind several times before I finally said it. "Dutch?"

He stopped, turning back. "Yeah?"

His eyes had an open look to them. A hopeful one. He was waiting for me to close the space between us.

"Were you at the house the other night?" I asked.

"What?"

"Two nights ago. Did you come by?"

Dutch's eyes narrowed as he shifted from one foot to the other. "Are you serious?"

I stared at him, clenching my teeth so hard that my jaw ached. I wanted him to deny it.

"I saw the paper, Em. I'm not a fucking idiot."

"That's not an answer."

He sneered, giving me a look I wasn't sure I'd ever seen before. It took me a moment to realize who it reminded me of—his father.

I exhaled.

"You need to stay out of whatever August has himself wrapped up in."

"Someone on this island set that fire, Dutch. That doesn't bother you?"

"You don't know that."

"I was there. I saw it."

His expression changed again, turning darker. "What do you mean you were there?"

"I could see the fire from the house." I wasn't going to tell him that I'd been with August when I saw it. The less ammunition he had, the better.

Dutch shook his head, staring at the ground. The muscles in his arms flexed, the veins in his hands surfacing under the skin. "So you thought you'd do what? Run over there and save him?"

"Are you saying if you'd seen a fire at Nixie's out your window, you wouldn't go over there?"

"He's not Nixie. And I know you went to the burial."

"What's that supposed to mean? It's not a secret."

"Then why didn't you tell me?"

"We haven't talked in days."

"Whose choice was that?" His voice rose.

I stilled, looking around us. Molly Tulles's husband was in the next row, watching. By tomorrow, she'd have even more gossip to spew at the market.

"The burial was for Eloise. You should have been there, too. And don't pretend like this is about the funeral. You're not even angry about August. You're angry at *me*."

"Is there a difference?"

"What?"

"It's all the same, right? Everything goes back to him. Like always."

My heart twisted as I remembered taking August's hand as we stood over Eloise's grave. I hadn't thought twice. I hadn't agonized over it or weighed the cost of that moment, I'd just done it. And I could still feel his touch on my palm, like sunlight pooled between my fingers.

It was true, what Nixie said. I'd never let August go, not really. And it seemed so foolish, so childish, that I could hardly stand to admit it to myself. I'd been eighteen years old. I'd known nothing about suffering or responsibility or loss, but somehow, I'd known this soul-deep kind of love that I now wondered if most people never found. It cut open a vein in me that never stopped flowing.

"I'm not going to do this here." I tried to go around him, but he stepped in front of me.

"If it were up to you, we'd never have this argument."

"We've been having it for years, Dutch."

"Tell me why you won't marry me." He blurted it out, making me wince.

"Because I don't want to be married. I don't want to have a family and make the life that everyone else on this island does!" I didn't care who could hear me now.

"I don't believe you."

"Of course you don't."

"You act like you don't want this life, but you're still here, Emery. You could have left at any time and you didn't."

"No, I couldn't. You know I couldn't. My dad was hurt. Then my mom was sick. Someone had to take over the shop."

Dutch was an expert at reading me, but I still didn't know how to be honest with him. He was there after August left. He'd understood me, but that had never been enough. It all felt like crumbling dust when I held it against the body-aching need I'd known before.

Dutch was the kind of man who told me what I wanted to hear. He played by my rules when the waters got rough so that he could be the one to swoop in and save me. But this was different. I shook my head, exhausted. I couldn't fight with him anymore.

"You have to stop asking," I said weakly. "Please. I'm never going to say yes."

Dutch leveled his gaze at me. I could see him searching for something to grab ahold of. Anything. "You don't know everything"—he swallowed—"about that night."

I went rigid, letting the words sink in, sure I'd heard him wrong. "What are you talking about?"

"I . . ." He scrubbed his hands over his face, breathing into them. "Jesus, I've almost told you a hundred times."

I could feel my insides turning to liquid. Whatever he was about to say was the first few drops of an entire ocean.

He stared at me, his face flushing.

"What?" I said, louder.

His eyes lifted slowly, and there was a coldness in them that I didn't like. "I lied, Emery."

My mind raced, my pulse quickening. But I wasn't putting it together.

"About August. I lied about being with him that night."

A sharp sting like needles under my skin rushed over me, making my stomach turn. This wasn't the last-ditch effort of a desperate man. He was telling the truth. I could hear it in his voice.

"Why?" I whispered. "Why would you do that?"

His lips pressed together. "Because he was my friend. I was scared for him."

I took a step backward, trying to fill the bottom of my lungs with air. They wouldn't inflate.

"I don't know why I did it, I just did. And then once I lied, I couldn't take it back."

I leaned into the tree, trying to feel the gravity beneath my feet. Nausea crawled up my throat as I remembered Eloise's words in the letter.

What August did . . .

"The only reason he wasn't charged with Lily's murder is because *you* said you were with him, Dutch. Do you get that?" But it wasn't just that. Dutch's lie was also the thing I'd clung to when everyone was convinced that August was a murderer.

"I know." He nodded. "But I'm telling you now because I'm worried about you, Emery. I don't want him anywhere near you."

"Are you saying . . ." My voice wavered. "Are you saying you think he hurt Lily?"

He was quiet for a long moment. Too long. "I'm saying that I don't know anymore."

I stared at him wordlessly before pushing around him, onto the path. The row of trees pressed in on either side of me, making me feel like they were closing in, and I walked faster, fishing the keys from the pocket of my jacket. When I made it to the truck, a sea of eyes in the orchard house were watching me through the opened doors.

I tried to slow my breaths, blinking furiously through hot tears as I turned to face them. "If you have something to say, then say it!"

They stared at me wordlessly. Abbott Wittich, Etzel Adelman. Nixie, Jake, and my dad. A dozen others whose faces I couldn't stand to look at.

I yanked open the door of the truck and climbed inside, swallowing down the cry breaking in my throat. I fumbled with the keys until the engine roared to life and pulled onto the road without look-ing back.

Almost everyone on this island had accused Dutch of lying that night. It had cost almost any chance he had at gaining anyone's trust again, until the town council put him in charge of the orchard. But he'd never wavered from his story, not once. Not until now.

But if August wasn't with Dutch that night, then where the hell was he?

Thirty-Four

EMERY

LILY'S STRAW-COLORED HAIR FELL from the edge of the bed, almost touching the wood floor. She was lying on her back, her feet up the wall and her arms outstretched over the quilts as she watched her toenails dry. "I still think she deserves it."

"What does it matter? I don't even care." I dipped the brush into the nail polish bottle and closed it. Lily had picked a dark crimson called *Wicked* for me—the last color I would have chosen.

"Well, I do."

She'd come over after school when she heard what happened from Dutch and I'd known as soon as I'd seen her face that she wasn't going to let this go.

Clara Murdoch had called me a slut in front of half of my history class, and I couldn't have cared less. Lily, however, was furious.

"Just *one* little black candle?" she pleaded, looking at me upside down with her bright blue eyes. "My grandmother has a whole drawer full dedicated to cursing Henry Salt."

I laughed. "Why does she hate the Salts so much?"

"She hates everyone."

"No black candles. No hexes, curses, or animal sacrifices," I said, mostly kidding. The downside of having a protective friend was having to rein her in. The truth was, it was exhausting, and the closer to leaving Saoirse I got, the more I realized that there was a part of me that craved being apart from Lily. I loved her, but she was more unpredictable than ever and I had less and less interest in getting sucked into her drama.

"It looks like blood," I said, leaning back onto my hands and letting my feet sway back and forth.

"That's what makes it hot." Lily flipped over, inspecting them. "What are the boys doing tonight?"

"I don't know. August is probably working."

"He's always working." She groaned.

I rolled my eyes. August did what he was told to keep the peace for his mom's sake, but Lily had no idea what it was like to do anything she didn't want to do. The way August looked at it, we would be gone in a few months, anyway.

"Let's go get Dutch. We can go up to Wilke's Pointe," I said.

Lily stuck out her bottom lip.

"What?"

"Nothing." She set her chin in her hands. "Let's just hang out, the two of us."

"Okay. Ice cream?"

"Yes"—she swung her legs off the bed and stood, pulling me up from the floor—"if you let me pick the flavor."

"It's your turn."

"You're right. It is my turn." She gave me a wry look before going to the mirror over my dresser. I watched as she combed her fingers through her hair.

I felt guilty suddenly that I'd thought I wouldn't miss her. She was impossible, selfish, and more stubborn than anyone I'd ever known. But it had always been the two of us.

When August and I first made the plan, there was a big part of me that thought it would never happen. But the closer it got, the more serious it became, and eventually I'd had to admit to myself just how badly I wanted it.

There were things I *would* miss. The little rituals that made this place strange. Bonfires at Imbolc, harvests under moonlight, the sound of my mother whispering over the tea leaves in the shop. I was finally old enough to realize that Saoirse was a place unlike any other. Across the water was a whole new world.

My mother would be angry when she woke and found my note, but the wild parts of her—the parts that had once dreamed of leaving Saoirse—would be proud. My father would be sad, but as long as he had my mother, I wouldn't worry about him.

Lily . . . she would be furious.

I set my chin on her shoulder, looking at her in the mirror. "You're so pretty."

It was true. Lily had always been beautiful in a perfect kind of way. But she didn't smile when I said it, like she usually did.

"A completely useless quality, it turns out."

"Huh?"

"Nothing."

I laughed, but Lily met her own eyes in the mirror, her mouth twisting to one side like she was trying not to cry.

"What are you talking about?"

She shrugged. "I'd rather be loved than pretty."

"Lily, everyone loves you."

"Not like they love you," she said, too seriously. There wasn't a joke behind the words. But just when I was going to argue, she kissed me on the cheek, breezing past me to the door. "Let's go."

Thirty-Five

EMERY

I DRAGGED THE KNIFE down the table, slicing the butcher paper in one clean line. Main Street was empty and the shop was dark, but I couldn't go home. Too many ghosts waited for me there.

The sea air swept in through the propped open door, touching every corner of the small room. I bundled the willow stalks together, tying their ends, before I folded the paper over them and taped it. They'd been waiting to be properly hung for days, filling the shop with a sweet smell that reminded me of my mother. This had been my job when I worked with her as a kid, trimming the herbs piled in her basket and drying them for tea.

I hadn't told a soul what Dutch said. Not even Nixie. And now that I didn't have Eloise's letter, I didn't know what to do. Go to Jake, like I should have done in the first place? Tell the town council? The more I thought about it, the sicker it made me.

The worst of it was that the lie had been so easy to accept for so many years. I wanted to believe it, so I did. I never pressed for details or prodded Dutch about that night and I'd told myself it was because I didn't want to remember it. I wanted to move on. But somewhere deep inside me, I'd also been afraid that if I did, I wouldn't like what I found.

Lily, August, Dutch, my parents, Eloise, Nixie . . . I was beginning to think there wasn't anyone on this island who hadn't lied about something. And I was no different. I'd been keeping that file in my bottom drawer for years.

The stool scraped as I moved it to the window and I climbed up, hanging the willow from the taut string that followed the edge of the ceiling. The bundle swung, casting a shadow over the floorboards, and when the subtle clink of china began to rumble, my gaze drifted to the hutch.

The teacups rattled on their saucers softly, making me still. The feeling of it was palpable in the air and on my skin—magic. The whisper of the island that bubbled up from the ground.

I climbed down, taking a tentative step toward the hutch. I could hear my own breath, my heartbeat thrumming as my hand lifted toward the green teacup I'd sworn I'd never touch again. I could feel the burn in my fingertips just when the light shifted on the wall beside me and I jolted.

"Oh my." Leoda stood in the doorway, eyes wide.

I pressed a hand to my chest, gulping in the air. "You scared me."

She stepped inside, watching me with a puzzled look. "A bit jumpy, aren't we?"

"I didn't hear you come up the steps."

Her scarf was wrapped up around her shoulders, hiding half of her mouth, but I could see the question in her eyes before she spoke it. "Everything all right, honey? You look a bit shaken."

"I'm fine." I cleared my throat, rolling the paper back up and dropping the knife into the can on the counter.

"Been years since I've seen you working with the tea leaves." Her eyes skipped past me, to the hutch.

Leoda hadn't approved when I took over the shop and stopped offering readings the way my mother had. She'd never let me forget it, either.

She reached into the deep pocket of her jacket and pulled out a small amber glass dropper. "Hans said you stopped by looking for this."

I stared at it as she held it out to me.

"The nightmares are back?" she asked, lifting it higher.

I took it, turning the little bottle in my hand so I could read the label. I'd tried every herb I had for sleep in the shop, but nothing was working. I needed something stronger. Leoda's tincture of valerian was a potent one that took months to make. If it didn't help, I'd have to break down and finally go to my grandmother.

"I heard there was quite a scene at the orchard earlier."

Of course she had. "Dutch and I got into a fight."

"Hmmmm." She sat on one of the stools, setting one elbow on the tabletop. "Everything okay?"

"Not really."

She gave me a sympathetic smile. "It's not been easy for anyone, all of this mess with August."

I stiffened, clenching my teeth. I didn't want to talk about August.

"You know I'm here if you need me," she said, more softly.

I nodded. "I know."

"Do you? Because it looks to me like you're carrying quite the burden."

We hadn't talked about Lily much through the years, but Leoda was one of the only people left on the island who understood what we'd been to each other. Thorns, and all.

"We"—I breathed—"Lily and I argued the last time we spoke. Did I ever tell you that?"

"No. You didn't."

"We were having lunch at the pub after graduation and we got into a fight about something. It was stupid, but she was angry with me." I swallowed down the pain in my throat. "It was the last time I ever saw her."

"Well, the two of you were like sisters, Em. Sisters fight."

I'd told myself the same thing many times. Lily was furious when she found out about the ferry tickets and our plan to leave the island. I'd known she wouldn't be happy, but the look in her eyes . . .

Leoda picked up one of the trimmed willow stalks on the table, rolling it between her fingers. "It's normal, you know. To replay it in your mind. To pick apart the moments and try to make sense of them."

"Do you remember the last time you saw her?" I sat down, placing the bottle between us.

She blinked, her lips pursing, as if I'd just pulled her from a memory. "Sure I do. It was at graduation, out on the lawn of the school. We were taking pictures and Lily was impatient, but she posed for the photos anyway." She suddenly smiled to herself. "The last time I saw her, she was running off, that graduation robe billowing out behind her."

I could see it, too. Her straight blond hair looked like gold in the summer, her fair skin dusted with freckles. We acted like sisters, but looking at us, we couldn't have been more different. Our temperaments weren't similar, either. Lily was all passion and fire. I'd been the quieter one who followed her lead.

"She wasn't a simple girl. She had her demons like anyone else," Leoda murmured.

My eyes snapped up, studying her, and I wondered for the first time if maybe Lily *had* told someone about her secret. If she'd gone to anyone after she found out she was pregnant, maybe it would have been Leoda. I waited, hoping she would say something to confirm it. But the tenor of things unsaid faded in the silence.

"You know, for years after the fire, I thought this town might not make it. There were some dark days. I would wonder what Greta Morgan would say if she could see what we'd made of her magic. But it turns out that sometimes, death is the only thing that can set things right."

"Set things right?"

"Never mind," Leoda said, setting a soft, warm hand on top of mine. "You'll tell me if you need anything, won't you?" She waited for me to answer with a nod before she shuffled back to the door, pulling the scarf tighter around her.

I watched as she picked up the lantern and turned the key. The propane hissed to life as the light inside the glass ignited, and the glow of it faded as she made her way down the street.

I'd never told anyone about that fight with Lily. Not even my parents. Maybe because I was afraid to remember it myself. We'd fought a thousand times about a thousand things, but that argument had been different. For a moment, as I sat across the table from her, I'd felt like I was seeing her clearly for the first time. For a split second, I'd even hated her.

The rattling began again, softly, and my eyes lifted once more to the hutch, where the green teacup was gleaming in the candlelight. The last time I'd held it in my hands was the first time I'd felt the full weight of the darkness that swelled beneath the island. It rushed in my veins, snaking through me like poison.

The lid of the teapot and the saucers clinked as I placed my hands on the table and leaned forward over the candle. The heat of it licked against my skin, and I focused, watching the flame dance on the wick. A single drip of clear wax beaded beneath it and I could taste the fire on my tongue, feel it boiling in my belly. My eyes burned with the light as I imagined the wick empty. And just as I thought it, the flame snuffed out, leaving me in the dark.

Thirty-Six

EMERY

I WOKE WITH A gasp, my hands clutched to my sweat-soaked night-gown.

I was home, enclosed by the four walls of my bedroom, but the dark sea still flashed before my eyes. The burn of fingernails scraping over my skin. I could feel the biting sting where they'd been only seconds ago.

I searched the length of my arms for the marks I'd seen there, feeling over my bones with shaking fingers. I could feel them, but they were gone.

First, the nightmares had returned in broken pieces. A frayed thread. But now, they were a fully painted canvas across my mind. My fists full of wet, tangled hair. The cold water lapping around me. The screaming. I could still hear the screaming.

I tried to slow my breathing, opening the top of my nightgown so I could feel the cool night air on my hot skin. I'd never told a soul what I saw in the dark between waking and sleeping. I'd never dared to utter it aloud.

I stood waist-deep in the water, my bare feet almost numb on the rocky bottom. And I could see my hands holding her under. Her hair floated around her as she kicked, trying to get her footing, and when she broke the surface and her screams pierced the silence, I pushed her down again, harder. Bubbles raced over my fingers as they twisted tighter, the muscles in my arms straining, until she stopped.

It wasn't until her hands were drifting lifelessly that I finally let her go, but when she floated to the surface and the moonlight hit her face, it wasn't Lily.

It was me.

I reached for the lamp on the bedside table and the room filled with light, erasing the dream from where it hovered in the darkness. Leoda's tincture sat beside it. But this wasn't a sickness of the body that needed to be cured with herbs. This was something else.

Deep down, I'd known that August was hiding something. After my father was taken to the city and my uncle Jake came to the house to ask me questions, August was waiting at the harbor. Nixie and I were taking the first ferry out to be with my mom at the hospital, and he'd broken into tears when he saw me.

But he wouldn't touch me as we stood on the dock. I remember wrapping my arms around him, but August just stood there frozen, every muscle beneath his skin like stone.

I had never believed it. Not when the first whispers about August not being at the party began. Not when everyone on Saoirse began to wonder. One by one, everyone we'd ever known became convinced, but I'd never believed that he killed Lily.

How could I? There was a blindness in me for August. A tether that bound me to him. I knew because I was the one who had put it there.

I'd first heard the tale about the blood moon from my grandmother. When I closed my eyes, I could see the page in her book of shadows, the delicate handwriting pulled across the thick paper in rows. But that night in the water, with August's bare chest pressed to mine so that I could feel his heartbeat against me, I had wanted to bind myself to him. It was a desperate, heartsick plea, born out of the fear that I would lose him. And that one decision had cursed me for all of my days.

I should have done it years ago, but I had never had the guts. This pain inside me was like broken glass clutched in a fist. I knew it was drawing blood. Bleeding me out, all day, every day. But still, I couldn't just open my fingers and let it go. Because this wasn't that kind of love.

I climbed out of the bed and stalked through the house with heavy feet, finding my boots and my jacket. The keys dangled from my fingers as I walked to the truck and opened the door. The moon was bright, the sky clear for the first time in days.

That was good, I thought. We would need the moon.

Thirty-Seven

ALBERTINE

BY MY COUNT, THE moon was nearly full. I could feel its tug on the island, in the soft rasp of dropping leaves and the sweet smell of withering blooms. It was even in the way the waves hit the shore. I'd never been able to see its light, but it was there all the same. And tonight, it sang in the darkness.

I'd woken to the owl.

My mind reluctantly stirred from the emptiness of sleep, and the thick scent of rain swirled in my head as I surfaced from a fragmented dream. I drew the air in as the sound drifted through the open window again. Three sharp calls from the highest branches of the white pine.

I sat up slowly, careful not to wake my aching bones too quickly. They were less and less forgiving these days, and as winter fell over the island, they would be more stubborn than usual. But there was no denying the island's summoning.

Bit by bit, the room came alive around me with the sounds and vibrations that I knew. My toes moved along the floor until they found my slippers and I slid off the bed, pulling my robe around me. The house was silent, but I could hear it—the movement of the air

down the hallway and its shift as the wind changed direction outside.

I let two fingertips drag along the smooth wall, leading myself to
the living room. When I reached the fireplace, I sat, rooting around
in the kindling bucket until I had what I'd need to get the fire started.
Something told me it was going to be a long night.

I stacked a handful of pine needles and leaves carefully on the
grate inside the fireplace and opened the soapstone box, finding a
match. It struck with the sizzle of a little flame and its warmth kissed
my cheek as I moved closer, letting it catch.

The crush of tires on the soft earth sounded before I'd even gotten
the last log on. Emery's truck.

I knew the sound of every set of tires, every engine on this island.
But tonight, she pulled into the house too quickly, the brakes squeal-
ing as she came to a rushed stop. I could think of only a few reasons
she'd be here at this hour, and none of them were good.

I turned myself toward the door with the fire at my back, waiting.
The beat of her boots came up the steps, but then she hesitated. She
always did that when something was wrong.

The ping of the handle was followed by the squeal of hinges on the
screen door and I felt the night air come into the house. I could feel
her, too. A heavy presence, like a stone thrown into the water, pulling down, down, down.

"You're up." Her voice was soft. Apprehensive.

I held my hands to the fire's warmth, letting the blood come back
into my fingers. "Of course I am." I turned my ear up, listening to the
pattern of her breath. The keys jingling as she fidgeted with them.
Her shifting weight as she leaned into the door.

It painted a picture in my mind—one that only I could see. I'd
never laid eyes on my granddaughter, but I was sharply tuned to the
things that people usually missed. I didn't need to see her to know
that she was upset. Swallowing down tears, I suspected.

"What is it, love?" I asked, patiently.

There was a silent second before her feet started moving toward me. In the next breath, she was tucking herself into my arms and I wrapped them around her tightly, squeezing. She smelled like the woods, but her skin was hot, like she'd been crying.

A small, broken sound muffled in my shoulder and I pressed my cheek to hers. I'd been doing that since she was tiny enough to fit into the crook of my elbow. But she wasn't a child anymore.

"I need your help." The words cracked as she said them.

"All right." I waited.

Her warmth slowly slipped from my arms. The fire was roaring now, the heat bleeding into the corners of the room around us. There was a steadying intake of breath before she began.

"Once, you told me that an oath made beneath the blood moon is binding. Is that true?"

"If it was made in earnest"—I tilted my head to one side—"yes, it's true."

A pause. "Do you know how to break it?"

My mind flitted from one unspoken question to the next. But I wouldn't ask them. This felt like before, when Emery was no more than a small bird, ready to take flight. One wrong step, and I'd lose her. "I do."

A long, heavy breath escaped her lips. Relief. "Will you help me?"

I hesitated, considering. I could think of only two times that Emery had come to me for the book of spells. Once, for the nightmares, and the other, when we learned her mother's sickness was not going to get better. I'd only opened the book for one of those requests.

I reached out into the air before me until her hand found mine and I gently wrapped my fingers around her wrist. Her pulse was racing. "August?"

Another broken breath. She pressed my hand to her face and she nodded, unable to speak.

I let it drop back into my lap, willing myself not to say what she didn't need to hear. One day, the book of spells would be hers, and she would use it how she saw fit. But today, she was asking for this.

"There are spells for breaking and spells for mending. But there are no spells for forgetting," I warned her.

She was quiet for a long moment. "I understand."

I got to my feet, leaving her at the fire, and followed the wall to the kitchen. The little doors and drawers in the old pine hutch held everything from butterfly wings to hagstones to ash of driftwood. But for this spell, we needed only three cords and a blade.

My hands felt for the items in question. I sniffed the bundles of herbs until I found the mugwort, and the salt was next, followed by a fresh candle and a small bowl. When I had what we needed, I shuffled back into the living room, where Emery was waiting.

"A bit of rainwater, love," I said, holding the bowl out in space until she took it from me.

My hand felt along the mantel for the book of spells as she went back to the door, but my fingers found the bound stone first. I stilled, picking it up and feeling its weight in my palm. The twine was wrapped tightly around the smooth, oval stone, unchanged from when I made it years ago.

There were also spells for binding, but I'd only ever had one occasion to use one.

I'd been able to smell the sick on Henry Salt before anyone else could see it. And it wasn't the kind of natural sick that hung in the air around withering bodies. It had the distinct scent of spellwork and I'd known almost immediately where it had come from.

I'd never cared for Henry, or his son Calvin for that matter, but I'd saved the bastard's life, like it or not. I also knew the cost of dark magic and was duty-bound to bind any witch on this island who used it. So I did.

Seven times I'd wrapped the stone, and with each one, I'd spoken the words. A few days later, Henry's cough waned, the gurgle in his voice disappearing. But I'd kept the stone long after he was well. Even after he died. The island gave us the magic, but there were some whose hands couldn't be trusted with the work.

Emery reemerged in the open doorway and I held a hand up to stop her. "Leave it open."

The air would only do us good. And this magic would need somewhere to go once we were through.

I set the stone down and lifted the book of spells from its place. The heavy cover opened across my lap as I sat, feeling the pages to find the sixth folded corner at the bottom right. Tucked into the spine of the book was a sprig of dried mugwort.

Emery returned to the fire and guided my hand to the bowl so I could take it.

"Sit down," I instructed, setting the water on the ledge before the fire.

She took the place opposite me and I gave her the candle to light while I poured the salt from the jar. The fine grains piled beside the bowl in a faint reverberation, and Emery placed the candle before it, waiting. The potent smell of mugwort filled the air as I twisted the bundle over the candle's flame. The smoke moved over my skin in a whisper.

The bowl, water. The salt, earth. The smoke, air. The candle, fire. We were ready to begin.

"Take the cord and cut three matching lengths," I said gently.

She took her time to measure each one carefully. When she was finished, she set down the knife. "All right. I have them."

"Knot them together, like this." I felt for twine, gathering up the three ends and showing her how.

"It's done."

I reached out, to where the three strands dangled from her hands, finding the knot. "This"—I held it tightly between my fingers—"is the oath you made." It was a point in time. A moment. "Now, take the three cords and braid them to their opposite ends." I held on to the knot as she wove the strands together in a slow rhythm. "Past, present, future," I murmured. There was one strand for each. A soft tug pulled the knot back and forth. I could feel her hands shaking as she folded one over the other. "Now, knot the other end. This is the present moment."

The room filled with silence again, despite the crackle of the fire and the hum of the rain. All around us, the air was alive. But the stillness was coming from Emery.

The braid stretched taut between us, her with one end and me with the other. I found the knife on the stone ledge, holding it up.

"Are you sure?" I asked heavily, hoping she would say that she wasn't.

I'd felt it in the air between them when they were young—the strike of electricity. It was a rare thing, but not a delicate one. And if she cut the cord, she wouldn't just lose August, she would lose a part of herself.

Emery was quiet so long that for a moment, I almost lost my hold on her presence in the room.

"I'm sure," she answered, taking the blade.

I sighed, closing my eyes. "Say the words."

Emery's fingers slid over the thick page in the book of spells and the sound of her voice deepened. "Past, present, future, I sever the bind."

I felt the braided cord pull against my fingertips as she set the knife against it.

"Again," I instructed.

"Past, present, future, I sever the bind."

"A third time."

Her voice rose, the sound of it changing with the words. I could hear it beneath her tongue—the magic. Emery hadn't always taken to the work like other women in our family had, but I'd sensed her time was near. Gooseflesh rose on my skin and the door tapped against the wall as the wind lifted. Outside, a strike of lightning filled the open house with a buzz.

When her lips fell quiet, I nodded, touching her hand that held the knife to the braided cord.

Her breaths rose and fell swiftly, like the sound of the sea, and another strike of lightning cracked through the night as the tension of the blade pressed heavier against the cord. I held my breath, waiting, but in the next moment, the sharp sound of the knife hitting the stone broke the roaring silence.

I froze, listening. But there was only the sound of the rain. The pages in the book of spells fluttering in the wind. When she said the words, they were like the thin touch of first frost on glass.

"I can't," she whispered. "I can't do it."

Thirty-Eight

AUGUST

HALO BEACH WAS OUR place. The four of us spent most weekends on its rocky shores our senior year of high school, when we figured out that it was the one spot our parents never came looking. The island was surrounded by beaches, but this one was all jagged shoreline and piled stones, with harsh winds that made the water crash even on the calmest days.

Standing there now, it had lost all its beauty.

It was nearly dawn and it was the last one I'd ever see on Saoirse. When the ferry left, I would be on it.

The thought put a stone in my throat, though I couldn't understand why. The day I left the island was the day I was freed. Not just from the suspicion and accusations about Lily. That was the day I was released from the orchard. From the Salt legacy that had been an ax hanging over me my entire life.

My mother said that the island would always call us back. That anyone who left would feel that pull for the rest of their lives. And it was true. I couldn't help but wonder if her final wishes weren't just a way for her to return, but a way for her to be sure I would return, too. Maybe both.

The dense tree line overlooked the beach below, the water bubbling and fizzing as it drew itself away from the rocks. In the distance, the black breaches that broke the water in waves were only barely visible, but they were there. The orcas. I used to watch them from the lighthouse in the fall when I had a rare day off from the orchard, and Emery had to work at the shop. In a few days, they would be gone.

I'd woken when it was still dark and started up the road, not really knowing where I was going. I didn't want to see the black stain on the earth that encircled the skeletal remains of the old Ford truck when the sun rose. I didn't want to see the caving-in porch or the photograph on the mantel. The remembering was worse than anything else.

Emery, Dutch, Lily, and me, spread out on the sun-warmed rocks like lizards. Sharing two swiped beers between the four of us or smoking pot Emery took from Nixie's barn and laughing over nothing until our bellies hurt.

Lily had this high-pitched screech of a laugh when she got going. But that Lily—the one from the beach—was a far cry from the Lily I'd last seen. I could still hear her crying. Still feel her hands twisted into my shirt, her knuckles white. They were the moments that trailed behind me everywhere I went, and even here, the roaring sound of the water couldn't drown them out.

I stared into the tide pool at my feet. The shape of my reflection fractured into pieces on the water's surface and then re-formed, creating endless versions of me.

I could blame the island all I wanted, but I was the one who'd fucked everything up. For my mom, for Emery. The whole of the sea wouldn't be able to wash out the stain of what I'd done. And I'd lived with that reality for years.

The woods were silent on the walk back to the cottage. When I reached the bend in the road, I could see Emery's drive through the trees. The truck had been missing since I woke, and I tried to push the thought from my mind. Still, it strangled out everything else, making me feel like my boots were heavier on the ground. Was she at Dutch's? How long after I left had they started seeing each other? Did she love him?

These were the questions I'd been asking myself since I'd seen them together at the shop. It was pathetic.

I'd wanted to believe that all this time, Emery was gone. That she left, like we said we would, and found a life somewhere else. But here she was, on Saoirse. With Dutch, of all people. Maybe that was my fault, too.

I willed myself to keep my eyes on the road until I reached the gate to the cottage, but when I pushed it open, I stopped short.

Up the path and framed by the two trees that arched over the pavers, Emery sat on the steps of the porch, watching me.

The stone walls of the cottage behind her were almost completely covered in the vines that snaked up and over the roof. I could see a flicker of light in the windows from where I'd left the kitchen light on.

I'd talked myself out of crossing the road and knocking on her door more than once since I'd seen her at the burial. A soft burn still traced over my knuckles where her hand had been, and I hated that it was one more memory I was taking with me.

She didn't move as I came up the path. It wasn't until I reached the porch that I could see how tired she looked. Her eyes and the tip of her nose were red, her hair only barely contained in the knot it was pulled into. It looked like she hadn't slept.

She didn't even have to say anything for my heart to start beating harder in my chest.

"Is everything okay?" I said, breaking the silence.

"No."

I waited, my pulse climbing by the second.

She bit down on her bottom lip, tucking her hair behind her ears nervously. In that moment, it felt like we were kids again. In a way, we were, standing there having a conversation that should have happened long ago.

"Why weren't you at the orchard before the party? Where were you?"

I drew in a deep breath, holding it. There were times when I'd wanted to tell Emery what happened that night. But the only thing worse than the barbed, cutting vines of the truth was the thought of Emery knowing it, too.

"I was at the lighthouse."

She looked me in the eye, silently begging me not to do it. But what would be the point now, after everything?

"With Dutch."

Pain knotted tight in my throat, sinking down into my chest. That was the well-rehearsed answer, but it hurt so much worse to say it now.

"I know, August," she said, her face unreadable. She didn't even blink. It was that small pause that made me feel like the ground would open up and swallow me whole. "I know that Dutch lied for you."

I stopped breathing.

"I defended you." Her voice wavered, and a tear slipped down her cheek. "I defended you when no one else did."

"I know." The words were a breath.

"I bore years of punishment for you. No one in this town would even look at me!" Her voice rose.

"I know!" I erupted. "You think I don't know that?"

"Then why didn't you tell me the truth?"

It was most likely the last time I'd ever see her. I'd leave Saoirse with that pain in my gut that I'd had for fourteen years. It never dulled. Never lightened. Wherever I went, it followed.

I'd accepted long ago that there was no healing for a wound like that. In many ways, I figured I deserved it. But I hadn't seen that pain in anyone else until Emery sat there with tears in her eyes, asking for the truth. Not just because she wanted to know. In that moment, she was asking me to free *her*.

I'd lived for so long with that weight. But seeing it on Emery . . .

"This is it, August. I'm never going to ask you again. This is your chance to tell me what really happened that night."

Despite everything, I realized, she was still taking care of me. Still trying to protect me. Even from herself.

"I have to ask you," she said. "I have to know."

I stilled, my eyes running over her face.

She'd never asked me. Not ever.

When the whole town wanted to know if I'd killed Lily, Emery had never said the words. She'd thought them. She'd wondered. I had seen it in her eyes a few times, and my heart would beat so hard that I couldn't breathe. I'd wait in agony, praying that she wouldn't ask, because I didn't know if I could do it. I didn't know if I was strong enough to look her in the eye and lie about that night.

Emery knew me too well. And maybe that's why she hadn't asked. Maybe she could tell just by looking that the answer would terrify her. That it would break the both of us. So she'd never asked and I'd never told her, and in the end, it broke us anyway.

"I guess it's about time." My voice deepened.

The look she gave me then felt like my soul splintering inside me. I knew what heartbreak looked like on her face, but there was no getting around that. Our hearts had been broken many times.

She rose from the step, standing so that she and I were the same height. She drew in a breath before she spoke. "Did you kill her?"

That small second of silence felt like my entire lifetime crushed into one moment. "No." I didn't look away from her. "I didn't."

She stared at me for a long time before she stepped down another step. The closer she got, the less I was breathing. I traced the outline of the star that bloomed in her left eye, like a faceted emerald stone cast into the sea. My heart was that strange, shooting star. Always falling.

"Then what are you hiding, August?"

It was the first time since I'd arrived on the island that she sounded like herself. I let that feeling sink deep inside me. I'd take that with me when I left, too.

"August?"

"Emery." I'd said the words a thousand times to myself through the years. Still, they were like knives in my throat. "Em, I set the fire."

Thirty-Nine

AUGUST

THE LIGHTBULB THAT HUNG from the ceiling had been burned out for years, but no one had bothered to replace it.

The small room in the loft of the barn was barely lit enough for me to see myself in the mirror. It had been my dad's room, before he married my mom and they moved into the cottage. Now, the only people who came up here were me and Dutch.

I pulled on the suit jacket my mom bought for me, straightening it over my shoulders. My grandfather had called me back to the orchard to work in the farthest row on the hillside after a fence fell down, and instead of helping set up for the party like I'd promised, I'd been cutting wire.

I hadn't argued. Even if I had, it wouldn't have done any good. My grandfather didn't believe in days off. The orchard wasn't a job. It was a life. Those were his words, not mine. I could either break my word to my mom to appease Henry or ruin this night for my mom by pissing Henry off. I'd chosen to avoid my grandfather's ire, figuring that would have the least amount of fallout.

My mom had gotten fairly good at walking on eggshells with him, but I hadn't.

I pulled the sleeve of my shirt down to cover the scrape on my wrist. Gloves or not, I always cut myself on the damn fence. I raked my hand through my hair, smoothing it back as much as I could. The heat and damp made it wave on the ends, but I'd pass for showered.

The music was already playing outside, and the sound of voices was multiplying. The island held this party every year after the high school graduation, one of the only rites of passage that resembled the lives of the kids on the mainland.

The party was supposed to be for all of the graduates, but this year it was at the orchard with my mom in charge, making it feel like one gigantic spotlight on our family. That attention had grown more acute in the last six months, with the town at odds with my grandfather over the future of the orchard. I was beginning to think this party was my mom's way of smoothing things over. The only reason I was doing any of it was for her.

One more day. That's all. Then Emery and I would be gone and Saoirse and the orchard and my grandfather would be nothing but memories.

All I had to do was get through the night without drawing my grandfather's attention. I'd spend thirteen more hours under his thumb. Then, we'd be on the ferry.

The wind made the wooden walls creak as it blew through the orchard, bringing the scent of soil and hay in through the window. I didn't think I would miss it. My dad sure as hell never did. If he had, he would have come back. But the bastard hadn't so much as called my mom since he left.

It had always been just the two of us in my memories. My father was the first Salt in generations to leave Saoirse and the orchard behind. And though no one knew it yet, I would be the second.

I let out a heavy breath, smoothing my hands over the jacket. She'd understand. I'd told myself that each time I thought about what it would be like when she woke up the next day to an empty house.

But she knew me. She often knew me better than I knew myself. That's what I was banking on.

I picked my work clothes up from where I'd dropped them on the bed, and I flinched when I caught sight of a figure in the dark corner of the room.

"Shit"—I let out a tight breath—"I didn't see you come in."

My grandfather leaned against the wall with glinting eyes, watching me. He was dressed in a clean shirt, which was a rare sight, and the silver-streaked hair that was usually covered by a hat was combed. But he had that look on his face, like he was ready for a fight. I knew it well.

I tossed the clothes into the basket against the wall. "Mom's going to kill me if I don't get down there. I'm already late."

"You're not going anywhere," he said.

I sighed, resigning myself to the argument, whatever it was. He didn't look or smell drunk, so I figured it couldn't be one of the bad ones. And I didn't think he'd risk a scene when the whole town was downstairs. My grandfather got away with most things because of who he was, but there were some lines even he wouldn't cross, if only for the sake of appearances.

I slid my hands into the pockets of my jacket, waiting for it.

He looked me up and down, his lip curling. "You know, August, you aren't the brightest Salt to ever grace this island, but I did think you were smarter than this."

I half laughed, already annoyed. "Thanks."

But he wasn't smiling. He looked at me straight on, with a coldness in his eyes that I'd only seen a few times before. It made me instinctively want to take a step back, but I kept my feet planted.

"Did you seriously think I wasn't going to find out?" he asked, looking suddenly taller.

But I still wasn't following. My mind raced, sorting through whatever he could be angry about. The list was endless. The fence. A tractor left in the rain. A mistake with the seed order.

"Saw Carl over at the pub."

The slow, sharp realization cut through my mind like a hot blade. Carl worked the ferry ticket booth at the harbor.

I wet my lips, trying to play it off. "So?"

"So"—he pushed off of the wall, taking his time as he crossed the room—"he told me you bought two one-way tickets for tomorrow. First ferry out of the harbor."

My heart thumped beneath my jacket so loud that I was sure he could hear it. I shrugged. "Emery and I are going to the city for the weekend," I lied.

"The city for the weekend," he repeated.

"She wanted to do something after graduation. I got us the tickets this morning."

"Why aren't they return tickets?"

"We haven't decided what day we're coming back yet."

He stared at me, his face blank. He wasn't buying it. "Do you think I'm an idiot?"

I clenched my teeth, trying not to do anything that would set him off further. But we were already past the point of no return.

"I'm not too proud to admit that your dad was a coward, August. I could see it from the time he was young." He moved closer, his eyes on the ground. "But I'm not making the same mistakes with you that I did with him."

Before I even saw it coming, his hands flew up between us, taking hold of my jacket, and he drove me backward, slamming me into the wall. His eyes were on fire, his nostrils flared as he peered down into my face. This wasn't one of his drunken rants. He was stone-cold sober. And that was far more terrifying.

When I tried to slip from his grasp, he put one hand around my throat, pinning me there.

"You listen to me," he growled. "You aren't going anywhere. You're going to stay on Saoirse, where you belong. And you're going to take over the orchard, like you're supposed to."

"I don't want the fucking orchard," I rasped. It was the first time I'd ever said it out loud to anyone but Emery.

His fingers clamped down harder, making me still. "I don't care what you want. This town thinks it's finally going to get its hands on our family's work and I'm not going to let that happen."

I shoved him off of me. "You can't keep me here."

"Yes, I can." He lifted a finger into the air. "Try and use those tickets tomorrow, and I will make sure you regret it. You leave this island, and your mother loses her job at the orchard. The cottage, too. Got it?"

My eyes searched his. He was serious. My mom had lived in that cottage for almost twenty years.

"You can't do that. The cottage is in her name now."

"I can do whatever I want to on this island."

He was right, I realized. If he wanted to, he could take it from her and no one would stop him. As long as he was breathing, everything on Saoirse belonged to Henry Salt.

"Bastard," I muttered, swallowing painfully.

My mom was the only person on this island who loved the orchard the way he did, but he'd never seen it. After my dad left, Henry refused to change his will to leave it to her. The orchard would only go to a Salt. Bearing the name wasn't enough; my mom didn't have his blood. And he knew I wouldn't make a single move that would hurt her.

He didn't say another word as he watched me think about it, and I could see the exact moment he knew he'd won. He let another nauseating silence fall before he finally turned and walked out the door. I listened to his footsteps trail down the loft stairs, biting the inside of my cheek so hard that I could taste blood. As soon as they were gone, I ran my hands over my face, pinching my eyes closed. The darkness of the room pushed in around my vision, making me feel like at any moment I was going to pass out.

I breathed, pulling in the air in one long draw, and then pushed it out, trying to slow my pulse. Thirteen hours. That's how close I'd been. But my grandfather knew me as well as I knew him. I wouldn't leave if I thought he'd take everything from my mom. And he would.

A numb, cold feeling inched its way through me at the thought, and I stared into the mirror, meeting my own eyes. I was an idiot for not realizing it before. The moment I left, he would punish her for it.

I followed the steps down from the loft, watching the shadows move over the ground below. They were spinning in the lantern light, the smell of food in the air and the clear starry sky stretched out over the island. Like it was any other night. Like my whole life hadn't just ended upstairs.

The side door of the barn swung behind me as I pushed through it, and I followed along the first row of apple trees, stopping to watch from the darkness. The whole town was gathered in the clearing, encircled by twinkling lanterns hanging from the branches.

I stopped breathing when I saw her.

Emery and her dad were dancing, and she was smiling in that way that made her eyes squint into tiny crescent moons. She'd trusted me. With everything. She'd been willing to leave it all behind. But that glow in her eyes would fade the moment I told her we weren't leaving. That we weren't special or different. That our lives would be exactly what we thought they wouldn't be. I didn't think I'd ever been more ashamed of anything. Ever.

Behind them, I could see my grandfather roaming the crowd with a wide smile. He looked smug, and I hated him for it. He'd spent the better part of a year before that sick, the life slowly bleeding from his body. I'd been sure that we would finally be rid of him, but just as quickly as the light began to leave his eyes, it had returned. We were stuck with him for God knew how long.

And I didn't only hate him, I hated the orchard. I always had. It was the heavy stone that pressed me to the dirt, the looming shadow that followed two steps behind me.

I set my back against the wall of the barn, staring into those godforsaken trees. They were like poison. And with every drop of blood in my veins, I wanted to cut them from the earth.

I took a step forward, watching the lantern swing on the nearest branch and staring into the orange flame behind the glass until its brightness overtook everything else. It washed away the night, the orchard, my grandfather. It filled my head with bright, drenching light. Before I'd even decided to, before I'd even thought it, I lifted a hand, taking the lantern from the branch. And as the breath left my lips, I dropped it.

Forty

EMERY

I WASN'T SURE HOW many seconds had passed since the words left his mouth, but I felt like I'd come out of my own skin. Like I was hovering in the air above us, not really there.

The light darkened and I looked up to the sky, where black clouds were creeping like a wave toward the island. I could feel the storm gathering overhead. The buzz of it in the air. The cold pushing in from the sea.

It was as if Saoirse had heard him say it. I was sure that she had.

August stared at the ground, his face flushed and jaw tight. He looked eighteen again, missing the years he'd spent away from the island. Away from me. I wasn't sure I knew the August who came in on the ferry, but I did know the one who'd stood beside me in that cemetery. It was the same one who stood before me now.

The pieces fit into the ones missing from the story. Why August hadn't been at the orchard before the party. Eloise's letter.

He hadn't killed Lily, but he'd set the fire that almost killed my dad. The fire that almost killed this town.

"Will you come inside?"

I blinked, remembering where we were. August still stood at the bottom of the steps, the set of his shoulders rigid. He looked afraid. Panicked, even.

When I didn't answer, he came up the stairs and unlocked the door behind me. It opened a second later, and I took a step back as the rush of warm air came seeping out. It wrapped around me, filling my lungs with a scent that I knew. It danced on my tongue as I stared at the threshold.

August disappeared through the doorway and the cottage suddenly felt bigger, looming over me. This place had once been like a home to me, but it had been years since those nights when I'd snuck into the empty house and climbed into August's bed. Even the echo of the memory hurt.

As soon as I stepped inside, I regretted it.

The door closed just as thunder rumbled in the darkening sky, and I turned in a circle, my lip quivering as my eyes flitted over the living room. The quilt draped over the back of the sofa. The wooden rocking chair beside the front window. A little clay pot in the windowsill above the sink. August stood before the fireplace, where a pile of fresh-cut firewood was stacked, watching me remember it.

It was exactly the same. Everything. But the two of us were far from the people who'd once stood in this room together.

To see August out on the street or in the shop was one thing. But to see him here, in this house ... my insides ached with a flood of images that I couldn't stop. That painful expansion in my chest was there now, as if my body could still remember those days even when all I wanted was to forget them.

There wasn't a single person on Saoirse who hadn't lied to me. But somehow, after everything, the one who cut the deepest was August.

"How could you do it?" I whispered hoarsely.

"I don't know."

"How could you just ..."

"I was a stupid kid, Em. I was angry, I felt trapped. I know that doesn't make it any better, but it's the truth. In that moment, I had no idea what I was doing."

I felt so tired and heavy that I wanted to close my eyes and disappear. This was why he'd lied. Why he'd hidden the truth about that night from me. He *had* been running from something when he left the island after all. But it wasn't murder.

The rain started to fall, hitting the tin overhang outside. In only minutes, it would be a downpour.

"No one knew except my mom," he said.

My eyes lifted. That's what Eloise was talking about in the letter. Not Lily—the fire. But if someone had it now, that's not what it would look like. Anyone who read Eloise's words would think exactly what I had.

"I wanted to tell you, but your dad . . . it was too hard. And then lying was harder. I thought, either way you would hate me, so leaving Saoirse seemed easier." He paused. "My mom was worried about something happening to me."

"Happening to you?"

"She got it in her head that we had to leave or someone was going to hurt me. That I just wouldn't come home one night."

The thing that had always been true about August and Eloise was that they looked out for each other. That's what she was doing when she took him away.

"Did you ask Dutch to lie for you?"

August hesitated, staring at his hands. "No. I didn't know what happened to Lily or your dad until I got back to the house late that night. When Jake showed up, Dutch had already lied. I just went along with it because I didn't know what else to do."

I shook my head, trying to understand. "Why would Dutch lie before he even knew you needed him to?"

August kept his gaze pinned on the window. A strike of lightning made the lights dim, before they brightened again.

"August." I pressed.

"He wasn't lying to protect me, Emery." He breathed. "He was protecting himself."

"How?"

He didn't meet my eyes. "You should ask him about it."

"I'm asking *you*."

His gaze finally met mine, and I could see him changing his mind, back and forth.

"God, what do I have to do to get you to tell me the truth?"

August reached up to rub his face with his hands. "They were seeing each other."

"Who?"

"Dutch and Lily."

My hands fell limply at my sides as I stared at him. That was the last thing I expected him to say. "That can't be true." I sank down into the rocking chair.

"They were. For months. A year, maybe. I don't think it was anything either of them thought was a serious thing. They were just sleeping together."

My eyes searched the floorboards in front of my feet. The thoughts were racing so fast that I couldn't catch hold of them. It was insane. All of it.

"Lily would have told me that," I said, feeling less and less convinced. They were the same words I'd spoken to my uncle.

August stayed quiet. He'd already said more than he wanted to.

"Why would she lie?"

"I don't know. Why did Lily do anything she did?" He paused. "Dutch asked me not to say anything, so I didn't. Lily was really paranoid about people finding out. She didn't even want him telling me."

I raked my hair back with one hand, thinking. "She was pregnant."

"What?" August gave me a confused look.

"Jake told me she was pregnant."

August stiffened. "And he told you it was me?" he guessed. "That me and Lily were . . ."

I nodded.

Something like a curse sounded under his breath.

"I didn't believe him. But Dutch . . ." My voice trailed off. "Why would he keep that a secret? After all this time?"

"I don't know. We all lied about something."

I went still, studying his face. It was true. Even I had lied about the deed to the orchard. But if August had any suspicions about that, I couldn't hear any sign of it in the words.

"Or, like you said, he was protecting himself," I murmured, a chill running up my spine as I thought it.

August's expression didn't change. He'd clearly already considered that.

I stood from the chair and squared my shoulders to the window, watching the storm rage. Beyond the trees, my house was veiled in the thick curtain of rain. Only two nights ago, someone had walked down that road and set a fire in front of this cottage. I was more convinced than ever that they had also taken the letter.

Dutch wanted me to stay away from August, but not because he thought August killed Lily. It was because August was the only one who knew the truth. I didn't want to believe it, but I did. He lied to Jake to cover for himself. Most of the town would jump at the chance to find evidence against August. But if people knew about Lily and him, and if August were cleared, there was only one person who could take the fall.

It was only then that I realized that when I saw Dutch at the orchard and I asked him where he was the other night, he never answered.

"I have to go," I said, moving toward the door.

I stopped mid-stride when I saw the packed bag on the floor. I looked at August, the question trapped in my throat.

He glanced from me to the pack, stiffening. "Yeah. I'm taking the last ferry tonight. My flight leaves from the city tomorrow."

"Oh."

"I was going to stop and say goodbye on my way."

"Really?" I said, doubtful. I hated how my voice sounded suddenly hollow. I hated that it hurt.

"Really. I was."

My hand tightened on the knob, and I leaned into the door. I had no right to ask him, but I had to. "Can you take the one in the morning?"

August's lips pressed together. Whatever he was thinking, I couldn't sift it from the look in his eyes.

"There's something I need to show you."

He hesitated. "Okay."

My grip instantly loosened on the knob, the knot in my throat unwinding. "Meet me at the pub. At six."

I waited for him to answer with a nod before I pulled the door open and stepped out into the wind. He'd told me the truth. Now it was my turn. But there was something I had to do first.

Forty-One

EMERY

THE CABIN SAT AT the bottom of the hill with only one window lit. I stood beyond the tree line of Nixie's property, watching the flick of movement behind it.

We hadn't said the words yet, but I knew that deep down, things had ended in the orchard when I told him that I'd never marry him. It was only now that it felt real. This thing between us had always been frail. I knew it, and so did he. But Dutch did love me. I had no question about that. He'd waited years for me to come around after August left, and then he'd waited even longer for me to start a family with him, convinced he could change my mind. I'd be lying if I said there weren't days when I thought, maybe even hoped, that he would.

The thing that had kept me with him was the fear of the future. Years down the road, when my dad and Nixie and Albertine were gone, what would I have left? *Who* would I have left?

Dutch had lied, but we all had, like August said. The worst part was that I didn't feel anything when I thought about losing him. I'd always thought of him as easy to unravel. He had all of his cards on the table. But if he'd really been with Lily, there was a whole decade and a half of secrets between us. Somehow, after knowing him my entire life and spending six years in each other's beds, I now had more questions than I had answers about Dutch Boden.

If he had the letter, I had to get it back. I didn't want to know what he might do with it.

He appeared at the door and the screen slammed behind him as he made his way down the steps. He was late, and although it would have been typical of the Dutch I'd known as a kid, it was unlike him now. He took his position at the orchard seriously, probably because it was the only reason anyone on Saoirse took *him* seriously. The look on his face gave away that he hadn't slept much, if at all. The fair scruff on his jaw was thicker than he usually let it get and his shirt was only half-buttoned, like he'd rushed.

The lights of his truck came on as the engine roared to life and exhaust billowed from the tailpipe as it warmed up. He waited a few moments before the brake lights glowed and the truck pulled out of the drive.

I didn't like the idea of sneaking around and trying to catch him in a lie, but I'd given him the chance to tell me the truth. I was done asking.

I waited until the truck disappeared around the bend in the road, and I came down the hill with quick steps, staying close to the fence. When I reached the door, I glanced once more over my shoulder, to the woods. The only sound was of the wind tearing through the trees.

The island had been restless all day, the air growing colder. Since the leaves had turned, nothing had felt right, and I had a feeling there was a deeper work at play. Saoirse was finally digging up the things we'd buried.

Inside, the only light that was on was the lamp beside the sofa. I let the door close behind me, and I turned in a circle, eyes running over the cabin. They focused when they landed on the desk.

I sat down in the rickety chair, pulling the lap drawer open. It was carelessly filled with pencils and scraps of paper, a box of staples, things that Dutch likely hadn't used in years. The next drawer was paperwork for the orchard. Files and agriculture records. Empty folders and order forms.

In the almost ten years that he'd lived in the cabin, he had yet to fill the place with a sense of being lived in. There were still blank walls and empty shelves and only two mismatched chairs at the little table in the kitchen nook. He was a simple man with a simple life who always seemed like he was waiting for something. That something had been me, I thought.

Once, the thought had been a relief. With Dutch, what you saw was what you got. Now, I wasn't so sure that was true.

I went to the bedroom, pulling open the drawer of the bedside table and then the closet, where the built-in shelves were stuffed with denim and work boots. It smelled of hay and soil. It smelled like him. I checked the pockets of his coveralls and jackets before feeling along the dusty top shelf with my fingers. Nothing.

If he'd taken the letter, I didn't know what he would do with it. Give it to Jake, like I'd almost done? Turn it in to the Seattle Police? My heart kicked unevenly at the possibility. August wasn't innocent, that was true. But he wasn't a murderer, and that thing in me that always protected him was still there. It had never gone to sleep.

"Em?"

I froze, and my breath caught when I heard his voice. I looked up at the mirror on the wall to see Dutch standing in the doorway of the bedroom behind me. His eyes went from me to the open closet and back again.

"What are you doing?" His gaze narrowed as his confusion turned to suspicion. I could hear it in his voice.

"I . . ." I swallowed, turning around. "I'm looking for something."

"I can see that." He dropped his keys on the bedside table.

I clenched my teeth when he took a step toward me, my eyes going to his hands. He looked suddenly different to me now. Once, he'd been a refuge. A place where I could forget, if only for an hour or two. But now I couldn't help but wonder if those hands had touched Lily. If they'd hurt her.

"What the hell is going on?"

"Nothing," I answered unevenly.

When he took another step, I backed up, pressing myself to the wall, and he paused, studying me. "You ignore me for over a week, won't take my calls, won't even look at me, and now you're in my house going through my stuff. Do you get how crazy this is?"

It *was* crazy. All of it. Me, August, him, Lily.

"Why didn't you tell me?" I watched his face carefully as I asked it.

Dutch sighed. "Em, we talked about this. I thought I was protecting August. I didn't want to—"

"Not about August. Or the lighthouse," I interrupted. "About Lily."

Dutch went rigid, his eyes widening. His hands dropped to his sides and all at once, the color drained from his face. It wasn't often I caught him by surprise. He could see the turn of my thoughts coming from a mile away. But that look in his eyes now was fear. "You've got to be fucking kidding me," he muttered. "He told you."

"What does it matter who told me? You lied. For years."

Dutch's chin jerked to the side. "No, I didn't. I didn't tell you, but I didn't lie."

"It's the same thing!" I shouted.

"She didn't want anyone to know, okay? I didn't think it was right to tell everyone just because she was dead." The enunciation of the last word made me shiver.

"You didn't keep the secret for Lily."

An emptiness filled his blue eyes, but he didn't deny it. "You think you knew her, but you didn't."

"I did know her. I was her best friend, Dutch." But I could feel how the meaning of the words had changed since I'd last said them. Dutch wasn't the only one who'd kept the truth from me. Lily had, too.

"She didn't tell you about us because she knew you would tell August. And she didn't want him to know."

"Why not?

"God, Emery, sometimes you are *so*..." He thought better of whatever he was going to say. "She was sleeping with me, but she wanted August."

"No, she didn't. I would have seen that."

"That's what I'm trying to tell you. She wasn't who you thought she was. She wasn't who anyone on this island thought she was."

I gaped at him. He would do anything to keep himself from holding the blame. He would even lie about Lily. "What else are you lying about?"

"Nothing."

"I don't believe you."

The muscle in his jaw ticked. "If I'd told anyone about me and Lily, who do you think they would have been looking at?"

"So you let August take the fall instead."

"He didn't take the fall for anything, thanks to me. I covered both our asses when I told Jake we were at the lighthouse."

"Did you know she was pregnant?" My voice shook unsteadily.

Dutch went still, falling silent for a long moment. "Where did you hear that?"

"Jake. It was in the autopsy report."

He turned toward the window, eyes skipping over the trees on the other side of the glass. He hadn't known.

"Where is the letter?" I asked.

He didn't answer. His attention was still focused on the woods. The muscles in his neck strained as he swallowed. He looked like he was going to be sick.

"Dutch."

He blinked. "What?"

"Where is the letter?"

He finally turned back to face me, and when he did, his skin was flushed. "What letter?"

If Dutch was lying now, it was convincing. I could see his mind turning with the question. But I couldn't risk giving him any more information. Not until I knew what was going on.

"Forget it," I said, stepping past him.

He grabbed my elbow, stopping me. "Are you serious? That's it?" His fingers dug into my arm, making me wince. "You just come here to drop that on me and you're just gone?"

I wrenched free of him. "Don't *touch* me." I spoke through gritted teeth.

We'd stitched ourselves together after everything happened. There was no one who understood what I'd been through like he did. No one who'd known how dark those days and nights had been. But that only made the truth hurt so much worse.

When I said nothing, he looked down at me with utter shock, his expression slowly changing again. "Well done. I guess you finally found your reason."

"What the hell is that supposed to mean?" I snapped.

"That you have never been in this. Not like I have." His voice rose. "You've been looking for a reason to bolt for years. You just didn't have one."

The words soured with the knowing. The weary reminder that I had never loved him. But that had never stopped me from letting him pull me into the dark of his bedroom. It had never kept me from trying to soothe the ache that lived inside me after August left. That was on me.

Forty-Two

AUGUST

THE FERRY TICKET SAT on the kitchen counter, staring up at me.

There weren't many times that Emery had surprised me, but when she asked me to stay, even if just for a night, I'd stopped breathing.

I'd owed her the truth about the fire. About her father and about Lily. But I'd also thought, as the words left my mouth, that it was the last time I'd ever see her. Ever talk to her. I'd secretly hoped that the truth might sever the thing that had tied me to this island and to her forever.

Bernard Keller had agreed to handle the paperwork for the house once I had the deed in order, and my bag was packed and ready. My flight back to Portland was booked, and I had a ticket for the six o'clock ferry. If I went to the pub, it wouldn't just be Emery there waiting for me. I'd have to do the one thing I should have done fourteen years ago: say goodbye. Not the knock-on-the-door-on-my-way-to-the-ferry goodbye. A real one.

I picked up my phone, dropping it in my pocket.

A knot coiled in my stomach as soon as I tossed the ticket into the trash can. It would have been easier to leave and be gone when the island woke. But I wanted to see her one more time. I always wanted to see her.

I snatched the keys up from the counter and started for the door. It was becoming too familiar, being in the house. I didn't feel misplaced inside it anymore, and I didn't like that feeling.

The woods were already alive with the sounds of night. The road was dark and the moon was hidden by the thick cloud cover, but there was finally a break in the rain. I could name the occupants of every house I passed, each of them illuminated by fireplaces or lamplight. Beneath those roofs was at least one person I could have killed in that fire. I'd been thinking about that a lot since I'd come back. And there was nothing that haunted me more than knowing what that single choice had cost.

My mom wasn't the real reason I left. Neither was Emery. If I stayed, I'd have to face what I'd done. Noah Blackwood may not have died, but I still had his blood on my hands, and I lived with it every day.

That night, I could smell the smoke the whole walk home, and only then did it really begin to hit me what I'd done. There was a color to the sky even though it was late at night. Like an orange glow reflecting off the haze. It cast the road and everything else in an eerie light, but it was the silence that struck me most. Everything was so quiet. Much too quiet.

I'd spent the hours at the lighthouse, where the sea crashed so loudly onto the rocks below that I hadn't heard the helicopters. In my mind, the orchard was finally gone. Wiped from reality like a smudge on a window. I'd watched the water foam white in the darkness for as long as I could stand it, and then I'd started the walk home, knowing I'd find my mother crushed by what I'd done. But every bit of power my grandfather held was in that orchard. Without it, he was nothing.

If I wasn't going to get what I wanted, then neither would he.

I was too young and too stupid to think about everyone else as I stood up there on the deck of the lighthouse. What would happen to the people who worked at the orchard. What would happen to the town. It wasn't until that moment when I smelled the smoke on the walk back to the cottage that those thoughts began to glow like embers.

Headlights appeared in the trees ahead, pulling me from the memory, and I moved to the shoulder of the road. The sound of a rattling engine grew louder as it came around the curve, and as it got closer, the brakes squealed. I stopped, lifting a hand to shield my eyes from the glare of the lights, but after a moment, it still hadn't moved. The truck sat there idling and I looked around me, to the trees. There wasn't a gate or a drive, just the woods.

I turned my back to the truck, finding my phone in my pocket and holding it at my side. The last time I'd crossed paths with someone on this island in the middle of the night, he'd beaten the hell out of me. But as I turned the phone in my hand, a sickening thought wormed its way into my mind. Even if I were lucky enough to get service, there was no one to call.

The driver's-side door opened and boots hit the ground before it slammed closed. I walked toward the sound, trying to make out the face. It was the blond hair that gave him away.

"Dutch?" I couldn't see him until he stepped past the hood of the truck.

"You told her."

His voice cut through the darkness and I instantly let out a heavy breath, letting the phone slide back into my jacket.

"Yeah, I did."

He laughed and the sound was uneven. It was only then that I realized he was drunk. His head tipped back just a little too far, the soles of his boots dragging a little too much. "Of course you did," he muttered.

"She asked me, and I told her."

"Same selfish bastard you've always been." He flung a hand at me.

"You're wasted, Dutch. Go home."

He propped himself up with one hand on the side of the truck clumsily, shaking his head. "I knew the minute you came back that this would happen. That you'd find a way to fuck everything up." He laughed. "Nothing changes. After everything I've done for you."

"I didn't ask you to lie for me. In fact, you didn't even give me a choice. And we both know you didn't do it for me."

He took three steps toward me, taking hold of my jacket and wrenching me toward him. "Fuck you, August!"

I shoved him off.

"Where were you when she had to take care of Noah? Huh?"

I swallowed down the nausea rising in my throat.

"Where the fuck were you when she buried Hannah? You weren't here. *I* was." He fumed. "But everyone wants you, right? That's how it's always been."

"What the hell are you talking about?"

"You think I'm an idiot? Lily was in love with you, you asshole."

"You're not an idiot. Which is why I don't believe for a second that you just happened to not go to Washington State. And then just happened to get with Emery. You were after her the second I left. You forget that I know you, Dutch. Lily wanted me, fine. I didn't want her. But *you* always wanted Emery. You were using Lily the same way she was using you, so don't act like it broke your fucking heart."

He leveled his gaze at me, his voice turning cold. "It doesn't matter now, does it? Emery's the same desperate whore that Lily was, looking for someone, anyone, to climb into bed with her."

I pressed my tongue to the back of my teeth, watching the glint in his eye. Before I could change my mind, I stalked past him, headed away from the truck. I wasn't more than a few steps away when he started laughing again.

"You're right. You were gone, August. And I didn't even have time to be pissed at you about it, because all I could think was, I can finally fuck Emery Blackwood."

I stopped mid-stride, watching my breath fog in the darkness before me.

"And I did. Over and over and *over* again."

I was already walking back toward the truck, the beat of my footsteps inaudible over the sound of my racing heart. I couldn't hear it when I took hold of his shirt and drove him backward. I couldn't feel anything as I watched him stumble and hit the ground hard. I lifted my fist into the air and brought it down across his face, sending a flood of something hot through my veins. When I hit him again, I recognized it—that steady rage that coursed through me when I dropped the lantern.

I hit him again. And again. It wasn't until his face was covered in blood and my fist slipped over his skin that I finally stood up off of him, the sound coming back into my ears. I blinked and the world came rushing back. The engine running. The woods. The pain in my hand.

I stepped backward until I was past the truck, eyeing the still shape of Dutch on the road. The headlights beamed over him, painting the road white, where only his boots were visible. And without a single feeling inside me, I turned and left him there.

Forty-Three

EMERY

I FLICKED ON THE lights and the buzz of the bulbs in the old outlets hummed in the still air. The pub smelled like ale, oiled wood, and freshly baked bread. Half of my childhood had been spent helping my dad serve beer to the tourists by day and to the residents of Saoirse by night.

After the orchard closed and the last ferry left, this place came alive with amber light, music, and laughter. In many ways, it was still my sanctuary. But I hadn't seen my dad in days, and I hadn't dared come to the pub when I knew he'd be here. After tonight, I doubted he would want to see me, either.

The ferry horn sounded in the harbor, followed by the call of seabirds hunting in the high tide. I willed myself not to look at the door. August hadn't said if he was coming, I only hoped he would. If he didn't, it meant that he was on that ferry to Seattle. That he was gone.

I didn't have the letter, and for all I knew, it was blown out the open door, into the rain that night. But I did have the folder from the bottom drawer of my dresser. And I figured I'd leave it up to fate to decide whether I ever gave it to him. If August showed, I'd tell him what I knew. If he didn't, I'd let it die with the rest of the secrets that strangled this place.

The door opened in a gust of wind, and August appeared against the dark backdrop of the street. His hair was windblown, his boots muddy, and I couldn't manage to pretend like it didn't matter. I was so happy to see him that I could feel the ache of it under my skin.

"Hey," I said, coming around the bar to take two clean glasses from the shelf. I had butterflies in my stomach.

"Hey."

"What'll it be?" I lifted my chin to one of the empty glasses with a smirk, reaching for the brass tap. I was trying to make light of the moment, and August looked relieved by it. We were both tired of hard conversations.

"Lager." He played along, making his way through the tables to one of the barstools. But the sight of him sitting there didn't fit the images of the sometimes-awkward teenager I had filed away. He was a man now. Comfortable in his own body.

I picked up the glass and tilted the tap down, watching the white gold liquid fan against the side. When it was filled, I set it down in front of him. "Remember when we used to sneak in here and steal beer?" I said, before thinking better of it. As soon as the words left my mouth, I wanted to pull them back in.

August smiled, but it fell a little, as if that particular memory stung when recalled. I knew that feeling. "I remember you puking off the edge of the dock in the middle of the night and having to hold on to you so you didn't fall in." He laughed suddenly, and the sound of it made me feel like the air was being sucked out of the room. I loved that sound.

"We were stupid," I said, filling my own glass.

He nodded, picking up the beer with his left hand and taking a drink. "Yeah, we were."

I let the quiet of the empty pub fall between us.

"Didn't know if you would come," I said.

"Me, either."

My eyes flicked up, meeting his. He really did look so much the same as back then. His jaw was squarer and covered in a thicker scruff, but in his eyes, he looked just the same. I didn't know why I hadn't really been able to see it then—that pain that seemed to live there. He'd done a horrible thing, but I had the feeling that this was the first time I was seeing August Salt clearly.

I searched for something to say. I could feel the clock ticking down, and when August left Saoirse again, he wasn't coming back.

"I guess you have to get back to your classes?"

"Not until next semester. I took a leave of absence when my mom got sicker."

I ran a finger along the groove in the wood countertop. They'd still taken care of each other up until the end. "What exactly do you teach?"

He smiled, as if he was amused by the interrogation. "I have two classes right now. 'Early Medieval History' and 'Archaeoscience and the Rise of Capitalism.'"

"Archaeoscience," I repeated. It wasn't what I would have guessed he'd end up doing, but somehow, it fit.

"What?"

"It's just funny. I was the one who wanted to go to college."

"Yeah. I think maybe that's why I went."

My hand slipped from the lip of the glass. I didn't want to know what he meant by that. "Are you . . ." I wasn't sure how to ask it.

"Married?"

I nodded.

"No. I don't have anyone serious in Portland."

I wanted more details than that, but I didn't have the nerve to pry. I'd noticed the first day I saw him that he wasn't wearing a ring.

"What made you stay?" he asked.

I shrugged. "I don't know."

It was a sad answer, but it was true. There was nothing I could tell him about my life that he couldn't guess, and the thought was embarrassing. I'd never had the reasons for leaving that he did, but I'd wanted a life that was my own. I'd wanted one with August.

"I guess when my mom got sick, I just stopped thinking about leaving. I felt like my dad needed me, but that's probably just what I told myself because I was too scared to go."

The words were more honest than even I'd expected. When he didn't press, I was grateful.

He reached for the glass again, and my eyes focused on his right hand that was still tucked into his pocket. When he caught me staring at it, his jaw clenched.

"What?"

"Nothing."

I gave him a knowing look and he gave in, reluctantly pulling it from his pocket. My mouth dropped open when I saw it. The back of his hand was busted up, his knuckles bloodied.

"What happened?" I reached for him, pulling the hand toward me and spreading the fingers across my palm.

But when I looked up, August wasn't listening to me. He watched my face from inches away, his eyes trailing down to where my hands were wrapped around his.

"What happened?" I said again, this time angrily.

"Dutch."

I leveled my gaze at him, tilting my head to one side. "You've got to be kidding me."

When August didn't answer, I dropped his hand on the counter and he winced as I turned on my heel, pushing through the swinging door into the kitchen. I pulled a clean towel down from the shelf and turned the tap to warm, soaking it.

"Guess you heard then," I called out.

August stayed quiet.

I wrung out the towel and went back out to the bar, where August was draining his glass.

"He's not a bad guy, you know," I said.

"I know."

I wasn't sure why I'd felt the need to say it. Maybe because I knew what I'd put Dutch through. But I'd always been clear about what we were. He just hadn't wanted to really believe it.

"Here," I said, holding my hand open.

August hesitated a moment before he set his into it again, and he watched as I wiped the blood from the skin and inspected each finger. I felt the bones one by one, making sure they weren't broken.

"He was drunk," he said finally, as if that was some kind of explanation. "It didn't go well."

Of course he was. "He was angry you told me about Lily. I guess I should have warned you." I dropped the rag on the counter.

We stared at each other, the ease that had been there between us a moment ago gone now. August lifted his empty glass between us.

"Can I get another or was that last call?" He was wearing a stiff smile.

I almost laughed. Now he was the one trying to make light of the moment. "Sure."

I refilled his glass and came around the counter to take the stool beside his. I couldn't help but notice that for the first time, it didn't feel like we were strangers.

"You said you have something to show me?"

My mouth twisted to one side. I stared into my glass, asking myself one last time if I was sure. It took several seconds for me to reach inside my bag and finally pull the folder free. I dropped it between us with a slap and picked up my glass, gulping until my eyes watered. There was no going back now.

"What is this?"

"Something you should see before you go."

His expression changed, eyes dropping to the folder for a moment before he picked it up. I watched as he opened it, reading over the words.

It was the deed to Salt Orchards.

He looked up at me again. "Where did you get this?"

"The records office," I answered.

August leaned onto the bar, waiting.

"I went after your grandfather died to look at the will. I thought maybe there would be an address for you and Eloise or something."

His mouth tilted as what I'd said sank in. I'd gone looking. He had to already know that, but it made me feel empty and naked before him.

"The deed to the orchard was filed, though."

I took the papers from his hand, finding the last one and setting it down. I said nothing as he read it over slowly. When he got to the bottom of the page, the muscle in his jaw ticked again.

I set my finger on the signature that sat on the last line. *His* signature. "You didn't sign this, did you?"

"No." I watched as he slowly put it together.

"I knew it wasn't your handwriting when I saw it."

"This doesn't make any sense," he said, almost to himself. "My grandfather left the orchard to the town when he died."

That's what everyone had been told. I bit the inside of my cheek, trying to decide how much to tell him, how far I was willing to go.

"If he did, then why would they need you to sign it over?" I said.

I could see him figuring it out, the way I had, as he read Nixie's signature below his.

He pressed a clenched fist against his mouth as he read over the document again. "What exactly are you saying?"

I drew in a long, measured breath. "I'm saying that Lily isn't the only reason they weren't happy you came back."

Forty-Four

AUGUST

THE MORNING FERRY HAD come and gone and in an hour, my flight would be taking off from Seattle.

I wouldn't be on it.

I cracked an egg into the pan, reading over the deed again as the kettle began to hum. The news that Henry had left the orchard to the town had surprised both my mom and me. He'd never wanted the town to have it, but in the end, I figured that he'd been forced to accept that I wasn't coming back to Saoirse and that there was no one to give it to. Now it seemed the stubborn bastard hadn't been so gracious after all.

I waved away the steam from the kettle when it began to fog my glasses, and I pushed them up my nose, reading my name again.

The date by the signature was almost four months after my grandfather died. According to Eric, that was enough time for the will to be probated and recorded. Once that was done, they'd only need a lawyer to transfer the deed and a notary as witness: Bernard Keller and Nixie Thomas.

If Emery was right, they probably weren't the only ones involved. To pull this off would have taken the entire town council.

Before the fire, my grandfather was convinced the town was after the orchard. Once he was gone and there was no one here to stop them, they'd taken it. They sure as hell didn't think I'd be back. And of all the people they could put in charge, Dutch Boden had landed the job. There was some kind of sick symmetry to that.

The kettle began to squeal and I picked it up, pouring as I finished the line of type I was reading. The water spilled over the rim of the cup and the kettle slipped from my fingers, splashing as it hit the counter.

"Fuck!" I flung the water from my hands, turning on the tap and letting the cold run over my knuckles. They were pink and swollen this morning, the skin cut up and stinging.

I set the kettle into the sink, abandoning the cup. I'd gone without a decent cup of coffee for more than ten days now. I could go one more.

A knock at the door sounded and I peered around the cabinets, eyeing the window. The top of Emery's head was visible through the glass and I moved the pan from the burner, cursing the fact that I could still recognize her like that. I'd know her anywhere. Her hands, her frame. I could pick out the sound of her voice in a sea of people if I had to.

I came around the counter, crossing the living room and glancing down at my packed bag still sitting by the door. Emery looked up at me with tired eyes when I opened it. She was wrapped in a thick gray sweater, her hair haphazardly braided over one shoulder. A thermos was cradled in her arms.

"Is that coffee?"

"Smelled the burned grounds when I was here yesterday." She handed it to me, staring at my face with an almost grin pulling at her lips.

"What?"

"Your glasses," she said, the smile finally breaking in a slanted line. "I've just never seen you wear glasses before."

I pulled them off, embarrassed, though I didn't know why. Why did it feel so familiar, her showing up at my door with coffee and commenting on my glasses? Just laying eyes on her made me feel grounded in a way I never did.

"Did you talk to him?" She didn't wait to be invited inside, stepping past me.

"Yeah." I went back into the kitchen, pulling down another coffee cup from the cabinet. I'd had to walk up and down the road to find a signal to call Eric, but I'd gotten him long enough to get the answer I needed.

"What did he say?"

"He won't really get a grasp on what's going on until he sees all the paperwork. He's requested the original will that was filed with the county. When he gets it, he's going to call me."

She nodded, but her gaze was on the countertop, as if she was lost in thought. Dark circles shaded the fair skin beneath her eyes and the angles of her face were more severe.

"You look like you haven't slept in days," I said, filling the mugs.

"I haven't," she muttered.

I watched as she picked at the loose thread of her sweater. She always used to do that. "What is it?"

"I just hoped he wasn't actually a part of this. My dad." I set down the coffee in front of her and she picked it up in both hands, like she was warming herself with it. "But he had to. They all had to know."

"Why did you tell me if you thought he might be involved?" I asked, studying her. That wasn't like Emery. The Blackwoods had always been tightly knit and loyal. I'd been cut out of that equation a long time ago. It had cost her something to give me the deed to the orchard. She didn't owe it to me, but she'd done it.

"I'm just so tired of all the lying," she said.

The pop of wood out on the porch made us both look to the front door. Emery's eyes slid to me before she got up, making her way to the window. Her hand fisted into the curtain when her gaze landed on something.

"What?" I said, following her.

I came to stand behind her, looking over her head. Outside, a white envelope sat on the mat. I reached around Emery, opening the door and stepping over it to come down the steps. In every direction, the woods were quiet except for the starlings that never seemed to leave the trees. There was no one.

When I turned back around, Emery was standing in the doorway, holding the envelope in her hands. She looked up at me, her brow pulled, before she turned it over and opened it.

I watched her eyes flit over the paper as she unfolded it, and the sound of her breath broke the silence. "Shit." She pinched her eyes closed.

"What is it?" I came up the steps, taking it from her and going back inside.

The paper was a crude xerox copy made of a letter, and as soon as I saw the handwriting, my stomach dropped. It was my mother's.

Hannah,

I've been thinking that I needed to write this particular letter for some time but I haven't been sure how to do it.

All I can think is that I wish that night hadn't happened.

I know what August did is unforgivable.

I swallowed, trying to steady the shake in my hand.

I've thought so many times about how you think you know your child, and then they do something that terrifies you. Something that opens a darkness.

"What the fuck is this?" I breathed.

I stilled when I reached the bottom of the page, where someone had written in all caps.

*LEAVE OR I CALL THE SEATTLE POLICE TOMORROW
ABOUT THIS LETTER AND WHAT HAPPENED AT THE
ORCHARD WITH LILY.*

Emery had one hand pressed to her mouth, staring at me. "It's a letter your mom wrote to my mom."

"You've seen this before?"

"I found it in the attic last week after you got here. A whole box of letters between them."

My hand went limp at my side. The single sheet of paper felt like it weighed a hundred pounds.

"Someone took it from my house that night the truck was set on fire."

I tossed the envelope onto the counter, pacing the kitchen.

Emery watched me from the living room. "What does that mean? What happened at the orchard with Lily?"

I stared at the message written on the bottom of the paper, biting down on my bottom lip. This was one part of the story I'd hoped I wouldn't have to tell her. "That day, after graduation, Lily came to find me at the orchard. After you saw her at the pub," I said. "She was upset and crying."

"Because of our fight?"

"Yeah." I sighed. "I mean, no. She was upset that we were leaving Saoirse and she was asking me not to."

"Not to what? Leave?"

I stared at her, wondering how much I should say. There didn't seem to be a point in lying, but there wasn't much of a point in Emery knowing every detail, either.

"Tell me," she said, reading my thoughts.

I crossed my arms over my chest. "I was working out in the orchard and when I came back to the barn loft, she was there."

"And? What happened?"

"She was really angry we were leaving and she begged me not to go. She was acting crazy, crying and screaming. I thought we were alone in the barn."

What I wouldn't tell her was that Lily had tried to kiss me. That she'd pulled down the straps of her dress and pressed herself against me with tears streaming down her face, reaching for the button of my pants. I'd never seen her act that way. Even thinking about it now made my stomach turn.

"What did you say?" Emery asked.

"I didn't know what to say. It was out of nowhere. I thought maybe she was on something." I shook my head. "I told her that she had to leave and when she wouldn't, I did. I didn't come back until an hour later and she was gone."

"So, Dutch was telling the truth." She laughed bitterly. "Lily was in love with you."

I'd suspected it more than once, but I'd never told Emery because they were friends. I knew it would hurt her. "Someone must have seen or overheard us. I don't know."

"Well, whoever it is, they're saying they'll use it to pull you back into this." Emery's eyes landed on the letter. The shadows on her face seemed to be getting darker by the minute.

"Who do you think took it? Dutch?"

Emery shook her head. "I thought maybe he did, but I don't think so."

"Then who?"

"I don't know. You aren't the only one with secrets from that night. I'm starting to think everyone has them. But I don't think this is about Lily. I think it's about the orchard. The will." She paused. "August, the police didn't have enough to charge you the first time, but they might if they had this. It would at least be enough for them to start looking into Lily's death again."

"You think I should leave," I said, following her train of thought.

But then her eyes lifted, meeting mine, and for the first time since she'd walked through the door, they were focused. "That won't stop whoever this is from using this against you."

I stared at the letter unfolded between us. "Then what?"

"I think we should find out what really happened to Lily."

EMERY

BLACK ELDER WAS MY mother's favorite for reading the leaves.

Lily hovered over the green, gold-rimmed cup, peering into the last few sips of tea before she raised it to her lips. We sat on the floor of the shop with the wind howling outside, but the flames on the candles we'd lit were calm.

She'd been begging me to read her tea leaves for months because my mother refused, saying that she didn't like looking into the futures of young people. That it never brought anything good. I finally agreed to do it as a kind of parting gift to her, whether she knew it or not.

It was the last day of school and the night before graduation. My last night with her in the world we'd grown up in together. The thought made my stomach drop a little.

My mother had been teaching me to read the leaves since I was a little girl, and the ritual of it was memorized in my fingertips. From the way I wrapped the towel around the handle of the kettle as I lifted it from the flames to the position of my hand as I turned the cup. But it wasn't until that previous fall that she finally let me begin reading tea leaves for customers who came into the shop.

"All right." I placed the folded linen napkin in front of Lily. "Flip it over. Carefully."

Lily did as she was told, tipping the cup quickly so that it landed upside down.

I sprinkled another handful of crushed, dried cedar over the coals in the brass bowl beside us and the smoke lifted into the air, filling my lungs.

"Now turn it clockwise. Three times."

She set her fingertips on the cup's bottom, rotating it with an excited gleam in her eyes. In that moment, she reminded me of the Lily I'd run barefoot with through the woods. The one who laughed all the time. Sometimes, I forgot about that version of her.

When she was finished, she set her hands in her lap, peering up at me.

"Ready?" I asked.

She nodded, lips pursing as I flipped it back over.

The herb was sprawled along the inside of the cup, sinking into a pool at the bottom. I tilted it toward the light and the shapes took form, glistening against the pale green ceramic.

But my hands tightened on the cup when I saw the only clear symbol in the swath of trailing black. I blinked, trying to clear my eyes, convinced that it was a trick of the smoke or the flicker of candlelight.

There, along the rim, a perfect circle looked back up at me, one straight line jutting out from its side. I'd never seen it in a reading, I only recognized it from my mother's *Herbarium*, where the hand-drawn symbols were listed with their meanings. It was Death.

My eyes flickered up to Lily, who was still waiting with a wide grin.

"Well?" She reached for the cup, but I drew back, holding it out of her reach.

She laughed, climbing over the smoking cedar and candles to take it from me, but the cup slipped from my fingers. It hit the wooden floor and bounced before it rolled under the table.

Lily was half-lying on top of me as she snatched it, peering inside. Half of the tea leaves were gone, scattered over the floor. "What did it say?"

I felt the blood drain from my face as the window rattled over our heads. Far in the distance, a rumble of thunder was creeping toward the island.

It wasn't just the symbol. It was its placement along the rim of the cup, away from the handle. It was Death. And soon.

"What's wrong with you?" She still thought this was a game.

I sat up, my tongue stuck to the roof of my mouth. I wasn't a skilled reader like my mother. And I'd only seen it for a moment. It was possible I hadn't seen it at all.

"Em?"

"Love," I lied, forcing a smile. "It says you're going to find love."

Her eyes brightened instantly, her grin stretching wider. "Really?"

"Yeah."

Lily settled back down, sitting cross-legged on the floor. Her wet hair was braided up over the crown of her head so that it would be wavy for the graduation ceremony tomorrow, and there was a warm glow to her cheeks. She was still smiling.

I pinched my eyes closed, shaking my head before I looked into the cup again. The black elder was now just a glob on one side of the porcelain.

But my eyes trailed back to the spilled tea leaves on the floor beneath the table, a sick feeling billowing inside me.

Lily took the second cup from the floor, setting it before me. "Okay, now let's do you."

Forty-Six

EMERY

IF THERE WAS ONE thing true about Saoirse, it was that almost nothing changed. That simple truth had been a source of pride for many of the people who lived on the island. While the mainlanders barreled ahead with the chaotic pace of the world, Saoirse was a refuge, a haven for those who lived by the old ways.

Today, it was the reason I knew exactly where Jake would be at eleven-fifty A.M.

He went to the pub three times a day, for coffee in the morning, a pint at noon, and whiskey in the evening. As soon as the clock's long hand moved to the ten, he would leave his little hole of an office, and I could even tell you what he would order—a pastrami sandwich with mustard and brown ale, his first public drink of the day. But anyone with half a brain knew about the bottle of bourbon he kept in his desk and tipped into his coffee cup.

He appeared right on time, pushing through the old metal door and out into the rain. The few parking spots in front of the building were empty, so Abbott Wittich, who ran the *Saoirse Journal*, was probably also out. But Sophie walked to work every day, rain or shine, and she ate her lunch at her desk.

Jake walked straight across the parking lot without so much as looking up from the set of keys in his hand, and as soon as his truck turned onto Main Street, I set out from the corner of the building. He'd be gone for at least an hour, maybe longer if he got caught up in conversation at the pub. That was plenty of time.

August had offered to come with me, but the moment Sophie laid eyes on him, she'd pick up the phone and call someone. Jake's niece, on the other hand, wouldn't give her much to talk about.

My reflection was bright on the big glass windows before I pulled open the stubborn door, and Sophie squinted behind her glasses as she looked up at me over the desk. "Em? That you?"

"Hey, Sophie." I smiled. "Is Jake here?"

She peered around me to the empty parking lot. "You just missed him, honey. He's headed to lunch."

"Oh." My gaze went to the hallway that led to his office. "He must have forgotten I was coming by." I glanced at my watch. "He was supposed to meet me."

"Well, anything I can help with?"

"No"—I sighed—"just some paperwork I need to renew a county permit. I know where it is."

Sophie opened her mouth to object, but I was already walking, disappearing on the other side of the wall. By the time she made up her mind whether she was supposed to let me in there without Jake's permission, I'd have what I needed.

I closed the door behind me, eyeing the brown glass bowl under the lamp in the corner. His other set of keys. That was another thing that never changed about Saoirse. No one but shopkeepers locked their doors, and even the town marshal had the keys to his file cabinet sitting on a shelf four feet away because he'd misplaced them too many times to bother hiding them.

I fished the keys from the bowl and fit the one with the red plastic head into the lock of the third cabinet. When the heavy drawer rolled out, I caught it with the palm of my hand, skimming through the tabs as quickly as I could read. The files were filled with reports of theft blamed on tourists, vandalism, or neighbor disputes about property lines, but I was looking for one name—Morgan.

I found it in the second drawer, in the very back. It was the thickest of all the files and I had to use two hands to wedge it up from between the others. When I finally had it out, I swallowed hard, the weight of it heavy in my hands.

I pushed the drawer closed with my hip and locked it, dropping the key back in the bowl. The file barely fit into my jacket, but I doubted Sophie had updated her glasses prescription in years. I snatched up a blank piece of paper from the corner of the shelf.

She was leaning over her desk as I came back down the hallway, the sunlight reflecting off the lenses of her cat-eye glasses. "Everything all right?" She frowned.

"Guess he didn't forget." I kept one arm pinned to my side to hold the folder in place as I smiled, waving the sheet of paper in the air. "Had it waiting for me."

"Oh, good." She grinned, unwrapping the wax paper around her sandwich. "You know how he is. Would forget his head if it wasn't attached."

"Yep. Thanks, Sophie."

"Bye-bye, honey."

I pushed back out of the door, letting the breath pent up in my chest escape through my lips. My face was hot, my hands slick as I searched my pocket for the keys to the truck parked around the corner. When I got inside, I pulled the folder from inside my jacket, setting it on the seat beside me.

I stared at it as I turned the key. The thick manila paper was stained and scratched around the edges, like it had been handled a thousand times. It likely had. Even when the news stopped talking about it, and the Seattle Police stopped showing up on the ferry, Jake had continued to pore over the details of Lily's murder. But the only answer he'd ever come up with was the wrong one.

I'd never blamed him, like everyone else had. And now, looking back, it was clearer than ever that no one had all the facts from that night. The only person who did was Lily.

My hand tightened on the gearshift before I wedged it into reverse, but as soon as the truck started rolling backward, my eyes went again to the folder.

Maybe I didn't know Lily either, like Dutch said. But I was sick of this town thinking they knew *me*.

I hit the brake, changing my mind, and put the truck into park. The papers slid as I pulled the folder back into my lap, opening it. For one of Jake's files, it was very organized, with tabbed sections separating everything from printouts of interviews and ferry manifests to what looked to be Lily's class schedule at school.

But I narrowed my gaze when the word *Blackwood* appeared on a sheet I was flipping past. I went back, thumbing through the corners until I found it, and pulled the clipped section from the others. My heart skipped when I saw my own face looking back at me. It was my school photo from my senior year. A young Emery smiled at the camera shyly in a simple blue dress. It was the same photo my mother kept at the shop.

My information was typed out beside it—address, parents, association to Lily. The next page was what looked like a timeline, starting at eight-thirty A.M. the morning of June 6. The hours followed me from home to graduation to the pub, back home, to the beach, and then to the party. It ended at home again, where Jake had first questioned me. Beside the time at the pub, there was a handwritten note.

Argument with Lily—see Abbott Wittich statement

And there was more. An itemized list of things they'd found in my bedroom. Cross-referenced interviews confirming my statements. I flipped to the next page. Test results for the clothes I'd been wearing that night. I hadn't even known they'd taken them or that the police had come to the house at all. But Nixie and I had spent days in Seattle. It was possible I'd come home and not even noticed they'd been there.

A feeling like a swarm of bees in my stomach surfaced, my skin flashing hot. This didn't look like the profile of a victim's friend. This looked like I was a suspect.

Forty-Seven

AUGUST

EMERY SAT LIKE THE eye of a storm in the center of her bedroom floor with the contents of the file fanned out around her. She flipped the page of another interview, one finger dragging across the words as she read.

I stood in the doorway, watching her with a fresh cup of coffee in hand. We'd been at it for hours, sifting through every piece of paper in Jake's records of the case, but there was one stack that Emery kept returning to. The one with her picture.

"I just don't get it," she said again. "Jake didn't make any secret of the fact that he thought you killed Lily. If he thought it could have been me, why didn't he tell me?"

I could see it getting under her skin. "He's your uncle, Em."

"I don't even remember him asking me. I don't think anyone ever did."

"Maybe that's why he wanted it to be me so badly."

"What do you mean?" She finally looked up.

I stared at the picture. I remembered it, because Emery hated that picture of herself. I kind of did, too. She looked timid. Nervous. That wasn't the Emery I knew.

"If I was the one who killed Lily, then you couldn't be," I said.

She tucked her hair behind her ear. "I wonder if my parents knew," she said, almost to herself. "Wouldn't be the only thing they hid from me."

The letters were another matter. They sat on the kitchen table with the lid off the box, but I had no intention of reading them. I didn't want to know what my mom had said about me or what I did. I didn't want to hear in her own words how much I'd made her suffer.

I wondered now if there was a box of letters in the attic at my mom's house. She'd never told me that she kept in touch with anyone on Saoirse.

When Emery caught me staring at them, she let the packet in her hands close. "One of them says you came back here after you left." The look she gave me was apprehensive, like she was afraid to know. "Is that true?"

I stared into the coffee mug, watching the steam lift up into the air. "Yeah, I did."

I watched as she picked at the staple in the corner of the packet. Deep down, I'd hoped that Emery would find me. That she'd just show up one day at our house in Prosper and make the decision for me. But she never did. It was torture being away from her and when I reached the point where I couldn't stand it any longer, I'd just taken off. I managed to drive the whole way to Seattle without convincing myself to turn around.

"Why didn't you come see me?" she said.

I let out a long breath, glancing over her head. "I did."

Emery followed my gaze to the window behind her. "You came here?"

I nodded.

I'd made it to the island on the last ferry, and I followed the road, keeping to the trees. The house was dark when I came through the gate. Emery's window was cracked open and as soon as I saw her through the glass, I knew I'd made a mistake. She was asleep, and I couldn't see her face, but the palm of her open hand was lit by a beam of moonlight.

In my mind, I was going home. To Emery. But standing there with my own dark reflection, I realized that I wasn't the same kid who used to climb through that window. And she wasn't the same girl who agreed to leave Saoirse with me.

Emery watched me remember the moment. I didn't want her to ask anything else. I didn't want to tell her what that moment had been like. What it had taken to turn around and walk away.

"I decided it would be easier for you if I didn't come back," I said.

Her mouth twisted.

"Would you have wanted me to? After everything?"

She was quiet for a long moment before she answered. "Yes."

I searched her eyes, not knowing what to say. I couldn't go back and change what happened or the decisions either of us made. I'd always wondered if she'd hurt like I had after I left, and I'd even wondered if it would make me feel better knowing she did. Like it would somehow justify or legitimize all that pain. But it didn't.

"Is it true that it calls you back? The island?" Her voice was suddenly hoarse and hollow. "My mom always said that if you leave, it will call you back."

"Yeah. It's true."

I'd felt it the moment we stepped onto the ferry and it had never left me. Not until I returned.

She stared off, the look in her eye growing far away.

"You look like shit, Em. You should get some rest." I changed the subject.

She nearly laughed. "Thanks."

"I mean it. When's the last time you slept?"

She shrugged, her eyes moving over the type on the page again.

I surrendered, stepping over the pile on the floor and finding a seat on the edge of the bed to read over her shoulder. "What is that one?"

She set it down in front of me. "A log or something. It looks like stuff that was found with her. She was dressed for the party, so she must have been headed there."

"Or to the beach," I said. "She left a note for you to meet her, right?"

"Right. But she never showed." Emery set her hands in her lap. "Let's go through it again."

"Okay."

"After the graduation, Lily was with me at the pub. We fought, and then she went to see you at the orchard, but at some point later, she came by my house and left a note telling me to meet her at Halo Beach." She looked over the papers again, picking one up. "As far as I can tell, the last person to see her was Etzel Adelman, who says she saw Lily at Leoda's shop sometime after four."

"She had to have gone home at some point if she was ready for the party."

"If she did, her parents didn't see her. They said the last time they saw her was before lunch. So, she had to have gone back home when they weren't there."

I looked at the log of what they found with Lily, line by line. It wasn't the original; it was a copy. And with the exception of a line that had been whited out, the items were listed one by one. A dress, shoes, a bracelet, earrings, a watch, matches.

"Why would she have matches?" I thought aloud.

Emery gave me a knowing look. We'd smoked a lot of pot in the lighthouse our senior year. That was one of the reasons the alibi with Dutch had checked out.

"Maybe she was at the lighthouse then."

"Maybe. But you didn't see her there."

"Maybe I got there after she left."

Emery rifled through one of the stapled packets, her brow wrinkling. "When they analyzed the dress, Jake said they found wax on it. Like, spilled on the fabric. And this is the weirdest part." She held another copied sheet in the air. "They found seaweed in her stomach when they did the autopsy."

I winced. The thought of them cutting Lily open made my skin crawl.

"This report is also what tipped Jake off that Lily was sleeping with someone. In his mind, that was you because you weren't at the orchard when the fire broke out. He knew that Lily and I got into a fight at the pub. Abbott saw us arguing. So, he put it all together, thinking you and Lily were sleeping together. That, and the history of violence and—"

"What history of violence?" I murmured.

Emery's shoulders straightened. Her fingers stilled on the paper.

"What?" I asked, studying her.

Still, she didn't look up.

"Christ, just tell me."

"Your family."

My hands tightened around the mug. So, Jake did know about my grandfather. Maybe everyone did. But no one had done a damn thing about it. "One drunk asshole isn't exactly a history."

She lowered the paper back onto the stack, setting one hand on top of it. "He wasn't just talking about Henry. He was talking about Calvin."

"My dad? What about him?"

"He said that before he left, Calvin was . . . hurting Eloise."

I pinned my eyes to the floor, that feeling on my skin turning into a pointed, sharp pain.

"Is that true?" she asked gently.

My throat was suddenly tight. "If it is, my mom never said anything to me about it."

"Maybe she wouldn't."

Maybe. I hadn't told her about my grandfather for the same reason. She'd never seemed broken up about the fact that my dad had left, but she'd never seemed happy about it, either.

It didn't matter if what Jake said about my dad was true. I wasn't Calvin. And I wasn't Henry.

"Then there are these loose ends, like Albertine calling the marshal's office that afternoon," I said, changing the subject.

"Yeah, but nothing ever came of it. Nothing was stolen from the house and I think the Seattle Police just chalked it up to an old blind lady hearing the wind rattle the windows or something."

I was skeptical. "They don't know Albertine."

"No, they don't." Emery raised an eyebrow. "There's no mention in any of this about Lily coming to see you at the orchard, so I don't think Jake is the one who threatened you with the letter. If he had information like that, he would have already used it against you. I don't think Dutch took it. So, who does that leave?"

"Your dad?" I said, carefully.

Emery didn't look at me. "A few days ago, I would have said there was no way he would do this. Now, I'm not sure. I'm not sure about anything."

I leaned down, picking up the photos of Lily. The first was a wide shot of her lying on the ground. It didn't look real, the black-and-white contrast making her look like a stranger. I flipped to the next one—a close-up of her open hand. The one after that was her from the side, and in the corner, three small numbers were imprinted on the photograph—388. I went back to the one before it, finding the next number: 386. The one before that one was 385.

The photos were in number order from 382 to 404.

"What are these?" I turned it around to face Emery.

She squinted, reading them. "The negative numbers, I think."

"Where's 387?"

She reached over the stack to her right to find the envelope of negatives. I waited as she went through them, holding each one to the light. "It's not here."

I took it, checking the numbers again. The film was cut before 387 in a diagonal line.

"Maybe it was an overexposure or the image was ruined somehow."

I turned the film over in my hands before I slid off the edge of the bed, searching the floor for the evidence log. I pointed to the one line that had been whited out. "Or it was something Jake didn't want anyone to see."

Forty-Eight

EMERY

JAKE'S HOUSE WAS A stone's throw from the marina and one of the only residences on Main Street. It wasn't a house at all, really. More like a two-level flat that shared a wall with the bakery. But the only entrance was the door in the alley that faced the water.

I knocked three times, shaking the icy sting from my knuckles as Jake's footsteps sounded inside. This time of night, he'd be a few drinks in. Maybe that was a good thing.

The door opened and he immediately drew back, surprised to see me. "Hey, Em." He blinked the blurred look from his eyes.

I stepped past him, glancing at the open bottle of bourbon on the coffee table. The pellet stove was going, but the kitchen window was open to the cold and he had the *Saoirse Journal* open beside an empty glass on the table. His place always smelled like fresh tobacco and coffee.

He ducked out to peer down the alley before he shut the door. "Everything okay?"

"No," I answered honestly. "It's not."

He reached up, scratching the back of his head. "All right. What's going on?" His speech was a little slower than it was in the morning hours.

"Was I a suspect in Lily's murder?"

It took a moment for my words to sink in, but when they did, his shoulders drew back. "What?"

I rubbed the spot between my eyebrows, impatiently. "I don't have time for this, Jake. Just answer the question."

"How did you . . ."

"I took the files from your office," I said flatly. What could he do about it now? "I've been going through them all night."

Jake paled, gaping at me. "What the hell were you thinking, Em?"

"I'm not a cop, but I'm also not an idiot. The file makes it look like I was a suspect. Is that true?"

"This isn't a closed case. You could get into serious trouble for—"

"And *you* could get into serious trouble for hiding evidence," I shot back.

He went rigid, his nostrils flaring. I hadn't been sure about August's theory, but it was clear on Jake's face.

"I want to know the truth, Jake," I said again. "Was I a suspect or not?"

His gaze went through me, his jaw working as he tried to think. I didn't know if I'd ever really seen him like that. Confused. Uncertain of what to do. In an instant, my uncle looked incredibly fragile, and I didn't like the feeling it gave me.

"They were taking a look at you, that was all." He spoke through a heavy breath. "The Seattle Police."

"Why?"

He walked back to his chair and sat with a groan. "They looked at everyone. You were Lily's best friend and you said you'd gone to the beach to meet her. She was drowned, for God's sake, so of course they were going to look at you."

"Then why didn't you tell me?"

"Because I knew it wasn't true. And you were shaken up enough.

Lily was dead and your dad was hurt. I didn't think it was right to tell you. Not then."

"Did my parents know?"

He shook his head once.

I sat on the corner of the sofa beside him, thinking. "Did they find something when they were looking into me?" That was the only reason I could think of that Jake would hide evidence.

Jake hesitated. "Maybe."

"What?"

The corners of his mouth turned down. "Just a statement from someone saying they saw the two of you fighting at the pub. Nothing that really added up to something substantial. There was way more evidence pointing to August, and they seemed much more interested in him."

"So you pushed them in that direction."

"I didn't."

Jake's hunch that August was guilty wasn't all wrong. He had set the fire. But everyone was so busy wondering who killed Lily that no one had looked too closely at what happened at the orchard.

"What was on negative 387?" I asked quietly.

Jake's eyes flicked up suddenly. Just when I thought he would dodge the question, he seemed to change his mind. "A necklace."

I gave him a puzzled look. "A necklace?"

"*Your* necklace. The one your dad gave you for your birthday."

Slowly, the weight of what he was saying sank in. My dad had given me a silver necklace with a butterfly on it that year. I wore it almost every day, but at some point, I'd lost it.

"It was lying in the leaves next to her." Jake's voice deepened. "At first I didn't recognize it. I logged it and snapped a photo like I did everything else, thinking it was Lily's. It wasn't until the next morning when I saw the film that I remembered it was yours."

"So, you hid it," I whispered.

"I cut the negative and burned it. The necklace, I tossed into the sea up at Wilke's Pointe. The Seattle Police never saw either of them."

The edges of the words blurred, making them hard to understand. He'd gotten rid of the necklace so that no one would ever find it. So that no one would have reason to think that I was there when Lily died.

I breathed, trying to sift through the hazy memories of that day. "How did it get there?"

"Are you sure you didn't see her that night?" he asked, but this time he looked me right in the eye. There was an unfamiliar tone to his words.

"Are you asking if I killed her?" I asked, hollowly.

Jake stared at me, unblinking. "I know you didn't kill her. But I think it's possible you know more about her death than you've told me."

"I told you everything I knew. She left me a note and I went to meet her but—" I stopped short, the words stuck in my throat. "She was in my room." The words trailed off.

"When?"

"That day. She came by to leave me the note that said to meet her at Halo Beach. Maybe she took the necklace then."

Jake looked skeptical.

"She took things without asking all the time. Clothes, shoes . . . Maybe she borrowed the necklace for the party. I don't know. But I wasn't there, Jake. I wasn't with her."

He said nothing, reaching for the bottle of bourbon and refilling the small glass that sat beside it. There was no telling how many he'd had.

"Would you have hidden the evidence, even if you thought I did it?"

He brought the glass to his lips, taking a sip. "I don't know. Maybe."

Everyone in the family, on the island, knew that I was the closest thing to a child Jake had. He'd always been a lonely creature, in love with a woman who either didn't love him or couldn't be with him. That didn't stop him from looking after both August and Eloise like they were his own. Then he'd borne the brunt of the town's anger after Lily and even more as we struggled in the aftermath of the fire. There were times I'd listen to him and my dad talk out on the porch and I'd heard him say more than once that maybe Saoirse was dying. That maybe it was the end.

And it would have been. Without the orchard.

If the town council altered the deed to the orchard, it wasn't likely that Jake had been kept in the dark. With the responsibility of Saoirse's welfare on his shoulders, it was also possible that Jake had made August's departure his top priority.

"Where were you the other night when someone set fire to Eloise's truck?" I asked softly.

He flinched, as if the implication hurt him.

"Did you do it?" I pushed.

"Do you think I did?"

"I don't know," I said, giving his own words back to him. "Maybe."

Jake shot the bourbon down and refilled his glass. He swirled the amber liquid as he stared into it. "Thought you knew me better than that, kid."

"So did I."

Forty-Nine

EMERY

I WATCHED HIM THROUGH the window, my breath fogging on the glass.

August was asleep on the sofa with his face turned toward the fire. I'd told him not to go back to his house. Not when people were setting things on fire and leaving threats at his door. At this point, we were in this together.

But the sight of him there in the living room was almost too much for me to pull my mind around. August Salt. Here, in my house. After all this time.

I opened the door carefully and hung my jacket on the hook as quietly as I could, but by the time I was stepping out of my boots, August's eyes fluttered open. He blinked a few times before they focused, as if he were trying to remember where he was.

"Did Eric call?"

He sat up slowly, rubbing his hands over his face, and I tried not to stare when the hem of his gray T-shirt lifted away from the waist of his jeans, uncovering the curve of his hip. His sleeve was cinched up his biceps, revealing the edge of a pointed shape inked into his skin.

There was a time when I'd known every square inch of August's skin and I was sure it hadn't been there before.

"No." His voice grated with sleep.

The will was the only piece of the puzzle we didn't have. Until we saw what Henry Salt wrote in the original copy, we wouldn't know exactly what transpired with the orchard.

August swung his legs from the sofa and I came around the arm, sitting beside him. It was warm where he'd been sleeping and I tucked my bare feet between the cushions. The room smelled like him.

"Did you find Jake?" he asked.

I stared into the fire, running my thumb over my bottom lip. "You were right about the log. Lily had something of mine with her when she died. A necklace. Jake got rid of it because he was afraid the Seattle Police would start taking a closer look at me."

August stared past me, expressionless.

It wasn't a surprise, but I knew it drove the betrayal deeper for him. August had looked up to Jake, seen him as a kind of father. But when Jake had to choose between the two of us, he'd chosen me.

"You should really sleep," he finally said.

"I can't."

August's eyes ran over my face. "Why not?"

I hugged my knees to my chest. "I've been having these nightmares every night. I used to get them a long time ago, after what happened, and they came back last week."

"What kind of nightmares?"

I clenched my teeth, trying to push the images away before they could fully form in my mind. But they were still there. They were always there. "I'm at the beach, standing in the water." I swallowed. "It's dark, almost completely black, and I can hear screaming."

August leaned forward, listening. I'd never told anyone what I saw in those dreams.

"It's so loud that it hurts my ears and it won't stop, just going on and on. Then I look down"—I breathed—"and I'm holding someone under the surface. My hands are numb and tangled in her hair. She's trying to come up and I keep pushing her back down." I pinched my eyes closed.

"It's just a dream, Emery. Lily—"

"It's not Lily. It's me. And it doesn't feel like it's just a dream."

August's expression turned wary. "What are you saying?"

"Sometimes"—I hesitated—"sometimes I wonder if I'm misremembering something from that night . . . I mean, it's all so incomplete now—the memories. That night, the next day. What if—"

"Emery." August's voice rose, more seriously. "You weren't there."

I shook my head. "I feel like I'm going crazy. Like I don't know what was real and what wasn't. I mean, there are things that I think I imagined or that maybe weren't the way I remember them."

"Like us?"

I blinked, surprised. But August looked right at me, his gaze unwavering. "Yeah," I admitted.

He ran a hand through his hair, his face turning back to the fire. "I do that, too. Try to make sense of it or spin it out into something it wasn't. It would have made things a lot easier if it wasn't real."

But it was real. So real that it had become a relentless, barbed vine. No matter how many times I ripped it from the earth, it kept growing back.

"Then why did you leave?" The heartbreak I felt was heavy between us. I couldn't help it.

August measured his words carefully. "I felt like I ruined everything, including us. I couldn't bear to tell you what I did, so when my mom said she thought we should leave and start over somewhere else, I didn't argue. I felt like it was the only way to make all of it stop."

"Did it stop?"

"No." August smirked, but he looked sad. "I know you feel like I left you here, but you followed me everywhere I went."

"Is that true?" I whispered, feeling the prick of tears at the corners of my eyes. I wanted it to be true.

"I wish it wasn't," he said, softly. "Sometimes I think you're the worst thing that ever happened to me."

The raw feeling inside me was like an open wound when he said it. But I couldn't even be angry, because I'd thought that, too. More than once.

I caught the tear at the corner of my eye with the heel of my hand. There was no point crying about it now. "Didn't you ever find anyone?"

"I've never been able to really be with someone. I've had hookups and people I've dated, but I always knew I would never spend my life with any of them. It was never on the table."

"Why not?"

He leveled his gaze at me, as if trying to decide on his answer. "You sure you want to go there?"

"I think we're there whether we want to be or not."

"It's going to sound crazy."

"That's okay."

He let out a long breath. "Because I'm somehow still connected to you. Like a part of me isn't there if you're not there. For years, I thought that would go away. It didn't."

I stared at him, speechless. I'd known what he was going to say but I hadn't expected him to say it like that.

"It shouldn't be like this." He paused, "Right? I mean, we were kids." He was looking past me again, his jaw clenching. "How long were you looking for me?" he asked.

"Too long."

Another silence. I let my head fall back and I watched the light dance over the ceiling.

"I still have the tickets." I sighed.

"The ferry tickets?"

I nodded, not looking at him. I wanted to laugh at myself. I also wanted to cry.

The burn of his eyes moved over my skin, but it was a long moment before he finally spoke. "I'm sorry. For not telling you the truth."

I swallowed against the ache in my throat. For the first time, it felt like us. The real us. Like the ocean that existed between him and me was just . . . gone. And the last bit of will I had to keep myself from touching him vanished into thin air.

I reached over, finding his hand with mine, and slipped my fingers between his. August stared at it for the length of a breath before his thumb brushed over my palm.

It was the same feeling I'd had when I held his hand in the cemetery as we watched Zachariah bury Eloise's ashes. Like the moment I touched him, the roaring wind inside me just stopped. And the moment he let me go, it would return.

August brought my hand up, pressing his mouth to my wrist and he just sat there, breathing. That single moment made the first of the tears streak down my cheek, and when I couldn't stand what was left of the space between us anymore, I climbed over to him, folding myself in his arms.

I closed my eyes, letting his scent wrap around me. I breathed it in, like it was the first breath I could remember taking.

"I'm sorry," he said, quietly. "I'm sorry I left."

I reached up, touching his face, like I was re-memorizing him. Every angle and shape. Before I could think twice, I let my mouth drift toward his. I waited for him to stop me, but he didn't. He sat there, so still, his hands tightening on me as I came closer.

My lips touched his and I closed my eyes, kissing him slowly. Carefully. Like I'd been waiting a lifetime to do it.

His mouth opened and I let him taste me as his hands dragged up my back. They found their way beneath my shirt, and his fingertips sent the heat flooding under my skin. We were already moving together the way we used to, like it was the most natural thing in the world. But I wanted to be closer to him. To feel him against me.

I pulled back, peering down into his face, and August's jaw was tight, his eyes strained as they jumped back and forth on mine. I pushed the wild hair away from his face, letting my knuckles trail down the back of his neck.

He looked more like the August I knew—*my* August—than he had since he arrived.

"I want you," he said, his arms tightening around me.

The words were so soft, so broken, that I almost couldn't make them out. His chest rose and fell beneath his shirt, his eyes still on my mouth.

I nodded in answer, my heart hammering painfully behind my ribs. Any minute, it would stop altogether. I reached up to unbutton my shirt and he pulled his over his head, dropping it to the ground. He slipped the straps of my bra down my shoulders and I unhooked it before letting my mouth find his again. His arms came around me as he stood, walking us across the hallway to the bedroom.

I'd dreamed it so many times, but this wasn't the half-empty ache that found me when I slept. This was really happening. He was really touching me. Kissing me.

He laid me down on the bed beneath him and his lips broke from mine as I pushed out of my jeans. Between us, his fingertips ran down my breasts, tracing the line of me, until they were trailing over my stomach. My hips.

The look in his eye was one I could remember so clearly. I remembered it the way I remembered the feel of his skin pressed to mine. The heat of his mouth. The smell of him that clung to me afterward.

He was moving too slowly. Too gently.

I tried pulling him closer, but he didn't move, his gaze still studying me.

"What?" I said between breaths.

His eyes made their way back up to meet mine. "Nothing."

"I'm different?" I said, guessing.

I was. My body wasn't the same one he'd last touched, but I couldn't find it in me to feel embarrassed about it.

"You're beautiful."

I held my breath as his touch moved over my thighs, between my legs, and when his fingers slipped into my underwear, a long, heavy exhale escaped his lips. I drank it in until I was filled with it. He watched me as my back arched and I bit down hard on my bottom lip, a small sound escaping my throat.

For a moment, everything that had happened since the last time I'd been with him like this was gone, wiped from time itself. And the whole world that broke into pieces when he left came back together. The smell of him filled my head and with it, every memory swirled. The first time he'd kissed me. Touched me. The night in the fishing cabin when I'd given myself to him, body and soul, bound by the blood moon.

This wasn't the distracted, hurried pleasure I'd found with Dutch. The desperate need to forget. This was the breath and flesh of what I'd known *before*. The thing I sometimes couldn't believe had ever been real, like August said. But it was. My whole body was singing with the memory of it.

This was why I hadn't been able to do it—cut the bind before my grandmother's fire. It would have been like opening my veins.

The words found my lips, as if some strangled force within me was clawing to get out and anchor itself to him. I pressed my hands to his face, my voice a whisper between us. "I missed you." The sound of it fractured. "I missed you so much."

His eyes traveled over my face before his fingers hooked into the band of my underwear, sliding it over my hips. I pulled at the buttons of his jeans, pushing them down until I could feel his warm skin against my hands. I still knew this body. I knew it like I knew my own.

He came low to kiss my collar bone, his lips finding the peak of my breast. His mouth moved over me, leaving a trail of cold on my skin in the sharp, winter air. But I didn't want to wait anymore. I didn't want to wait for another second. I wrapped my arms around his neck and his hands caught my legs, pulling them up around him. His forehead pressed to mine and when he pushed inside me, I wanted to cry, the relief of it like a wave I was drowning in.

August's mouth pressed to my throat as he leaned his weight into me and he groaned, that same sound of need deep in the resonance of it. More tears streamed from the corners of my eyes, disappearing into my hair.

For fourteen years, it felt like I'd been counting down the minutes, the seconds, to a moment that I thought would never come. He was an ache inside of me that would never be soothed. And it was a pain I didn't even want to be freed from.

The cadence of the woods drifted through the open window, where the wind in the trees sounded like a thousand whispers. But I could hear only him. The broken drag of breath in his throat, the helpless moan that escaped my lips.

I was drunk with it. Teetering on the edge of something shadowed.

I'd been in love with August Salt since before I knew what the words meant. I don't know when it happened—the narrow space between seconds, when a spark like the birth of a hundred stars found a home in my blood. Since then, every day had been colored with the glittering light of it dragging me in its wake, pulling me beneath its surface. And I didn't care. If this was what it was like to drown, then for the rest of my life, I didn't want to take another sip of air.

Fifty

AUGUST

THE BUZZ OF MY phone woke me from the calmest sleep I could remember.

I opened my eyes to glaring sunlight coming through the window. It filled the bedroom with specks of white scattering on the walls. Beside me, Emery was under the blankets, her dark hair spilling over the pale-yellow pillowcase.

I exhaled, giving it a few seconds before I would let myself believe it. I'd thought about it so many times. I'd dreamed it. And now Emery Blackwood was so close that I could touch her. I slipped one arm around her waist, fitting myself against the line of her body, and her feet moved to touch mine. She smelled like sun and the drying herbs that hung in the tea shop. She felt like home.

"Hi," she whispered.

She was so beautiful that I could hardly stand to look at her. It physically hurt to feel her skin under my fingertips. "Hi."

One hand came out of the blanket and she pushed down the covers, turning over in my arms. The light hit every curve of her. Her shoulder. Her breast. Her bare hip. I'd been with other women since her, and they were always hiding. Always drawing away from sight.

But Emery wasn't like anyone I'd ever met, and I'd never felt with anyone the way I felt lying beside her.

"What is that?" she said.

I glanced down, following the line of her gaze to my arm, where the seven-pointed star was tattooed on the inside of my right biceps.

She touched it, her eyes narrowing. "I saw it last night." Her finger traced the asymmetrical shape "What is it?"

"It's nothing."

"You tattooed *nothing* on your arm?" She arched an eyebrow. "Just tell me."

I waited a long moment before reaching up between us. She watched as my hand drifted closer to her and my thumb brushed along her cheekbone, below her left eye. The emerald green star in her iris was aglow in the morning light, blooming against the crystal blue.

I'd drawn it on a torn piece of paper and given it to a tattoo artist in Portland years ago. It hurt every time I looked at it, but I hurt anyway.

She looked up at me through her lashes, her lips pressing together.

"I missed you, too," I said.

The phone buzzed on the table and I reached over her, reading the screen. "Shit. Eric called. He must have left a message."

My phone had barely worked since I got to the island, and the cottage didn't have Wi-Fi. There was no telling what my email inbox looked like, much less my voicemail.

I sat up, finding my pants on the floor, and stood, tugging them on.

Emery propped herself up on one elbow, watching me. "You might be able to get a couple of bars on the porch."

I followed the hallway to the front door and tapped the screen, finding Eric's number. The outside air was cold and damp, but it was the first morning since I'd been back that it wasn't raining.

It took three tries to get the phone to ring, but when it finally did, Eric answered right away. "Where have you been? I've been trying you since last night."

"Sorry, the reception is shit here." When he said nothing, I pulled the phone away to check that the call wasn't dropped. "Eric?"

"Yeah." He paused. "I got the documents from the county. It's definitely not good news."

"Tell me."

"You're the owner, August. The orchard was left to you."

I leaned into the post at the corner of the porch, letting the words sink in. That was the last thing I wanted to hear.

"Hold on." Eric covered the phone, and his voice was muffled as he talked to someone else in the office.

My eyes focused beyond the window, to the kitchen. Emery stood at the counter filling the coffeepot with water in a buttoned-up flannel shirt that swallowed her. I traced the line of her bare legs beneath its hem, that heavy feeling returning to my stomach.

"August?"

I blinked, turning away from the window. "Sorry, what?"

"I said, if your signature is on the deed and you didn't sign it, then someone else did."

An engine rumbled somewhere in the trees and the screech of brakes sounded just before a truck appeared, the same red truck that had been in the woods the other night.

It slowed as it passed and when it reached the gate, Dutch was sitting in the driver's seat. He watched me, one hand hanging out the window, before he hit the gas, tearing down the road.

I looked down at myself. I was barefoot in only my jeans on Emery's porch. "Fuck," I muttered under my breath.

A crackle sounded on the other end of the line. "What?"

"Nothing." I pinched the bridge of my nose, trying to alleviate the throbbing in my head. "Okay, what do I do about this?"

"You need a lawyer."

"I'm talking to one."

"I'm not that kind of lawyer." He laughed, "Seriously, you're in deep shit here. I'll send you the name of someone in Seattle. It would be good to have someone local on it."

"Okay."

Eric fell silent again.

"You there?"

"Yeah," he said. "I have a bad feeling about this, man. I think maybe you should get back to Portland."

My eyes went to the window again. Emery was sitting at the counter, perched on one of the stools. She had Lily's file open, its pages spread out before her. "I'm working on it."

I watched the road where Dutch's truck had vanished around the turn. My grandfather had never really gotten along with the town, or any person, really. Growing up, I'd thought he was paranoid, fixated on a threat that wasn't really there. But he'd been right. The town wanted the orchard, and they'd taken it. What were they willing to do to keep it?

When my mom told me she wanted to leave Saoirse, I thought it was because she couldn't bear the rejection of the town, but maybe she'd known what I hadn't—that these people weren't just quiet, rural folk with strange superstitions who wanted to live in peace. There was a shadow on Saoirse. And it was growing by the day.

Emery didn't look up from the paper in her hand as I came in. The coffeepot dripped and sputtered beside the stove, but she ignored it, her eyes pinned to one of the photographs. "What does that look like to you?" She set it down.

I came to stand behind her, studying the image. It was the one of Lily's hand, where a bracelet around her wrist was no more than a blur. "Like a bracelet. Why?"

"It doesn't look like a chain. It almost looks like twine or something. Or willow." Her voice trailed off.

"Willow like the tree?"

"Yeah, my grandmother taught us how to make these twisted willow bracelets when we were little. We used to make them all the time," she said, distracted. "What did Eric say?"

"Exactly what you thought he would. The original copy of Henry's will names me the beneficiary. Of everything."

Emery's eyes widened. "So, you own the orchard."

The thought made me feel like the entire house was turning on an axis around me. I hated the orchard. Not just because of the expectations it had put on me, but because of what it had done to my family. It was a curse. A sickness. I'd never wanted anything to do with it, and to know that it belonged to me felt like a cancer growing in my gut.

Emery returned the photo to the stack, staring at me. "What are you going to do?"

"I don't know."

She tucked her hair behind her ears, a gesture that made her suddenly look so much younger. I kept forgetting that I hadn't seen her in so long. It felt like fitting a piece back into me that had gone missing. Like I could finally draw the air deep into my lungs again after fourteen years of shallow breath.

I came to stand on the other side of the counter, watching her bite her thumbnail as she tried to work it out in her mind. "We need to talk about this," I said.

"What?"

"Me and you."

She wet her lips, sitting up straighter as she closed the file in front of her. "Okay."

"I can't stay here," I began.

"I know."

"But after last night, I don't know how I'm going to leave if you're not coming with me." I just said it. We didn't have time to dance around this thing. I'd lost any shred of pride a long time ago when it came to Emery.

She looked stunned by the words. Her gaze moved over me, like she was remembering last night, and I had to clamp my hands down on the edge of the counter to keep from touching her.

"Do you *want* me to come with you?" she asked.

"Yeah. I do."

I knew it was crazy. That to anyone else, none of it would make sense. But Emery and I had always been something that didn't make sense, and I'd lived long enough without her to worry about the risk of sounding like an idiot.

She sat still, winding a strand of her hair around her finger.

"What are you thinking?"

She hesitated. "What if this is just unresolved feelings, like a need for closure? Or some kind of fantasy we're trying to play out or something?"

"It's not. You know it's not, and so do I." I could see that she was afraid. I couldn't blame her.

"Everything's changed. *We've* changed. We don't even know each other anymore."

"Yes, we do."

"I'm not the same girl you gave those ferry tickets to, August."

"But you kept them," I said

She shifted on the stool, her cheeks flushing a little.

"Dutch said you wouldn't marry him. Why?"

"Because I don't love him."

"You guys have been together for years. Why couldn't you love him?"

She stared at me, unblinking.

I'd known the moment I saw her standing in the road after I arrived on the island. I'd known it the first time I kissed her. The first time I'd told her that I loved her. I couldn't be anyone else's because I was hers. I'd always be hers. If she wasn't going to say it, then I would.

"I know we've both had a life since the last time we were together, but I'm so tired of being without you. I don't want to do it anymore."

The faintest trace of a smile surfaced on her lips. "Where would we go?"

The dread I'd felt as I said the words dissolved. She wasn't saying yes, but she wasn't saying no, either.

"My life is in Portland. But I'll make a new one anywhere with you."

She fell silent again, but I could see the flood of thoughts lit behind her eyes.

"I still love you, so how much has changed, really?"

"I don't know," she said, her voice small.

I wasn't asking a small thing. And it wasn't as simple as a yes or a no. There was her dad. Albertine. Nixie. The shop. And it would take time for her to trust me again, if she ever could. I hadn't thought for even a second when I got off the ferry that I would be standing here. But it was also all I'd ever wanted.

"Will you think about it?"

She pressed her fingers to her mouth, staring out the window for a long moment before she answered. Her hands folded beneath her chin as her eyes focused on me.

"Yes."

Fifty-One

EMERY

THE WHOLE TOWN WAS at the pub. I filled glass after glass with beer from the tap as my father took orders with a rag thrown over one shoulder. The sound of the busy kitchen clanged behind me. All the families had come for lunch after graduation, and my classmates were still dressed in their nice clothes. I, on the other hand, smelled like spilled beer and the stew that was cooking on the stove.

In a few hours, everyone would gather at the orchard for a bonfire and dinner before some of the parents ended up back here for a nightcap and most of the graduates would head to the beach.

I hadn't really thought about missing any of my classmates. As only children with no siblings, August, Dutch, Lily, and I had kept to ourselves for the most part through the years, making our own kind of little family. A few of the kids from our school would head to college in the fall, including Dutch, to everyone's surprise. The others would stay on the island and start working for their parents or for the orchard. Lily would be among them. As far as she knew, so would August and me.

Just as I thought it, she came through the door and a wall of sunlight spilled into the pub, pooling on the wood floor. She scanned the tables until she spotted me and her hand shot into the air, waving.

My stomach immediately dropped, making me feel sick. I hadn't told her yet that we were leaving, and it was less about the secret than it was dreading her reaction. She was fun and fiery and spontaneous. She was also self-centered, and terrified of being alone. Lily would be angry. There was no doubt about that. But I wouldn't have to be here, forced to endure the fallout of the news.

"Go ahead, honey." Dad took the full glass from my hand, jerking his chin toward the empty booth in the corner. "I'll bring you guys a couple of burgers."

"Are you sure?" I said, half hoping he'd force me to stay behind the bar.

"Go, Em. I got it."

"Thanks, Daddy." I reluctantly untied the apron from around my waist.

I grabbed two bottles of soda from the icebox in the back and followed Lily to the booth, climbing in on one side while she took the other. She immediately reached for a sugar packet and tore open the corner, sprinkling it into her mouth. It was one of those little rituals—things that never changed. Until now.

"Sorry I'm late." She groaned. "My parents made me take a million pictures in that stupid robe."

"It's okay. My dad needed my help anyway."

She sat up straighter, eyes sparkling as she tapped her fingers together in front of her. "Okay, so what's the big news? I'm dying here!"

I lifted the bottle from the table, staring at the wet ring it left behind. I hadn't really decided how to say it, but I was out of time to figure it out. There was no good way to break it to her.

"Come on!" She plucked another sugar packet from the bowl. "The suspense has been killing me."

"Well," I forced a smile. "It's big."

"Okay . . ." She was getting more excited by the minute. I didn't know if that was a good thing or a bad thing.

I leaned forward. "August and I are leaving tomorrow."

Her smile faltered a little. "Oh." She didn't even try to hide her disappointment. But she seemed more annoyed than hurt. "To go where?"

"Seattle."

"Okay. When do you get back?" She was already bored with it. That was like her, too.

"We're not," I said, lowering my voice. "We're not coming back."

In an instant, all of the color drained from Lily's face, making her blue eyes brighter. "What do you mean?"

I could feel the air around us shifting. The pub seemed hotter, more claustrophobic. "I mean we're not coming back. We're going to travel. I'm not really sure yet exactly where."

Lily's hand flattened on the table between us and she stared at it. "Are you serious?"

"Yeah." I was still trying to hold us above water with a smile, but Lily was sinking fast.

"You can't do that."

I looked around us, making sure that no one was listening. She looked like she was about to have a fit.

"He can't leave," she said, panicked.

"What?"

"The . . . the orchard," she stuttered. "August can't just leave the orchard."

"He doesn't want to run it, Lily. You know that."

"It doesn't matter what he wants!" She slammed her hand on the table, making me jump. Several people were staring now.

"Jesus, Lily, will you *shut up*?"

Tears welled in her eyes. "You're not going."

"Yes, we are. This is exactly why I didn't tell you. I knew you would freak out."

"How could you just lie to me?"

"I didn't. I was just waiting to tell you because I knew you would do this."

"Do what?"

I waved a hand between us. "This. Make it all about you."

She was breathing hard now, her eyes jumping around the table as her mind raced. "I'll tell your parents. I'll walk over there right now and tell your dad."

"Lily!" I whispered hoarsely. "What the hell?"

Her eyes traveled past me, to where my dad was walking over with two plates.

"*Don't*," I rasped. "I'm serious, Lily. Don't say anything."

A furious tear rolled down her cheek before she stood, hitting the table with her hip and nearly knocking the sodas over. My heartbeat sprinted ahead of my breath as I watched her walk straight toward my dad and I twisted the napkin in my lap until it burned against my palms. But just when I was sure she would stop him, she didn't. She pushed through the tables instead, storming out.

"What was that?" He watched as she disappeared through the door.

"Nothing." I swallowed hard, prying my hands free of the napkin. "Just Lily being Lily."

Fifty-Two

LEODA

THE LEAVES UNFURLED INSIDE the teapot, the fragrant steam curling up into the cold air as I set it on the wooden tray and replaced the lid.

This wasn't the kind of tea made for a social call. It was the kind you set on the table to make people more comfortable when there were uncomfortable topics to be discussed, and then poured out an hour later when it was cold. I'd made many pots of tea just like it through the years, and I suspected it wouldn't be my last.

The call had come just before breakfast, and there was a knock at the door a half hour later. I'd opened it to the last person I'd expected to be our ticket out of this.

I picked up the tray and the teacups jostled on their saucers. The gleam of sunlight on a windshield caught my eye through the window, and I watched the road through the lace curtains as the car drove past, waiting to be sure it didn't pull into the drive.

When it was out of sight, I pushed into the swinging kitchen door with my hip and made my way back into the dining room, where Jake and Dutch were waiting.

Dutch's busted, swollen face was purple on one side, the corner of his lip scabbed over. "If you come by the apothecary, I'll give you something for that," I said, frowning.

I set down the tray in the middle of the table, taking my own seat.

"Thanks, Leoda." Jake stared at the tea, but even he knew not to touch it.

I looked from him to Dutch. "Well, what is it?"

He gave Dutch a gentle nod. "Go ahead, son."

Dutch cleared his throat, sitting up straighter in his seat, and I resisted the urge to tap my finger impatiently on the table.

"Look, I'm not stupid enough to believe the bullshit reasons you gave when you offered me the position at the orchard. I'm going to guess it had something to do with knowing I wouldn't ask questions, and I haven't. So, keep that in mind when you're deciding whether to pull me back into this shit."

I arched an eyebrow at him. The arrangement with Dutch had been a kind of silent agreement between all of us—a truce. He took the chair in the manager's office and in exchange, we forgave him the sins he'd never admitted to. But sitting there now, he just looked like the fool of a kid we all remembered.

"Fair enough," I said.

He nodded, shooting another look in Jake's direction. "I lied. About that night."

"Clearly." My irritation laced into the words. I'd played these games with him and Emery long enough.

Dutch's eyes snapped up, focusing on me. The pulse at his neck was racing beneath the skin.

"I'd wager almost everyone on this island knows you *lied*. The question is about what exactly? And why?"

He stared at the table in a long silence. "About being with August at the lighthouse. I wasn't with him."

Finally, we were getting somewhere. "Did August ask you to lie for him?"

"No." He paused. "I told Jake I was with him because I knew he was looking for August. I wanted to protect him. And myself."

"Yourself?" My eyebrows raised.

He glanced up at Jake. "Lily and I were seeing each other before she died. I was afraid that if people found out, someone would think I had something to do with what happened to her."

The charming look that usually hung on Dutch's face was gone now, leaving only the scared little boy I'd known for thirty-three years. I'd delivered him, red and screaming, under a waxing moon and I'd known the minute I laid eyes on him that he would be trouble. Dutch had always been like a stray pup on the island, especially after his dad died. But anyone with a lick of sense could see that he was a coward.

I sank back into my chair. "If you lied about being with him at the lighthouse that night, then where was he?"

"I don't know."

"You never asked him?"

"No. I thought it was better if we just kept to the story."

Again, I looked to Jake. His face was unreadable, but I knew the way his mind worked. There was an undercurrent to the way he stood against the wall, his back rigid.

"The last time I saw him, he was working at the orchard before the party. I left to go home and change and when I got back, he wasn't there."

"All right." I folded my hands on top of the table. "Why don't you head over to the orchard. You'll be late and we don't need anyone wondering where you are. Jake and I need to talk."

Dutch hesitated, looking to Jake as if needing his permission. It made me roll my eyes.

"Go ahead," Jake said.

Dutch nodded, rising from the chair. We listened to his footsteps trail to the door before it opened and closed.

"Well? Now are you ready to do something about it?" I said, watching Jake from across the table.

He stared out the window. There was a reason he brought Dutch to me. We'd all done what we had to for the island, but some of us were more reliable than others.

"The lie that boy told was the only thing standing between you and charging August with murder," I said. "I don't think there can be any doubt now. He got away with it and now he's back, trying to take what's ours."

That godforsaken family had had us under a blade for years, wielding the orchard over the town to maintain the power they held. Now, almost every Salt was a rotting corpse, the last of them just waiting to be shot from the sky.

Jake finally turned to face me, running his fingers along the brim of his hat. "Maybe it's time we handled this," he said.

"Maybe it is." I pursed my lips, satisfied.

"I don't want my brother involved."

"He doesn't need to be." It was better that way, I thought. The mistake we'd made last time was involving too many people. This would have to be quiet.

He slipped the hat back on his head, pulling the keys from his pocket. He gave me one last, long look before he left.

I fixed my eyes on the steam still streaming up from the spout of the teapot, my mind turning. On Saoirse, we took care of our own. We'd been doing it for generations, and this was no different.

I stretched out my hands before me, waiting for the tingle to surface in my fingertips. Still, there was nothing. There hadn't been in years. Magic was a tricky thing. Fickle. And the last time I'd used it, it had failed me. But this was a problem that had more than one kind of solution.

Fifty-Three

EMERY

THE WILLOW TREE HUGGED the side of Albertine's little house, towering over it like a giant. The leaves had all dropped and now its long wispy branches swayed in the wind, tapping the windows like fingers drumming a song.

That house and the memories beneath its roof had been like an anchor for me. The thought of leaving them turned my stomach.

My boots stopped at the bottom step of the porch, pinning me there. It wasn't just the thought of my dad that had kept me here. It was Albertine. Nixie. The memory of my mother. Deep down, I also knew it was fear. I'd wanted to leave. I'd been desperate for it. But I'd also been afraid to go alone.

I hadn't given August an answer to his question or even made a decision, but I didn't know if I needed to. If he hadn't asked me to leave, I was almost certain I would have followed him anyway.

The feel of him was still alive on my skin, making me tremble. It was a kind of magic that scared me. Because if I lost August Salt a second time, I wasn't sure I would survive it.

I wiped my feet on the mat before I opened the door and stepped inside. "Oma?"

I called out, but there was no answer. No smell of jam simmering on the stove or beat of footsteps in the hallway. My heart always skipped just a little when that happened, reminding me that there would come a day when this house no longer had her in it. I feared that, too.

I made my way to the bedroom, where Albertine's patchwork quilt was spread neatly over the made bed. "Oma?"

A clinking sound echoed outside and I went to the window, pulling back the thin curtain to see the greenhouse at the bottom of the hill. The door was propped open and through the hazy glass, I could see the bright red glow of Albertine's coat.

The tension in my shoulders unwound just a little, and I went out into the hallway, following it through the house. I paused when I passed the mantel above the fireplace, where *The Blackwood Book of Spells* was resting in its place. Only a few days ago, I'd stood in that very same spot, holding the heavy book in my hands with tears streaming down my cheeks. But in the end, I hadn't been able to cut the bind that had been my agony for fourteen years. There were some things that were a part of you, no matter how badly they hurt.

I reached up and touched the thick leather cover, feeling the hum of it beneath my fingertips. Maybe I'd be leaving that behind, too— the magic. The quiet whisper of the island.

My gaze drifted to the window, where I could see a steady drip of rain was falling from the corner of the greenhouse in the distance. I opened the back door, following the stone trail through the tangle of climbing roses that lined the walkway. They reached across the path in wandering blooms, glittering with raindrops.

"Emery? That you?" Albertine stood in the doorway, an old, mineralized clay pot in her hands. Her plaid scarf was wrapped up around her head, her winter boots laced high up her legs over her jeans.

"There you are." I shook out my wet hair, letting it fall down my back as I ducked inside.

The mossy glass panes bathed everything in the greenhouse in an emerald light. The bright faces of dahlias and hyacinths and anemones peeked out from behind knotted vines dangling from the old metal shelves.

The plants were another one of those things about Albertine that defied her lack of sight. It wasn't just the herbalist in her that made the greenhouse stay filled with blooms, even in the dead of winter. She had never in her life seen any of the flowers she tended, yet she kept them going long after their season. The magic she wielded was rarely even spoken aloud. It touched every corner of her house and the land, like a wild vine.

"Didn't know you were coming up." Albertine went back to the potting bench with a bit of a limp in her step. Her bones weren't warmed up enough to loosen the stiff joints that flared when it was cold.

"Just thought I'd check in on you." I kissed her on the cheek before I slid onto the rusted stool beside her.

"Well, make yourself useful then." She pointed a crooked finger in the direction of another empty pot.

I obeyed, turning it upside down into the bin on the ground to empty it of the old, dry soil. The violets were waiting on the bench beside it, and I trimmed the spent stalk before setting it inside.

I caught her watching me. "What?"

"Something's up. I can smell it in the air." She leaned into the bench.

"Are you going to tell me what you came all the way up here for or do I have to pry it out of you?"

I gave her a look from the corner of my eye. She could smell bullshit from a mile away. "I want to ask you something."

"All right, shoot."

"It's about the night of the fire."

Her hands stilled on the pot and she turned toward me. "All right," she said, hesitant.

"You called Jake that afternoon because you thought you had a break-in."

"Yeah."

"Around three P.M., right?"

"I guess so. It was a long time ago, honey."

"Can you tell me what you remember?"

She set a hand on her hip, her blank stare drifting past me. "What is this about?"

"I just need to know what happened."

She sighed, flinging the dirt from her hands. "Well, I came in from the garden and there was someone in the house. I felt it right away— I was in the kitchen and I could hear footsteps, breathing. They moved from the living room to the front door and then they were gone. I called Jake and he came over a few minutes later and checked everything out, but nothing had been taken."

"Who do you think it was, then?"

She shrugged. "Beats me. It wasn't long after Beltane. The veil was thin."

There were two times a year that the veil was thin. Beltane on May 1, and Samhain, which was coming in only a few days. It was said that on those nights, spirits walked back and forth over the crossing to the Otherworld and I'd seen my fair share of strange things to believe it. "Ghosts don't use the front door, Oma."

"Well, after everything that happened that night, Jake looked into it again, but he didn't find anything."

"Maybe it was someone who lives here."

She grunted. "I don't think so."

"Why not?"

"Why would they sneak around? If it was someone from the island, then I knew them. No reason to skulk out and not say anything."

"Unless they were doing something they weren't supposed to," I thought aloud.

I packed in the dirt around the roots of the violets in the pot as I went through it again. If it was someone from the island, it could have been anyone. But there was nothing to steal in the house. I couldn't think of a single thing Albertine owned that would be worth anything.

She stretched her arthritic hands before her. "I don't like all this talk about the past, Em. No need to tempt the spirits. We should let sleeping dogs lie."

The faint sound of tapping rose over the wind outside and my eyes went to the house up the hill. On the far side, the branches of the willow were scraping against the kitchen window.

I went rigid, my fingernails digging down into the soil.

The willow.

Beside me, Albertine could sense my stillness. "What is it?"

"Lily was wearing one of those willow branch bracelets you taught us how to make. Do you remember?"

She frowned. "Yes, I remember."

It was an old practice that my grandmother had learned from her grandmother—tying a braided willow branch around your wrist to protect you from dark magic.

"She had matches. And wax, dripped on her dress," I whispered.

"Emery." Albertine's voice deepened, warping. I couldn't tell if it was her or if it was me. Everything was jumbled. Splintered.

"Lily was found in the middle of the woods, but she drowned. How did she get there?" My mind was racing so fast now, my mouth could hardly keep up. "If there was wax, then maybe there was a candle. And she was wearing a willow branch around her wrist," I murmured.

Albertine was suddenly careful to keep her face turned away from me.

"What does that sound like to you?" I swallowed.

"Well, that sounds like . . ." She fell quiet, pressing her lips together as if to keep herself from saying more.

"Oma?"

There was no mirth in her voice this time. No telltale smirk at the corner of her mouth. "I was going to say, it sounds like . . . spell-work."

"It was her," I breathed, pulling my hands from the pot and walking toward the door. "She was here."

"Em?" Albertine followed on my heels, her hand tapping the fence behind me every few steps to follow.

I climbed the hill and pushed through the back door, going to the fireplace. I took the book of spells from the mantel, cradling it in my arms as I carried it to the kitchen and set it down on the table.

"What's going on?" Albertine had her ear turned toward me, her brow wrinkled as she tried to decipher the sounds.

"She came here. For the book of spells," I said, flipping through the pages. "But she wasn't doing just any magic. If she was wearing the willow branch, she was doing dark magic."

"She couldn't have. There's no way she could have worked a spell like that."

"Exactly."

Albertine lifted a hand to her mouth, thinking.

"What could she have been doing?"

Albertine shook her head. "I don't know. A candle and a willow branch aren't much to go on."

"Seaweed." I said, remembering. "She had seaweed in her stomach."

Slowly, Albertine's expression changed.

"What? What is it?"

"There is a spell in that book. For drowning." The last word was almost inaudible. She reached over me, feeling the edges of the pages. "Somewhere in here." She held open a section and I started turning the pages, studying them one by one.

"Sailor's something."

My finger frantically dragged over the handwriting until I found it.

Sailor's Scourge.

It was an old spell. A very old one. The edges of the paper were brittle and yellowed, the ink blotted in places along a drawing of a branch.

"On a dark moon." I read aloud. "In the right hand, the anchor. In the left, a stalk of henbane. Spoken three times over candle's flame, with blood and seaweed on the tongue: 'air to water, water to lungs.'"

A sharp chill crept over my skin. "What do you mean it's a spell for drowning?"

"It's not all blessings and abundance charms in that book, love. You know that." She answered. "I suppose it was a spell crafted to drown someone. By the name it was given, I can guess it was a sailor. A fisherman, maybe?"

I read the words again. "What is the anchor? Like on a ship?"

"No. An anchor binds the spell to its intended recipient."

"How?"

"It's an item, usually. A possession. A lock of hair . . ."

"That doesn't make any . . ." The words disappeared on my tongue as it came to me. The necklace. A sick feeling roiled in my belly. "Oma"—my voice was brittle—"she had my necklace."

Fifty-Four

AUGUST

THIS TIME, I BOUGHT two tickets.

Emery hadn't said yet if she was coming with me, but if she did, I was going to be ready for the first ferry out in the morning. If she didn't, I had no idea how I was going to leave without her.

I came up the drive, shooting a glance in the direction of the burned truck. Maybe it would sit there another fourteen years, slowly eaten up by the vines and reeds. Like everything else, Saoirse would take it for her own.

The cottage was bathed in sunlight and it beamed through the windows as I came inside. The wood floor popped in a familiar pattern as I checked the rooms one last time. All I had to do now was lock the door and give the keys to Bernard. My stuff was packed at Emery's, along with the paperwork I was able to find in my mom's files, but I'd decided against taking anything else from the cottage. I'd gone this long without the keepsakes my mother had left behind, and now they felt like they belonged to another time. I wasn't sad to see them go.

But I stopped short as I passed the fireplace, my eyes pulled to the photograph on the mantel. The one of my mom and Hannah, with

Emery and me perched on their hips. Fishing boats bobbed in the gray expanse of sea behind them and their feet were bare on the sun-lit dock.

I picked it up, wiping the glass with the palm of my hand, almost smiling. Almost.

This, I'd take.

I looked over the living room and kitchen, surprising myself when I realized that I wanted to be sure I would remember it. The percola-tor on the stove, the rag rug beneath the sofa, the retro chairs at the kitchen table that looked like they'd once lived in a diner. The last time I left this house, I hadn't been ready to say goodbye, but stand-ing there now, I was. Maybe because I wasn't running this time.

I went out onto the porch and jostled the key in the temperamen-tal lock with the frame tucked beneath my arm. When I finally got it turned, the key stuck. I tried to yank it free, jiggling the handle until it rotated another centimeter.

The sharp flash of movement in the shadow at my feet made me freeze, and my fingers tightened on the knob. The slats in the porch creaked and I drew in a breath, listening. But by the time my eyes focused on the reflection behind me, it was too late. The heavy blow of something hard hit the back of my head, sending me forward, and the sound of shattered glass was the last thing I heard before it hit me again.

Then, there was only black.

Fifty-Five

EMERY

WE HAD TO GET off this fucking island.

I burst through the door, swallowing down the burn climbing up my throat. The house was dark, the fireplace cold. But if we hurried, we could catch the last ferry before it left the harbor.

"August?"

I went to the bedroom, opening the wardrobe and pulling the first bag I saw from inside. I didn't care which one. It landed on the bed before I took an armful of clothes from the top drawer: underwear, T-shirts, a few sweaters.

"August!"

I reached into the pocket of my jacket, finding my cellphone, and searched with trembling fingers for the number he'd given me. It took several tries, but when I finally had it ringing, I put it on speaker and went back into the room, pulling my winter coat from the hanger. We had a little more than twenty minutes to make it to the harbor. We couldn't wait until morning. We couldn't wait another hour.

When the call went to voicemail, I cursed, dialing again.

A soft buzz in the house made me pause and I abandoned the bag, following the hall back to the living room. There, on the table beside the sofa, was August's phone. My name was illuminated in white letters across the screen.

His packed bag was still on the floor, tucked under the kitchen table, and across the road, the windows of the Salt cottage were dark. The hair on the back of my neck stood on end when I saw the wall of black clouds tangling in the sky.

I hung up, pulling the door back open. I crossed the road, glancing over my shoulder to the darkening woods. The starlings were still singing, even though it was nearly night. The sound of it was like the cut of a blade in my ears, echoing in my head like screaming. They skipped through the branches overhead, moving from one tree to the next as I walked and I picked up my pace, trying not to look at them. They were following me.

The door to the cottage was closed, but when the sound of glass crunched under my boot, I didn't take another step. I hesitated before I looked down.

Scattered across the porch, shattered glass trailed to the left of the door, where a gold-rimmed picture frame was lying facedown. I crouched down slowly, picking it up and turning it over. It was us. August, Eloise, me, and my mother.

"August!" I shot back to my feet, trying the knob, but the door was locked. "August!"

My hands pressed to the window as I looked inside. Everything was dark, the lights off, the house tidied. He wasn't there.

I turned in a circle, suddenly feeling cold as the whispers of the woods found me. My eyes skipped over the trees, my heart beating so hard that the black pushed in around my vision.

The starlings weren't the only ones watching. The island was watching, too. I could feel it.

The truck engine roared as I plowed down the dirt road in the pouring rain, the dim headlights barely piercing the darkness. The sound of the ferry horn was far away as it drifted from the harbor. In minutes, it would be gone.

I took the two turns to the fishing cabin and the road narrowed before it came to a dead end. I slammed the gear into park, climbing out of the truck without even turning the ignition.

I ran up the walk and shoved through the door.

My dad nearly fell out of his chair, jolting when he saw me. "Em?"

"Where is he?" I spoke through gritted teeth, meeting his eyes with every bit of fury boiling inside me.

But he looked utterly confused, hovering over his open tackle box with a pair of small pliers clutched in his hand. "What? Who?"

"August!" I screamed. "Where is he?"

Dad looked around the cabin, getting to his feet unsteadily. "I—I don't know."

I raked both hands into my hair, trying to think. I was shaking.

"What's going on?" He reached for me, but I stepped back, a cry breaking in my throat. "Em?"

"August is gone."

"He left?"

"No—I"—I stammered—"I don't know. He couldn't have. His stuff is still at my house."

The question immediately surfaced on his face. Why was August's stuff at my house? What was he doing there? But he didn't ask.

"Someone left a note saying if he didn't leave, they were going to turn in evidence about Lily. He was looking into the orchard and—"

My father's hardened gaze settled on me.

"What?"

"You told him? About the deed?" he said, realizing it.

I didn't answer. There was no way around it. I'd chosen August over him. And I'd do it again.

"He's looking into the orchard?"

"Yes."

His expression changed as he dropped the pliers on the table.

"Dad? What is it?"

His lips pressed together in a hard line and he stared at me for a moment before he stalked past me, toward the kitchen. I watched as he picked the phone up off the wall and dialed with heavy fingers. He kept his back turned to me as it rang, but after a few moments, he hung up. His hand didn't leave the receiver as he stared at the floor, thinking. When he picked it up again, he dialed a different number. Still, no answer. After the third try, he slammed the phone down, heading for the fireplace.

"Where are you going?"

He went to the cabinet against the far wall, opening it with a steady hand. I watched as he pulled his rifle from inside.

"Dad?"

He was already shrugging on his jacket. I followed him to the road and he watched me over the hood of the truck before he opened the driver's-side door. "I can talk to them."

Them. So, I'd been right. This wasn't as simple as a jealous Dutch or a vengeful Jake. My dad knew exactly what was happening here.

"What's going on?"

He didn't answer, climbing inside and setting the rifle against his leg. When I was settled beside him, he turned the key and reversed without even so much as a glance in the mirror.

This wasn't about Lily. Maybe it had never been.

This was about the orchard.

Fifty-Six

SAOIRSE ISLAND

3:36 P.M.

The flash of Lily Morgan's flaxen hair flit through the trees like a fire spark as she ran.

There was a storm on the horizon. The smell of it seeped through the humid air, filling it with the sweetness of the oncoming summer. But it wouldn't reach the island in near enough time.

The front of her graduation dress was still unbuttoned, slipped over one shoulder, and the sound of her cries was broken and muffled, lost to the wind that snaked through the trees.

The burn was still there, alive on her lips, where she'd pressed her mouth against August's throat. He'd smelled like the wild thyme that grew along the rows of apple trees. He'd tasted like salt.

Another broken cry escaped her lips as she remembered it, clumsily pulling the dress closed with trembling fingers. In the next moment, he'd shoved her away, and the look in his eye had been the moment that the blade of knowing had twisted in her gut. More than every time she'd watched him touch Emery. More than every time he'd looked away when he caught her staring.

She had always been the pretty one and both she and Emery had known it. But Emery had been the kind one. The good one. And for as long as Lily had wanted August, all he'd ever wanted was Emery Blackwood.

Albertine's house appeared in the trees ahead and Lily stopped, watching the windows. Almost everyone on the island was either at the pub or getting ready for the party at the orchard. But there was still time to fix this.

The door wasn't locked because it never was. Lily let herself in, walking straight across the living room, to the fireplace. There, *The Blackwood Book of Spells* sat on the mantel.

It was the only book of its kind on the island. Most families had a spell book that was passed from one daughter to the next, but not like this one. *The Blackwood Book of Spells* was a complete and sprawling chronicle that went back for generations. And while some families had torn out the pages of dark magic in their books, the Blackwoods hadn't.

When Lily and Emery were children, they'd pore over the spells by firelight, reading them together. And she knew exactly the one she needed.

Lily pulled the book into her arms and sat on the floor, opening the heavy cover. The pages greeted her with the familiar smell of lavender and cedar. She scanned the handwritten words for the one she was looking for—Sailor's Scourge. It would have to look like an accident, and Emery wouldn't be the first person on this island to drown.

The thought put a pit in her stomach, but she swallowed it down. She was only doing what she had to. What the island wanted.

When she found it, she quickly copied the spell word for word onto the crumpled notebook paper she'd brought with her. But when the back screen door screeched, Lily's heart stopped beating.

Slowly, her eyes lifted to see Albertine's shadow on the kitchen floor. It didn't move as the door slammed behind her.

"Hello?" Her raspy voice echoed through the house. "Who's there?"

Lily lifted the paper from the book and closed it as quietly as she could before she got back to her feet. Albertine appeared at the end of the hallway, her ear turned toward the living room. Her gardening gloves were clutched in one hand, and the other followed the wall as she took a tentative step forward.

Lily hadn't thought to check the greenhouse.

"Hello?" she said again. Albertine couldn't see her, but Lily could swear that her eyes focused on her face, as if some part of her did recognize Lily's presence.

Lily set the book of spells back on the mantel, creeping backward with her heart hammering in her ears. In the next second, she was pushing through the door, onto the porch. She came down the steps, rounding the house before Albertine made it outside. And as she passed the willow at the corner, she reached up, snatching a branch from where it hung.

4:04 P.M.

Main Street was deserted. Lily kept to the cobblestone walk that hugged the shop doors, watching the darkened windows over her shoulder. The few businesses that were open this time of year closed up for the day. Even the pub would soon turn out its lights. The town's residents would find their fill of ale at the orchard with the sound of music on the record player in the barn.

Lily's reflection drifted across the painted window of her grandmother's apothecary before she slipped inside, eyes fixed on the glass cabinet behind the counter. The crowded shelves were filled with nightshades and poisons, teeth and scales.

She crouched down, pulling on the brass handle, and the door popped open. Her gaze ran over the labels quickly until she found the one she needed: henbane. The white fragile blooms were like crinkled tissue paper, their black centers like wide, open eyes.

A rush of hot blood coursed through Lily's veins as she picked it up, turning it over in her hands. It was followed by a trace of an involuntary smile on her lips. In her fingers, she held the key to everything she'd ever wanted. All Lily had to do was reach out and take it.

4:48 P.M.

Lily lifted Emery's bedroom window carefully, watching the road over her shoulder. She only came in this way when she told her parents that she was staying the night with Emery but spent the first half of it with Dutch at the lighthouse. Those nights, she lied to Emery, too.

It had started at the beach, when the four of them spent the night drinking ciders in the dark water. After an hour or two, August and Emery left Dutch and Lily behind. They were always doing that. And when Lily couldn't stand the idea of August's hands on Emery any longer, she'd pulled Dutch into her, letting him feel her against him.

It had taken him a moment to kiss her, but when he did, she closed her eyes. And she wasn't thinking about him. She was thinking about August. She was imagining that it was *his* hands underwater, finding their way beneath her skirt. The heat of *his* mouth open on her shoulder.

What she thought was one night turned into many and the longer it went on, the less Dutch wanted to keep the secret. Now, there was a soft curve to her belly. A swell to her breasts. The baby would be a problem to solve once Emery was gone. Lily would have to cross that bridge when she got there.

Beside the bed, Emery's clothes from the graduation were in a heap where she'd stepped out of her sandals and let her dress fall to the floor. Lily climbed inside the room and made her way to the dresser against the wall.

She tried not to think about how many times Emery had been with August in that bed. How many times she'd felt him inside her. In a few hours, it wouldn't matter.

A photo of Lily and Emery was taped to the mirror, a blurry polaroid of them on the dock. Lily lifted a finger and touched it, swallowing when pain surfaced in her throat. She loved Emery, it was true. But she was so tired of not being her.

She rooted through the jewelry box until she found it—the butterfly necklace Noah had given to Emery for her birthday. She wore it almost every day, and it was as good an anchor as any.

She dropped it into her pocket and then her eyes fell to the end of the bed, where the corner of a suitcase was sticking out from under the quilts. Lily's vision blurred, fury simmering in her gut. Emery was just going to leave and never look back. Like Lily had never existed.

She scribbled down the note and left it on the pillow.

I'm sorry. Meet me at Halo Beach at 6 and we'll go to the party together.

It would need to be timed perfectly. But Emery was never late.

5:57 P.M.

She'd chosen the spot for its circular clearing in the trees. It was a dark moon and Lily needed every bit of that power to summon the island's magic.

She sat cross-legged on the soft earth, setting out the things she'd brought with her. The candle, the matches, the necklace, the henbane. The seaweed she'd collected at the beach and the salt. And as soon as the long hand on her watch ticked to six o'clock, she got to work.

Her hands were steady as she pressed the candle's end into the dirt and struck the match, cupping her hand to protect its flame. When the wick was blackened at the tip, she lifted the pin, pressing it to her fingertip until the blood beaded there like a shining, crimson pearl. Once the henbane was smoking, she wrapped Emery's necklace around her fist so tightly that it bit into her knuckles.

Her eyes lifted to the darkening sky overhead. A slow warmth rose under her skin and she brought the seaweed to her mouth and swallowed it before she pressed her finger to her tongue. The metallic taste of blood made her mouth water and when she looked up again, the clouds were turning black.

A single tear striped her cheek as she closed her eyes, seeing Emery there. But there was a lightness in her voice as she said it. "Air to water, water to lungs," she breathed.

The wind picked up, pulling at her hair. She could feel the island and the sea that surrounded it. Feel it rushing in her veins.

"Air to water, water to lungs." She said again.

Emery's shape bent and swayed in her mind, and she focused, trying to hold on to it. When she said it a final time, the words burned in her throat. "Air to water! Water to lungs!"

All at once, the wind ceased, leaving the woods unmoving around her. Lily blinked her eyes open between heavy breaths, waiting. The sound of the starlings was in the trees. The distant hum of a car or maybe the generator at the orchard. In the sky, the black clouds had returned to white.

She exhaled, checking her watch again. 6:09. It was done. She could feel it in the air's stillness. In the steady pulse beneath her skin.

Her hands shook as she dug into the earth and buried the candle, the pin, and what was left of the henbane. When she got back to her feet, she brushed off her dress, Emery's necklace still dangling from her fingers.

There was no undoing it now. Emery was gone. There was finally room for Lily to find a way into August's heart, and she would. At the very least, she'd find a way into his bed. And when Lily bore a child that everyone thought was his, she would get what she deserved. For the first time in generations, things would be set right.

It was a Morgan who'd planted the first seeds of the orchard and it was a Salt who'd pried it from her family's white-knuckled fingers.

But there was one thing that Lily had forgotten—that the magic belonged to me.

The woods were quiet except for the sound of the starlings and Lily walked through the thick underbrush, back toward the road that led to the orchard. But before she reached it, a tightness tugged at the bottom of her belly, making her swallow hard. It was followed a few steps later by a shooting pain each time she inhaled.

Lily stopped, her brow cinching the moment she tasted salt on her tongue. When she tried to draw another breath, it wouldn't come.

A small sound escaped her throat, followed by a bubbling. She reached up, touching the corner of her mouth, where cold water was streaming over her chin. Her heart thumped painfully in her chest as she took another step, but she was choking now. Gasping around a throat full of seawater. And when she fell to her knees, the last thing she saw was a starling perched on the branch overhead. It looked down at her, eyes black and unblinking, as Lily Morgan drowned on dry land.

Fifty-Seven

LEODA

THE LAST TIME I stood in the barn loft, we were deciding a man's fate. Now, we would decide another's.

There would be no tea for this meeting. Zachariah, Nixie, and Bernard stood shoulder to shoulder in the cramped room, all looking to me. But if the task at hand was one I could do myself, it would already be done.

I peered through the crack in the door, watching the stairs. The orchard had been empty for hours and Dutch had sent the last of the farmhands home, but we couldn't afford to be seen here. Not tonight.

"What about Noah?" Bernard kept his voice low. He looked antsy.

"Couldn't track him down." I lied.

Emery complicated things for Noah and I didn't trust him to see reason. It had been hard enough to get him to look the other way when we dealt with Henry's will.

Bernard exhaled. "Probably best."

Zachariah didn't look as convinced. He didn't like it when decisions weren't unanimous. Bernard, Nixie, Noah, Zachariah, and I were the five votes of the town council, and it wasn't just road repairs, town events, and harbor matters we dealt with. More than once, we'd taken the very fate of the island into our hands. But this would be the first time we acted without one of our own.

Nixie would be the other problem. Her hands were tucked into the pockets of her overalls as she propped one shoulder against the wood beam at the center of the room. I'd almost left her out of it, too, but I needed another set of hands. And I had enough leverage to keep her in line.

She hadn't said a word since she arrived. Not when I told them about the letter, and not when I told them about Dutch recanting his story.

"It's no different than last time," I said. That uneasy look that was there anytime the subject of the past came up instantly surfaced in their eyes. There wasn't a stone-stomached one among them. "We know what we have to do."

"We don't *have* to do anything," Nixie was the first to argue, which came as no surprise.

I let out a frustrated breath, trying to temper my response. I'd have to handle this with care. "You weren't so reluctant when Hannah told us that Calvin was abusing his wife."

I didn't have the loyalty to Eloise that the others did, but I understood a thing or two about order on the island. I also saw the opportunity for what it was.

"Calvin was a drunk. He was hurting Eloise," Nixie said.

For me, it had never been about saving Eloise Salt and her baby. It was clear from the beginning that getting rid of Calvin was hitting two birds with one very well-aimed stone. One less Salt on Saoirse brought me one step closer to putting things right.

Calvin got warnings first, of course. A visit from Zachariah, Jake, and Noah. They'd hoped after a few broken ribs that he'd come to some sense, but I knew better. I knew the Salts. When he didn't stop hitting Eloise, we dealt with it. We took care of our own on Saoirse.

It was Jake and Noah who'd followed him from the pub and made sure he never made it home. They'd taken him deep into the woods and Jake was the one to pull the trigger. They buried him while Bernard and Zachariah ferried his boat across the Sound and left it to be found in the Seattle Harbor. It didn't take long for it to get reported, and by all accounts, he'd just skipped town.

It wasn't a huge leap for anyone to believe. Calvin was a selfish, cowardly excuse for a man who'd loathed his responsibility to take over the orchard. We were closer than ever to getting Henry to turn it over to the council, but when Eloise gave birth to a baby boy, all of that changed. He finally had his heir and we had nothing.

Calvin was out of the way, but we were still left with two Salts. I'd had plans for August from the time his mother's swollen belly first began to show. He and my own granddaughter Lily were born only months apart, and the natural course of things was to bring the orchard back to the Morgans the same way it had been stolen: marriage. But I hadn't counted on Emery Blackwood or the fact that Lily would do something as stupid as wind up pregnant.

August had never taken to Lily, and it became clear that I'd have to hasten Henry Salt's death. If he died with his only heir not yet of age, we'd have a chance.

I'd spent months preparing the curse for Henry, and I'd cast it by burying the spell deep in the woods. A few days later, the coughing began, and a month after that, the bleeding. There was a palpable relief among the town. We would finally be rid of him, and we were mere days from burying the bastard when I stopped feeling the draw of the island, the buzz of magic missing from my fingertips. And it never returned. Not a single spell or charm had taken life since, and I'd had to wait for his natural death to finally set plans for the orchard into motion. But August was about to destroy all of that.

It was my own fault. I'd delivered August after a thirty-three-hour labor, and I'd held the newborn in my hands the moment he took his first breath. He wasn't just a child. He was a Salt. Another pair of hands to inherit what wasn't his.

I remember looking down at him, hatred boiling inside me at seeing another soul born into the bloodline. If I'd done what I needed to do then, we would have buried an infant, and we wouldn't be here. But there was no going back and changing it now.

The town had a habit of looking the other way when it came to the Salts. They always had. No one gave a shit when Calvin showed up to school covered in bruises, and no one said a thing when the same started happening to August. I'd never liked either of the boys, but I had a responsibility to the orchard.

My great-grandmother planted the first five seeds of the apple orchard and my family line had tended it until one of them married a Salt and the Morgans were pruned from the vine. But I still understood my duty, which was more than I could say for any of this lot. It had taken a lifetime, but I'd done the thing I'd sworn to do. I'd lived to see the orchard untethered from the Salts. And by the time I was laid to rest in that cemetery, I'd rest soundly knowing I had fulfilled my purpose. Even if I'd lost my own magic in the process.

I was born a healer on this island, and the Salts were a bone-deep cancer.

That's why I told Lily exactly what to do when she came to my door, red-faced and crying about August and Emery leaving the island. I told her that the bond between them could only be broken by death. It was easy to reason with someone who was heartsick. It took only minutes to convince her to go to Albertine's for the book of spells, and then I went to the apothecary and unlocked the cupboard, just like I promised.

I knew that trusting her with the task was a risk. I'd have done the spell myself, if I could.

I let out a long, measured breath, looking from Zachariah to Bernard. I'd have to speak the only language these fools understood—a seventeen-year-old dead girl. The town's belief that August killed Lily was enough to get rid of him the first time.

"August killed my granddaughter," I said. "You know it, and I know it. The entire town knows it."

"Just because Dutch lied doesn't mean August killed her." Nixie shot a look to Zachariah, who would be her most likely ally.

I knew how this worked. If I was going to get them on board, we needed all of us.

"There's not an innocent among us," I reminded them, and that got their attention.

It was a dangerous shift in the discussion, but a necessary one. Every single person in the room had been guilty of crimes they'd gone unpunished for.

"We all have blood on our hands, some of us more than others." I eyed Nixie. She and Hannah had led the charge against Calvin, and Nixie herself had been the notary on the orchard's deed.

Zachariah cleared his throat. "We still don't know for sure that he did it. He *could* be innocent."

"Even if that's true—and it's not—we let August go, and it's only a matter of time before this all comes crashing down on top of us. He's on to what we did with the orchard, which means he isn't just a murderer, he's a threat to the island itself. If he goes to a lawyer or to the authorities, it's over. All of it. He could already have the will."

A deep silence fell over the small room and a moment passed before the first of them crossed the line in the sand.

"If we're going to do it, it needs to be tonight." Bernard was the one to say it, but I'd put those words in his mouth. There was a different kind of magic I was wielding now.

"How would it work?" Zachariah asked. Finally, things were moving in the right direction.

"Jake says August had a ferry ticket for the morning. If anyone comes looking, we'll say he left town. Another Salt gone missing. He disappeared before. No one will question it."

"So, what? You're just going to go pull him out of his bed?" Nixie scoffed.

"We don't need to." I lifted my chin. "Jake's already got him up at Wilke's Pointe."

"What?" Bernard's voice filled the room.

Nixie tipped her head back, staring at the ceiling. "Jesus Christ, Leoda."

"Grabbed him this afternoon. This can be clean and tidy. Quick."

"There's nothing tidy about it. He's got a job in Portland. Friends. People who will come looking for him," Nixie said.

"Fine. Then we play it differently this time. Make it look like he took his own life."

She arched an eyebrow at me. "And why would he do that?"

"Guilt," I answered. "We have more than enough evidence to convince anyone of what he did to Lily." I took their silence as a good sign. "Bernard and Jake will take him up to the cliffs at Wilke's Pointe. We leave the body to be spotted by a fisherman. They're in that cove every morning this time of year. Nixie, you can go to the house and make sure there's nothing there that will complicate things. Zach, you keep an eye on Noah until this is all done. We need him to believe the story."

"And Emery?" Nixie asked.

Emery. She was always the problem. Getting between my plans for Lily and August. Never giving up the search for him after he left. She'd been ruining things from the beginning. But I would never convince Nixie that she had to go, too.

"We'll have this taken care of before she wakes up in the morning. She mourned him once. She'll do it again."

I waited for more questions, but they didn't come. The six of us looked at each other, silent. Jake, Bernard, and Nixie still had a lot of years left between them, but Zachariah and I were old now, white hair and wrinkles. Aching bones. Still, there was one thing that bound us to the task—the island.

We'd all made sacrifices for Saoirse. No one more than me.

I found my own eyes in the mirror that hung over the dresser and the light glinted in them. When the words finally made it to my lips, I could feel the decision settling in their minds. "All in favor?"

Fifty-Eight

AUGUST

SMOKE DRIFTED PAST THE open doorway, a spinning plume of white against the black sky.

I couldn't see Jake, but the butt of his cigarette glowed amber in the darkness as he took a final drag and flicked it onto the rocks.

Behind him, a sea of stars stretched and disappeared on the horizon, where the water touched the sky. The bluff overlooked the city far in the distance, and we'd come up here as kids when we didn't want to be found. We weren't the only ones, I realized.

My wrists burned beneath the ropes he'd tied behind me, and the small wooden chair was like a blade against my back. It was nothing to the ache in my head where he'd hit me, or the sharp pain in my ribs every time I drew breath. At least one of them was broken.

"Are you going to tell me what we're doing up here?" I said, watching him pace before the door.

He stopped, scratching his jaw before he finally turned toward me. It wasn't the same Jake I'd grown up with who looked at me from across the room. The one who'd left an ice bucket of fish on our porch at least once a week or the one who I found fixing my mom's truck early in the morning before she woke up. There was a different man behind his eyes now.

"I'm not gonna play games with you, August."

"Really? That's a relief. Because that's what you've been doing since the night of the fire."

His eyes hardened, focusing. That pissed him off. Good.

He stepped inside and closed the door. The tiny room was outfitted with two armchairs before a cold fireplace and a bookshelf built into the wall. It was one of the oldest houses on the island, erected by someone up the Blackwood line.

He sank into one of the chairs, setting both hands on his knees. I couldn't help but notice that his eyes were clear for once. Whatever he was doing, he was doing it lucid.

"You've made a real mess of all this, August. You should have listened to me."

"This place was fucked up long before I was born, Jake."

It was true. Saoirse was like poison. A thick, creeping sickness. And at the heart of it all was the goddamn orchard. My mother had never been able to see that, either.

Jake's eyes ran over me, landing on the trail of blood that had dried stiff on the shoulder of my white T-shirt. I could feel it like scales on my ear and neck.

"It's not the first time someone's beat the shit out of me," I said flatly. "But you already knew that, didn't you?"

He stared at me, clearly uncomfortable.

I smirked. "I thought so. But you never did anything about it, did you? You're good at looking the other way when you want to."

"I figured if you needed my help, you would ask for it."

I swallowed hard against the burn in my throat. Because he was right. I knew that if I had gone to him, he would have helped me. He'd been there for me and my mom for as long as I could remember. But I hadn't gone to Jake because I didn't want my mom to get involved. Maybe he didn't, either.

"You know, I always thought you loved her," I said.

"I did."

I couldn't hide my surprise. I hadn't expected him to answer at all, much less admit it. People had been saying it for my whole life. That Jake had been in love with my mom for years before I was even born. That was one of the reasons the town believed he didn't want to find the evidence to have me charged with murder.

"I don't think it was any kind of secret." His head tilted a little to one side. "I would have done anything for Eloise. And I did."

My brow cinched. Whatever he was referring to filled the room with a deeper cold. The look in his eye was hollow, his voice distant.

"Then why'd you turn against her?"

"I didn't."

"All right. Why'd you turn against me? You know I didn't kill Lily. You knew it the very first time you sat me in your office and asked me."

His eyes shifted away from me. "We do what we have to do, don't we?"

We weren't talking about me or my mom anymore. "Emery." The moment I said her name, his jaw clenched.

Emery was maybe the only thing in the world Jake cared about more than my mom. He'd had a choice, and he'd made it.

"Was she happy? Eloise?" he asked, studying my face for the answer.

If there was ever a soft underbelly to Jakob Blackwood, this was it. Right here. And if I wanted to, I could gut him. But I couldn't pretend like I didn't understand what he'd done and why. All these years, I'd thought he abandoned us, but he'd been trying to protect Emery. At risk to himself and anyone else who got in the way.

"Maybe, in a way," I answered honestly.

He let out a long breath, giving me a nod. "Good."

I had no idea if my mom had been happy in Prosper. She hadn't been herself, that was true. But sometimes I'd thought she'd become someone else and she'd found a way to live with that.

"You know, if all of this is about the orchard, you can have it."

"I'm afraid it's too late for that."

I swallowed hard when his expression didn't change. He'd already made up his mind about whatever we were doing up here. "Then what are you going to do?"

"I told you, we do what we have to."

Bright, white light flashed on the window behind him and Jake stilled. I could just barely hear the sound of tires as he stood and paced to the door.

My pulse climbed, my hands slick where they were tied behind me. Two car doors slammed, followed by footsteps. My breath hitched as Jake turned the knob and the door opened. But when I saw who stood there, I froze.

Leoda Morgan.

The hood of her jacket was pulled up over a knit hat, and her small face was turned toward me. Jake stood well over a head taller than her and he opened the door wider so he could step outside.

She said nothing before the door closed and then there was the sound of voices. It was too muffled to hear over the roar of the wind and the waves crashing at the bottom of the cliffs.

My heart was at a sprint now, the sting of gooseflesh rising on my arms. Whatever was going to happen, it was bad. I could feel it.

I jerked at the binds tied around my wrists, rocking the chair with the force of it. But then the door was opening again, and Jake came back inside, pulling the knife from the pocket of his jeans.

"What are you doing, Jake?"

He didn't answer, coming around me. A second later, I could feel the tug of the ropes as he sawed through them. When my hands were free, he yanked me up by my shirt, shoving me forward.

"What's going on?" I glanced to the open doorway, where the headlights still glared.

Jake reached into his jacket and pulled the gun from his holster, holding it at his side. "Walk." There was a finality in the way his eyes met mine, making my stomach drop.

I turned slowly before the sharp click of the gun sounded behind my ear. If there was a way out of this, I couldn't see it. We were up on the east side of the island, where no one would hear a gunshot or the sound of shouting.

"Walk," he said again.

I took a step toward the open door, then another. When I came down the stairs, Leoda was waiting, her breath fogging as she watched me. Behind her, Bernard Keller was standing with only his legs awash in the headlights.

Jake shoved me past the truck, toward the almost full moon that was rising over the cliffs. The tall grass that filled the meadow swayed back and forth around us and when we reached the edge, I stopped. Below, the foam of white crashed and dissolved on the stretch of black rocks.

"Give me your wallet." Jake's deep voice was closer now.

It settled in my mind, all at once, what was about to happen. He hadn't brought me up here to scare me or threaten me. I was about to die.

The wind jutting up the rockface whipped around me as I turned to face him. "You don't have to do this, Jake." Nausea climbed up my throat.

I couldn't feel my hands. Or the ground beneath my feet. I wasn't even sure my heart was beating anymore.

"You shouldn't have come back here, August," he said. And he looked as if he meant it. As if he didn't want to do what he was about to. But he was going to do it anyway.

The churn of the water and the scream of the wind filled my head before the faint sound of something else made me flinch.

"August!"

Somewhere, in the flood of racing thoughts, the sound of my name found me. It was ragged and broken.

Jake stilled, his eyes widening before he turned, looking back to the wall of darkness. Across the meadow, the house was still illuminated in Bernard's headlights, but a figure moved toward us. Fast. No, two figures.

I didn't see her until the clouds drifted and the moonlight touched her face.

Emery.

Fifty-Nine

EMERY

"SHIT."

My dad's voice was a grating whisper as the house on Wilke's Pointe came into view. The windows were lit and Bernard Keller's car was parked out front, its lights on.

The truck slowed as Dad hit the brake and Bernard appeared in the open doorway of the house, eyes wide as they shot into the darkness, toward the water. I followed his gaze, turning in my seat until I saw what he was looking at.

They were ink-black silhouettes against the night sky.

Jake. Beside him, August stood at the edge of the crumbling rock that abruptly dropped to the beach far below.

"Oh my God." I breathed, reaching for the door handle. I slid out of the truck before it had even stopped. Then I was running.

"August!" I shouted, my throat burning. But the sound of my voice was swallowed by the wind.

My dad's boots hit the earth behind me and I tore through the tall grass, the scream trapped in my throat.

"August!"

When I saw the glint of moonlight hit the gun in Jake's hand, I gasped, slowing. August's hands were in the air, the side of his face covered in blood. It soaked his shirt at the shoulder.

"What the hell are you doing?" I stared at my uncle in shock.

"You shouldn't be here." Another voice sounded and I turned to see Leoda standing behind me.

I looked between them, unable to put it together. None of this made sense. "What is this?"

My dad appeared at my side, the rifle tucked under his arm. But he didn't look confused. He knew exactly what was going on.

"How could you bring her here?" Jake spat, his furious gaze fixed on his brother. My uncle stood like stone, fingers clamped tight on his gun.

"You both need to leave. Now," Leoda said calmly. She took a step toward me, her silver hair dancing around her face in the wind. The angles of her usually rosy cheeks made her look like a skeleton.

I lifted a hand toward August. "Come on."

But he didn't move, looking to Jake.

"He's not going anywhere." Leoda watched me with glistening eyes.

Dad took a careful step forward. "We're not leaving unless August is coming with us."

"I can't let you do that," Jake answered.

"This isn't like before, Jake." My dad's voice changed, the words slowing.

Something unspoken passed between them, and Jake hesitated. His eyes jumped back and forth between my dad and me before he lifted the gun, pointing it at August's chest.

I shot forward, throwing myself in front of him, and Jake instantly froze, the gun tipping down.

"Get the fuck out of the way, Emery!" he shouted.

"Emery"—August's unsteady voice was at my back—"*move*."

I could hear my dad cocking the rifle in the dark, the sound of Leoda's voice rising. But I didn't take my eyes from Jake's.

"Whatever is happening here, it doesn't matter." I shook my head. "Just let us leave."

In the distance, a pair of headlights bounced in the trees and I watched as Bernard's car disappeared.

"We don't have time for this." Footsteps moved toward me and Leoda suddenly appeared beside Jake. She reached up, wrenching the gun from his grasp. "If you can't do it, I will."

August's hands took hold of my jacket and he shoved back, sending me stumbling into the grass. By the time I got back to my feet, Leoda had the gun trained on him again.

Behind her, my dad lifted his rifle higher. "You pull that trigger, and I pull mine."

"You think I give a shit about dying?" Leoda scoffed. "I'm an old woman, Noah. I was born on this island to do one thing, and I'm going to do it."

In the time it took me to draw another breath, the pieces clicked together.

The orchard.

The Salts.

Lily.

"We have the will!" I stammered, searching for the only thing I had to grab hold of. "A lawyer on the mainland has it."

That made her pause. She looked from me to August.

"If anything happens to him, this will come out. All of it."

I'd never seen Leoda the way I saw her now as she stood there in the dark—a hollow husk with icy blue eyes.

I'd always thought of her as a kind of grandmother. Everyone did. She'd brought most of us into the world, watched our first breaths of this life. Now I wondered if she'd watched any take their last, too.

"You left it open, didn't you?" I said, realizing it.

Leoda's eyes snapped up, finding mine.

"What the hell are you talking about?"

"The last time you saw Lily wasn't at the graduation." My own voice sounded unfamiliar in my ears.

Understanding settled in Leoda's eyes, but she didn't move.

"She always went to you. About everything. So, when she was upset after our fight at the pub, after she'd gone to see August, she went to find *you*." I spoke evenly, recounting what I'd riddled out from Jake's files. "There's only one place on this island to get henbane—the locked cabinet in the apothecary," I said. "Did she remember the spell from the book of shadows or did you point her toward it?"

Leoda's chin lifted defiantly and the glimmer of something vicious shone in her eyes. I wondered now if I *hadn't* seen it before. There was something familiar about it because I'd seen it in Lily.

"But Lily didn't have the skill for a spell like that," I began again. "And instead of killing me, she killed herself."

Leoda's gaze was empty now, completely vacant of the warm, protective woman who'd fluttered over me like a hen for my entire life.

"And when Lily died, you had to change the plan. You may not have been able to get him charged with her murder, but August left Saoirse. So you got what you wanted. All you had to do was wait for Henry to die so you could be sure the orchard ended up in the right hands."

She didn't deny it. How could she?

"That orchard belongs to the Morgans. Not the Salts. Lily was the sacrifice the island required." She said it with an unnerving conviction that sent a chill up my spine.

It had always been about the orchard. Everything on this island was. That's what August had been thinking as he stood with the lantern in hand, staring into its flame. But not even the fire had been able to kill it.

Leoda hadn't known what would happen when Lily cast that spell. But long before that night, she'd put her own granddaughter on the island's altar. And she justified her death with the outcome—at last, the orchard was free of the Salts.

"Let us go or I will take this to the police myself."

At that, the set of her mouth faltered, her nostrils flaring. "You wouldn't dare. This island is in you, blood and bone, just like the rest of us."

"And I'll burn it to the ground if you hurt him."

Leoda's eyes narrowed.

"We have the will," I said again. "And you have Eloise's letter, right? If Henry's will ever sees the light of day, you can use it."

Reopening the case against August when Jake had already stacked it against him was something we wouldn't risk. She knew that. As long as both of us stayed quiet, everyone would get what they wanted.

I took a step toward her. "And it won't just be you who falls for this. It'll be anyone else who played a part. By the time it's over, this place will be a ghost town."

Leoda blinked, lowering the gun.

I reached behind me, not taking my eyes from hers, and a second later, August's hand found mine.

"I'm taking him with me," I said, watching her carefully.

She didn't like it, but she couldn't argue, either.

My dad jerked his chin back toward the house. "Get him out of here."

My hand tightened around August's and Dad didn't lower the rifle until we were swallowed by the dark. I didn't look back, measuring my breaths as we crossed the meadow. The truck was still running when we reached the house and the headlights broke into flickering beams as August rounded the hood with one hand pressed to his ribs. The look on his face made me feel sick. If we'd gotten there even a minute later . . .

I climbed inside, my hands shaking on the steering wheel as I waited for his door to close. As soon as it did, I hit the gas and the tires spun in the mud. The truck rocked over the uneven road, headed for the tree line.

"Are you okay?" I barely got the words out, watching the house disappear in the rearview mirror.

August stared out the window, to the moonlight spilling over the black water below. He didn't have to say it. The answer was no. I wasn't sure we'd ever be okay again.

Sixty

EMERY

We began the way my grandmother had—with earth, air, fire, and water.

Colored stars hung in the window over the dining table, casting a rainbow of light on the floor beside my feet. The window faced east and the moment the sun rose over the buildings downtown, that slice of warm light filled the kitchen of our little apartment.

I flipped the griddle cake on the cast iron and the batter sizzled as Norah climbed up into one of the chairs, crayon in hand. Her sister was sitting on the tabletop, bare feet swinging into the air as she finished the pile of blueberries I'd set beside her.

The red brick building on East Street looked out over the park, and on clear days, you could see the mountains in the distance. They were the same ones you could see from Saoirse, but the island felt a whole world away these days.

I hadn't been back in the six years since August and I took the ferry. Neither of us had. That was better, I thought. To cut Saoirse from me like the rotten part of an apple.

But I had taken one thing with me, and in turn, I'd given it to my daughters. The old ways. I taught them as Albertine and my mother had taught me. Our apartment sat in the middle of the bustling city, but inside, it held the magic of herbs, bones, stones, and shells. Ash and black salt and sigils carved into candles. I still dried my sage and lavender in the window, and I still made the infusions I'd been taught for my neighbors. I'd even begun to read the tea leaves again, though it had been a slow return to the practice.

In a way, leaving the island had helped me find my own magic for maybe the first time.

There were letters from Nixie and Dad. Seeds and pressed flowers that found their way to my mailbox from Albertine, and I still made her griddle cakes every weekend. But sometimes entire days went by without me thinking about Saoirse, and that was something I never thought possible.

August appeared in the hallway as I took the griddle cake off, setting it on top of the stack. His T-shirt was hiked up on one side, revealing the olive skin that stretched from his hip to his ribs, like he'd just pulled it on but hadn't bothered finishing the job. His hair was longer now, more like it was when we were teenagers, and every once in a while, I saw that August in a flash on his face, like a passing shadow.

He picked up an edge of the steaming cake and instantly dropped it, hissing. "Shit. That's hot."

"Don't say *shit*." Liv's straight brown hair fell like a curtain beside her face as she scribbled on the thick white paper she'd fished from my desk.

I stifled a laugh and August kissed me on the shoulder before he picked up the plate, setting it on the table. He scooped Norah up next, propping her on his hip as he cleared another chair for her. She looked tiny in his arms, peering over his shoulder at me with big blue eyes.

I'd imagined him as a father many times, but I hadn't foreseen the quiet tenderness he would have. The way he read beneath the surface of things with a gentle touch or a sideways smile. I'd underestimated him in a way. I'd underestimated *us*.

We'd had no beginning, I realized. We just always were. When I thought about it like that, it was comforting. Like there was no waiting for an end, either.

He'd kept his job at the college and he continued teaching when I enrolled in classes. It took me three and a half years to finish my degree in psychology, of all things, and I walked across the stage at graduation with Norah kicking in my belly.

Now, life had grown into something new. August taught classes on Mondays, Wednesdays, and Fridays. He had papers to read and grade on Tuesdays and Thursdays when I took classes for my doctorate. The weekends were spent like this—lazy mornings in golden light and a haze in the air from the cast iron. After a lifetime of hungering for things to change, I'd settled into a life that I hoped never would.

The apartment was chaotic, no more than a few cramped rooms littered with the evidence of our simple but very full lives—books, paintbrushes, a slew of colorful scarves the girls used for dressing up. And I loved it so much that every time I thought about it, it felt like my heart was going to burst inside my chest.

"What is that, baby?" August leaned over Liv, moving the paper she was coloring into the light coming from the window.

I set down two juice glasses, coming around them with a damp towel to wipe Norah's blueberry-stained fingers.

"It's Saoirse." Liv's little voice made a jolt go through me.

When I looked up, August's eyes were lifted to meet mine.

"What did you say, honey?" I said, dropping Norah's hand with a constriction in my throat.

August slid the paper toward me slowly and my heart kicked up when I saw it. Trees. A thicket of crude, green and blue pines was drawn in Liv's four-year-old hand, the green branches tangling into one another.

August sank down, crouching beside her chair as he stared at it. "Saoirse?" he asked, studying our daughter's face.

"Mmhmm," she chirped, reaching for the syrup.

I picked up the drawing with trembling fingers and August followed me back into the kitchen. We'd never told them about Saoirse. We'd never uttered the name aloud, afraid that even here, the shadow of the island would find us.

We stood there staring at each other, each of us not wanting to say it, before our gazes drifted back to the girls, sunlit and glowing in the window with the stack of griddle cakes between them. After a moment, August took the drawing from my fingers and lifted the lid of the trash can, dropping it inside without a word. When it closed, I let out the breath I was holding.

There were many stories told about the island. We'd grown up with them, and we'd been careful not to pass them to our children. But there in the kitchen, almost three hundred miles away, I could hear my grandmother's time-worn voice recounting the oldest of Saoirse's legends: That if you left the island, it would always call you back.

Acknowledgments

WHEN THE FIRST GLIMMER of this story found me, there was just a man on a ferry, headed home to bury his mother's ashes. I had no idea where he was going to take me.

Working on this book has been an incredibly growth-filled experience as a writer and I have many people to thank for their support along the way. The lion's share of my gratitude, as always, goes to my family—Joel, Ethan, Josiah, Finley, and River. You are the best home and I love you.

My agent, Barbara Poelle, played a significant role in the development of this book when I sent her an early version and she sent it back to me with a challenge—to dig deeper and lean into the story's darkness. Without her, *Spells for Forgetting* would not be the book it is today. I'm very lucky to have you in my corner, Barbara.

This book brought me into the orbit of an exceptionally talented editor, Shauna Summers, who was able to see its magic before a first draft was even finished. I'm so happy that it landed in such good hands. Thank you for helping me weave this story into something I am incredibly proud of. Thank you also to Mae Martinez, for your valuable role in the editorial process.

Thank you to my critique partner, Kristin Dwyer, who helped me get through the weeds of the first seed of this project all the way to the final draft. Has a book ever taken us on a path as winding as this one? Thank you for taking the journey with me, even when we can't see the destination.

A very heartfelt thank-you to Stephanie Garber, who, at a time when I was at a significant crossroads, pushed me to return to this book and see it through. I am so grateful for a friend who seems to truly believe that I can do anything I put my hand to and who won't stand by silently when I'm letting fear keep me from following my heart. My thanks also to Isabel Ibañez who kept patiently reminding me that this story was waiting for me to tell it. August and Emery also thank you for your unwavering loyalty.

Thank you to Diya Mishra, brilliant storyteller and dear friend, who generously gave of her time and energy as I worked on this story in script form. Your contributions helped break open the soul of this book and without you, I honestly don't know if I would have found it. Thank you also to Jordan Gray, whose creative input was invaluable in the revision process. Thank you for your incredible insight.

Thank you to the entire team at Random House for bringing this book into the world with such enthusiasm. And also to my assistant, Carolyn Schweitz, and Gold Leaf Literary for their support over the last year. Thank you to the two beta readers who read very early versions of this book: Natalie Faria and Vanessa Del Rio.

I have many other friends, family, and colleagues who make up the support system that keeps me writing the stories that I believe in. I am so grateful for each and every one of you.

ABOUT THE AUTHOR

Adrienne Young is the *New York Times* and *USA Today* bestselling author of the Fable duology and the Sky in the Deep trilogy. Her books have been published in over twenty-five countries around the world. When she's not writing, you can find her on her yoga mat, on a walk in the woods, or planning her next travel adventure. She lives and writes in the Blue Ridge Mountains of North Carolina.

ABOUT THE TYPE

This book was set in Albertina, a typeface created by Dutch calligrapher and designer Chris Brand (1921–98). Brand's original drawings, based on calligraphic principles, were modified considerably to conform to the technological limitations of typesetting in the early 1960s. The development of digital technology later allowed Frank E. Blokland (b. 1959) of the Dutch Type Library to restore the typeface to its creator's original intentions.

Discover the next spellbinding novel
from Adrienne Young . . .

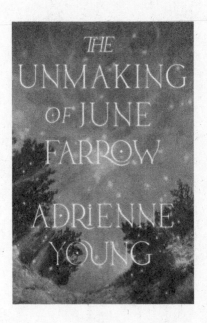

One woman risks everything to end her family's centuries-old curse,
solve her mother's disappearance, and find love in this mesmerizing
novel from the bestselling author of *Spells for Forgetting*.

Coming in Autumn 2023

QUERCUS